LOVE is a WILD ASSAULT

ISBN 0-940672-58-8

Jacket illustration by JOHN WILSON

Design by WHITEHEAD & WHITEHEAD

by ELITHE HAMILTON KIRKLAND

Divine Average
Love is a Wild Assault

Love is a distant laughter in the spirit.
It is a *wild assault* that hushes you to your awakening.
It is a new dawn upon the earth,
A day not yet achieved in your eyes or mine,
But already achieved in its own greater heart.

—KAHLIL GIBRAN
The Earth Gods

Elithe Hamilton Kirkland

LOVE
IS A WILD
ASSAULT

Shearer Publishing
Fredericksburg

Published in 1984 by

Shearer Publishing
406 Post Oak Road
Fredericksburg, TX 78624

Library of Congress Catalog Card Number 59-6362

Reprint of the 1959 edition published by
Doubleday and Company, Inc., Garden City, NY

Manufactured in the United States of America

To My Husband R.D. KIRKLAND

Man of Purpose and Strength
A Doctor Who Supplements Science
With a Wisdom Beyond Formula

FOREWORD

Heroic Harriet, the central character in this novel, made her entrance into my life through the Texas State Historical Association. Dr. George W. Salmon of Houston, a member of the Association, and Dr. H. Bailey Carroll, its director, were her escorts.

This was back in 1953. And now, I present her to you, the reader.

> Harriet the Brave . . . *a woman caught in the vortex of the Texas Revolution and shaped by danger and desertion into an example of remarkable personal courage—a memorable exhibition of strength and endurance.*

> Harriet the Beautiful . . . *a woman of magnetic personality, compelling sudden loves and strange loyalties amidst the fierce passions of wilderness conquest and the political storms of a newborn republic.*

Never doubt her reality. In the fascinating Caddo Lake region of Northeast Texas the inhabitants hand down stories of Harriet and her romantic entanglements with Robert Potter (the Senator from Red River) like treasured family heirlooms, kept burnished with the repolishing of each generation. Her status in these stories varies all the way from "Potter's paramour" to "the bravest woman in the Republic of Texas."

The sensational scandal set off by Rob Potter before he met and loved Harriet—while he was serving the state of North Carolina in the Congress of the United States—has no match in history. It forced him to flee from the violence of his own creation to a different brand of violence on the Texas frontier, where he launched a new political career with the Independence movement and found a new love with a refugee in the Runaway Scrape—our provocative heroine.

Through Potter, Harriet became heir to a legacy of such puzzling treachery that to this day it remains unexplained to haunt any historian, professional or casual, who probes this phase of Texas history.

George Salmon is one of the haunted. Being history-conscious, and having grown up in Northeast Texas, he found himself much in the company of the intriguing ghosts clustered around Harriet at Potter's Point on Lake Caddo. They pursued him with the idea that tall tales should be sifted and recorded matter studied for a book that would do justice to their high courage and thrilling exploits.

In 1951, A. L. Burford, a Texarkana attorney, gave Dr. Salmon a copy of a manuscript written by Harriet at the age of eighty-three. This personal chronicle had first been discovered among Harriet's relatives in 1936 by J. H. Benefield, another Texas lawyer, while investigating land titles in the area where Harriet had been a property owner. As a matter of family confidence, her documentation had been protected from the public eye, but a few copies had limited circulation among attorneys and historians.

Here in Harriet's personal history, Dr. Salmon realized, was a perfect outline for a magnificent romantic story based on actuality but translating the sensational events into the human values that only time can refine and interpretative fiction can present. Her story, he decided, must be written, and he would see that it was. His medical practice and writing for professional journals left him no time for such an undertaking, so he decided to take his problem of finding a storyteller for Harriet and her "cast of characters" to Dr. Carroll at the University of Texas. He was delighted to find that Dr. Carroll was no stranger to Harriet's story—was, in fact, a fellow admirer. He learned also that a copy of her autobiography had filtered into the University's Texas History Archives long before it had come to his hand. But in deference to its personal content it had been under seal here for some years, though no longer restricted.

Dr. Carroll agreed that it was time to release Harriet from historical limbo into the more heroic domains of Texas personalities. And it was at this point that these two gentlemen—under the banner of the Texas State Historical Association of which I am a member—escorted this charming and dynamic woman into my writing life. I had other books under way at the time and no eagerness for more story ideas, but when I agreed to read her account, her sponsors settled back content, knowing the power of Harriet's presentation.

Once fully acquainted with the century-old mystery and controversy in which she was involved, I was committed—as they expected, unable to resist Harriet's appeal in such statements as:

> It seems to me that my life was spared these many years in order that I might write this history and let the truth be known about much that has been falsified and misrepresented.

Harriet considered her account just "an outline of what it was like to live in that wild country in those early days," and, thus far, no writer had tried to fill in her colorful outline so rich in dramatic dialogue and poetic description. So I emerged from my "interview" with Harriet as her aroused defender and storyteller.

Dr. Salmon conferred with me on his findings; and then, with Dr. Carroll's advice and assistance, I plunged into such exhaustive research that it placed me among the missing for several years as far as my own personal life was concerned.

Although I was a familiar of Harriet's period, having done years of intensive research on the Texas Republic as background for my novel, *Divine Average*, the great amount of contradictory material to be studied for this present book—involving court cases, political and personal feuds, crime and scandal—presented an entirely new mountain of research.

In the Texas State and University libraries and archives, I examined multiple books, periodicals, newspapers, census reports, court records, personal records and documents, political papers and broadsides, theses, and other scholarly reports on the personalities of the period.

In the clerk's office of the Supreme Court of Texas, I studied the largest single source of data for the framework of my novel: a 400-page transcript (in longhand) of the proceedings in a case involving Harriet (her property and her reputation) that had been in and out of East Texas courts for twenty years. In Harriet's testimony and the many depositions for and against her, most of the facts and hearsay about her life up to sixty-five years of age were set forth.

There was one elusive publication—Potter's defense of his crime, an eighty-six-page booklet written while he was in prison—that was finally located in the library of the University of North Carolina. This filled in one of the most exciting segments of Harriet's account wherein she referred to a "small book" that Potter gave her to explain the motives of his crime.

The state library of Oklahoma, Indian City U.S.A., and the Smithsonian Institution gave assistance with details concerning the Caddo Indians. Everywhere I probed, librarians and their clerical staffs gave me laudable support in my detective work.

And now LOVE IS A WILD ASSAULT is ready for you. As you accompany Harriet through a lifetime of courageous living, may the journey make you friends and allies . . . Tejas! . . . forever.

Elithe Hamilton Kirkland

Austin, Texas

1.

Some women measure life by the men they have loved, Harriet reflected, and some by the children they have had.

Others, in summing up, evaluate by a creed or code, considering the rewards of conformity and the penalties of violation (or vice versa!).

And then there are those who know no other measurement than the accumulation of possessions (How many *things* do I have now at the end of gathering-time?).

In measuring her own long and eventful life, Harriet decided to examine each of these standards before starting to write what must be documented—certain personal matters to be set down while mind, eye, and hand were mutually responsive.

Fortunately, one didn't need a sense of hearing to remember and record accurately. Audient memory required only the ears of the heart, and hers were ever receptive to sounds of the past—vibrations awesome and sweet, always a part of the montage of reflection: a panther's scream, a whippoorwill's cry—gun of battle, and cradle song.

She picked up a pencil for annotation of her thoughts:

Consider men loved

There had been many guests in the big house of her heart. And with them much richness of shared understanding, ornamented with jeweled moments of inspiration and adoration. To three of them she had given residence and the full union of her woman self.

> *The gambler* . . . in merchant's disguise . . . with the face of a hero. False spring love. Sudden flower and withered dreams.
> *The statesman* . . . duality of dove and serpent . . . Summer tempest in her heart. Violence and near destruction.
> *The trader* . . . the searcher . . . hands of goodness . . . eyes of wisdom . . . All the seasons of love!

But physical communion was far from the full measure of man-love in a woman's life, if she computed honestly. In the tinted mists of Harriet's memories, those others waited to be counted, and would come close when she beckoned.

The minister . . . He looked like Christ clothed in buckskin and had saved her from starvation.

The lawyer . . . A trusted friend and able counsellor through years of scandal and treachery.

The purse maker . . . (She chuckled as this one leaped to the front of her mind in such clear imagery and so fantastically garbed.) Wilderness mongrel who called her "kishi-woman" and kindred of Ina, the Mother Earth.

The rest she would bring closer when the events to be recounted demanded their presence.

Consider children

Perhaps no one alive besides herself knew the full count (she smiled in grave amusement): eighteen in all. And she was certain that her four now alive, moving with dignity and influence through the higher stratas of financial and social structure in New Orleans would be embarrassed by any personal awareness of the fact and humiliated by any publication of it.

It had been a long time since she had brought the fourteen departed ones into her memory room, called them by name, redefined their features. Their life spans ranged from infancy to maturity. She began to list them, chronologically.

1. *Joe Boy* (child of strength and comfort—little partner!)

2. *Ginny* (angelic baby Virginia, the merry toddler, stricken in war's shadow, and, she had to remember, so crudely buried on Galveston Island.)

3. *Infant Son* . . . (possessed for one sad morning, and yet the image so sharp: black hair abundance, and the face a paternal miniature . . . his shroud, a deerskin . . . if she hadn't been alone in childbirth——)

4. *Lakeann* (O piercing fragrance of hawthorne! O knife of agony undulled by time!)

As she wrote the name "Lakeann," Harriet's hand became afflicted; she lost control of the pencil; it rolled, and dropped to the floor. She sat very still, her hands vaguely clutching. When she had conquered the emotion, she recovered the pencil and with firm composure finished the list without pausing between names.

> 5. *John David* (and the awful row about his name.)
> 6. *Douglas Daniel* . . . 7. *Eva Jean* . . . 8. *Lena Loyce* . . .
> 9. *Thomas Claude* . . . 10. *Lockett* . . . 11. *Sally Sue* . . .
> 12. *James Freedom* . . . 13. *Felicia* . . . 14. *Alsheena* . . .

"Alsheena," she murmured the name. And the young woman whose life had been to her mother like an uncompleted poem of love and beauty, seemed to come from memory into reality—seemed to enter her mother's presence. Between Alsheena and her mother there was a sharing that death had not touched. For this daughter had given Harriet the ultimate joy of the encircling years: A namesake grandchild, Harriet Ann—"Tricky" the family called her because of her precocious insight into the motives of adults. When Harriet began to see in Tricky a replica of her own child self in looks and thoughts, she felt that life had paid her a vast compliment. Here was an extension of her own personality more positively exhibited than in any of her eighteen children. The supreme flattery. Tricky was her pride and vanity . . . Then when Tricky, orphaned, came to be her daily companion, she found that she must look upon more than her own child self in her grandchild—there was an idealized adult self shining in the worshipful mirrors of Tricky's eyes and just as faithfully reflected in devoted attendance on her grandmother's needs. This was disturbing.

"Alsheena," Harriet said gravely to the lovely shadow in her presence, "I had thought I was done with responsibility. But this unexpected quirk of the life force, this duplicate of self with which you presented me, imposes a duty I can no longer evade. There are some things I must write down for Tricky before I leave her—things I had thought to spare myself the discomfort of remembering. But because she is so much like me and adores our mutuality, I must fortify her against a future that might too much resemble my past. Also, I must provide her with a weapon of truth to wield in my behalf for I have just had occasion to realize that one does not outlive certain types of notoriety. Tricky is too young for explanation . . . yet, she must understand."

It seemed that Alsheena nodded in agreement.

Harriet turned back to listing her children. Now the four living ones. She wrote with pleasant deliberation.

15. *Charles Paul* (Harvard graduate . . . reputed to be one of the most competent surgeons in the South . . . practicing here in New Orleans, thank goodness.)

16. *William Patrick* (business man . . . substantial . . . builder . . . importer . . . like his father skilled with woods and full of quiet wisdom.)

17. *Edward Yancy* (Tulane graduate . . . physician turned industrialist and financier . . . labeled in public life "a prominent man of the New South" . . . "E.Y." was family power and prestige.)

18. *Addie* (Adeline, youngest daughter . . . wife of Dr. Frank Marreo—good man, skilled physician, prominent family . . . the beautiful Marreo home—my home and Tricky's . . . surrounded in my old age by prosperity, influence, integrity.)

"Blessed in my children," she said aloud, and looked up to find Alsheena still there, apparently as real as any of the four she had just listed.

"Alsheena, I could always talk to you freely about the past—the times before I met your father. But you were the only one of my children I could trust to understand fully, especially about those six stormy years in wilderness country. Just the other night at the big dinner party your brother E.Y. gave, I realized that the clouds which gathered over me during the Texas Revolution will never completely break away from my life. Now you would think, wouldn't you, Sheena, that in a life as long as mine, a six-year segment more than fifty years behind me could be cut out and discarded and the scars ignored. But I find there is no surgery for the body of experience that makes up a life. It must remain intact and whole, forcing acceptance and understanding. I am trying now to analyze the whole by measuring the parts . . ."

Harriet penciled two more words:

Consider code

"It's amazing, Alsheena, that I have lived so long without asking
myself what rules I live by, what beliefs I hold. A personal code, I
suppose, assembles and forms outside the conscious mind, for the
most part. It is made up of compulsions, influences, and individual
thought or drive. If we don't do much thinking for ourselves, then
we have just a copy-cat code. Too often we let others set the rules,
and we pick a creed from various merchants of morality as we would
pick a garment, for comfort and appearance—sometimes it isn't even
comfortable, just stylish. We want only to be assured that if we observe
the tenets passably well, we will attain heaven and escape hell. It is
troublesome to have to search our hearts for purpose, probe our minds
for truth. To accept a leader and blindly follow is the easy way along
any path—but what of journey's end?"

Harriet was thoughtful for a moment, then wrote *"Searching"* and
underscored it. After a while, she continued her discourse with Alsheena.

"I think that each of us was meant to seek and search our whole
life through for truth and righteousness and that we will be rewarded
for effort. Certainly, we err frequently and all stand in need of informed guidance and inspired leadership, but this should be accepted
to stimulate and support searching, not to end it. Guidance un-
questioned becomes dictation. Leadership unchallenged becomes
tyranny. This part of my code has made me unable to live by dogma,
certified and hidebound, with a go-to-heaven guarantee. Once we
reach the age of thought and effort, I think our Maker intends for
us to *grow* to heaven. Growth follows birth in every cycle of life. Why
shouldn't it be the same for moral and spiritual development? Height,
branching, and fruiting of each spirit has its own dimensions. So it is
a part of my code to consider life in all of its aspects as *growth
through searching.*"

She stopped her soft monologue and wrote *"Fearless."*

"I don't mind saying to you, Alsheena, that I have been called
brave and courageous many times in my life. I admit that such praise
pleases me. But I must thank my mother for that part of my code
that rules out fear. I was only ten years old when she instructed me
from her deathbed, 'Don't be afraid for me or for yourself. Fear is

weakness. I leave you in God's hands.' As I have met crisis after crisis in my life, I have examined fear and found it weakness; I have exercised courage and found it strength—a special strength from God's own hands. . . . One time a stranger came to my wilderness home on Mulberry Shore. When I greeted him at the door, he just stood staring at me, dumbfounded. Finally, he said, 'In my mind you were pine-tall, Brave Woman, and now my eyes behold you only flower-high.' He had made a long journey, he said, just to see 'the bravest woman in the Republic of Texas.' . . . It was this fearless trait in my nature that the Indians recognized and respected—without it, they would have preyed upon me, possibly destroyed me. . . . Truly, I can say, I have lived by the rule: *Be not afraid.*"

She paused again, smiled whimsically, and wrote "*Sky-minded.*"

"That phrase must be the Indian influence, Alsheena. The god of the Caddoes was called Caddi-Ayo, chief of the sky, and resembled our Christian God more than it is comfortable to admit. I wonder if true religious thought isn't always upward-reaching. Gods dwell on heights. God reigns above. Well, whether the approach be pagan or Christian, we all seem to have the urge to identify ourselves with the Universe and the Creative Force back of it all, a Power we call God— otherwise, we feel insignificant, helpless. Since youth, I have identified myself with nature, felt a part of the vastness, the mystery, the wonder. There are so many exalting expressions of sky-mindedness in nature . . . plant life reaching upward, foliage and flowers loving the sky, seeking the sun . . . waters spread out to reflect the color glory of the heavens . . . hills and peaks yearning toward the upper reaches . . . birds in the patterned ecstasies of flight . . . clouds caressing the face of the sky . . . stars and planets the ornaments of space. In communing with these things, I find myself in touch with the Power of God. I find assurance of eternal Beauty and Goodness. On the other hand, in witnessing the destructive forces of nature, I am reconciled to man's exhibitions of brutality, believing that when all is finished, the love force will somehow bring perfection out of it all, and the final equation will be good. In the meantime, since everything in nature seems to express incessant striving against adversity—whether it be a new blade of grass or an ancient oak, smallest insect or lordly beast— I am challenged to do the same. So, I believe it is important to be *sky-minded and ever striving.*"

The clock on the mantle in Harriet's room clanged three times. She was dimly aware of it, and surprised. Then the door opened, as she expected it would, and she was annoyed. It was Addie. And, of course, Alsheena disappeared.

Addie had rules about naps and such. So Harriet knew what Addie wanted. Nevertheless, she inquired, "What is it, Addie?"

"You aren't taking your nap, Mama. I thought Tricky was in here. I was going down the hall and I heard you talking to someone."

"Tricky is not here. I was only thinking aloud. I'll get my nap, don't fret. And don't begrudge my wakefulness. I've got all eternity to rest in."

"But, Mama, Frank says——"

"Addie, you are married to a good doctor and I respect him. But don't quote him just now. I'm thinking about other things."

"I could write your letters, Mama." But Addie knew her mother hadn't heard her. She never heard you unless she was looking at you. Addie wondered what her mother was writing. But she turned and left the room. Harriet had rules about prying.

When the door closed behind Addie, Harriet made a notation on the fourth category of measurement.

Consider possessions

Land . . . my beautiful home in Texas . . . Mulberry Shore . . . Lake Caddo . . . How I loved it! . . . frontage of waters . . . background of forest . . . fields fresh-cleared and rich-soiled . . . season color and weather mood spreading an ever-changing beauty over it all. . . . All of it taken from me . . . betrayed . . . defrauded . . . dispossessed. . . . I must be thankful that age has diluted the bitterness of loss . . . but now I know that I loved land more than any "thing" I ever possessed . . . Perhaps we are not intended to possess land, forever in conflict over ownership. Perhaps we should all be custodians of the land, letting it possess us (There I go again, thinking like an Indian).

Slaves . . . There weren't many . . . I recall no pride of possession. Hannah I loved. Delia I distrusted. The others, I forget. But they abide in my mind as people, not property. I was relieved when I no longer "owned" them—equally relieved that Hannah never left me.

Livestock . . . What a joy they were—horses, cattle, poultry . . . the care of them rewarding work . . . faraway, gracious memories . . . Sukey Blueskin, my favorite riding mare . . . Socrates, my pet rooster . . . Now I own none of these things. All emancipated.

Adornments . . . Important things to the female of the species and I am no exception. Jewelry, fine cloth, style still have meaning to me, but I'd gladly exchange all I have or ever had for a chance to spend the rest of my life in the country . . . in the simplest abode . . . in the simplest garb.

Comforts . . . A variety of them according to the time and place . . . and now the only one that I place any kind of value on is my feather mattress.

Out of all my possessions, the one remaining, the one truly cherished, *a feather mattress!*

Harriet glanced over her notes, muttering, "I would not like to be a recording angel, keeping books on everybody's life." Then she sat thinking over E.Y.'s dinner party, the event that had prompted this self-analysis.

It was one of those elaborate evening affairs that her son hosted for men of influence, their wives, and a few selected guests who were usually newcomers on the New Orleans business scene. It was Edward's way to have all the adult members of his family present, showing them off to the best advantage. Tricky, as usual, was the only child present, there by her grandmother's request and need, and it was their custom to stay together and to leave together soon after dinner. "All eyes and ears," the family characterized Tricky, proud of her perceptions, relieved at the convenience provided by her loyal service to her grandmother. Harriet, though hard of hearing, had good sight and could read lips. It was just that her mind was not always on the scene at hand.

Tricky's powers of observation and memory were remarkable not only in the matter of names, or what was worn and said, eaten and drunk, but also in an awareness of adult attitudes toward one another —especially those they considered hidden. She and her grandmother had some grand times reviewing these occasions together. The family would have been shocked indeed could they have listened in on the revelations and conclusions of a perfectly frank eight and eighty.

At this particular party, the dinner was over and clusters were visiting here and there, in the casual interlude between eating and dancing. Musicians were performing the soothing cadences calculated to aid digestion. Harriet didn't hear the music. She was studying faces and occasionally reading lips. Tricky had left for a moment on some small errand for Addie. Then a face came into focus that jerked her senses back to a scene of fifty years ago. The Slidell face. Not old enough to be the one she remembered so well. So it must be the boy—the one who had stared at her so as she walked by the stream with Mrs. Slidell that day—that awful day of ordeal and revelation. Yes, this was the one. The same clawlike stare. For a brief moment, she saw him again as she had seen him that day: a stringy boy, perhaps twelve years old, with a gun nearly as long as he was, and clutched in his right hand a great bundle of dead squirrels, held by the tails. The Slidell features and disposition were clearly stamped on him. Mrs. Slidell hadn't presented him, just muttered bitterly, "Saddled with orphan kin—on my husband's side—his kid brother"; and they had moved on up the trail with the boy's stare still hooked on to them . . . So, Harriet concluded, this Slidell staring at her now must be the wealthy Texan that E.Y.'s banker friend, Mr. Gates, had asked to bring to dinner—another newcomer scouting for financial connections. Mr. Gates was standing beside Slidell, and it was obvious to Harriet that the banker was giving his prospect a who's-who briefing on the personages about them. Slidell wasn't paying much attention—he was staring at her. Mr. Gates became aware of this.

"You are observing our host's mother, Mr. Slidell. Amazing charm, striking figure for one her age, don't you agree?"

Harriet, concentrating on their lip movements, knew exactly what was being said.

"Mr. Gates, this will amaze you, as it does me. I saw that woman nearly fifty years ago when I was a boy living with my brother in the piney woods of East Texas. Are those real pearls she's wearing?"

"Very real, I assure you. Her son can afford them. You say you knew her in Texas?"

"I saw her only once. But I've heard tall tales about her all my life.

24

Much big fiction about beauty and bravery. Indians and wilderness riff-raff called her 'kishi-woman.' "

"What does 'kishi' mean, Mr. Slidell?"

"Kishi means panther, Mr. Gates. Vicious. Cunning."

"Perhaps they meant something else—some kind of compliment." Mr. Gates was disturbed.

"Whatever they meant, and regardless of tall tales and real pearls, she was just——" Mr. Slidell licked his lips in malice. "If you will pardon me, Mr. Gates—she was just a common prostitute."

Mr. Gates felt that he might collapse. He looked furtively around to see if anyone had heard.

The room reeled for Harriet. And then she started walking toward the two men.

Though they saw her coming, it did not occur to them that she knew what had been said.

Her purposeful approach made Mr. Gates very uneasy. O God, why did I bring this barbarian here? And why has she singled him out? he thought desperately. He knew that Harriet had long ago given up receiving with the family at such large gatherings and that she felt no social compulsion to meet and greet strangers. He told himself: E.Y. and I are such good friends—she's just coming over for a little chat with me. But when she came up quite close to them, this comforting possibility fled. For she was ignoring him and stood facing Slidell with a clear measuring gaze that stripped him down to the bare character.

Now neither man could doubt her full knowledge of what had just been said. And neither could speak. Slidell could not unlock his eyes from hers. The claws in his stare were loose and bleeding, and his tortured look accepted her evaluation and begged for release. But when she spoke, her eyes still held him—and her words were addressed to Mr. Gates, deliberate and precise, as if reading from an account sheet.

"Mr. Gates, if this man has money to invest, you would be wise to investigate the source. He grew up with Zack Monk's gang that headquartered in the old Neutral Strip. They maintained equipment for making fraudulent bills and operated a string of way stations for an international ring of robbers trafficking in stolen slaves and horses. Mr. Slidell's brother, who raised him, was a strong link in this evil chain, and doubtless the same proclivities reside in this man. If he is using your firm and your reputation to promote his advancement, shouldn't you know if his fortune was made by honest endeavor or criminal intrigue? I think you will find that he is just a——" She paused to let the misery of her victims mount. "He is just a common thief."

Tricky came up and grabbed her grandmother's hand, alert to the tension in the air and alarmed that Harriet's hand, usually so warm, was icy cold.

"I'm ready to retire, Tricky," Harriet said. "Good night, Mr. Gates."

She and Tricky left the reception room, hand in hand, nodding graciously to other guests as they departed.

"Gram," Tricky said, as soon as they were clear of the room, "Mr. Gates and the gentleman with him looked as if they were about to choke."

"I hope they do. And the biped you are referring to is not a gentleman!"

"You must have said something very shocking to them, Gram."

"I did."

"I'm sorry I was not there to hear for you."

"There was nothing to hear. They didn't talk back."

"Do you want to tell me about it?"

"Not now."

As Harriet reviewed this scene, she was reassured within her own mind that she had seen the last of Mr. Slidell. Mr. Gates had no doubt facilitated the exit of this unsavory newcomer from the New Orleans business scene. But there was no charmed circle she could draw about herself to keep out other messengers of calumny. She had lived too long to ever rule out the mysterious pattern of coincidence. And it was only self-deceit if she thought for a moment that her Texas ordeals could be buried in time or distance. The controversy in which she had been a central figure had been too prolonged, too sensational to be soon forgotten. Accounts would be distorted and exaggerated indefinitely.

When escape is impossible, defense is imperative, Harriet told herself, and documentation will be my defense, with Tricky the custodian. I will begin this very day . . . after my nap, of course. I wonder *how*

Addie knows *when* I lie down. I must be making some noise I am unaware of. It would be fun some day if, when Addie peeps in to remind me, I could say, "Don't bother me, Addie. I've *had* my nap."

She moved stealthily to the high bed, stepped up on the footstool that was necessary to bring her small figure to the right level for climbing in. She lay back slowly, easily, and sank with blissful relaxation into the softness of the big feather mattress. The fact that she protested the nap did not keep her from enjoying it. She was happy, too, over her decision. She sighed and slept.

When Harriet opened her eyes, Tricky was standing on the footstool at her bedside.

"How long have you been standing there, child? Climb up beside me."

Tricky in one quick bounce ascended to her familiar perch on the edge of the great bed, her legs dangling, her face bent close to her grandmother.

"What have you been doing?"

"Practicing piano."

"I wish I could hear you."

"It's better that you can't. I'm not very good . . . Gram, do you consider Aunt Addie a smart woman?"

"Well, there are smarter women, I'm sure. But, in most respects, I'd say she is smart enough."

"Do you think she knows much about heaven?"

"I couldn't say, Tricky. Addie and I have never discussed heaven in specifics."

"Well, she has some specifics about what I should and should not do to go there. So today I asked her, 'What is heaven, anyway?' and she said, 'The beautiful city of God.' And I said, 'I don't care for cities. I shall probably have to live in New Orleans all my life. When I die, I want to go to the country—country like where Gram lived in Texas. If heaven is all city,' I said, 'I don't think I'll bother about going there.'"

"What did Addie say to that?"

"She said, 'Don't be irreverent,' and made me practice an hour longer to get the 'nonsense' out of my head . . . What kind of a place do you think heaven is, Gram?"

"I believe it's a sort of glory-place, my dear."

"And what is a 'glory-place,' Gram?"

"A place of love."

"Like you and me here together, and happy."

"That's right."

"Different things make different people happy, Gram. So it doesn't seem like God would make heaven just the same all over."

"God makes countless pleasant variations in nature, Tricky. I don't think it is illogical to expect the same in his heavenly creations. Your grandfather always said that heaven to him was a beautiful lakeside with mulberry trees on the shore and great wavy cypresses on the lake islands . . . and a morning view of the sun reaching out with deft fingers to pull back the curtains of mist from the face of beauty . . . and an evening view of the sun throwing a mantle of gorgeous hue over the body of shining water . . . and with me there by his side to enjoy it all."

"Do you like grandfather's idea of heaven?"

"Very much."

"I like it too. Do you think it will really be like that when you go to meet him?"

"I hope so."

"Do you think my mother and father will be at that particular place in heaven?"

"Your mother was born at Mulberry Shore. She loved the lake like a water nymph. And your father loved your mother so much that her very presence was heaven to him."

"Aunt Addie and Uncle Frank and the rest—they like it so much here in New Orleans—they would expect to dwell in a heavenly city, don't you think?"

"Very likely."

"No one around here seems to care for lakes and trees and such but you and me."

"Our family loves us very much, Tricky, but they don't love the same things we do."

"What did you look like when you were a child, Gram?"

"Very much like you."

"I thought so."

"Why?"

"It seems to me sometimes, Gram, that you are me old and I am you young."

"It seems that way to me too, Tricky."

The old woman and her grandchild meditated for a while on this good companionable thought.

"When you go to glory, Gram, may I have your lovely feather mattress?"

Harriet was startled. It wasn't the first time that Tricky had seemed to reach into her mind as if it were a box of visible thoughts and pick out the subject right on top!

"Yes, Tricky. It has been on my mind to tell you that was my intention. I shall instruct your Aunt Addie and Uncle Frank that it is yours from the moment I breathe my last upon it. And it is to be cared for and handled by you alone."

"Thank you, Gram. . . . I remember the first time you asked me to help you make bed, and we took all the covers off and looked at the beautiful mattress. I'd slept with you and had a most wonderful dream and you said it was because of the magic mattress. You never let anyone else help you make bed, do you, Gram? No one ever touches the mattress but you and me?"

"No one. It is the secret treasure of my life and your dreams."

Tricky reached down and pulled the bed linens back to reveal a bit of the mattress, allowing a peek at their treasure.

"Gram, I like this thick golden cloth. I never saw any mattress covered like this."

"You probably never will."

"It looks like something for a queen."

"Better than some queens have had, I suspect. Your Uncle Edward bought the material in Paris before you were born. It was something to bring me from his travels in Europe because he knew I have always loved to work with fine cloth. He was rather shocked when I covered a mattress with it."

"Uncle E.Y. is very rich, isn't he?"

"Yes. Very rich."

"I expect he paid a lot of money for it."

"Indeed he did. It is a very expensive and durable piece of true brocade."

"I love Uncle E.Y."

"Who doesn't? Those who don't love him for himself, love him for what he has."

"I love him for both. I love him for himself—although his self is rather high and mighty sometimes. And I love him for having enough money to buy this beautiful cloth."

"Enough of magic—help me up and back to solid ground. I have some work to do at my desk. Smooth the bed for me and run along."

"May I bring your tray up at suppertime and eat with you?"

"You certainly may."

Tricky took a final peek at the mattress, running her hand over the brocade caressingly before tucking the covers back properly. Then she skipped to the door, but stopped in impulsive thought before going through it. She turned and walked over to the fireplace which was graced by two narrow decorative mirror panels on the outer framework. She stood studying her reflection, then went to the desk where her grandmother was preparing to write.

"Gram, am I beautiful?"

"Tricky, since we are agreed that you appear to be me young, it would be unseemly for me to compliment myself. But you are not homely. Remind me to tell you the story of the young Indian whose excess of vanity caused him to turn into a tree."

"Oh, Gram! What kind of tree?"

"Don't try to trap me, just remind me."

"At supper?"

"All right." She gave a shooing motion with her hand, and Tricky obediently withdrew.

Harriet dipped her pen and wrote . . .

A LETTER TO MY GRANDCHILD, HARRIET ANN PURCELLE

New Orleans
April 15, 1890

Dear Tricky,

You have just left my room, an eight-year-old child, but this letter is for you to read as a grown young lady. Since it is the privilege of old age to see visions, I am now addressing Harriet Ann, a renowned

30

New Orleans Beauty (*it will not be your Uncle Edward's way to let you go unnoticed*). *Suitors are the biggest concern of your life at this time. You would like to discuss your various admirers with me. You would like to ask me many questions about men and their ways. It is my intention that in my experiences and opinions recorded here you will find some of the answers*—before you marry.

Let me say right off, *watch out for the young man with heroic face and hungry hands*—*with the look of lost dreams in his eyes and a great need. He may be another Solomon Page. I want you to know all about Solomon . . .*

2.

If some part of my past that concerns Solomon Page should ever touch any part of your future, you might hear that Solomon was a brave patriot in General Houston's army and fought for the independence of Texas . . . and that while he fought, I dallied—took up with another man, deserted my home and husband. I want you to know how it came about that my name was linked with a scandal that has become linked with the history of a state, and why it is that I cannot expect time to give me the sweet anonymity that would bless my old age and cast no shadow after my death.

I will not describe Solomon by coloring and dimension. It is the effect of him that we will consider, so that you may identify his counterpart by more subtle measurement than height or hue.

I was seventeen years old when Solomon entered my life. He had come to see my father, Francis Moore, who was a physician. Father's office was in our home in Nashville. I often received the people who came to see him, and it was thus I met Solomon. He had come about some minor injury to his hand and was overly distressed about it. He rushed in, without introduction, and was much disturbed at finding the doctor too busy to give him immediate attention. He paced the floor and nursed his hand like it was some twitching, dying thing. At first, I was secretly amused. Then I began to share his distress and feel that I must quiet and comfort him. I surmised that only a musician could be so concerned about his hands.

"The doctor will put your hand in shape," I said. "Don't worry. You will be able to play again in no time at all."

He stopped dead still and turned a most startled stare on me.

His scrutiny embarrassed me. "I was thinking—you must play something——"

"I do play something," he said and gave a small smile, "but not very well."

Solomon's smile, like a banished hope on his sensitive features, is one of the clearest memories I have of him. Perhaps because that was the first signal to my senses that this nervous young man could arouse in me such an attraction as I had never before experienced. Anyway, at our first meeting, it was this special smile of his that caused me to come up close to him and ask to examine his hand that I might further reassure him. It was a beautiful hand—slender, long-fingered, pale and utterly unblemished, except for the bruise along the upper palm—as if the fingers had been bent back and a blow struck with a rod. As his distress was out of proportion, so was my compassion. He didn't tell me how the hand was injured. I never asked him. The fingers trembled, out of all control, and it was natural that I should support his hand with mine as I looked at it and spoke with certainty about the doctor's abilities to make it good as new in a few days. When I paused from my comforting and persuasive chatter to look up at him, his eyes met mine with a glow of gratitude that for a moment had me feeling that I had done no less than save his life. A pulse began to throb from his hand to mine.

"You are very helpful and kind," he said, almost in a whisper, then added "Miss——" and waited for me to supply my name.

"I am Dr. Moore's daughter, Harriet Ann."

"Charmed, Miss Moore." (I was the charmed one. I could not let go his hand.) "Solomon Page, at your service." The pulse between our hands grew stronger, and the tremor of it seemed to spread all over me.

It was on the third trip to my father's office that Solomon said to me as he departed, taking his hat from me at the doorway, "You are the woman I need."

To me this was the same as a declaration that he loved me madly. I had yet to learn that need alone does not define love. I had yet to learn that the maternal as well as the mating instinct requires recognition and control if a woman is not to betray herself in one way or another.

Solomon's abrupt statement so filled me with a surge of urgency to meet all his needs that I stood quite speechless, my hand still held out after his hat was on his head. I became acutely aware of every detail of his clean-shaven features, his movements, his clothing—he was dressed all in shiny black and soft gray: dark shoes, frock coat and tall hat; light pants with gloves and waistcoat matching. While I stood so immobile, his restless hands were adjusting and smoothing his gloves. Solomon always wore gloves, soft as skin.

As he turned and left, I still could find no words to call out after him. I fled upstairs and locked myself in my room. There I sat with my hands to my burning cheeks in an agony of regret for not saying what I wanted him to know—that this woman he needed felt as if her whole being were a magic pitcher, full to the brim, that he might tip and pour for all satisfaction, all happiness.

Up to this time, he had never called on me, only my father. In the weeks before he came again, I suffered in that way especially reserved for youth in the grip of a new emotion that cannot be expressed—a feeling that is banked ever higher and higher with wild imagining and uncertain expectation—and because it is accompanied with the burning conviction that no one, no one ever before, has endured anything quite like it, it is peaked with a desolate aloneness. I was tortured by the thought that my silence had offended Solomon— that my dumb gaping had been interpreted as dislike and I might never see him again. (I look back on this picture of myself with sad pity—that I could ever have reasoned thus about Solomon Page, so schooled in countenance reading that my feelings were perfectly plain. He must have considered the possibility that such intensity of devotion might become a burden. But his needs were greater than his cautions.)

Daily I planned what to wear, what to say, what to do should Solomon come that day. But I exhausted myself to no purpose, for when he actually did appear, I did not run out and change to a more alluring frock, I spoke none of the sentimental phrases that had sounded so captivating when I rehearsed them. His demeanor was so casual that I felt chilled and sick and ran away again in hot shame to hide in my room. I was there when my father knocked and came in to tell me that Solomon was coming to call on the family that evening and had asked permission to pay court to me. Suddenly I was out of the abyss and into the clouds. I hugged my father, kissed him again and again, laughed and cried, danced around him with many antics about what I would say and do to bring Solomon to an early proposal. I was stopped short when I became aware that my noisy exhibition had brought Sarah, my stepmother, to investigate. She was looking at me as if I were demented.

"It's just an excess of spirits," father explained.

"Animal spirits!" Sarah amended, her disgust sharp and plain.

Joy drained out of me. Was life as one became adult all disguise and restraint and decorum? The six years that I had been under Sarah's watchful eyes had been lean ones for my lively and affectionate nature. She was not a cruel woman, but she was strict and critical and unimaginative.

My father explained to her about Solomon—that he was five years older than I—that he was set up in business and able to support a wife, his business being that of a distributor, trading in the wholesale district, supplying outlying shops and stores with certain goods. Sarah nodded approval at his eligibility. Then she reminded me that I was unattractive when I laughed because my mouth was so big, and cautioned me not to scare the young man away with bold eagerness, and by all means to brush my hair so that my curls did not escape in that ragged fringe that made me look like an untidy child.

My father said, with dignity and mild reproach, "It is already quite evident that the young man considers my daughter attractive." The "my daughter" phrase was always the signal to Sarah that she had said quite enough.

They left me alone in uneasy anticipation. Solomon was my first serious suitor. I had had a few beaus my own age, but none had excited me beyond a bit of flirtation.

That evening when I was coming into the parlor where we would receive Solomon, I overheard a conversation between Sarah and my father. They were talking so earnestly, they failed to hear me approach.

"You have kept her from knowing she is beautiful," my father was accusing Sarah.

"I have done her and you a great favor," Sarah answered. "Beauty is a dangerous thing—dangerous to have—dangerous to be close to. It breeds arrogance and conceit. It causes contention and jealousy. I say she'll be safer, better off in every way, if she never knows what she can do with it or cause others to do because of it."

"Sarah, I disagree with you. Beauty is a wondrous thing. We should accept and enjoy it in human nature as we do in other manifestations."

"In a woman it can bring her soul to perdition quicker than any other fleshly thing."

"Puritanical nonsense!"

"Nonsense or not, you'd better get her married and settled. Coddle her beauty and you'll regret it."

"Sarah, you have not had enough parties for her. She has not met enough eligible young men."

"Francis, may I remind you that being mother to two families and wife to a doctor who eats and sleeps at any hour of day or night leaves little time for frivolity. Hatty has been helpful and obedient, but it's time she was safely married, and if this young man is as sober and sincere as you say, I advise you to encourage it, and forget any ideas of offering her beauty to the highest bidder."

"Sarah, you can be so wrong and so right at the same time that I despair——"

By this time, having moved well out of sight, I had loosened a few of my curls because of what I had heard, and now came into the parlor purposely to silence them. I was altogether content with the whole development. My self-confidence soared. My mouth wasn't really too big. I was beautiful! I could get Solomon! My stepmother would help me! For once I blessed her narrow mind. And I added to my love of Solomon a great gratitude for taking me away from all this: from restraints, dullness, family duties. He was bringing me freedom as well as love: I could cook, sew, dress as I pleased—love and be loved to my heart's content. I also felt very astute and discerning. I realized that Sarah loved my father very much and wished she were beautiful—that though I gave her a lot of help, she would be glad to have me gone. My presence was too constant a reminder that my mother had been a beautiful woman. She hoped to possess a little bit more of father with me gone.

I sat down primly to wait for Solomon while giving respectful attention to Sarah's final admonitions. At the same time, my heart was thumping and my thoughts were giddy: *Come on, Solomon. Come on, my lover. I'm waiting for you—the beauty in bondage. Waiting for you to free me. Waiting for you to court me. Hurry, Solomon.*

Waiting. Waiting for Solomon. This was to become the refrain of my life. If I had only been as discerning as I thought I was, I would have glimpsed on that very first evening what lay ahead. Before Solomon arrived, more than an hour late, I was sick with anxiety, my father was angry, and Sarah, tight-lipped and knitting frantically, was suffering in her own secret way. But our irritation was erased when Solomon arrived with apologetic explanation of business delays and carrying presents for all. It didn't matter that the gifts were all wrong: tobacco for my father, who didn't smoke, a red knitting bag for Sarah, who loathed red, and confections for me in a flavor that I didn't care for.

(Study the gift-bearers, Tricky. There will be many among your suitors, I'm sure. Much of the true nature of a man is revealed through the gifts he brings to a woman.)

All during the courtship, Solomon brought me gifts, every time he came to call. I treasured every one as a special offering at the shrine of love. It mattered not that the flavors and flowers and ornaments were not my preferences. I was too full of romantic notions to realize that his giving me always what he wanted me to have, without any attention to what I might want, was really an expression of self-love. He loved me, yes—but he loved me for himself and not for myself. Even the pearl ring that was something I could truly admire and treasure—so beautiful and so valuable that it reminded me of the Biblical "pearl of great price" and seemed the perfect symbol of love —even this was no true gift, never really mine. But it was indeed a pearl of great price! I will tell you more about this later.

It seemed to me that Solomon cruelly delayed proposal. Sometimes he seemed impersonal and detached in a manner that tortured me, and my high spirits would gradually deflate in his presence. At other times, he would study me with an impassivity that made me uneasy. But all this was forgotten when he rushed in to see me one day, all gaiety of spirits, in a mood completely new and exciting to me, demanding that we get married at once. Everything was just right, he said, all his worries gone. He drove a new carriage and a beautiful span of bronze sorrels. He told me that a home was waiting for us—that he had been able to get a good house at a great bargain—and that best of all, he had a very special gift to present me. We would take a drive into the countryside. . . .

I had never seen Solomon so happy—I had never been so happy myself. That day was all laughter and light . . . and I remember till yet the glow in Solomon's eyes: the dreams in his eyes were no longer lost—they were coming true—and I thought it was all a part of the miracle of love. . . .

He stopped the carriage beside a pond along a shady lane (I remember there were some lively ducks sailing about gaily diving for underwater delicacies—I saw them through a sort of haze—for Solomon kissed me with a fervor he had never before exhibited) and he brought out the ring—a pearl, a golden bronze with pink lights—it reminded me of the sheen on the shoulder of one of the sorrels. He slipped it on my finger. It was a perfect fit. How had he known? He said with a sort of wonder, "I never expected it to fit so well." And I thought it only another sign of love's greater perceptions.

"It is a very valuable ring," he said. "Promise me that you will never remove it from your finger, except in my presence."

I promised. He held my hand, studying it, caressing it, murmuring, "lovely, lovely." Then he raised it to his lips, and finally laughingly kissed the ring, "for luck," and took me into an ardent embrace that convinced me heaven lay just beyond the gates of marriage.

We were married in my father's house. He provided generously for my wedding wardrobe and gave Solomon a hundred dollars for our wedding trip. And I drove away with my handsome husband, behind the sorrel team, to "freedom." We decided to delay our honeymoon travels until we had inspected our new home. It was some distance from my father's, and I had never seen it. Solomon said he had been there only once. He had told me it was furnished because the owners had removed to another part of the country and did not want to freight so many possessions. I was surprised to find it in such disorderly state as if its occupants had moved out in unhappy haste. Solomon explained that he had intended to bring out help to clean and repair but had been too busy to arrange it. The house was an attractive two-story frame, the furnishings were in good taste, some even luxurious, and the yard and garden well planted. All only needed tending. I settled down to work, love, and happiness, wedding trip unimportant and indefinitely postponed.

But this flawless state of bliss did not last long. I soon found out that I could not expect Solomon home at any particular time in the evening or night. He explained that his business took him to outlying shops and that the keepers would often delay him with conversations, games, or drinks that he could not refuse and remain on profitable and friendly relations. This I could understand and was not too disturbed for a while. But the house was lonely, I was impatient for his company, and I always waited up for him. One night it was three o'clock before he got in. I thought he must have been set upon and robbed, perhaps murdered. When he arrived haggard but safe, I embraced him with a great outburst of weeping, protest, and relief. He expressed nothing but annoyance at my concern, lay down on the bed in utter weariness, still fully clothed, and went to sleep as I questioned him. He slept until noon the next day, then changed his clothes, ate what I set before him, and left without giving an explanation. I retaliated by going to bed early the following night and pretending sleep when he came in, again in the early morning hours. I heard him sigh deeply as he undressed for bed in the dark. He was depressed! He needed me! I told him at once that I was awake, offered to get him food, said I was sorry I hadn't waited up.

"Sorry?" he said, as if surprised that I was there. "Sorry? I'm relieved that you've decided to be sensible."

So I tried to appear to have decided to be sensible—tried to convince myself that his business was a troublesome one, full of irregularities, and that I shouldn't pry into a man's world—that he had come home early at first only because we were newlyweds—that I must settle down, as it were. This reasoning made even better sense when I realized that I was pregnant. I wanted to find no serious defect in my husband. I felt comforted and not nearly so lonely in the evenings. I visited neighbors, worked hard, and found at last that I could sleep without Solomon by my side.

Then one evening he surprised me, coming home unusually early. He brought me some confections, the wrong flavor, and some ribbons, the wrong colors, but, oh, I was so happy! He looked hollow-eyed and pale and I felt contrite—felt that I had failed him somehow.

"Business has been bad," he said.

I did everything I could to lift his spirits, banish his worry—told him how much I loved him, poor or rich. He seemed cheered. That night I was so reassured, so happy in his love, that I yearned to talk about the child we would have, but delayed telling him, lest he worry more about business being bad.

The next morning just before he left, he asked me for the ring. It was so valuable that he could get a good loan on it for his business. It was only for security. We'd have it back in a few days, he said.

I did not share my uneasiness with my family and soon they were beyond my reach, for my father, with Sarah, my brothers, and my half sisters, removed to Mexico. He hoped to make a fortune as a colonist in Texas; the land was rich and free and physicians much needed around the Brazoria settlement—so he had been advised by his good friend, Dr. Anson Jones. He brought the family to visit Solomon and me before their departure, and was pleased with our apparently happy circumstances. I tried to hide the alarm and grief I felt at his going so far away, completely out of my life. In those days we had to accept the fact that such separation of families was often permanent. There could be no visiting, no presence for births, weddings, sickness, or death, and little communication. There was always the hope held out, however, that if the "promised land" proved up, the ones left behind would follow. In our case, this seemed unlikely. My father made a chance to be alone with me. He reminded me gravely that my maternal grandmother lived in Kentucky, that she had told him at mother's funeral that her home was always open to her daughter's children and her heart and purse to their needs. "So if you are ever in distress of any kind, call on your grandmother. I have had some recent correspondence with her. She wants you to write to her." I promised I would do this. Then he asked me if I knew the condition of Solomon's finances. I told him I did not. He asked if I had money on hand—had Solomon given me money for my own? I had to admit he had not—that I only had the money that I had brought with me—some savings of gift money. Solomon did all the buying, I said, without saying what precious little he bought—just staples to supplement what came from the garden. Father frowned at this. Then he gave me a hundred dollars. "This is your money, yours alone. Call it 'reliance money' and never spend a cent of it unless your personal need is imperative and Solomon absolutely can't supply you."

I hid the money carefully and I did not tell Solomon about it.

The pearl was back on my hand before long, as Solomon had said it would be. But not more than a week passed until it was gone again. Then daily I watched the nervous tension build up in him until it culminated in the matter of the gloves. Solomon loved fine gloves and had many pairs. I always laundered them very carefully for him. This particular pair had shrunk and when he put them on, the fingers were too short. His hands were perspiring and the gloves wouldn't come off easily—the more he tugged, the more he perspired and the tighter they stuck. Finally he managed to rip one down the palm, then with his free hand he ripped the other one. But he was not done; he deliberately tore the gloves to shreds, finger by finger. Then he looked around in a sort of frenzy, saw the other pairs drying on the table, and approached them as if they were something hateful and alive. In horrible fascination, I watched him tear up six pairs of gloves. Then panting and flushed, unaware of me it seemed, he left

41

the house, and for the first time since the day I met him, he departed without pulling on gloves. I watched him from the window and wept. His hands looked exposed and helpless. He himself looked ungroomed and wounded. . . . I became very sick at my stomach.

It was dawn the next morning before I saw him again. Neither of us mentioned the episode of the gloves. That day someone came for the carriage and horses. Solomon said he got a fine price for them—that he could better afford to hire a rig then feed the team.

It was only a short time later that Solomon asked me if I had any money. I told him only a little that father had left for emergency use. He pressed me until I told him the amount. Then he became excessively, unnaturally gay and said the business was saved—that one hundred dollars would get him out of the hole. When I asked him to explain his business crisis, he told me a long story about customer credit and payments due to wholesalers and being cut off from his stock. I realized with a sense of shock that he was not telling me the truth and that I must start thinking with my mind instead of my heart. I flatly refused to let him have the money. He argued with me—then he begged—then he wept. I had never seen a grown man cry before, except my father at my mother's funeral. After all, Solomon was just twenty-three, but he had seemed like such a man to me, and here he was sobbing before me like a desolate child—sitting slumped in a chair, in utter despondency, his arms hanging, his face crumpled, crying! I couldn't go to him and comfort him, for I still didn't intend to give him the money. So I sat down in another chair, looking at him, and cried too.

Then he said something that effected me more as a verification than a revelation: "It's a gambling debt, Hatty. The cards. A gambling debt."

When I said nothing, he finally cried out to me, "For God's sake, Hatty, can't you see? Unless you let me have the money, we're ruined!"

I felt old when I answered him, old and painfully wise. "All you have made out of your business, if you still have one, and the ring and the horses and carriage—and perhaps this house—are already gone and have not appeased the debt. My few dollars would not reclaim any of these. You intend to gamble with it in the awful hope that you'll win. Why do you think you will win?"

"I've lost so long, it's time for a turn. Besides, I was cheated out of some of it. I know what to watch for. Trust me, Hatty. I'll get it back—all of it."

"No, Solomon."

"Hatty, you're cruel. You're selfish. You've hung around my neck for these months telling me how much you love me. Now you have a chance to prove it and you say 'No, Solomon' in that cold heartless manner. How could you, Hatty, how could you?" He was crying again.

"It's my money, Solomon. Reliance money my father said it was. I have no money that has come from our marriage. You have given me no money; I have been too timid to ask for any. I haven't gone shopping a single time since we were married. I have been wanting to ask you for some money to buy goods for baby clothes, but——"

"Baby clothes! Baby clothes! Oh my God, Hatty, not that too!"

"That too. And if your gambling brings us to ruin, I have to think about having the baby—not just us. I won't let you gamble with that hundred dollars."

"What will I do, Hatty? What will I do?"

"You'll have to make out the best way you can." I left him and went to bed, lying in miserable, sleepless stillness. After a while he came in. I pretended to be asleep. He crawled in bed, restlessly turned for a while, then sat up and seemed to be studying me and my breathing to be sure I slept. Then he got up and began to prowl the house. He closed the bedroom door, but I knew what he was doing. He lighted a candle. He hunted for the money. For several hours he hunted, taking the bedroom last and most cautiously. I had no fear of his finding it. But in those hours I had to lie there and become acquainted on a new scale with the man I had married: he would lie, beg, weep, steal from the needs of his wife and unborn babe. All the things he had provided for me that I thought were from a loving husband's hands had been really given from the bounty of his other love, his greater love: gambling. The house that had been vacated in such disorder—the ring that was not bought or made for me, but just happened to fit—and all the rest. It was like being beholden to a man's mistress. My sense of shame and disillusionment became something alive and liquid, hot and painful, that trickled from my throat into my chest, and through my stomach, completing its course with a cramping sensation, low and agonizing. I thought of my child and tried to compose myself. Did I still love Solomon? I asked myself—and realized I did. The awful pain seemed to dissolve in yearning to help him. I must help him. But how, without compromising this new practical self that I hadn't known was within me. This night I was learning much about myself as well as Solomon. Then I thought of the gift money—bits I had saved in the years before I met Solomon, birthday and Christmas gifts of small amounts. There were fifty-seven dollars in all. I had been planning to spend some of it on baby garments if Solomon did not offer me the money I needed. But I had a number of fine petticoats from my trousseau that would make up adequately for the baby. Perhaps the gift money would buy back a little of all that had just been lost between us. . . . When he finally came to bed and lay down with a great sigh, I stirred and asked if he were awake.

"Solomon, I do love you. I want to help. Would fifty dollars——"

"Oh, yes, Hatty. Oh, yes!"

"And besides that, seven dollars for new gloves——"

"Oh, my dear, my sweet girl." He turned to me, all affection, all contrition. "I made a sorry spectacle about the gloves, and put myself in bad grace with lady luck besides. Without gloves I have no luck, no confidence. And I've been too dead broke to buy new ones. Many a time new gloves have put me back in the luck. They'll do the trick this time! I know it! I'm sure of it!"

"Solomon, you do have a respectable business, don't you?"

"Of course I do, Hatty. My family have been successful merchants of one kind or another for generations. I told you that."

"Then why do you make a business of gambling?"

"It isn't business. It's something I like to do. Many gentlemen gamble."

"Many gentlemen like whiskey and drink regularly. Some like it too much and die drunkards. Don't you think you like gambling too much, Solomon? Why don't you quit? Leave it alone?"

"I will. I will, Hatty. I promise you. But not now. Not when I'm stripped. I'm due a winning streak. And I've got to get the ring back. Don't you realize—that ring's worth a fortune—the greatest luck I ever had. If I hadn't won it and all the other stuff with it, we might not have been married even now. Oh, what a game that was, Hatty!"

"And you married me just to celebrate!"

"Don't say such a thing. It sounds trashy, common."

"Why didn't you quit when you had so much? or at least before you lost it all?"

"When you're winning, you feel like you'll never lose again—and —well—when you're losing, you must try to win back what you've lost. And then, a gentleman must always consider fair play and self-respect."

"Self-respect?"

"Certainly. When you're winning the heap, it doesn't seem fair to pull out. When you're losing, it's cowardly."

"Do all gamblers play fair?"

"I guess you know what a silly question that is. Are all men honest in business? Is any game without its cheats? Life is full of greedy guts and cutthroats. One of them has that ring. I intend to win it back and I won't quit till I do!"

"Maybe the man you won it from feels the same way about you."

"I won it from the man who has it now."

"I see." But I didn't see. I didn't understand. I only knew quite well that gambling had us on the brink of disaster and I must do everything possible to get Solomon to quit.

"Would you want your son to be a gambler, Solomon?"

"I hadn't thought about it."

"Well, think about it."

We were both silent for a while. I waited for some comment, some expression of concern for the child we were to have. Finally, he gave a little chuckle.

"Hatty," he said, "we're all born gamblers. Life is a continuous game of chance with big bets on survival and success. The gambling we do with cards and other forms of betting entertainment is simply indulgence in condensed living. There can be all the despair of loss, all the glory of gain in one evening. Within a few hours, sometimes minutes, a man can rise from pauper to prince. It's tremendously exciting, Hatty! Condensed living, that's what it is! The essence— without all the tiresome deviations and delays that must go into everyday plodding toward good or bad fortune. Do you know, Hatty, when you're *really* gambling, you don't think of another thing in the world. Nothing outside the game is with you—no persons—no problems—no awareness of time. I wish I could explain the feeling."

"I think I understand."

He chuckled again. "You know, Hatty, if you were a man, I think you might not be so averse to the cards . . . you're willing to take a chance and parlay a stake of fifty dollars into a pearl that a princess would envy . . . so tomorrow you'll be a poker player by proxy. I shall consider that you are holding my hands—that should bring me a special kind of luck." He laughed outright.

"It's not the pearl I'm gambling for, Solomon. It's you. And I don't feel lucky at all." I turned away from him and wept.

"Hatty, dear." He touched me gently. "Don't cry. I'll quit. I promise to quit when I get the ring back."

My weeping did not mar Solomon's happiness and relief at having fifty dollars and a new chance. He was soon asleep. And before I slumbered, he had some pleasant dream in which he broke out laughing (such a ghostly sound, sleep-laughing)—and he spoke in his sleep.

"Too bad, Mr. Howard," he said with playful sympathy. "Too bad. But you can see for yourself that I am a man whom kings obey and queens love."

Who was Mr. Howard? I wondered. Unfortunately, I would soon find out.

At this point in her narration, Harriet was transported from past to present by a close rich fragrance, the aroma of hot chicken gumbo. She looked up and Tricky was standing beside the desk with the supper tray.

"Chicken gumbo and snow pudding, Gram. Where do you want it?"

"Right here. I'll clear the desk." She opened the drawer and swept the desk top clear of the scattered pages so closely filled with her small fine handwriting, thinking as she did so: I must be more careful.

"What a long letter, Gram!"

"Yes, and writing has tired me. But gumbo and pudding should revive me enough for the Indian story I promised to tell you."

"Let's hurry, Gram. Hurry and eat."

"We will not hurry. Your Uncle Frank says it is not healthful to hurry with eating. We will sit here quietly and relish every bite of this wonderful, beautiful food. Then you will call Marcus to take the tray and light the fire, and I will be ready."

"Gram, why do you always talk about food like it was a beautiful picture or a bouquet of flowers?"

46

"There's a very special reason. I'll tell you sometime, when you're older."

"How much older?"

"Considerably."

"There's certainly a big pile of things for you to tell me when I'm older, isn't there, Gram? You'll be getting older and older too. And you're pretty old already. Do you suppose——?"

"I don't know what you're saying, Tricky. I'm eating."

Tricky concentrated on the gumbo and pudding. She didn't want to finish behind her grandmother. That would delay the storytelling. . . .

"It was the custom of the Caddoes for the children to be taught by the grandmothers of the tribe," Harriet began.

"I wish we were Caddoes, Gram, and you were the only teacher I had to have."

"If that were the case, I would be explaining to you certain things about your conduct—about being good—about the dangers you would encounter on the way to the spirit land of eternal happiness—and how to overcome them."

"How to get to Indian heaven, you mean."

"One of the teaching stories I would tell is the story of a young brave named Ha-ah-hot-shoo-we-da, The Perfect One. He was flawlessly made: his features were godlike, his skin the luster of polished bronze, and his hair like purple-black satin. In his limbs was the grace of a young stag, and his muscles held the strength of an eagle's claws.

"This handsome young brave was also accomplished in manly things. He was fleet of foot, sure of his arrow's mark, and full of energy and skill for games and ceremonies. And as for his voice—it was pure melody—and such whistling: oh my! he could cast a spell with his whistling, so high and sweet. The Caddoes loved an accomplished whistler."

"He must have been wonderful!"

"Well, he appeared to be—he was—almost. Of course, his attentions were sought by many maidens. He was pampered by the womenfolks of the village and imitated by his brothers and companions. But alas, this youth was not as perfect as he outwardly appeared to be. All his beauty and accomplishments could not conceal a big flaw in his nature.

But because it was so hard to look upon him and find fault with him at the same time, no one spoke to him of this fault except his grandmother."

"Oh dear. What was wrong with him? Was he mean to animals?"

"I don't think so. He was hardly aware of them—hardly aware of anything except himself."

"Oh."

"And his beauty. He would stand by the clear water and gaze at himself for hours."

"Oh."

"And when he was not admiring himself, he was critical of others. He would tell his sister that her nose was too big. He would tell his brother Na-wotsi, that his fingers were too short for proper skill with bow and arrow. And he told his best friend, Tasha, that with his big feet, it would be better for him to straddle a log in the water and use his feet for paddles, since they were much too big and flat for running on the trail. Ha-ah-hot-shoo-we-da laughed often at one whose eyes were set too close together for comeliness, telling him that surely Caddaja had put a bug's face on a man."

"Who was Caddaja?"

"The Evil One. Ha-ah-hot-shoo-we-da's grandmother told him that in her opinion, the Evil One had twisted the tongue of her grandson, else he would not speak so much of his own perfections nor dwell so often on the flaws of others. And she warned him of the consequences . . . Well, it happened one time that Tasha became so enraged with Ha-ah-hot-shoo-we-da's derision of his big flat feet that he challenged The Perfect One to a race: If Tasha could catch Ha-ah-hot-shoo-we-da before he reached a certain spot, there would be an end of this mockery."

"How?"

"Tasha would cut out Ha-ah-hot-shoo-we-da's tongue."

"Oh my!"

"Ha-ah-hot-shoo-we-da said to Tasha, 'That is a very wicked thought, tejas. Though I have no fear that you can catch me to perform such an act, just imagine how dreadful it would be if the tribe were deprived of my beautiful whistling.'

" 'Better to be deprived of the pleasure of such music than to endure the misery of such mockery,' Tasha replied.

"Ha-ah-hot-shoo-we-da agreed to run, for he was brave and self-confident. So after another had set the proper distance between the contestants for starting such a serious race, the drums beat a signal, and the runners dashed ahead.

"Ha-ah-hot-shoo-we-da found, as he had expected, that it was not at all difficult to keep well ahead of his awkward-paced friend. To tease Tasha, Ha-ah-hot-shoo-we-da would slow down, and allow his opponent by supreme effort to get so close that he was ready to reach for his victim—then Ha-ah-hot-shoo-we-da, laughing, would sprint far ahead. Along the path to the spot designated for ending the race, there was a rushing stream to be crossed. Ha-ah-hot-shoo-we-da decided, in order to make his performance more spectacular, that he would take a short cut and make a dangerous crossing of the stream above the place regularly used. At this danger-crossing, there was a large rock in mid-stream and deep violent waters around. But the stream was no wider than a man's two leaps, if that man were agile and sure. So Ha-ah-hot-shoo-we-da, with the grace of a winged buck, leaped to the great rock in the center of the stream. Then he paused to look back and laugh at Tasha.

"And he called out: 'What good are paddles without a canoe?' Then he leaped for the other bank. But his eye had stayed too long in pleasure at Tasha's dismay; his laughter had thrown his head high. So he did not see the bit of moss at his toe—the small patch of slickness that was his downfall. He fell into the stream. His head struck a stone. The swirling waters pulled him down, and his spirit was released from his body and started on its journey to Caddi-Ayo."

Harriet paused and looked at Tricky, sitting in a posture of pure wonderment on the stool at her feet.

"Caddi-Ayo . . . Caddi-Ayo . . . " Tricky repeated after her grandmother. "What a beautiful word, Gram."

"It means Chief-of-the-Sky, The God One. In the teaching tales of the Caddo grandmothers, there were many tests of the spirit described —tests that would be encountered along the journey to paradise. Your ability to pass these tests depended, of course, on your conduct in earthly life."

"What happened when you couldn't pass the tests?"

"You would be turned into a certain plant or animal, as befitted your virtues and your faults."

"What happened to Ha-ah-hot-shoo-we-da?"

"Well, he was able to pass some of the tests without any difficulty. Then he came to a place where a voice called out to him to stop and talk a while. He shouldn't have stopped. He should have pressed on. But he liked to talk, and the voice was a gossipy, inviting one, inquiring about Ha-ah-hot-shoo-we-da, his family, and friends. So he recited at length his own perfections. Then he spoke of his sister with the big nose.

"The voice said, 'She also had a great generosity, did she not?'

"And Ha-ah-hot-shoo-we-da replied, 'I suppose so.'

"Then he told of his friend whose eyes were set so that his face looked like a bug.

" 'But his eyes were sharp on the trail, were they not?' the voice inquired, 'and his head full of forest wisdom?'

" 'I suppose so,' Ha-ah-hot-shoo-we-da said. 'And that Tasha, whose big flat feet are the cause of my being here much sooner than I expected or desired, he should have been a turtle instead of a man.'

" 'But were not the feet of Tasha willingly used for errands useful and kind? It was not the feet of Tasha, but your own feet misguided by vanity and mockery that brought you here, too soon and unprepared.'

" 'I suppose so,' Ha-ah-hot-shoo-we-da murmured, at last abashed and silent.

" 'You are not yet ready to dwell with Caddi-Ayo,' the voice told him. 'You will be turned into a tree—a very beautiful tree with gracious trunk and branches, and leaves of intricate and lovely design, like a mulberry tree, and creating a cool, heavy shade, giving pleasure to man and beast. It will fill with pretty blossoms, lovely to look upon. But the flowers will fall and the sweet fruit of the true mulberry will not appear. For the spirit yields no fruit to vanity and mockery.'

"And so that is the reason we have the tree called the *shade mulberry* which to this day bears no berries from its false blossoms."

Harriet sat back in her rocker and sighed, pleasantly weary, drowsy with the warmth of the flickering fire.

"Were there any shade mulberry trees where you lived on Caddo Lake, Gram?"

"All the trees at *Mulberry Shore* were true mulberry, Tricky, true mulberry. And the fruit so sweet, so very sweet. The trees big and bountiful, haven for children and birds . . . a regular haven . . ." Harriet's voice trailed off, and her eyes closed.

"Gram, tell me——" Tricky saw that her grandmother was asleep. She sat gazing into the fire for a while, occupied with visions of Ha-ah-hot-shoo-we-da. After a while, she got up and stood close to the fireplace mirror panels and studied her reflection there. And her thought was, perhaps I am as perfect as Ha-ah-hot-shoo-we-da. I have heard Uncle Frank say I am dangerously bright. Aunt Addie's friends are always saying, "What a beautiful child! You will soon have a New Orleans belle on your hands, no doubt about it." So, I am beautiful and I am bright.

Tricky removed her apron. She slipped the bows from her black curls, and found some of Harriet's combs for securing her hair high on her head. She removed a fancy umbrella from the rack near the dresser, and using it as a sort of walking-stick accessory as she had seen ladies of fashion do, she strutted before the mirror, glancing at her grandmother from time to time to be sure she still slept. After a bit, she replaced the umbrella, and then unbuttoned her shoes, removed shoes and stockings, and, raising her skirt above her knees, gave close scrutiny to feet, ankles, and legs. "Perfect," she said aloud. "Perfect and beautiful." A log in the fire popped open and sputtered, sending out new flames. The light danced on the mirrors, making waves. Tricky thought of Ha-ah-hot-shoo-we-da gazing at his reflection in the water for long hours. She hastened to get back into her true self and costume. She brought a shawl and put it over Harriet's knees.

As she left her grandmother, she was thinking of the cook. I must go find Jennifer. I must tell her she is a wonderful cook. I must tell her that I'm quite sure she makes the best snow pudding in the whole wide world. I'll never, never again, talk about what big funny-bunny ears she has.

3.

As Harriet continued the preparation of the letter-manuscript that she intended for a post-mortem confidence with her granddaughter as a young lady, she found her days filled with an unexpected zest. Looking out over her life from the vantage point of purpose in old age was like viewing from a height something examined heretofore only at eye level. At any time when she could be alone and pick up her pen, the story flowed from her mind to the page in a steady stream of writing. She would bring her mind to focus on any part of the scene, like a spyglass, and it would leap into clarity through all her senses. When she did pause occasionally, and hold the pen in idleness, it was not in an effort of recalling, but a pleasure of reliving—an indulgence of the senses.

Now, when she was fully rested at night after a few hours of sleep (as had been the case for some years), she did not lie in self-imposed apathy waiting for daylight, she arose and in happy stealth made fire and light and continued her work. If Marcus wondered what so often became of the wood that he left ready for the morning fire, he was too considerate of her privacy to inquire and too aware of her cheerful disposition to be concerned. Addie, with no knowledge of her mother's nighttime activity and busy in her own affairs, accepted the explanation that Harriet's contented seclusion was a preoccupation with copying some family papers and piecing a velvet and satin log cabin quilt for Tricky. Harriet kept the quilt close at hand to work on when Tricky and other callers were around, and no one observed her slow progress on it.

Harriet approached the story of Mr. Howard feeling like a patron of the theater taking a choice seat at a familiar but ever-exciting performance.

I got very little rest that night, my mind in such turmoil with the full revelation of Solomon's passion for gambling, and added to that, Solomon's restless slumber at my side, talking in his sleep about a Mr. Howard and laughing in such an eerie way. I started to waken him and ask about this Mr. Howard. And then I decided I would be better able to go to sleep if I didn't know.

The next morning, before Solomon was dressed and downstairs, Mr. Howard was knocking at the door.

I was hanging out clothes in the back yard at the time. I had been up since dawn, trying to work away my worries with cleaning tasks. And although it was not wash day, I had gathered up several tubs of clothes and started a washing. Each dirty spot rubbed out made me feel more hopeful, and the sweet fresh scent of clean things waving in the morning air was invigorating.

When I heard the knocking, I walked around to the front, clothes-pin bag around my waist and a wet garment in my hands, expecting at this time of day to see one of the neighbor's children sent to borrow something. As I rounded the corner, my bonnet blew off, and there was a man catching it for me, laughing at my confusion with no place to put the garment and free my hands.

"Shall I put it back on for you?" The man had a strange effect on me, the pale blue eyes so very bright in the swarthy face, the teeth so white and even exposed in a merry grin. "On second thought, I think not. My eyes rebel at being deprived of the view."

I did not like his familiarity, and my look told him so.

"Can you tell me if Solomon Page lives here?" He still held my bonnet.

"He does, and I am Mrs. Page."

His manner changed. He apologized for the intrusion, introduced himself properly, explained that he did business with my husband, and having been unable to locate him lately had decided to call at his home. Though his words were proper and his tone respectful, his eyes made me uncomfortable—they were so probing and so accented by heavy dark eyebrows and abundant sideburns that I found myself staring into them without intending to. I quickly asked to be excused until I could call my husband and unlatch the front door . . . When I let him in, he was still holding my big pink bonnet, and we both laughed.

Solomon had seen Mr. Howard arrive and was trying to get dressed in a nervous frenzy. He kept saying, over and over, "He's the man, Hatty, he's the man." I told Solomon to be calm, dress properly, and come down to the parlor for coffee. In my father's house, I had become adept at conversing with strangers. I would see that Mr. Howard didn't get annoyed with waiting. "For God's sake, Hatty. Be careful what you say. He's the man!" Solomon clutched my arm, instructed in stealthy tones. "Make him like you. He could take the house, put us out this minute if he wanted to. He could ruin me. Maybe that's what he wants to do. O God!"

"Solomon, the fifty-seven dollars, I put the pouch in your coat pocket."

"The fifty-seven dollars—oh yes, oh yes, the fifty-seven dollars. Such a little bit! Such a damnable little! But a little money and a lot of luck . . . you've got to bring me luck today, Hatty, you've got to. Kiss me for luck . . . now get down to Howard. No wait! Wait, Hatty! Gloves! I have no gloves yet. I may have to leave with Howard, and no gloves! Oh, God, no gloves!"

"Solomon, there is a pair with your wedding suit. You know, I put them away to save."

"Get them. They'll do. Get them."

I got the gloves and then rushed down to Mr. Howard, resolved to learn all I could about this man who frightened Solomon so. I felt fiercely protective, as if running to a dear one's rescue.

Mr. Howard was older than Solomon, by perhaps ten years; his figure was larger and stouter and his grooming in the height of fashion. I remember that he wore a blue silk waistcoat with black stars embroidered on it, and a large blue crystal stone for a watch fob that sparkled as he toyed with it. I recall also that he wore an impressive diamond ring. He told me that he was in the wholesale jewelry business and he and Solomon had some dealings in jewelry stock. I said, "Yes, I know," being careful not to reveal what I really knew and what was dawning upon me with awful clarity: Solomon was no match for this man in business or gambling. He was shrewd and self-confident, and exuded an unsavory sort of attraction or power. I felt disturbed and rather helpless in his presence. I could not see what benefit it would be to Solomon for Mr. Howard to like me. I could sense, on the other hand, how it might compound our troubles. While I chatted to him of house and garden and the flower borders I had planned for the yard, I was thinking it would be safer for Solomon to take his losses and break from this man—just quit gambling and start over. I could go to my grandmother's until the baby came. Solomon could go to work. We could start over.

Suddenly, I was aware that Mr. Howard's tone had switched from polite to personal as he inquired, "Do you have no life apart from this house and yard? Are you daily tied to all the menial tasks required here? No servants? No pleasures?"

"I don't need servants. I enjoy work."

He didn't reply at once, just sat watching me, playing with his watch fob so that it flashed and glittered, and I watched it with a sickly sort of fascination to avoid meeting his eyes.

Then he said, "I know a real jewel when I see one," and paused, expecting the blush that I could not hold back. "It hurts me to see a precious gem in the wrong mounting. I make it my business when I find such a gem to get possession of it and put it in a proper setting that it may be seen and appreciated for its true worth."

I didn't know what to say. Oh, why, why, was Solomon so slow! I must flee or say something to break the spell of intimacy this man was so brazenly creating. I kept staring at the glittering fob, feeling more helpless and embarrassed every moment.

"I have offended you. I'm sorry. I spoke of jewels simply because precious stones are my business. I have often said that a jewel is a flower in stone, preserved beauty, as it were. My impulses regarding true beauty are really rather high-minded, Mrs. Page. When I see a flower blooming in isolation, its loveliness hidden away, I want to pluck it, place it in a vase that fits its beauty, and put it on exhibition."

"It would probably last longer left on the stem," I said.

"But what of all the pleasure lost? . . . Have you never considered the relationship between beauty and pleasure, Mrs. Page? Tell me, can it be possible that such flawless——"

Solomon was coming down the stairs. Oh, how thankful I was! I quickly got to my feet and started pouring coffee. Mr. Howard was at my side in an instant.

"Forgive me, dear little lady, forgive my forward speech as I forgive the rare beauty that provoked it." Then he moved away from me and toward the door to greet Solomon with a geniality that I am sure was very surprising to him.

I served the coffee quickly and made my escape through a fog of polite phrases, while Solomon, bemused with Mr. Howard's friendliness, stirred his coffee and stared into the cup, smiling faintly, scheming what to do and say—leaving Mr. Howard free to use his eyes on me, like a pale blue flare, lighting up, appraising, penetrating, following me with no abatement until the door closed behind me. I rushed

56

through the house and on out into the back yard, where I stood leaning against a tree, panting, bewildered, perspiring, as if I had been in a dangerous chase and narrowly escaped being caught. I had thought to rush to Solomon's rescue. Now who would rush to mine?

The events that followed so quickly upon Mr. Howard's visit were like a fantastic theatrical. That very afternoon a serving woman appeared at my door. She looked like something out of a gay drama. She was an attractive mixed-blood, caramel colored, gaily dressed. She carried an enormous bouquet, the flowers in mixed shades of pink. She presented me with the bouquet and a note from Solomon saying, "Lady Luck is smiling. Don't worry. All is well. I'll be late." The unnatural concern for my welfare, and the awareness, never before expressed, of my fondness for pink, made me more uneasy than happy. And I was still more surprised at the woman's announcement that she had been sent to serve me.

"I need no one," I said.

"But I was told to stay."

"I'm sorry. I have no money to pay you."

"I have been paid, ma'am."

So I admitted her, a minor character, and the play was begun.

Meeta was so cheerful, expressed such concern and interest in me, somehow surrounding me with luxurious attention, that I relaxed and slept soundly that night and didn't know when Solomon came in. The next morning, more odd things were happening: deliveries of more pink flowers, a large order of fancy groceries, assorted meats, fine wines, whiskies, and brandies. I rushed up to Solomon and shook him awake. He laughed and teased—was very gay. "From Lady Luck's horn of plenty," he said. When I chided him about the extravagances, he said promptly that they were Howard's extravagances. "All of them?" I inquired.

"All!" he replied jubilantly. "I didn't spend a dime of what you gave me except for gloves and the game. That would have been bad luck. And I was simply shining with luck, last night, my love, simply shining! Your luck!" He gave me a hug.

"How much did you win?"

"A very respectable stack, a *very* respectable stack. I am well fixed for this evening, for a really big game."

"Hadn't you better give me the fifty-seven back—for safety?"

"Heavens no, Hatty, that's not the way you play along with Lady Luck. We mustn't break the run by anything like that. We've started out to parlay that into the pearl, remember?"

"Yes, and I don't feel right about it at all, and I think it is quite wrong to accept all these things from Mr. Howard."

"Hatty! You don't think Mr. Howard would be courting a pregnant woman, particularly a married one, do you?" He laughed uproariously at my red face!

"Explain it to me! Or I'll throw it all out into the street, the woman included!"

"We're playing at my house tonight, Hatty, that's the explanation. A really big game. Howard and four other men. It's going to be a stamina game—we play as long as we can, financially or physically. We may play into tomorrow. Howard and I planned it and decided to play here. My premises, his provisions—I see nothing wrong with that. He's a man of means and no responsibilities that I know of: Why shouldn't he furnish the provisions?"

"Or use the house, since it's his."

"That's not the way it is, Hatty. He just loaned me money. The house is security. He doesn't possess it."

"Then why were you so scared yesterday that he had come to move us out?"

"I was nervous, that's all. He's not the bloodsucker I thought. I got to know him better yesterday. You know, Hatty, I think he likes us. I told him jovially that I was in a pickle about the ring since I had given it to you before we married. He said he'd throw it in the game tonight and give me another chance at it. I've watched him play that ring off and on before I won it. He must have some superstition about it—he plays it even when he has money. It always seems to heat up the game, you might say."

"And always gets back in the game, it seems."

"When I get it back, I'll never gamble with it again. I'll cash it in and be done with it."

"You gave the ring to me, Solomon."

"Of course. I'd buy you another one. After all, you don't want to be wearing a ring around that's worth thousands of dollars and may be carrying a gambler's curse."

I decided not to speak my thoughts on this. But I could not leave the subject of Mr. Howard's "provisions" alone.

"Why did he send Meeta?"

"Meeta?"

"The serving-woman."

"Do you think it would be proper for you to be preparing and serving food and drink to six men all night, and cleaning up after them?"

"I don't even think it's proper for Meeta to do it."

"Don't be fussy. These men are gentlemen, not ruffians. I'm just trying to point out to you that in providing this help for you, Howard was doing the considerate and proper thing. We planned it together, I told you that. When I am in better circumstances, I will provide these same things on some other occasion. He knows that. I told him."

"When you do, be sure you provide an abundance of pink flowers for the gentlemen," I said, with sarcastic implication. He laughed at my "joke," and as I left the room called after me, "Send Meeta up with a cup of coffee and a pink bud for my boutonniere!"

Such was the dialogue in *The Drama of Mr. Howard* at the end of the first act.

For the rest of the day I was possessed with a mood of defiance—defiance of Solomon's blindness and Mr. Howard's intentions—defiance of the "stamina game" with its masculine threats and excitements. I spent most of the day altering a rose-colored "half-dress," that had been made especially for my wedding trip and never been worn. When it came time to dress for the evening, Meeta took a big interest in my appearance and showed a fine talent for hair dressing. I had a large comb which she used to secure a cluster of flowers among my dark curls, and she selected a large pink rose that I would carry in my left hand, which was a fashion touch of the times. . . . My preparation was out of all proportion to my participation. As Solomon pointed out, I was not going to a party. He would present me, and after I was introduced and had served coffee, I would not rejoin the men unless he summoned me. They wanted no interruptions beyond Meeta's serving of food and drink when they asked for it. I must see that she did this promptly and that the food was well prepared. I did not care for the role assigned me. So when the men were gathered and I was being momentarily the charming hostess, I exerted myself, even beyond decorum, to be so charming that the game would be delayed. And there I made another discovery about gambling: the fever of it is more compelling than a woman's charms. The men were polite to me, but their minds were on each other and the contest ahead . . . with the exception of Mr. Howard. *I* was his game. And after a while his concentration upon me made me feel that he and I were alone in the room, engaged in a contest of our own—a type of contest in which I was altogether inexperienced.

Through the fevered hours of that night, Meeta was my informant. After my initial appearance, I didn't re-enter the presence of the players. But Meeta's descriptions were so detailed that I felt I had observed the whole thing. She even produced a deck of cards from somewhere and explained the game to me. Solomon was a steady winner throughout the evening, and then shortly after midnight, Meeta announced that Mr. Howard had the pearl in the game. Sometime later, Solomon came into the kitchen. He was slightly drunk, very triumphant, and more—I hardly know how to explain it—more masterful and admirable in appearance—I suppose more like the inner vision of himself, momentarily realized by the stimulant of his winnings.

"Hatty," he said. "Hold out your lovely lucky hand."

He slipped the ring on to my finger, but it wouldn't go on over the knuckle. I had not had it on for sometime and had been gaining weight.

"Hatty, what's wrong?" He was alarmed. I knew what he thought. It was a bad omen.

"Nothing's wrong. I'm supposed to gain weight. The ring always did fit tight."

"Oh." It took him a moment to realize what I was talking about.

"Meeta," he called her to him. "Let me see your hand." The ring fit perfectly. "Why the pearl is the color of your skin. How lovely! Look Hatty, isn't that lovely? You keep it on, girl, for as long as I play. You'll be close to me. You'll bring me luck."

Meeta's eyes met mine. She was saying to me plainly: "Humor him. He's a little drunk. You can trust me." And strangely enough, I did trust her.

"Is the game about over, Solomon?"

"Over? Hatty! When the pitch is this high? Why, the best is yet to come. Two are about ready to fall out. With just four in the game, we can bleed faster and heavier. Don't worry, Hatty, it's my night, and I'll have Old Man Howard ready for a shroud by daylight. Meeta, bring in a pot of hot coffee and some solid food." He strode from the kitchen like a confident, successful businessman.

Meeta came to me, pulling off the ring.

"Keep it on," I said. "I want neither credit nor blame for whatever luck eventually befalls him."

While Meeta was gone to serve the food, Mr. Howard came to the kitchen.

He came directly to me and stood looking down at me, his hands thrust in his pockets, his eyes smiling as if we shared a secret. And we did.

"You planned all this, didn't you, Mr. Howard? Even to Solomon's winning back the pearl?"

"I'm glad your beautiful head is not an empty one," he said.

"And what now, Mr. Howard?"

"That's for you to decide. That's why I am in here—to consult with you."

I looked at him steadily, waiting for what he had come to say.

"I maneuver for what I want. It is not my policy to engage in mayhem, nor to leave wide tracks of trouble behind me. Also, I recognize what I want when I see it, and do not rest until possession is accomplished."

I had made up my mind that anything he said would not startle or frighten me, at least not outwardly, for after the silent appraisal he had given me earlier, I was not unprepared for this interview. I have Mr. Howard to thank for one bit of valuable knowledge in the man-versus-woman relationship. As I flitted about among those six men, all shadows except Mr. Howard, I realized that the female of the species is equipped with a certain awareness of male intent, and if she will let this awareness communicate with her senses rather than ignoring it as evil or absurd, she will be much more able to cope with all matters that arise, pleasant or unpleasant.

So I didn't ask Mr. Howard what it was he wanted. I just turned my face away from his direct gaze and continued to wait for him to explain fully.

"I want you. I want you not for a moment's pleasure—but for years of pleasure. And I want you to share this pleasure, for a part of my enjoyment of your beauty would be in showing you what the rewards of beauty can be. I have no ties, and there are ways of bringing about a dissolution of those that bind you. I am aware that you have fooled yourself into thinking you love this weakling Solomon Page. He's no good at either business or gambling. He has lucky streaks, but he goes wild with them. You'll never mean as much to him as gambling. That pearl excites him more than you do."

He was trying to anger me into speech and almost succeeded.

"On the other hand, I (whose chief excitement in life has been fine gems, and I have traveled to far places to see them, even when I couldn't buy them)—I find you more exciting than any jewel I have ever beheld or bought. Don't you respond, just a little, to this excitement!" His voice was husky, compelling, and to my horror, I realized I was excited—my heart thumping so, my throat tight, my body recording an unwilling fascination. (Lesson two from Mr. Howard: you do not have to love, or even like, a man to be pulled into the net of his maleness.)

At that moment, I wondered desperately what had become of Meeta.

"You do respond. You do. You do not need to say a word. I know it. Now listen to me: We will humor Solomon along in this false prosperity. I'll hire him, send him to some foreign port on a gem-buying assignment. He will have letters to connections of mine. He will be in games wherever he is, and he'll gamble with *my* jewels, and we'll never see him again."

He knew Solomon's weaknesses. His diabolical scheme would work!

Anger cleared my throat, released me!

"Mr. Howard, your scheme is worthy of Satan himself. And if Solomon Page should cease to exist this minute, if I were as free as the day I met him, I would avoid you as if you really and truly were the Devil!"

And the devil laughed—laughed at me—and turning to the cabinet, poured himself a brandy and drank a toast:

"To the game," he said, "the game between me and you. What a worthy opponent I chose! What a challenge! You are just as I imagined and my pleasure begins sooner than anticipated."

Then he came back to me. "I would like to touch you but I won't. I will take my pleasures gradually and savor each one. Since you could stop my scheme for deporting dear Solomon, I have another move to make—and you cannot stop this one. I will go back in there and stay until Solomon Page is more in my debt than he was when I came . . . but I will not be through with him . . . I'll give him chances to get in even deeper . . . then I'll close in on him, and you know as well as I do what he'll do. He'll run out on me. He'll desert you. I'm as sure of that as I am of sunrise—and so are you."

"I'll tell him—I'll tell him this very night."

"Not this night. You would not humiliate yourself so before six men. Any time that you tell it, I can explain it away as misunderstanding, or feminine wiles to separate him from his gambling. And if you should convince him, do you think Solomon is the type to rush to your defense with gun or sword?"

I couldn't answer.

"That fact alone—that I am so sure he would not defend you, fight for you to the death, for insult or danger—makes me despise him and have little regard for the method of his removal . . . And now I set out to prove these things to you. Never fear for yourself. Whatever extremity I bring him to, you will be cared for."

I was unable to protest or cry out. I felt as if I had turned to stone.

He leaned toward me until I was sure he was going to touch me, but he didn't. "I will make up for the pain," he said. "Pleasure is sweeter after pain."

He left me, and Meeta came in while I was still standing in a daze.

"Are you ill, ma'am?"

"Why were you so long?"

"Long, ma'am? I just served the food. You're so pale and fagged-looking. Let me fix you an egg brandy." She led me to a chair at the kitchen table.

"Yes," I said. "Do that. I'll share it with you, and we'll drink a toast to the devil."

This was the curtain line on Act Two, Tricky. And when the curtain came up several hours later, it was daylight, and I was still sitting at the kitchen table, my head resting on my arms.

Meeta shook me gently.

"Let me help you to bed ma'am for some real rest."

I roused and listened. I heard only the faintest sound at the front of the house.

63

"They're still playing," she said, "but several are asleep on the floor. It'll be terrible quiet from now on. Let me take you upstairs."

I looked at her left hand. The ring was not on it. I asked no questions.

Meeta got me to bed, insisted that I drink something that seemed like hot milk. She held the glass for me, and her face so close to mine seemed to resemble Mr. Howard's but in a benign fashion. Was she a part of Mr. Howard's plot, I wondered. I didn't care. It was all very muddled. What a sweet smile she has, I thought, and went dead asleep.

When I awoke, the room was dim and Meeta was sitting in a rocker nearby.

"What time is it?" I asked.

"Mid afternoon, ma'am." She went to the windows and opened the shutters.

I sat up. She put pillows behind me, handed me hot tea. I sipped it gratefully.

She said, "I must leave for a while, but I'll be back. Mr. Howard said to give you this with his compliments—something returned to you, he said."

The pouch was the one I had given Solomon with the fifty-seven dollars in it. I examined it with amazement. How had Solomon happened to reveal that I had given him the money? But the money was not all! The pearl ring was there too, with Mr. Howard's initialed handkerchief run through it and tied.

"Meeta, Mr. Howard trusts you and you know each other in some way you have not revealed to me. Please take him a message for me. Tell him I am keeping the money because it was originally mine. But the ring was never mine. And as God is my keeper, I hope I never see him or the ring again!"

"Are you quite sure, ma'am?"

"Quite sure."

She took the ring and prepared to leave.

"I'll be back before late night."

"No, Meeta, don't ever come back."

"But, Mrs. Page, I'm hired—I'm paid——"

"Not by me. Good-by, Meeta."

"You should know, Mrs. Page, that Mr. Page is not here. After

64

the game, he drank heavily, then slept, and a while ago I prepared food and coffee for him, and he changed and left. I don't think he'll be back tonight."

"I can manage."

"The house is clean."

"Thank you."

"Don't dismiss me, Mrs. Page. You need me. I can make things easy for you. I can be with you—through anything."

Her face was so sad and appealing—she was so genuinely concerned for me—I was tempted to accept the comfort of her presence, the luxury of her attentions. She sensed my hesitation. She rushed to the bedside and fell on her knees.

"Don't spoil it all, ma'am! Don't send me away. I can be happy serving you—someone beautiful and kind like you. Like Mr. Howard says, we go together, you and me, the beautiful lady and just the right serving-woman to keep her beautiful. He's matched us well, ma'am. Don't make me go. I'll never cross you. I'll wait on you day and night. I'll protect you. I'll——"

"Hush, Meeta, hush!" I closed my eyes so I couldn't see her. I felt weak and lonely. I had no idea what Solomon would do. There was one thing certain: he could offer me no help or comfort. Why must I send this woman away—deny myself the solace of a devoted servant, the satisfaction of living as a beautiful lady properly attended? Even in my state of dejection, I had to face the answer, for it was plain: In accepting Meeta, I would be yielding something to Mr. Howard. Could he possibly have known the extent of the temptation he offered me in Meeta? Not only that we were suitable to the positions in which he desired to place us, but that we felt the mutual need for the security of such a relationship? I cannot know. I only realized through my misery that I couldn't violate the personal code that demanded I reject all connection with Mr. Howard.

"Go, Meeta. Leave me at once!" My eyes were still closed, my face turned away from her.

"No," she said. "I will stay."

So I couldn't hide my face like a distraught child. It would be a contest of wills.

I sat up straight in bed and faced her. "Get up!" I ordered.

She obeyed me. My eyes held hers, and I sensed again some kinship

with Mr. Howard, some resemblance, and this gave me the courage to
be harsh with her.

"For your connection with Mr. Howard, I pity you," I said. "I want
no part of anything that is a part of him. Do you understand? No part
of anything——"

Her face drained of all expression. She turned from me and walked
out the door without a backward glance. A final swish of bright skirts,
a soft click of the latch, and I was alone—utterly, desperately alone. I
cannot help but wonder, as I toy with this memory, what might have
happened if I had accepted Meeta as a part of my life that day. And
how I yearned to! There was some bond between us unrelated to the
circumstances. There have been times in my life, both of need and
elation, when I have thought: I wish Meeta were here. That is strange,
is it not? It is quite likely that in putting aside the favor of Mr. Howard
and the luxury of a devoted servant, I also shut out that most rare of
human relationships, a true friend. Sometimes I think this life is a
test in proper balancing—gains against losses.

To my surprise, Solomon came home that night, and we slipped into
a pattern of living that was pure delusion. We ignored all that had
happened relative to his gambling and walked on the thin ice of pre-
tence: that things were going smoothly in his business—that the lavish
supply of groceries delivered at the house from time to time was of his
own provision. My only touches with reality were the child I carried
and the hundred and fifty-seven dollars I had hidden away. When Mr.
Howard's plot had run its course, surely Solomon would be cured of
gambling for good, and somehow we would escape together—somehow!

It was only a matter of weeks before the thin ice broke under us
and we were floundering in another crisis. I awoke one night to the
awful sound of Solomon panting and gasping as if he couldn't breathe.
I hadn't heard him come in, but there he was, fully clothed, staggering
around in the candlelight, like he was drunk, but moving with purpose
from wardrobe to dresser, and stuffing things in a carpet bag . . . and
the horrible gasping, gasping, as if he were being chased and couldn't
get air into his lungs.

"Oh, Solomon, Solomon, what is it?"

"Howard! Howard! He turned on me like a mad dog! I've got to get
away! Got to get away!"

"I know. I know."

"You don't know anything about it! He called me a thief! He's the thief! He's robbed me! Robbed me of everything! I wish I had the guts to kill him, but I don't. And if I can't kill him, I've got to get away from him. He tricked me . . . he'll prove I'm a thief . . . send me to prison . . . let me rot there . . . have me in court, he said . . . prison for life, he said . . . or hanging . . . He'd like to see me hanging!"

"Solomon, listen to me. Don't be so frightened. Howard is only trying to scare you away—to make you desert me. We'll fool him. We'll go together."

For a moment I was calm and purposeful. I was out of bed, moving about, enumerating in my mind a few articles I'd take. "We'll leave everything we can't carry in that bag. We'll go right now. We'll get away from him—if we have to run all the way to Mexico. Papa will help us. Papa——"

"Are you crazy? I wouldn't get to the city limits dragging you along. I may not anyway if I don't hurry. Get me that fifty dollars—and I'll make it—if he doesn't have someone after me—some hound-killer right behind me—and I did feel followed—I did!" He leaned against the wardrobe panting.

I stood dazed and chilled. What I had said conveyed no meaning to him except that I might encumber him.

"Don't just stand there—get my things—what you think I'll need— in God's name, where are my gloves?" He staggered back to the dresser and jerked out a drawer so far that it fell to the floor.

"Solomon, listen. Believe me." My teeth were chattering so I could hardly talk. "Howard isn't after you. He's after me. I've wanted to tell you——"

"After you! Come to your senses!" He tried to laugh and couldn't. I realized that his misery was compounded with brandy, for the bottle that had come with the groceries that day stood empty on the dresser. He began digging in the drawer muttering, "Coward. Coward. Run. Run. When you ought to kill him. Kill him."

"Solomon! He deliberately planned to ruin you. Scare you. Make you desert me so I'd despise you. Don't you see? If we go away together, he'll leave us alone. We can make it. I have a hundred and fifty-seven dollars. That will take us a long way. That will——"

"A hundred and fifty-seven dollars? And where did you get all that, my fancy?"

"The fifty-seven I gave you was gift money I'd saved. I still have the hundred Papa left with me. Mr. Howard gave me back the fifty-seven you lost——"

"You lied to me—you cheated—you tricked me just like Howard ——"

"No, Solomon, listen——"

"You listen to me!" He grabbed me, shook me roughly. "Get the money."

"I'll get it," I said. "Turn me loose. Bring the candle."

"Get the candle yourself," he said, shoving me away. "I want my hands free. You're tricky. Confounded tricky. Conniving with Howard. But don't try anything—anything at all. I'll be right behind you, right after you."

"I hate you!" I said, and was surprised that I had given the scalding emotion that rushed over me such a name. I walked out the door and down the stairs in the darkness, my sense of outrage burning so bright that I made no misstep, touched no object. He came stumbling after, carrying the candle, bumping into things, panting and swearing.

I went into the kitchen. I said, "It's in the pantry." But my hiding place was actually in the basement, and the basement door could be barred from either side. While he was making his way toward the pantry, I quickly slipped through the basement door, taking the loose bar with me and dropping it into place on the inside.

Then I sat down on the basement steps, my dumb rage matching his abusive fury from the other side of the door. Finally, I heard him crying, and my hatred dissolved, leaving me sick and weak. After a while, I could hear him climbing the stairs, and then coming back down with a new alertness, as if sober fear were upon him, and out of the house by the back door.

It was daylight before I responded to the aching stiffness of my body and moved about. Feeling that my life was blighted and my heart broken beyond possible mending, I crept upstairs and into bed. And when I began to cry, tears didn't seem adequate to my despair . . . so I searched for and found some primitive cave of my emotions and brought forth from it wailing and mourning, beating and thrashing about until utterly exhausted and ashamed, I fell asleep and into fitful dreaming. And Meeta appeared to me, disheveled and wild-looking, as if she had fought her way in. But she straightened the covers, smoothed my tangled hair, offered me hot tea. The fragrance of it pleased me, and I opened my eyes. I saw Solomon. I closed them and opened them again. There was Solomon, real enough, looking white and dazed.

He's come back to me, I thought. He couldn't desert me. He loves me, after all. And there was tea. I didn't even know he could make tea. We stared at each other. He brought me a steaming cup. His hand trembled. So did mine.

"Don't spill it."

"I won't."

He didn't kiss me. Didn't say anything. Just sat back down. I sipped at the tea, welcoming the hot trickle down my throat.

"I'm glad you're home."

"Me too. And it's just luck that I'm not running, or in jail, or even dead. The purest luck—the most fantastic luck of my life."

"What do you mean?"

"He's dead. Good and dead."

"Who?"

"Old Man Dirty," he said. "Howard. Shot right through his craven heart!"

I felt rigid. Couldn't speak. Couldn't breathe. Couldn't move.

"And I'm glad," he added. "Very glad. Don't try to make me feel any different."

I held tight to my cup. I thought I must still be in the nightmare—still asleep and dreaming Solomon had killed Mr. Howard. I closed my eyes and moaned.

"Oh, come to, Hatty. Be thankful that he's dead—that we have a home—that I'm out of his clutches. All the papers he made me sign are burned—no record of any kind. I'm out of the trap. Nobody knows who did it."

And I was out of the trap too. But all I could feel was horror. "How can you be so sure that nobody knows you did it?"

"Oh, for God's sake, Hatty! I didn't kill him. I wanted to. But I didn't do it."

His statement was so matter-of-fact that I accepted it.

"It was luck's perfect timing, I tell you. I was hiding out last night

in a wholesale place that belongs to a friend of mine. I figured when
he came down this morning, he'd help me out of town. He did better
than that. He brought me the news: Howard's fine fate—his private
safe cracked—jewels and cash taken—papers burned. Bless the brave
heart that did it! Papers burned!" Solomon smiled and looked into
his teacup with a dreamy withdrawnness.

So it was his luck, not his desire, that had brought him back to me.
Now I wanted him to express some special concern for me—excuse
his conduct of the night before—say he was out of his mind for the
moment with fear and drink—that he wouldn't really have deserted
me—anything, anything to make it easier for me to forget his exhibition of naked concern for himself, and himself alone. But he said
nothing. I had to speak of it.

"After last night . . . why did you come back?"

"That's a silly question," he said. "With the dragon dead, there's
no cause for flight."

I wanted to accuse: But if it had been otherwise, you would have
fled and left me to be devoured. But my emotions were used up. I
could not quarrel or make demands. I took several big swallows of tea.

And Solomon said to his teacup: "He will not take this house. He
will not rub my nose in the dirt. He will not hold me to forced debts
I couldn't pay in a lifetime. He will not bring me into court as a thief.
He will not send me to prison. He is dead. Stone dead. And I am a
free man. Thank you, Lady Luck.

"Hatty," he looked up at me, "Lady Luck delivered me. I have had
many a lucky break, but nothing to compare with this. Dear Lady
Luck, my guardian angel!"

"Too bad she isn't visible so you could embrace her."

He chuckled. "Yes, isn't it? . . . You know what, Hatty. I can get
back to business now. I'm through with gambling." He waited, expecting my applause . . . "Doesn't that make you happy?"

"Yes, Solomon." . . . not happiness really, just weary relief.

And thus ended *The Drama of Mr. Howard*. The villain dead.
Poetic justice done. And Solomon Page, with Lady Luck by the hand,
his heroic face animated with good intentions, taking the curtain call.

(There was an epilogue to the little drama, but it was of no consequence. I was the only one who heard it and I ignored it . . . It was
spoken by an Imp of Wisdom in a soft aside: *So you think he has*

70

quit gambling, the imp laughed slyly. *The whole experience with Mr. Howard is proof to him that things will always come right in the end, for Solomon Page—his Goddess Luck will see to that. This is not really the end, not really!*)

4.

The next month or so, I saw Solomon through a haze of maternal concerns. My grandmother came from Kentucky to visit me and stayed until after Joe Boy was born. I had so much to ask her about birth and babies, so many new sensations to revel in when at last I held our son in my arms, that all I could feel for Solomon was gratitude for being The Father of such a wonderful baby as Joseph Page.

But the baby was only a few months old when I had to face up to the evidence that Solomon was back at his gambling. His moods began to reflect clearly his winnings and his losings. And Joe and I entered only the fringe of his thoughts—a remote, detachable part of his life. I began to feel as if my home were a rug on which I was precariously camped—that it might be jerked out from under me at any time.

Then one evening Solomon came in early and very jubilant. It was like the day he gave me the pearl.

"Hatty, we're going to New Orleans! Fabulous New Orleans! Isn't that wonderful! We'll make a fortune there! The place is on a big trade boom. Some say it will be a greater city than New York. I just talked to a man from there—you wouldn't believe the things he told me about the great frontier export business, and import demands never satisfied, money flowing like the Mississippi. A man who knows merchandising can get his own price for his goods—get rich in no time at all! And we're going there! Aren't you excited?"

"Why, yes, I'm excited. But how can we manage such a trip?"

"It's managed! We're on our way! Leaving tomorrow."

"No, Solomon, no!"

"The coach will be here at daybreak. I've sold the house with all the furnishings. Get busy and pack our clothes."

"You've done all this without considering, I suppose, what might happen to a baby, not even six months old, on such a long hard journey?"

"What's wrong with Joe? Strong, healthy baby. Just the right age to travel—won't have to bother about strange food and water making him sick. All you have to do is hold him on your lap and feed him when he's hungry."

"What if I should get sick?"

"When have you ever been sick? answer me that. You're strong as

73

a mule and you know it. I traded for a fine comfortable coach for us to ride in. What more could you want?"

He'd wanted to go to New Orleans for a long time, he said. And the opportunity to trade the house for the coach and enough cash for the trip seemed to be the big chance he'd been waiting for. Coaches were needed on the frontier—so he'd sell it for a big profit. Also, we'd have three paying passengers, young gentlemen he knew who, like himself, were desirous of locating in New Orleans.

Solomon exerted himself to win my full approval to the move—and he had many winning ways with which to erase my hesitations and doubts.

"It'll be our wedding trip, Hatty. A regular honeymoon adventure. Stopping at inns and plantations, camping out when we need to, sheltered in our good coach, secure with weapons and supplies. One of our passengers is quite a marksman—there'll be game. We'll take our time. No strain, no hurry."

It did sound rather wonderful.

"Funny honeymoon," I said. "With a baby and three strangers along."

We laughed. I was won over.

And it was a wonderful journey. My happiest time with Solomon Page.

The only flaw was the gambling. "Just for fun . . . just a little spree . . . small stakes . . . friendly game."

The whole trip was a long winning streak for Solomon, until finally his companions in the coach would seldom sit in a game with him. But it was easy to find a game at any stopover, and there were many, for we took almost three months for the trip. Solomon was completely happy. Each day brought new scenery, new games, no work, and more winning. He assured me time and again that he was not really gambling. He was through with that. These were just sociable games, casual hands, no sharp stuff. And I must say in all honesty that I didn't worry much. A gambler who is winning is very easy to live with. And our three passengers looked up to him as one especially gifted. They nicknamed us the King, the Queen, and the Little Ace. The one named Fad made up rhymes about us and chanted them from the driver's seat. Fad was the cotton-headed, gay-hearted one, and a genius with the reins. You should keep the teams happy, he said. And this he did with talk and song in the tones and tempos befitting the roadway.

I find the jingles and tunes of youth among the freshest of all memories. I can hear Fad singing and calling so clearly . . . every word and the music of it. . . .

Harriet stopped writing and began to clear her desk. Tricky and her best friend Tanya Gates were coming in for chocolate and cookies this afternoon—and hoping for a wilderness story, she knew. She wished they weren't coming. She was reluctant to leave the memory coach and Fad's singing . . . sometimes when he'd repeat, she'd join in . . . what fun it had been, that singing. . . .

> Now on this coach in the passenger space
> Is a King and a Queen and a Little Ace,
> A Man-of-Ten-Hearts and a Princely Jack,
> A royal flush from a lucky pack.
>
> Oh, we're on the road with a happy load
> For a journey long with a jolly song.

The door opened, and Tricky and Tanya rushed in, exclaiming, "Sing some more, Gram. Sing some more!"

Harriet was startled. She had thought she was only remembering. Was I really singing? she started to ask. But the excitement of the little girls was proof enough that she had been. She laughingly protested against their insistence that she finish the song. What a ridiculous thing that would be, she thought, a deaf old woman singing, even for the amusement of children. She was relieved that Jennifer was bringing the chocolate and cookies. That would change the subject to eating. But she was mistaken.

Tricky stopped Jennifer to tell her of the fine song Gram knew and to ask, "Did you ever hear that song, Jennifer, about the coach and the cards?"

"Nebber did, chile, nebber heard a such a song."

"Of course Jennifer never heard it," Harriet interrupted impatiently. "It was Fad's own song—only those in the coach heard it."

Tricky and Tanya became persuasive again, begged her to complete the song. Jennifer wanted to hear it too.

"All right. All right. But close the door, Jennifer. I don't want any-one else to hear. This is to be a secret performance, mind you. If you promise to tell no one about it, I'll sing the rest, but softly. Another verse was . . .

> Oh, the Little Ace is a ball of fire,
> Queen for a mama and King for a sire—
> And I'm the driver, a deuce that's wild,
> Friend of King and Queen and Child.
>
> Oh, we're on the road with a happy load
> For a journey long with a happy song.

Harriet was singing much louder than her deafness allowed her to realize. Marcus came in and pretended to check the wood supply.

Harriet broke off. "Why did you come in here, Marcus?"

"Jes checkin' yo room fo chill, ma'am, and seein' to the wood."

"It's too early for that. You were curious about what you heard in here."

"P'rhaps so, ma'am. That what yo singin' soun' mighty fine. I'se quite a song-man myself."

"Is that so? Do you ever sing bass?"

"Sho' do, ma'am. Mighty, mighty low bass."

"Fad had a part that he used some low notes on, after the verse that went like this . . .

> Oh, the team out there is four of a kind
> And I'll sing them a song if you don't mind,
> They don't play poker, either draw or stud,
> But they're drawin' this coach right through the mud.
>
> They're on the road with a heavy load,
> On a journey long and they need a song.

And then he went real low on these words—listen Marcus—and then see if you can do it, as Fad did it:

> Here's a place for the bass
> For the pace is very slow
> Very slow—slow—slow
> While we go—go—go
> Singing low—low—low.

Marcus could do it. So they all repeated the verse together and let Marcus come in solo and full force.

"And there was another verse . . ." Harriet was no longer self-conscious, nor for the moment aware that she was a deaf old woman.

> Of the coach and the cards as we roll along,
> Of the wheels and deals I sing a song,
> While we cross the lands of three great states
> No dead man's hands of aces and eights,

> For we're on the road with a happy load,
> On a journey long with a happy song.

> Here's a place where we race
> Such a pace we almost fly
> Almost fly—fly—fly
> Whizzing by—by—by
> Singing high—high—high.

"Sing it so I can hear," Harriet shouted. "Don't mumble."

So they gathered closer around her and sang their loudest. And then she recited Fad's finale:

> Look at 'em go! Like an inside straight!
> Hey there, Five! Six! Seven! and Eight!
> Pull it together! Deal to the wheel!
> I feel lucky! How do you feel?

"I feel turrible," Marcus confessed in a sickly whisper.

They all looked around and there stood Addie in a posture of frozen outrage.

Jennifer and Marcus disappeared like fog in a hot oven.

Tricky became very busy at the chocolate tray.

Harriet sighed and said, "Won't you have some chocolate with us, Addie? Tricky is ready to serve."

"No thank you, Mother." Her tone brought Harriet the full impact of her daughter's anger and indignation.

She won't dare speak her mind in front of the children, Harriet thought. And her self-control has her close to tears. But she mustn't cry in front of the children either. That would be weak and undignified. I should just let her suffer—not give her a chance to express her feelings—but I'd rather just have it over with.

"Girls, run down to the kitchen and ask Jennifer for the nutmeg. I want some for my chocolate this afternoon."

Tricky and Tanya, relieved, scampered out.

"All right, Addie. Let go."

"Oh, Mother, you were shouting—something dreadful—before the servants—*with* the servants—and teaching the children, those innocent little girls, a vulgar gambling song. How could you do such a thing? How could you?" The close tears spilled over.

"Just a jingle, Addie. Don't exaggerate. Your servants are incorruptible, and I don't think the experience will make casino girls out of Tricky and Tanya."

"Mother!"

This is strange, Harriet thought, that I resent her prudishness so much. I was the one hurt by gambling, not she. She has never suffered from it and knows nothing of what I have suffered. I also resent deeply her embarrassment over my shouting. Of course I can't sing. But why couldn't she laugh about it?

Harriet herself laughed. "It might not have been musical or proper, Addie, but surely it was funny. . . . Now, dry your tears. I reform. For your sake, I give up singing—at least until more people in this house are as deaf as I am—or as foolish."

Addie didn't smile, and the tears she wanted to control were still sliding down her cheeks. "Mother, I didn't mean——"

"Now you're compounding your misery by being ashamed of being ashamed of me. Addie, what does it matter, as long as——"

Addie turned away and fled down the hall.

"I love you, Daughter," Addie didn't hear, "and when I die, I shall bequeath you a laugh and a tune."

Harriet turned back into her room, muttering to herself, "You old goose. You old goose. Just write it from now on—just write it. You lived it once, and that's enough."

When the girls returned with the nutmeg and over their chocolate and cookies begged for other songs—just whisper them—she told them firmly there had been enough commotion for one afternoon. But somehow she felt cheated. There had been another song . . . about a Chickasaw maiden. It would have been fun singing it with Tricky and Tanya, Jennifer and Marcus. The words kept singing in her head.

So that night when she sat down to write of her life with Solomon Page in New Orleans sixty years ago, she first finished what she wanted to say about Fad's songs.

There was one song that must have a hundred verses, or more. If he had a name for the song, it must have been "On the Way from Nashville to New Orleans." It was a singing narrative of the scenes and events along the way. It's the part about the Chickasaw maiden that you'd like, Tricky. There were still some Chickasaws left in western Tennessee when we made that trip, and at one of our stops, we met up with a family of them. They camped near us at a lovely watering place. And there was a young girl in the family who looked like a legendary princess of some kind. Fad sang about her time and again on the rest of the journey—things along the way would remind him of her, and he'd tell the teams about it. Like this . . .

> On the way from Nashville to New Orleans,
> My eyes they feast on some grandly scenes:
> Saw a great—saw a great big grizzly bear,
> Saw a Chickasaw maiden with long black hair——
>   Chickasaw maiden so young and fair.
> Now I wouldn't want to hug the big grizzly bear,
> But I'd like to hug the Chickasaw maiden fair.
>
> On the way from Nashville to New Orleans,
> My eyes they feast on some grandly scenes:
> Saw a house—saw a house that made me want to sing,
> Like a castle it was such a stately thing——
>   A castle it was and fit for a king——
> In Alabama State and it made me want to sing
> And made me want a house like a castle for a king.
>
> On the way from Nashville to New Orleans,
> My eyes they feast on some grandly scenes:
> Saw a tree—saw a tree, such a wonderful tree——
> Had the biggest white blossoms I ever did see——

79

Biggest white blossoms that ever could be
In Mississippi State on a magnolia tree;
Made me think of a love that never could be.

On the way from Nashville to New Orleans,
My eyes they feast on some grandly scenes:
But my heart—my heart will hold to three:
The Chickasaw maiden, the house, and the tree——
  Black-haired maiden, how lovely was she!
And in my dreams she'll forever be
The queen of my castle by the white-blossom tree.

We arrived in New Orleans near the end of the summer, 1830. . . .
One year and one baby later, we had settled down—Solomon to regular gambling and I to making a living for myself and two children.
We lived in the Upper Faubourg, and Solomon made of the place
where we lived a sort of distribution center for his goods. But the
trade suffered because he gave it such weary and irregular attention;
so I decided to learn all I could about his business and make some
use of it. All the time I could spare from Joe and Ginny, my baby girl,
I devoted to studying the goods, the prices, and the accounts. And I
dealt with the customers in Solomon's absence, which was most of the
time. There was a long stretch—it must have been a year or so—when
Solomon was completely absorbed in New Orleans night life, and
indifferent to both family and business. He asked me no questions
about the business. He came home in the early morning hours, slept,
ate, changed clothes, occasionally made small unfeeling talk, and left.
It was like living with a sleepwalker, someone never fully awake. His
wakeful self, his energies, whatever feelings he had were in a world
the children and I did not inhabit. He brought the children no gifts,
not even a garment of any kind. When I came to realize that neither
affectionate attentions nor angry protests could penetrate the indifference, I accepted it, built my own wall of unconcern and concentrated
on caring for the children and accumulating some money. I was handicapped in the business because the customers were all men and many
would rather deal with a man and have merchandise delivered than
come for it, and some of the goods were in lines women were not
expected to handle or understand. And there were even more handi-
caps in the necessary buying that must be done in the wholesale dis-

trict. But I managed, and I made money, in spite of embarrassments and obstacles. Finally, I had all the goods paid for, most of it moved, and was able to sell the surplus to another distributor. Then I took the money on hand and carried out a plan that had been forming in my mind. The Upper Faubourg needed a shop—a shop for women. I found the house I wanted on Camp Street, next to the corner of Julia Street, and I rented the house. Then I bought some dressed planks, borrowed a hammer and saw, and put up the shelves and counter with my own hands. When I had everything in readiness, I went down to some of the principal wholesale houses on Chartres Street and bought the stock for my little shop and had it delivered. Then I moved my family into our new home. I consulted Solomon about none of this. I was not being obstinate. I had simply learned that the matter of taking care of the children and myself was entirely up to me. He accepted the change as casually as he would have accepted a change in bed covers and continued completely self-engrossed. Whatever his gambling luck was, he managed to keep himself well dressed in shiny black and soft gray with innumerable pairs of fine gloves, and I continued to care for the gloves, press his pants, and wash and iron the white shirts that he changed every day. The spotless white shirts, ironed without a wrinkle, the stacks of soft gloves —why did I accept this ritual of labor? Why didn't I refuse to do them? scorch them? carelessly handle them? I suppose I still cared for Solomon in some way, and still hoped he would change. A white shirt, starched just so, and perfectly ironed can make a man look so much better than he really is!

It is amazing how persistent a dream can be, how it can survive though starved and bruised and trampled upon. I know now that Solomon and I both had our dreams—mine of a good true love—his of a great good fortune. And we let our dreams drive us on and on, over paths of pain, and into separate ways of desolation and danger, made more desolate because there was no sharing . . . no sharing of anything but shame.

(Tricky, I have, in writing the above lines, had a revelation, you might say. I am nearer to understanding Solomon Page than ever before in my life. What an unexpected development, that in my attempt to enlighten you, I may attain some deeper perceptions for myself. Have I done Solomon an injustice in my memory with the one-word epitaph, "Coward"? Will this disinterment of the past expose some remnant feeling of kindliness or even gratitude for Solomon in the deep wells of my heart? I cannot say until the story is done. And the part I am about to relate will not be told from a controlled time-tempered viewpoint but will be drawn from the intensity of its own span.)

Solomon's negligence did not abate, even when I was very ill with yellow fever. I was attended by my father's good friend who was in New Orleans at that time, Dr. Anson Jones. I suppose the neighbors who cared for the children told him something about Solomon, for as I recovered he told me of his plans to go to Texas and offered to escort me and the children there to my father's home at Brazoria if I wanted to remove to the colony; or, if I desired to visit my grandmother in Kentucky, he would see that I had proper passage on a boat up the Mississippi. I told him that my little shop was prospering and that I thought it best to remain where I was. He looked at me with a doctor's probing intensity and said, "Loyalty is a commendable virtue, but it can be misplaced."

I could not explain to Dr. Jones that it was my sense of pride and independence rather than loyalty to Solomon that kept me from taking refuge with my father or grandmother. Bound to an indifferent husband, I possessed a certain freedom that I could not possibly have had as a dependent relative. I was providing more for myself and the children than I could request or expect to receive from anyone besides a husband. I had even been able to purchase some nice furniture and put aside some savings. Since men seldom admire a woman of independent thought and action, and seem naturally resentful against any manifestation of female self-sufficiency, I did not reveal, even to Dr. Jones, the extent of my accomplishments or sense of security.

"What shall I tell your father?" he was asking me.

"That because of your excellent attentions, I will soon be my strong self again—that the children are beautiful and healthy—that we are not in need of any kind."

"Shall I tell him that apparently it is by your efforts alone that you and the children are able to live in comfort?"

I had been away from my father so long, I had forgotten how much the mind-eye of a good doctor can see.

"No . . . no, please don't. It is possible—I think—I hope——"
(What exactly was my hope, I wondered?) "I hope, Dr. Jones, that
my husband may come to realize his responsibilities—that he may in
time discover the fickleness of Lady Luck."

He made no comment on what he thought of my husband. He
patted my hand and said, "Hope alone can be a starvation diet. It is
energy and courage that will sustain you, and I will inform Francis
of your adequacy in this respect."

It saddened me to part with Dr. Jones. His nearness and friendly
interest had been a great comfort to me, a close tie with my father.
But I truly had no desire to leave Solomon and again become a part
of my father's household.

The months sped by. I was much occupied with the children and
the shop. My place became, in a sense, a small social center for
women. I kept informed on the romantic trends of European dress
and hair styles and kept fashion plates on display for my customers to
study and discuss as they made their purchases. I designed and made
pretty clothes for myself and the children, making of our appearance
models that the ladies could copy. I wore the above-ankle lengths,
the low necklines, the puff and sheath sleeves with the shawls and
ornaments that were the fashion of the period. My black curls were
easily arranged in the piled-up mode of the times. I found the work
pleasant and profitable, and my time for loneliness and disappointment over Solomon became more and more limited.

In addition to sewing supplies such as needles, threads, trimmings,
and cloth, I carried a small line of ornaments, perfumes, and powders,
as well as a few tonics and snuffs. I will never forget a certain regular
customer of perfume and snuff. She confided to me that she had
dipped snuff for thirty years and none of her family knew it—that
her husband had often remarked that he wouldn't live with a woman
who had such a nasty habit and all eight of her children were very
critical of women who dipped. "Though my husband is impetuous
and my children affectionate, I have never been discovered," she
would boast. "A certain combination of flattery and high grade scent
does the trick. No apothecary has ever matched the perfume that rises
from a well-placed compliment to pleasantly daze the recipient."
Then she would explain how a certain floral essence could enhance
and prolong the "daze."

She would take a big dip in my presence, then the little tin box would disappear in a graceful gesture that seemed to be an unconscious adjustment of her low-cut dress.

She would preen before my mirror and say, "Regardless of my appearance, I shall always be adored by friends and family for my wonderful disposition," and add with a chuckle, "developed by snuff and deception."

It never ceased to amaze me how many women enjoy discussing highly personal matters while they are working out a new hairdo, testing color combinations before a mirror, sniffing perfumes, or surmising what a certain tonic will do for them. Some of these were very entertaining, some quite embarrassing. There was the long-faced Mrs. Hoodey who insisted on nursing her five-year-old child whenever it became fretful, wherever she was. And any sign of disgust or disapproval from anyone brought forth her blunt explanation that she had good enough reason: longer nursing meant fewer babies. I told her outright that it didn't seem decent or natural to me, and that I'd rather have five than nurse one for five years.

She laughed at me. "Wait until you have five, dearie, and you won't be such a saucy little prude. You'll let one suck until it leaves home if it keeps you from having another one."

Mrs. Hoodey was there, rocking and nursing this child bigger than my Joe Boy, and a half dozen other customers the afternoon Solomon surprised me so. He had never been in the shop when I had customers. I know the women gossiped much about this husband of mine whom few of them had ever seen and then only at a distance. On this day he had left the house earlier than usual. But I didn't expect to see him again until his usual predawn entrance. When he rushed into the shop by the front entrance, I expected some dreadful news and braced myself for a shock. One of my customers, embarrassed that her hip-length hair was down and in complete disarray, rushed behind the counter and got on her knees to be out of sight. Another who had removed her skirt to try a new color with her shirtwaist, unraveled the bolt and clutched the cloth around her. Another lady dropped a bottle of my most expensive perfume and incensed the whole room. Mrs. Hoodey alone remained perfectly placid, rocking and nursing her youngster.

Solomon was in one of his rare transformed states. He looked altogether handsome, excited and wonderful. He spoke a proper apology to the ladies and seemed to see only me.

"Hatty dear, I must talk to you at once, alone. Your customers will excuse you for a few minutes, I know!" He went quickly out of the room and into our living quarters and I followed, fully aware of the highly perfumed excitement I left behind me, and that Miss Longhair had her head above the counter staring in fascination.

"Harriet Page, guess what!" Solomon's hands were tight on my shoulders. He kissed me, then pushed me away to look at me. "Your hair looks wonderful that way—and those bright bows on your bodice —they are a sweet touch. No wonder this place is crowded. Your customers hope to buy something that will make them look like you." I tried not to respond.

"Snuff and deception," I said. And I thought with bitterness: I will not let you bridge long months of heartache and neglect with a bright moment of pretense.

"Hatty, we're going to Texas! To Texas, I tell you!!" His hands flew out in a wide gesture and then grabbed mine while his eyes were fixed on my face with sparkling entreaty.

I jerked physically at the impact of the announcement and tried to pull my hands away. But he held on to them while enthusiasm and explanation streamed out.

"I've been talking to the captain of the ship *Amos Wright*. He knows the land around Brazoria. It's rich land, he says. And settlers can get it free. Free! Do you understand! A great acreage! They make such cotton crops on the land that men grow wealthy in a single season. 'Why, young man, you can be a plantation owner and have folks callin' you "Colonel" in no time at all if you'll just put forth some go-and-git.' That's what he said. And he told me about the wild cattle that can be herded in for nothing. And they grow fat on tall prairie grasses and bring big prices in the New Orleans market. He says he knows a man personally who made thirty thousand dollars on a single enterprise like this."

"Solomon, we're city bred. We don't know anything about farms or cattle. And besides, that's wilderness country. We'd—we'd be lost."

"Hatty, where's your spunk? And there's something else. If you go along you can get land too—free—a lot of it—for yourself. (He didn't explain it exactly as it was—that a family man got more than a single man.) You've got a business head. You'd like that. You'd be able to make real money—not just little dabs like this shop brings us."

"The little dabs from this shop feed and shelter your family, Solomon."

"I know, Hatty, I know. And that's one of the reasons I want to change things. I want to go where we can do something big . . . have a grand home like some of those plantation houses we saw in Alabama —and lots of servants and fine things. You'd like that, wouldn't you?"

"That's just dreaming. We can't just go there and be rich from the minute we step off the boat. What would we do until we got the land and had things growing on it?"

"I'll get work of some kind. I know that's what you want me to say, and I'll do it. There's lots of jobs for newcomers, the captain said. I'll go to work as soon as we get there, I promise! I'm through with New Orleans. I want a new start. You can have your little shop in Brazoria, if that would make you feel better. And you'll be near your father. Had you forgotten that?"

I hadn't forgotten. I wanted to see my father. Letters had been few and very sketchy. I knew that my father had taken on Mexican citizenship and had been allotted some good lands. But I knew also that his health was bad and sensed that there had been more hardships than the letters revealed. It would be good to live near my father and brothers again, and Sarah wouldn't begrudge me the pleasure of their company—not if Solomon and I had means and lived apart from the family. And could it be that Solomon, away from big city life, might be a different man? Might be the kind of man before me, holding my hands so tight, imploring me to give him another chance? In one respect, I did not deceive myself. I knew it was the money I had accumulated that would take us there. But there was enough. I could take with me most of my furnishings and from the shop less bulky notions and supplies that would surely be much in demand on the frontier.

"I'll go, Solomon," I said. "I'll go with you to Texas."

He hugged me and kissed me hard. "You'll not be sorry, Hatty. You'll not be sorry." As he kissed me so ardently, I had a memory flash of the pond in Nashville and the lively ducks, and the feeling I had for Solomon there started to rush over me again, but the thought of the pearl he had slipped on my finger came back too. I shuddered

86

and pushed him away and told him I must get back to my customers.

I'm sure I was looking flushed and much disturbed when I re-entered the shop. "We're going to Texas," I explained to the ladies.

What a commotion that set up! *Texas* . . . there seemed to be some magic quality in the name. It set off all sorts of comments and surmises. It was big adventure, both threatening and promising.

"You'll be living right out among the Indians! They'll be your neighbors!"

"They're friendly in those parts, I understand."

"A fashion woman like you, with all your finicky habits, is liable to find the wilderness road too rough for travelin'," Mrs. Hoodey said.

"Maybe I'll learn some new fashions from the Indians—probably start wearing feathers in my hair and carrying Ginny like a papoose."

"You'll start havin' babies like an Indian, that's what . . . by yourself . . . not even a neighbor or a midwife around. I guess you don't know what unsettled land in a raw country is like. I had a cousin died out there. I pity you."

"My father lives near Brazoria, Mrs. Hoodey," I informed her with dignity. "He is a doctor. And his best friend, Dr. Anson Jones, has recently removed to Texas. With two doctors to call upon and other white settlers for neighbors, I do not expect to suffer any special privations, although I am perfectly aware there will be inconveniences."

"Neighbors! Inconveniences! Pah! That country's so spread out and jungley that chances are you won't see any more of your pa than you do here. If you take up land, you're liable to be housekeepin' on a dirt floor, livin' on bear meat, and totin' your water from a muddy bayou—and all so far removed from folks that if you scream for help, nobody'll hear you, except maybe an old painter will scream back at you."

"What's a painter?"

The customer with the long hair removed some pins from her mouth to answer me before Mrs. Hoodey could reply.

"Painter is a low word for 'panther.' It's a wild cat, big like a lion, big and slick, and no mane. My brother killed one on a hunt up river. He says they scream like a woman sometimes. Curdles your blood and softens your bones, that scream, he says."

"Feeds on Indian babies sometimes too." Mrs. Hoodey cut in, "And if they ever get a taste of a white baby——"

"Mrs. Hoodey, what did your cousin die of?" Someone tried to change the subject.

"Drownded. In one of those mean Texas rivers. Pregnant too."

"The river or the woman?"

"Both you might say. The river was on a rise."

"I thought maybe a painter ate her," another woman said.

"Might have." Mrs. Hoodey was unperturbed. "They never found the body. I hope you aren't expectin', Mrs. Page. If you are, with that boat ride, and all, I pity *you!*"

The loud smacking sounds of the child in her lap revolted me. I turned my back on her, and the other ladies surrounded me to chatter and complete their purchases. I pretended to be gayer than I was. It was a relief that Mrs. Hoodey soon departed without addressing any more depressing remarks to me.

I closed my shop the very next day and began to pack for the trip to Texas. I had little knowledge of frontier needs and limitations. I took all my furnishings except a large wardrobe. There were two large beds, a trundle bed and cradle, a walnut bureau with good mirror, dining room table and benches, two straight chairs, two rockers and two small tables. There were trunks and barrels that carried our personal belongings, the household supplies, and a selected stock from my shop. I made an arrangement with a friend to dispose of my surplus stock. We also took along two barrels of flour, several hundred pounds of sugar and coffee, and some other necessaries in the grocery line that we had been advised were hard to come by on the frontier.

Under all my high hopes for the Texas adventure and reunion with my family, there was a caution; so I prepared a well-padded reticule to conceal my savings. I fitted it with strong drawstrings that I could wind securely around my wrist and this became as fixed a part of my clothing as my stockings.

The trip to Texas on the *Amos Wright* was for Solomon and me, and many others aboard, a maiden voyage. This made for a general mood of happy surmise. A ship under sail is a lovely thing, and to be a part of the movement picked up from wave and wind is an exhilaration hard to describe—it is like a great hope, made visible and in motion, bound for a land of fulfillment. As we skimmed over the pleasant waters, catching glimpses of a shore line green and mysterious, the breeze would from time to time become more spirited and cool and seemed to be pushing us along and urging, "Hurry! Hurry on! The wonders of a new life and land are just ahead!"

I remarked to one of the ship's crew, "It's like a ship of dreams." He was winding a stack of rope and gave me a startled look. Then he looked around at the clutter and crowd.

"Most folks feel that way going out for the first time," he said, "but when they're coming back after a rough time, they act like they're on a rescue ship. They're cryin' for white flour and a soft bed, they're cussin' Indians and Mexicans, and pinin' to set foot back on certified American soil . . . Better not count on—I mean—this old ship's not anything fancy—and Texas is—well, it's not what you think —and you shouldn't be plannin' on—what you're plannin' on—a woman like you shouldn't be—out there."

Confused by his attempt to warn or enlighten me, he fled before I could question him.

Card games and drinking were the chief diversions for the men, and I knew by the way Solomon's eyes began to glitter and his hands moved restlessly that he wouldn't long refuse to participate. The games were just "to pass the time away," he said, but by the third day, the time he was passing away included a good part of the day and most of the night. So over my pleasure in the trip was a film of uneasiness, but I fortified myself with the thought that when he was settled in a job and removed from temptation, matters would be different.

When we reached Velasco near the mouth of the Brazos, some of the passengers left the ship and hired horses to ride the rest of the way, since the progress of the boat upriver to Brazoria was so slow. It was through some of these that my father learned we were aboard the incoming vessel. Dr. Anson Jones was with him when he received the news, and the good doctor rode in haste to meet the boat and came aboard as soon as we landed. I had expected to see no one I knew and was so happy and relieved to see his familiar kindly face that I could hardly refrain from embracing him. He told me that my father was ill and under his care and not able to come into Brazoria for me, but that he was sending my brother John with a saddled horse for me so that I could come to him at once. He said that it was best for Solomon to stand guard on our possessions until a wagon could be sent the next morning, since the day was too far gone for freighting.

Before we went ashore, Dr. Jones learned of the furniture I had brought. It was his opinion that I surely wouldn't be needing it all, since we would be fortunate to secure as much as a one-room shelter with a floor in it. He offered me a hundred dollars for my best bed, and I readily parted with it. In this strange new country I was looking out upon, money seemed more reassuring than furniture.

We had to wait a while for my brother. I checked over all the things we had brought to be certain everything was together, and was concerned about leaving Solomon to watch over them. Many of the men gathered on shore to watch the landing did not look trustworthy. I tried to tell myself that they were not as bold and greedy as they appeared, that it was their frontier garb that made them look as if they had just emerged from Ali Baba's cave. Knowing from Dr. Jones' conversation that the things I had brought were very real treasure on the frontier and that Solomon's love of gambling was always stronger than any sense of responsibility, I tried desperately to think of some further precaution to take, but there was none.

I implored Solomon to avoid any kind of betting—that he might be challenged to gamble with some of the goods, but not to touch them under any circumstances. In my anxiety, I probably said too much. Anyway, he promised that everything would be safe and that he would stay on board until my return in the morning.

Then John arrived and all was happy excitement. The children had never had a horseback ride and they were gasping with delight and astonishment over the whole procedure. John held Ginny in front of him and Joe clung behind. The horse brought for me carried a comfortable sidesaddle and I was almost as enraptured and inexperienced as the children with this form of transportation.

That five-mile ride from the Brazos to my father's house gave me my first impression of the land of Texas, and it was engraved on my senses with a depth and clarity that makes recollection simply a matter of thought direction . . . to springtime, 1835 . . . the rocking-chair gait of the gentle creature that carried me . . . the surprising comfort and conformity of the padded quilted leather under me—the poised feeling it gave to have one leg supported by the firm set of the foot in the stirrup and the other relaxed in the cradle of the horns.

"It's as if I had climbed upon a cloud," I told John, "and then had a support slipped under one knee so I could set my foot down upon the air without falling through."

He laughed at me and said Texas affected people different ways.

It was a day that seemed to bloom radiant and lush in the fullness of an April afternoon. The turf was so springy that the horses seemed almost to bounce. The long grass sent up a fresh protesting odor as it was crushed under the horses' feet. The soft rush of wind from the gulf bent the flowers and grasses in graceful swirls and brought wave after wave of fragrance from the bright spreads of exotic color patterns, gaudy reds and golds, pink and blue profusion. I was glad that John was not talkative and the children too awed for their usual chatter, for there was no interruption of the ecstatic, sensuously beautiful sounds that were a part of the experience: the soft thud of horses' feet on the productive earth—the clear, painfully sweet cry of the field larks, calling, responding, calling, responding—and the caressing sound of wind through eager grasses.

Riding to the west, we came to a curving belt of timber, like a great protecting arm around the vibrant waist of the prairie, and on the edge of the timber stood the comfortable log house, boarded inside and out, that was my father's home.

I was shocked to find my father so gaunt and ill, too weak to walk about. He was so glad to have us with him that the next morning he would not let me go back to Brazoria. When I was discussing with him what I had brought to Texas, he interrupted to ask if there was any white flour.

"Two barrels," I said, "and one of them is for you."

He was so happy that tears came to his eyes. "Bless you, Hatty. Bless you! Fresh white flour! Good bread once more. This will make me well again." He became very excited and called to John to hitch up the wagon and go into town for it at once. I thought he would let me go too, but when I started to move from his side, he held on to me.

"No, Hatty, no. I need your presence. It's been so long and you strengthen me. John can bring some of your things today with the flour, and the rest tomorrow. No need for you to go at all."

"But Solomon——" I couldn't explain to him, while he was so ill, about Solomon's gambling.

"Solomon won't mind another night in Brazoria. John can explain that you're humoring me by staying here. Nothing to be done there that the two of them can't manage. Solomon, no doubt, will pass the time to good purpose, getting acquainted. The people are friendly, and the boat is the center of interest while it's there."

This didn't comfort me, but I couldn't leave without upsetting him, so I settled down to wait for John to make the trip. Father lay on a couch by the front window so he could watch the road and I sat in a rocker by his side. Together we watched the wagon grow smaller and smaller out on the prairie until the speck of it was finally out of sight. I tried to divert my father while we waited but I began to share his suspense. And finally, after several hours, when the speck reappeared, I strained my eyes anxiously to make out what the wagon brought.

At last, I made an awful discovery. There was no load. And there was a passenger on the wagon seat beside John. It was Solomon. As they came closer, I saw one lonely piece of freight on the wagon bed. A barrel. I felt sicker and older than my father. I knew what had happened.

I hid my feelings from father. He saw only the barrel and was satisfied. I rushed out to meet the wagon. My thoughts were such an agony I could hardly breathe. And what if the barrel were not flour? But it was. That helped some. At least my sick father would have his white bread.

I could tell that John was controlling his anger with great effort. I was at the wheel when Solomon got down off the wagon.

"What have you done? Why didn't you bring more?"

"I got into a game of cards and lost all your things," he stated calmly.

I couldn't speak.

John said, "I'm going back in the morning, Hatty, to get your things. They weren't his to gamble with, and there's not many men around here, even the renegades, so low as to take from a woman. Dr. Jones said he'd help me. One way or another, we'll get them, except the groceries—probably a lot of sweetened coffee and white biscuits have gone the belly route by now."

I started crying and John kept talking. My tears seemed to loosen his anger.

"I'd like to know if you intend to put up with this rot-gut gambler for a husband. He's stripped you and the babies down to beggars."

Solomon said, "I was swindled by a bunch of thieves. Just plain swindled. I could have won in a fair game. I knew I could. But those swindlers——"

"You're the swindler, the lowest of the lot!" John yelled. "You swindled your own wife and children!"

"Oh, John, hush!" I protested. "Father is so sick and he'll hear you." Father had gotten up from the couch and was standing in the doorway.

John lowered his voice but didn't hush. "If you stay with him, he'll probably put you up for wager someday—or Joe—or Ginny. He's not a husband. He's a leech. If you can't pull him off, then take him away and stay out of my sight. He makes me sick!"

And John did indeed look very sick. His face was so white and his voice so violent that I knew a word from Solomon would start a fight.

But Solomon ignored him and went on in to meet father. And I begged John to keep quiet and spare father and we'd work things out later when he wasn't so ill.

I rushed on in to explain to father, "Solomon unloaded the things from the ship and found a place to store them before John got there," hoping that I was keeping the bitterness out of my voice. "John wanted to hurry on out with the flour. He's unloading the barrel now."

5.

It was several days before my father learned the truth. John did manage, with the help of Dr. Jones, to recover the furniture and the trunks, but the groceries were all lost.

Sometime after, John and I were discussing the matter when we thought we were alone. But father came upon us quietly in his stocking feet and heard too much before we were aware of him. He asked some questions that we had to answer, and then he too said that I must leave Page—that there could be nothing but trouble ahead for me and the children until we were parted from him. I found myself defending Solomon, saying he might do better now that we were in a country where he couldn't gamble so much, and they reminded me that this was the first thing he had done upon landing. I insisted that if he got a job—got land of his own——

Father pointed out that getting land would not be as easy as we had been led to believe—that with Stephen F. Austin in prison in Mexico, relations between the American settlers and Mexican officials were very strained and the mood of the colonists gloomy and rebellious. There was no settled land policy, and a revolution was brewing.

When I mentioned the possibility of opening a shop in Brazoria, he objected that it would be neither safe nor respectable. The best thing, he said, would be for me and the children to remain with him, and tell Solomon we were through with him. I could not explain to my father that I had rather take my chances with Solomon than with Sarah. Pioneering had not agreed with Sarah. Her frugality had sharpened to stinginess, and her critical quality had ripened into doomlike predictions. Dependence on her would be an awful price to pay for safety and respectability.

So when I told him I could not accept his support—that he was much too burdened already—he insisted that we must stay on for a while—that he would put up with Solomon if I would only stay with him until he was well again—then we would somehow resolve matters.

We were at my father's house most of that summer. Father loaned Solomon a horse to ride and he was away much of the time, looking over the country, doing a few odd jobs, bringing back news of the unrest among the people, and the possibilities of war with Mexico. He elaborated on what a fine thing an independent Republic of

Texas would be, with its own government and land policies. I was surprised at Solomon's interest in this direction. Now I see it as an expression of his desire to have something important happen to him simply by taking a chance—courting Lady Luck and enjoying the thrill of suspense, by-passing preparation and patience. So, for the time being, war seemed to him a good game to get in on. Thus he might draw a hero's card and rake in a land bounty.

And war did seem most imminent. Santa Anna had come into full power in Mexico and was showing himself a complete despot. He had decided to become the Napoleon of the West. The liberalism that freedom from Spain had initiated throughout the Mexican domain began to fade before his pronouncements, like a tender vine in a desert gale. Mexican regulations had been antagonizing the settlers in Texas for several years, and by the time we arrived much of the feeling was openly rebellious. Mr. Austin had gone to Mexico City in the winter of 1834 in the hope of working out some peaceful agreement and had been thrown in prison. At the same time, the Texans were expected to submit to customs duties imposed on them for supporting a Mexican army of occupation. Now, in the summer of 1835, they were waiting in anger and suspense for Mr. Austin's return. He had finally been released on bond, then further delayed. The colonists respected his leadership and were reluctant to take any kind of action until they had his report and advice. And the desire for a war of independence was far from unanimous. The people were divided into a war party and a peace party. The war party wanted immediate revolution. The peace party wanted to work for legislative remedies. My father was at first in favor of a peaceful line of action. He said that the settlers from the United States were trying to repeat the American Revolution on a smaller scale and with less cause. He pointed out that many colonists, like himself, had benefitted by the generous land policies of Mexico and had readily agreed to the legal and religious requirements in order to get the land. He himself had title to several thousand acres and felt that he owed a certain loyalty to Mexico. Solomon, on the other hand, had no such ties and found it easy to cultivate animosity to everything Mexican. He had come to Texas hoping to become a Colonel Groce overnight (the Colonel had arrived on the Brazos in 1822 with one hundred slaves and had established a cotton kingdom). All Solomon had was restless hands and empty pockets.

One morning at breakfast time, late in the summer, father announced to the whole family that he had plans for moving to one of his farms on Chocolate Bayou where he thought the surroundings would be healthier. He said that if I wanted to settle near him that he would give me a half section of land and twenty cows.

I saw Solomon's face flush in anger when my father looked at me directly and said with particular emphasis, "This 320 acres of land must be *yours*, my daughter, and the twenty cows *you* may select from my herd. Cared for properly for a few years, the increase can give you a substantial income."

If father thought that addressing me as "my daughter" would keep Sarah quiet, he was very mistaken.

Before I could express the wonderful relief and gratitude I felt, Sarah exclaimed, "Francis! That is not right! These children all have to be educated. You should not give anything away until they are all grown. Then whatever is left, you can divide equally. Hatty's got an able-bodied husband. Let him support her."

Sarah was right enough that my father had no ready reply. And I was so hurt at her lack of concern for my plight that I spoke too hastily.

"Sarah, I want you to know once and for all that I have no desire for anything that belongs to you or the children. Please do not concern yourself about my father's generosity. I will not accept anything that he offers. I have always made the living for myself and my children and I shall continue to do so." I got up from the table to rush out, for I didn't want to burst into tears before them all.

But before I could escape, Solomon shoved his chair back and stood up to have his say.

"I'm tired of having this family treat me like a leper, or a ghost that haunts the place. Just because I was swindled out of a few pounds of groceries and let some rowdies carry off the furniture, you've all acted like I was an imbecile or a crook, not fit to wipe your feet on. And Hatty!" He screamed out at me, almost in tears himself. "I'm sick of your high and mighty independence! I'm getting out of here. That's what you all want. But I've got a surprise for you. I'm coming back! I'll be back with a freight wagon before the week's out. And

I'm taking my family with me. And you'd better be packed and ready, Harriet Page, or there'll be a revolution in the Moore's righteous back yard!"

And he did walk out, and right on down the road to Brazoria. No one tried to stop him. John said, "Thank God. Sit down, Hatty." Then he brought the coffee pot from the kitchen and poured hot coffee all around.

I said to Father and Sarah, "He may never come back. I'll wait a week. If he isn't here by then, John can move me into the settlement and I'll open my shop."

Father said, "There'll be no need of that," and gave Sarah a straight, hard look.

She said, "You couldn't find a place. Why don't you stay put? We'll make out."

"I'll find a place or I'll build one," I said recklessly.

It was a strained unhappy week we spent, waiting for Solomon. I got everything ready to go and did not waver in my decision to leave, with or without Solomon.

None of us really expected him back, but a week to the day, he returned. He had found a house over on Chocolate Bayou, he said, and was taking us there. He began loading at once. My father said he knew the Chocolate since he owned some land there, and besides his own small house, there was not a dwelling suitable for habitation on the whole bayou. Solomon told him the location he had been given.

"That's just a waste house," father said. "No respectable man would take his family there. It's unsafe—unhealthy! Hatty, don't go!"

Solomon ignored him and kept on with the loading. I told father I'd manage—not to be fearful—let me try to work things out. So he said no more. He brought a sack of flour from the barrel I had given him and put it on the wagon and sent the children to the cellar for some jars of black-eyed peas that I had put up for him. Solomon told him not to worry about what we'd eat—that he had supplies waiting in town.

We were soon ready to go. Solomon refused to have another meal with the family. The leave-taking was an ordeal. John was not even present. When my father and I embraced, our cheeks were wet and we clung together as though we might never meet again. Our hearts seemed to know what our minds dared not forecast.

The supplies we took on at Brazoria looked dangerously inadequate, and I had no chance to inspect them. But since Solomon had somehow made the money for them and was at last trying to provide, I held my peace.

I had not realized that there would be no sign of a road to the place we were going. Solomon reckoned by certain features of the landscape, as he had been directed, and had a small compass loaned by the man who hired out the wagon to him, for on the prairies it was easy to lose your way. Most of the time we were in sight of the forested region that marked the banks of the water course we were following, and finally we turned from the prairie toward a bend in the bayou. You can imagine how we felt, so fresh from the city, so alone in this wilderness, with no sign of human habitation anywhere. We had traveled most of the day and though we hadn't covered many miles, it seemed we were at the end of the world. I thought surely we had been misdirected. And then we saw the house! Such a dismal sight! It reminded me of a little old man, witless and lost, eyes vacant, mouth ajar, hair matted. A tree had fallen on it, knocking off part of the chimney and crashing in the roof. Whatever had been used to cover the two high small windows and the doorway had been removed.

"Are you certain this is it?" I asked Solomon before we got down.

"Yes," he said, looking all around. "It has to be."

There was no flooring, only the hard-packed earth and that had been broken by a growth of weeds where water had dripped in from the roof and blown in from the openings. There were great stacks of long-legged granddaddy spiders in the corners and in the fireplace, bird nests in the chimney, and plenty of signs that animal life had found the place a convenient shelter.

"We can't stay here," Solomon said.

"Where can we go?"

"I'll find a place."

"Tonight?"

He didn't answer me. The day was almost done. We were stranded. We were able to make a fire in the fireplace and get water.

I will not detail how we dispossessed the spiders and other occupants, finally prepared food, and put up the bed where we all four slept in exhaustion. We used the dining table to cover the door.

Next morning we had a visitor and it was a great relief to discover that a family lived about a mile away. They had seen the smoke from our chimney. The man who came to investigate was most anxious to be helpful. He said that he had found keeping stock a very good business—that he had a friend named Merrick who was keeping a much larger herd over on Austin Bayou—that Merrick was needing help. Solomon might get a job with this man and work into the cattle business, he said.

This was something to act upon. So we unloaded our belongings and stacked them in the old cabin, hoping it wouldn't rain until we could get out. First, Solomon must return the freight wagon to Brazoria—then he would go find out about work with Merrick and living quarters. This meant that I must camp out with the children in this desolate spot until his return. But I urged him to go. I was comforted that the friendly family was nearby. They invited me to stay with them. But since their dwelling was only a one-room cabin for a family of six, I preferred my own soft bed in the privacy of my primitive quarters.

It was five days before Solomon returned. I was thankful to see that he had come in a wagon for moving us out. We were going to a good house over on Austin Bayou, he said. Mr. Merrick himself had built the place and occupied it for a while. Now the owner lived on a farm further up the bayou and wanted tenants in this house.

Would Mr. Merrick give him steady work, I inquired. He hadn't even seen the man, he said, but the freighter in Brazoria had instructions from Merrick to send any family in that would come. It didn't sound quite right to me. But there was no choice. We had been warned that rains would soon put a stop to all wagon travel.

It took us two full days to make the trip. On the first night we lodged with a Mrs. Abit. She was a weakly little woman, in very poor health, but her frail body supported a gallant spirit. We shared the same bed that night and talked until nearly daybreak. It was such a relief to me to be in the company of this woman that I told her my whole plight. She gave me some advice I've never forgotten.

"Don't feel sorry for yourself," she warned. "There's no strength in self-pity—and you'll be needing all the strength you can muster.

. . . And don't hate either. Hate is just a trap. You get caught in it, and you tear yourself to pieces."

She thought the Merrick cabin would probably please me. "I've heard it's better built than most—neatly sealed and finished, with one room and a shed, but you won't be having company—you'll have to come out to see folks—you're not just off the beaten path—you're off any path a-tall. Even Mr. Merrick, who lived there until his wife died, is twenty miles away, and there's no sign of a settler any nearer than that." She tried to prepare me for what lay ahead.

"Since your man will have to be gone from home to work for Merrick, you'll find your blood chilling when the painters scream and the wolves cry. But the wolves are shy creatures, and, like the painters, they're harmless as long as they're well fed—and in these parts, there's plenty for them to feed on."

I told her about Mrs. Hoodey's tale of panthers eating babies.

She laughed. "Lots of whoppers told about the old painter, all the way from eating babies to kidnapping them and raising them like kittens. You don't let those big cats worry you. They got plenty to eat without bothering your babies. It's that cottonmouth you want to watch out for—the moccasin with the white ring around his mouth. He's deadly. Don't be afraid—just be rightly cautious."

Mrs. Abit refused the payment I offered her for our lodging, saying it wasn't her way to take payment for hospitality. So I brought out my stock of pins, needles, and threads and told her to choose something for a present.

"Honey, don't expect me to refuse anything so tempting as these large needles and some of that good thread," she said with a big smile. "It's thirty miles to Brazoria, you know, and we never go a distance like that for little things."

The visit with Mrs. Abit fortified and cheered me. I had found a friend in this wilderness and I was moving into a good house. I didn't know enough about isolation really to dread it.

But my good spirits were considerably trimmed down after we met the traveler on horseback. He was a bearded, droopy fellow who said his name was Grimes. When he learned we were moving into the Merrick house, he gave a groaning sigh.

"Just hope you got plenty of provender, that's all. Last family moved in after Merrick's old woman died, plain starved to death.

'Bout this time of year, it was, just before the rains spread the old bayou all over the country. The man drowned tryin' to get back home to the woman and kids. They starved to death. Wouldn't catch me squattin' in a place like that even long enough to scratch up a fire. But maybe you got more provender than them folks had."

He looked over the wagon for what obviously wasn't there, then stared at Solomon and me before he finally pronounced, "You all look mighty city-tender to be headin' in here." And I'm sure in our stylish New Orleans clothes, we didn't give the appearance of being hearty pioneers. We had no answer for him.

He heaved another gusty sigh of pity. "But then maybe you got more luck than some," he surmised, and rode on.

And we drove on . . . and on . . . and on . . . until we seemed to have a whole vast unoccupied world all to ourselves. It was a beautiful world, but I felt as if we were intruders on this trackless prairie covered with glowing flowers and tall grasses. It seemed a sort of dangerous sacrilege to crush and trample a trail across it, leaving a scar upon the face of beauty.

We approached the bayou in the afternoon and came upon the cabin just at sundown. It was located on a good rise with a long view of the prairie in the front, but protectively tucked into the edge of the timber growth along the bayou. There was a branch in front of it, like a moat for a miniature castle, and over the branch a sturdy footbridge. If the branch were running full, the cabin could be approached only on foot. As it was we were able to drive up to the door. Hawthorne grew tall and luxuriant about the entrance, and the scarlet bunches of parsley-haws gave the place an appearance of fruitful abundance that was pleasing to me. The flavor too was sweet and refreshing at journey's end. I had had my first taste of parsley-haws earlier that summer and found it especially appealing. I did not realize, however, that soon it would come to haunt my sense of taste with a ferocity that would endure to my dying day. It is a sated sweetness cloying my throat right now, and that summer is fifty-five years behind me and I haven't tasted parsley-haws since!

Harriet stopped writing and rang a bell that brought Marcus to her side.

"Marcus, tell Jennifer to make a large glass of lemonade for me, strong and sour. And bring with it some sharp cheese and salty crackers, a pitcher of thick cream—also a plate of sliced meats, beef, ham, chicken, whatever she has—and some boiled eggs with a dish of those little pickled onions she made last week. Bread—thickly buttered. And a pot of my favorite black Ming, very strong."

Marcus didn't move. He was shocked and frightened. He alone knew how much time Harriet spent at her writing desk. Now her eyes were so bright, yet she looked weary, and the pages of writing all around—he was sure she'd gone out of her head! She'd been at it all day, and Miz Addie not at home to make her take her nap. She'd hardly touched her lunch—of course, she could be hungry, but it wasn't mealtime and Miz Addie disapproved of anyone in the whole household eating between meals. Something was mighty wrong with ol' missus.

"Marcus, don't stand there like you'd been hit between the eyes with a poker. I am completely sane. You and I both know Addie won't be back until late this evening. Do as I say! Do it quickly. And don't forget a single thing." She enumerated the items again and added "some of that Mediterranean anchovy extravagance that E.Y. sent over."

"Mr. E.Y.'s comin' to visit ya tonight, ya know." Marcus reminded her.

"Of course I know. And I want to get some more done before he gets here." She looked up at Marcus, and smiled winningly. "I trust you, Marcus—in every way." They both understood fully what she meant.

Marcus nodded.

"Now hurry with my refreshment!"

"Refrushmunt!" Marcus rolled his eyes. "Ise glad Mr. E.Y.'s a doctor and Mr. Frank's a doctor. Youse liable to need 'em bof!"

His comment was lost on Harriet, back at her writing. . . .

The man who owned the wagon came on horseback for it. He brought news of Mr. Austin's arrival in Brazoria, and he and Solomon talked excitedly about war with Mexico, for it did not appear that Mr. Austin was in any mood to compromise with Santa Anna. Then Solomon hired the horse the man had ridden out, agreeing to return it as soon as he saw Merrick and got lined up on his job. He was sure his employer would furnish him with a mount. Solomon was out of money, and so I paid for these things.

I had been worried all along that our supplies were so low, but Solomon didn't seem concerned—said he'd work out all that with Merrick. He couldn't even get any wild game for us. His only weapon was a pistol and he had only a whiff or so of powder left for that. As he prepared to ride off to Merrick's farm, I gave him ten dollars, and told him somewhere, somehow, he must get groceries and bring them back—that we now had only one quart of black-eyed peas and some musty meal. That in three days we would be entirely without food. He promised that he'd be back—there was no cause to worry or be alarmed.

Then he left us.

Heartsick and weary, feeling more desolate and helpless than I'd ever felt in my life before, I watched him go.

"Oh, Solomon, please hurry back!"

"I will, Hatty, I will. Take it easy."

"Take it easy!" I knew no kind of ease in the days that followed. The little house was comfortable and secure, but brush and grass were so thick around it, I couldn't allow the children to step outside lest the snakes or wild beasts harm them. My only weapon was a good ax. Solomon had cleared a path to the bayou and cut a small stack of wood for cooking fire. But it offended him to use his hands in this way, and he always gave them worried examination when he laid the ax aside. So there had been no clearing made around the cabin before he left.

At the end of the third day, Solomon had not returned. The peas and the meal were gone. I gathered the ripest of the haws and fed the children with these along with the last crumbs of the cornbread on the fourth day. On the fifth day they ate nothing but the parsley-haws. On the sixth day, they were very fretful, and Joe would talk of nothing but food.

"Will Daddy bring meat? . . . Will you make brown gravy, Mama? . . . Will he bring some sugar? . . . Do you promise to make some sweet cornbread?"

I recklessly reassured them that he would come back and bring us food.

The wolves howled at night, and the panthers screamed, as Mrs.

Abit said they would. And it seemed that I was caught in a nightmare of unreality. I glimpsed a bear and deer and wild turkey and longed for a gun. I lamented my stupidity. If I must blunder into the wilderness, why hadn't I had the forethought to have a gun of my own and to know how to use it?

Daily, I watched from the doorway, my eyes burning and straining. I couldn't believe the prairie could remain so empty of human life. And then at the end of the sixth day I saw him, just as the sun dipped out of sight, and the whole landscape turned a sort of shimmering gold. As he rode on and on toward me, everything was golden in the glow of my relief: the grass and trees, the waters of the bayou, everything! Golden flood of relief! And a golden man and horse riding closer and closer from the rim of twilight to the cabin door.

Food and protection at last!

And then he was there—a presence in the almost-dark. I watched him anxiously as he dismounted and staked his horse and then came across the bridge toward us. I could hardly believe it was Solomon. There was something so strange about his appearance. When he was close, the children drew back, hardly recognizing him. He wore the plain clothes of a frontiersman and they were not becoming—they did not even fit well.

We stood looking at each other. He was empty-handed!

"Food," I said. "Where is it?"

He didn't answer me.

"We're starving!"

He looked away from us and explained that he hadn't been able to get anything. He hadn't even seen Merrick yet. Instead, his curiosity about the war had taken him to a settlement and he had learned that everybody was volunteering to fight Mexico. He had to say he would go too or be called a coward. His clothes were not suitable for going to war and he'd been unable to trade for the ones he had on. He'd had to use my money to get them.

I listened, quiet as death, while he spoke.

He finally looked at me and said, "I did not want to be called a coward."

I felt the wildest sort of anger. A rage of indignation and hate seemed to grip me and shake me and almost send me out of my mind.

"You're a coward already!" I screamed. "Dragging your family out to desolation's end and then deserting them—leaving them trapped to starve in the wilderness! Have you eaten since you left us? Of course you have! You don't look hungry! And you don't care that we've had nothing for three days but haws. If you don't care about what happens to me—think of those hungry children, and nothing but haws, nothing but haws, I tell you!"

He went on into the cabin and sat down. The children whimpering huddled on Joe's trundle bed.

And I couldn't stop the flow of angry words. I elaborated upon his cruelty and selfishness until I was exhausted and had to sit down too. He mumbled something, and I told him what I thought of his abilities as a fighter.

"What a warrior you'll make! Fighting for Texas! What in God's name do you know or care about Texas! There's no love in you for anything but your precious hands and a game of cards. Don't tell me you have any sense of patriotism or duty! You want to get with the men and the cards, that's all—and going to war is the only way to do it! You don't really intend to fight. But I hope you have to. I hope you get into a war so big and so hot that you can't run! I hope you get trapped somewhere where you have to wait and wait without anything to eat—and that what you're waiting for never comes—and you just rot there. That would be a fitting end for you—just rot!"

I said all this, and much more. I forgot Mrs. Abit's admonition about the trap that hate sets.

It was an awful thing, this fury and hate I felt there in the dark, not being able to see Solomon, hearing the rocker squeak under him now and then. It was like throwing myself against an iron cage. He never admitted the gravity of the situation, offered a remedy, or acknowledged that he heard. I had the awful feeling now and then that he was napping. Once in a while he would mutter something meaningless like, "Why don't you get off your high horse?"

In a final outburst, I asked him over and over why he had come back.

"You brought no food. You have no way to take us out. You're going to war. Why did you ride back—just to let us know that we would be left here to finish starving? If you want to be rid of us, why not kill us off some more merciful way? Why did you come back, just answer me that, why?"

He didn't answer me. And then I sat quiet a moment and had my own awful answer. He had come back for my money. I was not frightened. Cruelly indifferent he might be, but there was something in his nature that made him incapable of physical violence. This contradiction had once given me hope. I had always classified cruel husbands as wife and child beaters. Solomon had never struck me or even spanked the children.

I wonder what I would do now if I could go back to that dark night there in the cabin with Solomon and relive it in the light of my present understanding of both myself and Solomon. Would I praise him for his impulse to be a soldier? How would he have reacted to: "How brave you are! How wonderful!"? Would I work out some rational scheme—such as having him take the children to Mrs. Abit and then come back for me (and the money!), assuring him that I'd be glad to finance his patriotic expedition as a Texas volunteer? Would he have accepted such a plan? He might have. But if I were as hungry and weary and disillusioned as I was that night, might I not still lash out with the same temper and condemnation? I might. At any age or stage of experience, hunger and hate are the enemies of reason.

So I made my final declaration into the darkness: "You won't get my money—not a cent of it! You can't beg it out of me or frighten it out of me. I'd throw it in the bayou first!"

Later, he fumbled his way to the bed, fell across it and slept. The children were asleep in the trundle bed. I sat on in the rocker, feeling hollow and dazed, dozing now and then until dawn. I found that I was so weak and sore I could hardly get to my feet. I stood in the doorway a while and then went to the bayou to fetch water. I washed my face there and tried to think what could be done.

I heard the horse whinny and turned to see that Solomon was unstaking and preparing to ride off. I ran back up the path. The children were standing in the doorway, looking so pitiful and hungry that heartbreak and wrath engulfed me again. I rushed down to the bridge.

"If you go off and leave us here to starve, I hope the first bullet that's fired, pierces your heart!"

He quickened his preparations to mount.

"You're treating us like bait for a beartrap. You know another family starved to death in this very cabin!"

"You can manage," he said. "You always have."

"Manage? Do I kill game with my bare hands? Grow a garden overnight without even a seed to plant? Set up a shop here on the bayou for bears and alligators? Can't you realize that we're already starving!"

"You'll have to make out the best you can." With that, he climbed on the horse and started off.

I had the impulse to run after him, begging him to come back, offering the money I had, anything if he'd just come back. And a little way off he did stop the horse, as if about to change his mind. I held my breath but did not call out. Then he started on again, and I screamed out after him, "Don't come back! Don't ever come back!"

He was getting too far away to hear me, but I couldn't stop screaming.

"I don't want you! Your children don't want you! Do you hear? God smite you Solomon Page! God smite you dead!"

He disappeared from my sight without God making any move to simplify my future by smiting him.

Joe called to me and I went running back to the cabin.

"Ginny's awful hungry, Mama."

I sat down in the doorway, put my hands over my face and abandoned myself to grief. Ginny plucked at my hands and began to cry loudly in accompaniment.

Joe patted my shoulder. "Don't you cry, Mama. I'll grow up to be a big man, and I'll go and bring you a big bag of meal myself."

I just cried harder, and so did Ginny. It was Joe's utter stillness as he stood by waiting for us two distraught females to subside that made me conscious of the injury I was doing the children by indulging in lament and woe. I wiped my face on my apron, looked at Joe, and managed a smile.

"Wash your sister's face, Joe Boy, while I gather some haws. I've been watching a cluster very red and plump and it should be just right this morning. We'll not eat just plain haws. We'll try some with cinnamon and some with salt and see which we like best."

Ginny was still crying.

"Listen, Ginny, you have company. Someone has come to see you."
Somewhere in the cabin a cricket had started a gentle, friendly chirping.

I picked up a pail and went to gather haws. Joe took Ginny by the hand. "Come on and we'll find Mr. Cricket after you get your face washed."

As I picked the haws, carefully selecting the ripest and reddest bunches, tasting and testing them as I went, the storm of my despair began to calm. I was able to let loose of Solomon and think of something else. Of Mrs. Abit who said, "There's no strength in self-pity, and you'll need all the strength you can muster out there." . . . Of my mother and her last words to me: "You cry too easily, Hatty. Control your tears. Always use the good mind God gave you." She was dying and told me so. "Don't be afraid for me or for yourself. Fear is weakness. I leave you in God's hands."

I kept selecting the haws carefully—none must be wasted. "In God's hands." It seemed more like I was in the devil's grasp . . . "Don't feel sorry for yourself." . . . How long would the haws last, I wondered? How long could we live on them or endure to eat them and nothing else? . . . "Don't be afraid . . . fear is weakness . . . I leave you in God's hands." Left in God's hands and delivered up to Solomon Page! . . . But after all, should I blame God for my own rash judgment—in selecting this man for a husband—in leaving my security in New Orleans to follow him to Texas—in pridefully rejecting my father's help and advice, deliberately trailing disaster?

This bit of self-analysis restored my balance, and it seemed that the brilliant cluster of haws that I reached for was a manifestation of God's care—that this sweet, rich juicy fruit was provision from His hands. And I felt thankful and hopeful. So many good things could happen before the haws were gone: a roving hunter, someone lost in the woods, might happen by. I might be able to find other things to eat. I would keep busy. After all, I had the ax. I'd clear a better and safer path to the water's edge; I'd cut more wood. We didn't need the heat for either warmth or cooking, but a bit of fire was cheerful and would light the cabin for a while at night. I had only a small piece of candle left and must save it for emergency lighting. But the glow of the coals on the hearth at night could be infinitely consoling.

6.

I met the days one by one—each of them a sort of battle with nature and with myself. Sometimes I was covered to the point of smothering with blankets of difficulty and pain and loneliness. There was the necessary watchfulness against danger, the eternal listening for shot or yell that would indicate human presence in the neighborhood, the efforts to reassure the children and divert their minds from hunger. And in the discipline of my surroundings, there were things learned, inwardly and outwardly, impressed upon me with a vividness that will never be dimmed. The nights were the hardest, fortifying myself against the eerie, lonely, threatening sounds of the night: the warning sounds, the mating sounds, the combat sounds . . . the owls with their wandering-soul calls . . . the wolves, howling, barking, answering, challenging.

"They're talking and singing. . . . They're in a big argument," I'd tell Joe when he'd wake and listen and then ask if I heard too.

Worse than all else, were the panther noises. They had the full range of cat calls and cries magnified to giant proportions, reaching uninhibited and terrifying peaks of protest, outrage, and defiance, resembling nothing so much as the human voice in some ultimate agony. To soothe the children in their fright, I kept explaining they were just big cats, and I began to identify one especially ferocious voice as "Big Tom," making him the central character in a series of animal stories that I invented for their entertainment.

But there came a night when I could not speak soothingly to them or reach into my imagination for another tale. It was a night that brought me a double ordeal. . . . A dark, awesome night when the voices of the wilderness came closer than ever before, seeking, protesting, crying out in terror and conflict as if a spirit of rapaciousness moved through the forest and every creature was either preying or being preyed upon. When an especially vicious conflict between two big cats settling a dispute over meal or mate seemed to come right up to the cabin door, the children awoke and clung to me. We were all three in the big bed and I had one on each side of me. I pulled them up close to me.

"Don't be afraid," I said. "It's just Big Tom. He's got into an awful fight. He has a very bad temper, you know."

"It sounds like somebody, Mama," Joe insisted. "Are you sure it's just the big cats? It sounds like somebody hurt awfully bad."

One of the cats uttered a loud, piercing prolonged scream. Virginia cried out and Joe huddled close, his whole body trembling. I considered lighting the precious candle, or getting up and building the fire high to comfort the children with a lighted room. But there might be a greater need for the candle and my hands were so sore from using the ax I must make the firewood last as long as possible. I decided to comfort them as best I could in bed. I moved Virginia over between Joe and me, turning her so that she could cuddle close and hide her face against me.

"Joe, put your hands over Ginny's ears," I instructed, "so she can't hear the bad cats and their ugly noises." It always steadied Joe to be called upon to help his sister. "You and I know we won't be hurt, but she can't understand."

I encircled both the children tight in my arms and was able to place one hand over Joe's ear, pressing his head gently into the pillow so that the appalling sounds would be shut out some for him too.

Soon they were both asleep, and in my relief at the accomplishment, I lapsed into a state of relaxed exhaustion that failed to record the fearsome sounds outside and allowed me to escape into slumber also.

As I slept, I dreamed. And at first it was a pleasant dream. I was back in the security of my little house in New Orleans. I had cooked a fine breakfast and Joe sat happily stuffing himself. I sat in a rocker, the one I had bought especially for rocking Ginny soon after she was born. I held my baby girl in my lap, feeding at my breast. The contentment I felt at nourishing my child from my own body was a deeply pleasant, highly physical sensation. I pushed the damp locks back from her forehead and said, "Don't hurry so, my lamb. Don't act like a starved pig. I'll let you get your fill." And the elation at feeding the dear hungry baby rose high in me again. Then it all changed. I felt a pain in my breast and nightmare sensation of inadequacy and shame. The child in my arms became fretful and insistent and the breast empty and hard—and the baby lips were sharp teeth. The pain shot through me and I cried out and leaped up. And as Virginia wailed out in protest and bewilderment, I knew the awful reality of what was happening. My little girl, weaned for two years, had been driven by her fear and hunger back to babyhood's source of comfort and nourishment while I slept and held her close.

My sense of shock at Ginny's deep need and my inability to supply it was so overwhelming that a suffocating nausea swept over me. She reached for me again. I cried out for the help of God, pushed her from me more roughly than I intended, and leaped from bed. Her wails redoubled.

Joe awoke, greatly alarmed.

"Get Ginny a drink, Joe. She's thirsty. I'll go get some haws."

It was daylight. I had to get out of the cabin, and hide in shame from the clutching hands I couldn't fill, the hungry mouths I couldn't feed, the sad eyes I couldn't change. I was their mother and I had failed them—in every way! The sharp pain was still like a knife in my barren breast. I stood with my back to the door so that if Joe looked out, he couldn't see that I was crying. I reached out blindly for the haws, pretending to pick them, crushing them in my hands. The nausea continued to surge through me. And with me was the hateful memory of Mrs. Hoodey and her suckling child. It was an accusing memory. If I had kept Ginny nursing, perhaps now, in this extremity, I could have satisfied her.

Joe called out to me. "Mama. What are you out there for? You got plenty of haws yesterday."

"I'll be right back, Joe," I said. "I'll be right back." My knees were trembling. My heart was thumping hard and slow. And I saw my hands were red with the crushed berries. I still couldn't go back in the house.

"Mama, you're barefooted," Joe protested as I walked on down to the bayou, completely incautious of danger.

"Mama, you don't have your dress on."

The dew-drenched grass felt good to my feet. "Don't worry, Joe," I answered him. "Nobody will see me. I'll be back. You stay there."

And to myself I said: This is our own private wilderness, Joe Boy, our own private little hell. It doesn't matter whether we wear day clothes or night clothes, or no clothes at all.

I crouched by the edge of the bayou, gazing numbly at my reflection there as it became brighter and brighter in the sunrise. My gown fell around me, making me look like a white bundle with a black head sticking out of it. My face in the water was distorted and bony, and the black hair tumbling around it heightened the weird effect.

"Black witch!" I said to the reflection, hating myself. And then I gasped in astonishment as a large catfish swam lazily across my re-flected face.

My depression vanished, and my mind came instantly into focus. Here was food! Meat! I almost leaped into the water after it. Why hadn't I thought of this days before? Surely, I could catch a fish! I stooped to wash my hands and sent the fish scurrying away. I dashed water into my face and ran back to the cabin.

"Joe, I'm going to catch a fish for us," I announced, as I scrambled into my clothes, some high shoes and stockings.

"Oh my," Joe said. "That's wonderful, Mama. How do you catch a fish? Have you ever caught a fish before, Mama?"

"Why, no, I never have, Joe." My hopes dipped a little. But there wasn't much to catching a fish. "Your grandfather and Uncle John used to go fishing once in a while when we lived in Nashville. They used poles with lines on them, and at the end of the line a hook, and on the hook, a worm!"

"We don't have any of that."

"Oh, but we do. Any good stick will do for a pole. I have some good strong thread for a line and a bent pin will do for a hook. And you can help me dig for some worms right by the cabin door."

Joe was entranced with the big earthworms he was able to turn up with a dinner fork.

"Maybe if you don't catch a fish, Mama, we can eat some worms."

I almost laughed, and then realized that if it was a joke at all, it was too grim for laughter.

When I had my fishing pole ready, Joe begged to go to the bayou with me, but I told him he must care for Ginny, and besides too much watching would scare the fish away.

Realizing that sewing thread might not be strong enough to hold a fish, I had used a piece of ropelike dress braid for the main line. I had used thread to wrap around the head of the pin and tie it to the braid. But there were two things I hadn't picked up in the casual observations of my father's and brother's fishing poles: weights and corks. When I submitted my bait to the bayou, the braid floated on top of the water, the pin dangled just below the surface, and worm after worm wiggled free. I was glad that Joe wasn't on hand to witness the dismal results of my efforts. Finally the braid became soaked enough to go down further and the pin held on to a very inactive worm. I forced myself to patience and waited. And finally a fish came. I held my breath while he eyed the bait. Then there was a quick flick, a little jerk on the line, and fish and bait both were gone. I repeated this game several times. It was maddening. One time I was so certain I had the fish, and jerked so hard on the line, that I lost my balance and fell. I alternately felt bleak disappointment and unreasonable anger at the placid and tricky fish.

Weak from the ordeals of the night, wanting so desperately to provide something for the children expectantly waiting, I was enraged at having food so near and yet so unattainable.

I stuck my finger getting another worm impaled on the pin and threw the line back in with such force that the braid sank to a better level. It had hardly come to a quiet position before the largest fish of all rose to investigate. It seemed to me that he actually sniffed at the bait dangling so temptingly there, then rejected it and swam languidly on—not away, but directly toward me—directly to the spot where I was perched in frantic expectation. Then it seemed to rest in the water, just out of my reach, its glassy eyes mocking me, its tail movements back and forth, back and forth, taunting me with its repleteness—as if it might be saying, "Take away your silly worm. I'm not hungry!"

"So you're not hungry," I yelled and leaped into the water, grabbing for my tormenter, feeling a sharp fin under my hand as I almost caught him.

Then I found myself thrashing about, fish forgotten, only one thing in my mind: to keep from drowning. The water came to my shoulders and the bank was slick and without incline. My shoes and clothes were heavy and restricting. There were snags underfoot, and as I struggled, I became more and more entangled. My skirt caught and I could not free it. Gasping for breath, my whole body quivering, I realized how near to death I was—how my children were about to be left alone in helplessness and fear because of my careless, impulsive behavior. The crisis of hunger was suddenly diminished. We were far from starvation. The haws were not gone. To stay alive was the important thing. I caught hold of a snag and willed myself to be perfectly still, save my strength, and work with my mind. I made a plan and began to execute it. I loosened the belt of my skirt and my full petticoat, and slowly, carefully got free of them. I unbuttoned my waist and pulled off the long tight sleeves that were so much tighter wet and held my elbows stiff and unbending. Then very cautiously, I worked out a few steps to a point on the bank where some long reeds grew. My wet shoes were like stones tied to my feet. I held to the reeds and rested, and then when I felt I had sufficient strength, I began to twist about so that with one hand I could undo my soggy shoes and throw them on the bank. Some more rest—then kicking, tugging, lurching, sliding, I was finally out of the water and onto the bank. I lay face downward, breathing heavily, thankful for deliverance, calmed by escaping a calamity worse than the one I had been dwelling on. I thought how wonderful it was to be alive and restored to my children. I turned and sat up, still too shaky to rise to my feet. I saw my bulky clothes in the water and thought how stupid it was for women to encumber themselves with so much unnecessary clothing, so foolishly restrictive—and how ridiculously unfair the social dictum that swimming was not for ladies. I pronounced a vow to myself that if God let me live long enough, I would learn to swim. This resolution seemed to refresh me. I got to my feet and set about recovering my waist and skirt and petticoat, using the fishing pole. My fishing in this respect was more successful. When I had the three pieces on the bank, I removed the pin, braid, and thread from the pole, for these items were irreplaceable. As I stood winding the thread about my finger, I became aware of a most unusual sound. It seemed quite near. It was like a purr—an enormously big purr.

The sound was on my left. I turned to look in that direction and found I was facing the largest cat I had ever seen. He was sitting at the base of a huge cypress tree, and even in this position he was almost as tall as I and possibly twice as heavy. His attention was all on me, and the sound he made, though hoarse and rasping was unmistakeably a purr. Big Tom, in the flesh, and purring with pleasure! He was not looking at me as though I were strange to him, so he must have watched me many times when I came out for water.

"The painters are just big cats, shy and harmless, long as they're well fed," Mrs. Abit had said. And somehow he seemed so much more friendly than the slippery tangled bayou from which I had just escaped. I was excited but not afraid. In fact, I felt a sort of companionable interest in him. At the same time, I realized I must be cautious in my movements. If I ran away, he might be inclined to pursue.

If I moved toward him, he might be aroused to defense. So for a moment or so, we just stared at each other. My close scrutiny brought a stop to his purring as if he too realized the necessity for caution. But he continued to sit on his haunches, still and brown as the tree trunk beside him, his black ears alert, his expression docile, the hair along his belly gleaming white.

On an impulse, I shouted "Scat!" and shook my wet garments at him. With one great leap he bounded into the brush and away. The motion was so sudden and easy and left such little sound for a creature so big that I was inclined to wonder if he had really been there. I turned my back on the spot and began to walk slowly toward the cabin, clad only in my undergarments, soaked clothes and shoes heavy in my arms. I felt that somewhere behind me, Big Tom watched, but I did not look back.

Harriet's son E.Y. found his mother asleep in the chair at her writing desk. It was a comfortable high-backed, lightly-cushioned chair. Her hands were at rest on the arms of the chair, her head was tilted back a little, the lips almost smiling, the breathing gentle and regular.

Her pen lay at the end of the page where she had written "I did not look back," as if she had become too weary to replace it in the holder. Several pages were scattered about, face up, on the desk. E.Y. was curious. He had no compunctions about reading the scattered pages. Where his mother was concerned, he felt possessive, proud, and privileged. His treatment of her was indulgent and occasionally high-handed when he made up his mind that a certain course of action was best for her interests or health. E.Y., now forty-four years old, had been a married man only seven years but had been his mother's stand-by for the twenty-five years since his father's death. They had come through some hard times together and had realized a mutual dream when he had received his medical degree from Tulane, though he was thirty-seven years old at the time. Then he had married Gracie and she had given him a son. Claud was only six years old. So E.Y. sometimes felt very old and very young at the same time. But he always felt close to his mother. They both knew that in temperament and interests they were much alike. For four years he had practiced medicine—then he had turned to business investment and been amazingly successful. On this evening he had a big piece of news for his mother. A company he had organized only three years previously with a quarter million capital had just been sold by his own efforts for a half million. He was eager to relate his triumph to her. He wanted to keep making up for what had happened to her in the past—at least the part he knew about. As he scanned the pages before him, he realized that his mother was writing about her life, and detailed here was an episode he knew nothing about. He began reading at the place where the fish scurried across her sad reflection in the water.

His mother's poetic use of words had always delighted him, and he was pleased that she was writing these memoirs—writing them for him, he felt sure. But he must be watchful that they didn't fall into other hands. He must not let anything happen that would lead to a revival of public interest in her past. He intended to make certain that she lived out her days in serenity and comfort. Her description of the fishing escapade disturbed him deeply. He seemed to share it with her, actually experience her desperation and struggle, and when he had finished, there was a clear picture in his mind of her diminutive figure in scanty wet garments walking the path from bayou to cabin door, her back to the perils she had conquered, her face to the waiting hungry children—her beauty and bearing incongruous to the wild surroundings, but the courage that sustained her quite compatible with wilderness requirements. E.Y.'s eyes clouded with love and adoration and he shook his head to clear them. He saw the food tray where his mother had dined and went closer to examine it. He smelled of the empty glass, and of the bowl that had held the anchovy—here his eyebrows raised and he smiled with satisfaction that she appreciated his treat. He picked up the one remaining pickled onion and chewed it thoughtfully, nibbled on a shred of cold meat, used the tip of his finger to identify what had been in the other empty bowls and plates, lifted the lid from the teapot. He frowned, leaned over his mother in concern. He was afraid her appetite had been dangerously active while writing of her hunger ordeal. He picked up her wrist to check her pulse. She opened her eyes, smiled at him, and raised the free hand to touch his cheek lightly.

"How long have you been spying on me, Edward?"

"Only a little while. You were sleeping so peacefully, I hated to rouse you."

"I didn't intend to doze off like that. How're Gracie and Claud?"

As he answered her, she looked at him, but at the same time casually pushed the sheets covered with writing, back under the pigeonhole section and out of sight.

"And what financial wizardry have you been up to?"

He pulled a chair close and sat leaning toward her so that their faces were close together, and related the details of the half-million-dollar sale. His mother was the only member of his family who thoroughly understood and enjoyed a discussion on the intricacies of business manipulations, and it pleased him to give her a full account and not have to disguise his self-satisfaction with what he had accomplished.

"You amaze me, son, and make me very proud. I think it is a surprise to us both that finance and not medicine calls forth your most lively abilities. You look so much like your father, Edward, and you have your grandfather Moore's fine talent with the sick, but neither of them ever evidenced any particular shrewdness in a business way. This takes a special kind of sharp discernment. Where did you get it?"

"You know as well as I do where I got it—where I'm getting it right now. You just want to hear me say it. From you, of course!"

"Such things are not for a woman's mind, son, you know that."

They both smiled at what neither believed.

"I'd like to do something special for you, Mama, to show my appreciation."

"There's something I've been intending to discuss with you—something that would involve a bit of financing—and some conniving."

E.Y. knew better than to make rash promises until he had heard her out.

"It's about Tricky. It appears that she's going to be the only girl in both families, Addie and Gracie having each left off with one child, and that a boy. I know Addie and Frank will give her the supervision she needs, and I know you'll make a big thing of her beauty—she'll want for nothing your money can buy her to make her queen of your social world, but that isn't enough.

"Tricky is a lot like me—more than you realize. I want her to have some training that I needed and missed out on. There are many things in which I can instruct her, but these things I have in mind are a little too strenuous for me now."

"What do you have in mind, Mama?"

"I want her to know how to swim and how to fish. I want her to have some excursions into the country and learn something of nature firsthand. I want her to be able to ride and shoot like a man."

"And you expect me to bring this about?"

"I do, and some of it, like riding astride and handling a gun, without other members of the family knowing."

E.Y. didn't particularly like his assignment. He didn't like women out of their place, and an independent, lively little thing like Tricky might easily become a rowdy. Ordinarily, he would have been firm and direct with his mother, explaining why he thought such procedure improper and unwise. But the account of her wilderness ordeal was so fresh in his mind that objections to her proposal were difficult for him to express. She had handicapped him. For a moment he wondered if she had done it on purpose.

"Mama," he said gently. "This is some leftover from your experiences long ago on the Texas frontier. Those times are past. Tricky will have no need for so rugged an existence. She will have money, position, education, travel, the best marriage opportunities. Let her be trained as a lady, as a beautiful lady, a gracious lady."

"She has a mind too, you know."

"I know. I know. Probably one equally as keen as yours. Feed her mind on books and music and travel, and if she is alert on money matters and such, that's all right. She'll make a fine banker's wife."

"But suppose she should choose for a husband some army man or government scout and follow him to an outpost on the frontier."

"Ridiculous. We'll carefully select the young men she meets."

"We will?"

"Indeed we will. And remember, Mama, wilderness life is almost a thing of the past. The Indians are confined on reservations. With forty-four states in the union and Oklahoma Territory opened up for settlement, the next generation will come into a national heritage of civilization and unity from coast to coast."

"A fine statement for a public address, Edward, but far from the truth. You and I will not live to see the Great American Wilderness an orderly domain. Tricky may see it—she also may have a part in charting it—or become its victim. And I maintain that whether male or female, in wild or civilized surroundings, everyone should know how to swim. Don't you agree?"

"I don't know that I do."

"But you will, because I want it, see that Tricky learns?"

"And how will I do this? I have neither the time nor inclination to loiter at resorts, and my interests are such that a country estate would be a burden and inconvenience."

"I'm not asking you to reorganize your life for a whim of mine, Edward. You have a fine pond in that showy yard of yours. House it, make it private, if your sensitivities demand such false modesty, and hire someone to instruct both Tricky and Claud."

"I suppose I could."

"But will you?"

"Yes."

"Thank you, Edward. And you do intend to have Claud taught to handle horses and guns, don't you?"

"Yes, but he's young yet. In another year or so, I imagine."

"Then Tricky may learn at the same time. It will be more interesting for both her and Claud—put a bit of competition into their training."

"It won't be easy to arrange."

"It wasn't easy to arrange for the sale of that company at half a million either, was it, Edward? But you wanted it done, and you did it."

"That's different."

"Not so different. Just approach it the same way—with resolution and careful planning. I'm sure Tricky will co-operate."

"I have no doubt of that."

"Then it's settled."

"I shall see if it can be worked out within the bounds of safety and good health for the children."

"Oh no, Edward. I want no slipping-out words. Say you'll do it or you won't do it. I want a contract with your conscience, in case I'm not around to give you the prod personally."

Edward laughed. "All right, Mama, you have my word, though not my full approval."

"And one more thing——"

E.Y. sighed and prepared to get firm.

"It's about the mattress."

"Mattress?"

"My feather one—covered with the brocade you brought from Europe."

E.Y. frowned. It still displeased him that his mother had put his valuable gift to such commonplace use.

"I know you didn't like what I did with that expensive cloth. But the mattress is my special treasure. And Tricky knows both the sentimental and material value of it. I want it to be her inheritance from me. I have told Addie this but wanted you to know my expectations because of what you have 'invested' in it." She gave him a sly smile. "And somewhere down the generations when feather mattresses are outmoded, some descendant will take the brocade and display it properly—by that time it will have aged enough to be a precious antique. In the meantime, I dream upon it."

E.Y.'s frown disappeared. "I'll see that it goes to Tricky, Mama, never fear."

When E.Y. was gone, and Harriet lay in drowsy comfort upon the yielding softness of the feather mattress, she was thinking: It isn't an easy thing to get around E.Y. . . . . I wonder if he suspected that I purposely left those pages out for him to read . . . Now, I must be cautious . . . he's seen quite enough . . . he's the only one who knows I'm writing a personal account . . . what if I should die before it is complete?

Before falling asleep, she had perfected her plan for proper concealment of her manuscript.

The next morning, after breakfast, Harriet bolted her room door, which she did so rarely that it made her feel like a conspirator. Then she quickly got out her sewing basket and placed it on the bed. On the far side of the bed, she exposed the mattress and quickly ripped out a corner seam. The brocade had been put on over a durable cotton ticking and so secured at the ends that a long pocket existed at top and bottom. Into this pocket, she slipped the numbered pages, stitched together and folded so that they could not easily become rumpled.

When the bed was made and the door unbolted, she sighed in relief, returned to her desk, placed a new stack of paper conveniently at hand, and put time-wings on her imagination for instantaneous transportation to Austin Bayou in Texas, late September, 1835.

I called out to Joe as I came up the path, carrying my wet garments, "I didn't catch any fish and I fell in the bayou. When we get out of here, we're going to get Uncle John, or somebody, to teach all three of us how to swim."

"We are?"

"We certainly are!" Oh, how happy I was to be alive and coming back to my children! "And guess who was down there keeping me company while I tried to fish?"

"There was somebody down there?"

"Big Tom himself!"

"Big Tom!" Fish forgotten, his eyes were big with excitement.

"Purring away, sitting under a tree, watching me, laughing at me, no doubt."

The haws tasted different and better that night, eaten as I detailed a new story about Big Tom, so much easier to build around the reality.

This was the beginning of a closer acquaintance with Big Tom. Acting as though our meeting at the bayou had given him further privilege, he sometimes came to the very door of the cabin in the night and lay down close to the wall, purring in great loud gusts, moving his claws rhythmically in noisy scratches of pleasure; and once he reared up against the cabin wall to sharpen his claws on the hard surface of the logs.

When the moon was especially bright one night, I opened the shutters on one of the windows and let Joe stand on a chair and look out at Big Tom. The cat showed no alarm at our observation—only increased the tempo and volume of his purring. Another time we were awakened at the sound of the big cats fighting nearby and were able to watch Big Tom chasing another panther from the premises.

Even though I liked Big Tom and somehow felt less forsaken because of his attachment, I did not allow myself to trust him and always carried the ax on my excursions outside the cabin. But it was several days after my tumble into the bayou before I had another daytime meeting with him. I had gone out for water, and because of some drift that had moved in, I had to leave the path and go to a spot several yards below my regular dipping place. I sat my bucket down and started to chop away some reeds to give better access to the water. As I raised my ax, I was startled by a low growl and spitting sound, such as a cat makes in threat or defense. My grip tightened on the ax. I turned without moving from the spot where I stood. My eyes searched the tall grass and underbrush. Then I saw him—so near and so astonishingly big that the scene seemed distorted beyond reality.

Big Tom was stretched out on his belly, flattened against the earth, and the distance from his nose to twitching tail tip must have been fully eight feet. His ears were laid back, his greenish yellow eyes glared malevolently, and his open mouth showed a hostile baring of teeth. One forepaw was raised for striking, the long retractile claw extended for ripping. There was no doubt about the animosity and intent of his posture. I almost threw the ax, but just in time I observed that Big Tom's eyes were not focused on me. At the same time, I realized that the growl and hissing were contradictions to a cat's stalking stealth, and the pure silence it achieves before pouncing on its prey, and I had been entirely vulnerable, my back to him. I shifted my glance in search of his enemy and saw the death-dealing cottonmouth, the broad flat head with the white rim around the mouth raised from the coil, ready for striking. The ghastly closeness of this evil serpent sent a shiver over me and I felt the skin of my whole body roughen. I was within its striking distance—a few inches and an instant from death's door. I literally held my breath. Big Tom made a movement with his up-lifted paw, inviting the deadly snake to strike—and when it did, he dodged the fangs with an easy motion, and then pounced to rip and claw out the serpent's life before it could strike a second time. With a playful motion, he slung the shreds of it aside and moved around sniffing the place where it had been. I could have reached out and touched him. I didn't move a finger, hardly breathed. He moved back to the snake and sat on his haunches looking at it, sniffing, using one forepaw and then the other playfully pushing it about, seeming amused with some movement in a segment of the tail end. Once he looked up at me curiously, then went back to mauling his gruesome toy. I realized that while he was thus occupied might be a good time to make my departure unobtrusively. So with studied indifference to him, I dipped my water bucket and walked at my usual pace back to the cabin and the children.

The parsley hawthorne was near the end of its fruiting when Solomon left for the army. Nine days later, the ripe red haws were hard to find and I was in competition with the greedy birds who seemed especially hungry for this delicacy as the season faded.

The children had ceased to fret. They didn't have the energy to complain. We all three became very quiet, our movements slow and apathetic. I kept a bit of fire going most of the time in the hope that the chimney smoke might prove a signal to someone. Providing wood and water took most of my strength. Clothes and shoes seemed heavy and cumbersome. So most of the time I was barefooted and without petticoats, wearing only a lightweight house dress that I had made lighter by removing the tight sleeves and trimming the full skirt off to almost knee length.

I left the cabin door open in the forenoon as I did what must be done outside in the little flare of energy that morning brings. In the afternoon, I closed the door. I no longer spent hours scanning the prairie. Most of the afternoon, the three of us lay quietly on the bed, trying to make rest a substitute for food.

On this afternoon of the ninth day, the children slept, and I lay half-dreaming, a sort of waking torment, in which I envisioned what it would be like, starving to death. Would I live longer than the children when we were deprived of all food? I mustn't die first. I must watch them die and then let go. I tried to put aside my nightmare. I must hope. I must pray. I got up to stir the fire. I'd drink some hot water. That often helped, especially when I could imagine it was tea or coffee.

There was some new sound outside—slight but different. I listened.

"Hello!"

I couldn't believe it was a human voice. My heart pounded. I wondered if I was going to faint in this delusion or dream.

"Hello, in there!"

The children both awoke.

"Mama! Mama! Somebody—somebody——"

I rushed to the door and unbarred it, all my weakness gone. The children were at my heels. When I flung it open, there was a man—a big man, middle-aged, friendly, astride a fine gray horse. He looked most wonderful to us, a hero and savior. I'm sure we looked rather terrifying to him, but at the moment I had no thought for my bare feet, uncombed hair, and short dress.

"Are you Mrs. Page?" he asked.

I nodded. I found my throat was too tight for speech.

"Your husband around?"

I shook my head.

"My name's Merrick. I heard you folks had moved in. Been wonderin' why he hasn't shown up."

I struggled to say exactly the right thing. I mustn't let him get away, must be careful and polite.

"Won't you get down and come in, Mr. Merrick?"

He dismounted as if he were in no hurry, dropped his reins that his horse might graze, and came towards us.

Suddenly, I was no longer stiff and staring. I was possessed with a feeling of wild relief and gratitude. I ran to meet him (ran into him expresses it better), threw my arms around him, holding to him fiercely, sobbing, "You've saved us, you've saved us!"

He stood, stiff and awkward, patting my shoulder, murmuring, "There, there."

But I did not long embarrass him. My balance was soon restored, and I drew back with an apology for my looks and my action. And I explained that we would have starved if he had not come—that we had had nothing but haws for two weeks and they were about gone.

Mr. Merrick said, "That's too bad," and went to remove his saddlebags.

"I brought you a few little things," he said. "You build up a cooking fire and I'll go get some meat."

He took his rifle from the saddle, staked his horse to browse, and without another word disappeared into the brush east of the cabin.

A man—and a gun—and "I'll go get some meat." Was deliverance ever so positive and so sweet!

I rushed into the cabin to make myself respectable, explore Mr. Merrick's saddlebags and get the fire going. There was meal and coffee. I had the water heating and was mixing the cornbread when I heard his gun. A short time later, he came in carrying a turkey, skinned and gutted, and several sharpened sticks. We didn't speak as he cut off chunks of turkey meat, stuck them on the pointed sticks and began to broil the meat over the fire. I continued with the preparation of the bread and coffee. The odors were so tantalizing to the children's hunger that I gave them some coffee beans to chew in order to appease the agony of their waiting.

126

It was hard not to eat the meat and bread while it was too hot—hard not to swallow it whole without chewing—hard not to eat like ravenous animals.

When the first edge was off our hunger, Mr. Merrick opened the bottle of brandy and poured a generous gurgle into the big blue cups I had filled with coffee. Then he unwrapped some rock candy and gave it to the children. Their utter pleasure and gratitude caused him to turn away to hide his feeling, for I could tell that he had the impulse to gather them into his arms.

The food made the children excessively drowsy and soon they were fast asleep. But it had the opposite effect on me. Mr. Merrick and I sat long at the table sipping from the blue cups and talking, talking. He seemed almost as starved for companionship as I.

When I asked him how it was that he had brought the supplies to us, since he had no knowledge of Solomon's departure, he hesitated to explain, but finally told me.

"I kept wondering why Page didn't show up to work for me. With help harder to find than gold in an alligator's teeth, I was willing to give him a job, no matter how tender-footed he was. I thought maybe he wouldn't get the war-fever, being a newcomer, and I'd be able to hang on to him.

"I got no pleasant memories about this cabin here where my wife departed this life, and I kept putting off coming over. But finally I couldn't put it off no longer—on account of the dreams."

"What dreams, Mr. Merrick?"

"For three nights in a row, I dreamed—awful things—about this place. In the first dream I rode up and looked in the window. I saw a woman and two children. They sat at a bare table. I thought at first they had no clothes on—but that wasn't it—they had no flesh on—they was just skeletons."

He looked at me, wondering if he should go on. I was amazed at his revelation and the manifestation of so mysterious a force. But I was not frightened. I wanted to hear the rest.

"And what were the other two dreams, Mr. Merrick?"

"Well, on the second night, I was here at the cabin again. But I couldn't even get near. It was surrounded by wild beasts, thick as ants. The door was open and the beasts crowded inside. I heard a child scream and awoke. Then I heard the scream again, and knew I had been awakened by a painter, probably had been hearing it in my sleep. So I figured I couldn't put any stock in that dream. Never thought much about dreams meaning anything anyhow.

"But when I had the third dream, I woke up feeling I couldn't rest till I knew for sure what was going on at this cabin. It was so—so very real, ma'am—so very real."

He hesitated to go on. He fumbled with his empty cup and I refilled it.

"Tell me about it—your third dream—Mr. Merrick. Please do."

"I rode up to the cabin—I rode up and called out. And I waited, knowing the smoke in the chimney meant life, most likely. But my heart was in my throat, so to speak, about what I'd find. And then the door opened—and a girl was standing there weeping, black curly hair, big eyes, and two little ones with her—at first I thought it was a girl—she was so small and——"

"Was she bare-footed and in a short sleeveless dress, Mr. Merrick?"

"Yes, she was, Mrs. Page."

"And did she rush out to you—and did she——"

"Yes, she did, Mrs. Page. Exactly what you did when I got here. Gave me an awful strange feeling when it came true—just as it was—in the dream—holding you there—and you crying against me——" he poured more brandy into his cup and averted his eyes, deeply embarrassed. "Like I say, I never put much stock in dreams—but a man don't want it on his conscience that he's been warned and done nothing about it. So I just rode over with a few things in my saddlebags——"

"Even rock candy for the children."

"That was—in Mrs. Merrick's things—something she left behind. She had a sweet tooth . . . Now, Mrs. Page, tell me more about yourself."

It was awfully easy for me to talk—and talk. It seemed I couldn't quit. And Mr. Merrick was so interested—he kept me talking. Finally I was telling him the whole truth about Solomon, about his gambling, about his deserting us, leaving us in the wilderness to starve. And finally, how wonderful that he was here now and could make arrangements for getting us back to the settlement.

At this point, I became aware that Mr. Merrick was looking at me sympathetically, but without understanding.

"You believe me, don't you, Mr. Merrick? You understand my predicament? You'll help me to get out. I can pay you."

"It isn't that, Mrs. Page. I know how hard it's been for you, cooped up here. But your husband didn't desert you like that. He's left some word somewhere—sending a wagon perhaps or some supplies. There's just been a delay, that's all. It's that way out here—nothing comes about on time. If I moved you out and he come back here to find you gone, things would be in a pretty mess, now wouldn't they?"

"My husband is a gambling man, Mr. Merrick. He volunteered more to be with the crowd and get in the game than to fight for anything. He's not giving a thought to his family. If he's thinking of a game, or in one, we simply don't exist."

"Don't be too hard on him, ma'am. Lots of good men like the cards."

He actually thought I was being unfair to Solomon!

I made another appeal: "Mr. Merrick, I have no one—absolutely no one—to come to my aid. My husband was too angry to visit my father or brother. He brought me out here principally to spite them. He would avoid them. I don't say he expected me and the children to die. He expected me to find a way out—I've been finding ways out ever since I married him. But now I'm trapped. You must get me out!"

My desperation only convinced him I was pushing my excitement into hysteria.

He tried to pacify me. "I'd like to accommodate you, Mrs. Page, you know that, but I don't think moving out is the right thing to do. And even if I did, I couldn't get off to move you right now, and there's no one in these parts to call on. You'll be all right. I'll get you some more meat in the morning and check back when I can."

I thanked him and withdrew into cool politeness. I told him I'd try to make him comfortable for the night in the shed room. He told me not to go to any trouble. He'd bring in his saddle and blanket and bed down on that.

He went out to unsaddle and I moved Joe's trundle bed into the shed room. I put a bench by the bedside with my bit of a candle on it in a graceful copper holder. Then I refilled the blue cup and set it by the candle. When he carried his gear into the room, he returned to the entrance and looked in on me. The cabin was lighted only by the fire I had built up and I stood in front of it. He stood there, stooped in the low doorway for a moment, as if he were searching for the right words.

"You shouldn't have troubled. But thank you, ma'am. I haven't seen soft clean covers like that—haven't had anyone think of my comfort like that—since my wife passed on. You might not believe me if I told you I haven't even so much as passed the time of day with another woman in more'n a year—been livin' in a man and animal world—I'd just about forgotten home comforts—and a woman around." He was very confused.

"Goodnight, ma'am." He stood for a moment longer. "Don't worry —don't worry—about anything."

He closed the door—with much more force than necessary.

I sat down in front of the fire to rock and think—think about Mr. Merrick and how I might influence him to take us away. Even if he would just bring another horse and take us to Brazoria, I would leave everything behind. But he would not be easy to persuade. He was a man perhaps twice my age with a deep sense of propriety. He had decided not to meddle with the Page family. He did not think we were really deserted. He did not want an irate husband tracking him down.

But I was on his mind, I knew that. I knew he was lying there on the bed in the shed room, thinking about me, and the satisfaction it had brought him coming to my rescue, passing the evening in my presence. He was probably disturbed at the thought of leaving us alone again in the morning. I heard him turning restlessly in his bed and this made me more hopeful.

All at once, it seemed that nothing was more important than sleep— blessed sleep—in comfort and safety—hunger appeased—good man and gun nearby. I was in bed and sound asleep without knowing how I did it, and I did not awaken until I heard Mr. Merrick's gun at daybreak. He had slipped out to hunt without awaking us.

I felt refreshed and exultant. I wanted to shout for joy. But as I dressed quickly and carefully I became sobered by the thought that I might soon be alone again, waiting for some other chance deliverance. I prepared to be as cheerful and charming as possible, for I must change Mr. Merrick's mind. But I soon found this would be no easy matter. He brought in another turkey and a fat buck. He declined breakfast, drank a cup of coffee standing, then occupied himself exclusively with dressing the meat, salting it, instructing me how to keep it from spoiling, preparing some strips for drying. I was with him as he worked, helping when I could, asking many questions, for this was a task quite new to me.

He answered me in short impersonal phrases. He would not look at me nor converse with me in the open direct manner of the evening before. He was overly cautious not to get too close to me. And once when our hands touched in the work, his face reddened. I realized then that his feelings for me were such that I had become a threat and a danger. And because of his personal distress, he could not comprehend mine. I was temptation, another man's wife, and he must be done with the meat and away from me as soon as possible.

The irony of it! Deserted by one man because he cared nothing about me, and about to be left by another because he cared too much! Woman, forced to depend on man for protection and provision, is sometimes offered a strange choice. Mr. Merrick was good and kind. He represented safety for me and the children. I must not let him go. I stayed close to him, placed my hand upon his arm several times. I realized that I was distressing him and I felt sorry, but the nearer he came to the end of his task, the greater my resolve. He became fully aware of my intent. Once he stopped his work on the meat and gave me a long level look as he wiped the sweat from under his eyes. He said nothing, but returned to his work with such purposeful haste that I could neither assist him nor think of anything to say. Then he went down to the water's edge to wash his hands, and before I knew what he was about had unstaked his horse and mounted for departure. He looked toward me, tipped his hat, mumbled something I couldn't understand, and turned his horse to go.

I called out "Mr. Merrick!" and ran toward him.

He stopped and looked at me. "Yes, Mrs. Page?" His voice was grave and strained.

I had intended to plead, "Come back! Come back and stay with me!" I was even holding out my arms to him.

But my hands dropped to my sides, and what I really said was: "God bless you for your kindness!"

He gave his horse a jab that sent the animal leaping away. Mr. Merrick himself was hunched down over the saddle horn as if in pain. I think he was crying.

As for myself, I felt that there was two of me: One stood very still and understood Mr. Merrick's motives for riding away, sympathized with the hungry loneliness that the children and I had aroused in him, truly blessed him for feeding us. The other writhed in humiliation at what I had tried to do and failed to accomplish, and felt a searing resentment that a deliverer had come and gone, refusing to believe that we were really forsaken. And this one of me prayed that regret would be Mr. Merrick's companion, night and day, giving him no peace.

I don't know how long I stood there with my miserable contemplation. I was aroused by a faint roaring sound. It seemed to come closer from across the prairie somewhere. Then I saw it. Rain. A heavy, unhesitant, marching wall of rain, approaching with no fanfare of lightning and thunder, just the warning roar, more and more distinct.

I hurried frantically to get in dry wood, estimated the speed of the cloud very poorly, and was caught and soaked with the second load in my arms—an initiatory baptism into another season of endurance.

7.

The heavy rains had set in, and the bayou rose and reached around our log shelter, embracing it with a fateful finality of detachment. The few remaining haws were pelted off the bushes and washed away. There were a few tablespoons of coffee to be used over and over, and cornbread that might be stretched over three days. And beyond that meat—just meat. The weather was too warm to keep the meat properly, there was not enough salt for curing, and no sun for drying. I was inexperienced at fire-drying. The fires I created were spiritless things, for I had to miser the wood on hand and bring in wet grass and sticks to dry and then feed the contrary coals. I became more smoked than the meat, and my eyes streamed as I worked.

"I'm not crying," I kept telling Joe and Ginny. "It's just the smoke." And the smoke was also a good disguise when I was crying.

After three days, I had to throw all the meat out except a few salted pieces, and some strips finally smoked dry. It was an awful decision, throwing away the rotten meat, standing the offensive odors as long as possible. Properly preserved it would have sustained us for weeks. And the damp air held the scent in the room with us after the meat was gone, and made what we had to eat a nauseous and difficult diet.

Virginia became listless and pale and lay on the bed most of the time, sleeping much more than she should have. Joe sat for long periods just rocking, back and forth, back and forth, his eyes wide and staring—gazing inwardly upon some child's world of escape.

As I listened to the dreary downpour, the gloom pressed heavily upon me, and I too would seek escape in my thoughts. I would walk into a beautiful garden where vegetables and fruits were plentiful. I would gather them, prepare them, and set them before my children. I would pour milk from a pitcher, spread fresh bread thick with butter and brown sugar. I would slice a tall cake, dip into a deep fruit pie, still hot and juicy. I would watch the expressions of Joe's and Ginny's faces as I served these things to them. It seemed at times that I actually smelled and tasted these imaginary things. But I must always come back to the stale meat and the coffee that was no longer a color or a taste in the water, just an exhausted fragrance.

One time Joe said, "Mother, who will there be to mourn for us when we are dead, this cabin for our coffin?"

"I suppose the painters will scream and cry," I said in an attempt at lightness.

"No," he said. "They aren't here any more. The animals have gone to safer, dryer places. But there will be mourners, Mama."

Was he in a delirium, I wondered. I waited a moment, not answering.

"Guess, Mama, guess who?"

"I don't know, Joe Boy. I don't know."

"The trees, Mama, that's who. Listen, when the rain is thin, how they drip and cry, drip and cry, drip and cry."

After a long week of darkness and rain, we awoke one morning to brightness and clear skies. The penetrating sun seemed to arouse us from our dismal lethargy. But we looked out upon a watery world. Most of the land around the house was under water. The branch ran deep and rapid under the footbridge. A small mound covered with a thick growth of broom corn was the only spot above water that could be reached without wading.

In the afternoon, searching for something to amuse the children, I asked Joe what he'd like to do. He said he wanted to set fire to the broom corn. I doubted it would burn, but there was no harm in letting him try and no danger involved. Wild life had deserted the bottom land, and the fire couldn't spread. I helped him take a burning piece from the fireplace and gave him a handful of dry grass. He was delighted to be allowed to make the fire himself, and soon had great swirls of smoke rising and a few tongues of flame from the dry tops. It was pleasant to look upon—our signal of defiance to the encroaching waters.

We were so revived by the fire and fresh air that pride and hope returned. We had baths and changed our clothes. But these conditions also made our appetites stronger, and chewing the strips of dried meat only seemed to make us more ravenous.

Joe had to believe something could be done about it. He stood in the door and watched for Mr. Merrick to come with another turkey. He assured me and Ginny it would be just a little while. He watched on and on and I couldn't dissuade him. I was busy putting the cabin in order and wondering why I bothered.

Finally he said, "Here he comes, Mama," so calmly that I almost believed him, though I felt sure Mr. Merrick wouldn't be checking up on us any time soon.

"He's riding a different horse."

This time, I went to him determined to get him away from the door. But instead, I stared in amazement—stared and trembled. For there was a rider.

"It's not Mr. Merrick, Joe," and I was so relieved to say this.

But oh how important it was that I make no mistakes this time. I controlled my impulse to express elation—to rush out to meet the stranger. I waited for him to tie his horse across the bridge, and come up the watery path to the cabin door. I had time to study him well, and I liked all I saw and concluded about him.

He was tall and straight and bright blond hair showed under his wide black hat. There was youth and confidence and wholesome friendliness in his bearing. And when we were face to face, his eyes showed a vivid blue in his bronzed face. The beard on his face did not conceal the strong bone structure nor disguise his gentleness. And the wide happy smile with which he greeted me said plainly that he was no chance visitor.

He removed his hat, extended his hand. "Mrs. Page, I am rejoiced, madam, to find you alive and well. My name is Cloud. Your friend, Mrs. Abit sent me to you. I've had my troubles finding you."

"Mrs. Abit! Dear Mrs. Abit! How wonderful!" I turned to hide the agitation of my joy. "Do come in and sit down. I'm sure the long ride has wearied you."

As he made friends with the children, my thoughts rushed around in sweet panic—so glad I was properly dressed—so glad the room was in order—happy that I had a good chair to offer him. And I kept saying to myself: What a strange sort of beautiful-looking man he is—I haven't seen anyone in so long, I must be addled. But his hair glows so, and his eyes are so very blue—he has a holy face—Christ could have looked like that. I must compose myself.

"Do tell me about Mrs. Abit, sir. Is she well?"

"Mrs. Page, I am a minister of the gospel, and not long ago, Mrs. Abit sent for me to come and pray with her, watch by her deathbed, and give her a Christian burial."

"Oh!"

"Yes, the weak body released the strong soul at last. And what a rich spiritual estate hers must be! Try not to be shocked or grieved. Let me tell you about it and about her concern for you."

And so he told me in his gentle way and without haste or lament about his deathbed visit with Mrs. Abit.

Mrs. Abit had more for him to do than conduct her from this world to the next. She required a promise and a mission of him. She had heard of my husband's departure and feared we might be starving. She had tried to get word to my father only to learn that both Father and John had gone to join Stephen F. Austin at Gonzales where the Texas army of resistance was being organized. So, although she could not give Mr. Cloud specific directions about finding the Merrick cabin, and Mr. Cloud did not know his way around in the area, she had asked him to promise her that he would go in search of me just as soon as he had laid her away. Moreover, she used her last energy to supervise the pack he should bring with him to me. In it she had him place sugar, coffee, dried beans, hard biscuits, brandy, candles, cheese, and rice, the choicest of her stores.

And when she knew the light of her life was burning low, for only a few more flickering moments, she asked for no personal reassurance or comfort from Mr. Cloud. Instead she whispered, "Don't forget your promise, Brother Cloud. Pray that you reach her in time."

He told her that his promise was a sacred trust and he would not rest until it was fulfilled.

"She paid you a very special tribute, Mrs. Page," he told me, giving me a direct look from his shining eyes. " 'Brave and beautiful,' she called you, and added 'I think all earthly beauty is God smiling, Brother Cloud. God was smiling the day she crossed my threshold. He is smiling now,' and then she herself smiled and departed."

We were silent for a bit and then he asked me how it happened that we had made the fire in the patch outside. I told him it had been Joe's idea—that we were simply in search of something cheerful to do.

"God moves in mysterious ways," he said. Then he told me how he had literally prayed his way through the wilderness to us, going in the general direction Mrs. Abit had indicated, notching trees as he went, reluctant to venture out on the prairie.

"The landscape seemed to hold not the slightest sign of human habitation," he said. "I had been riding since daylight, had met no one. Finally, I simply rode out onto a stretch of the prairie, stopped my horse, closed my eyes, and said 'Lord, I am in Thy hands. Show me the way.' And I rested a while there, then raised my head and searched the landscape. And I saw——"

"The smoke from our fire!"

"Yes, long, lazy curls, reaching up into the sunshine above a distant strip of timber . . . And I came."

A long look, full of greatest satisfaction and gratitude to the Power we couldn't see or understand, passed between us.

"God is smiling," he said.

"Indeed, He is, Brother Cloud." It seemed to me that He was smiling through the eyes of Mr. Cloud himself.

Then the expression in his eyes changed. He looked at me more intently, turned and studied the children.

"What have you done for food?"

I told him of the parsley-haws and the meat.

He arose quickly. "Forgive me. I should have realized—the things Mrs. Abit sent—they're on my horse."

The children rapturously munched cold biscuits while I prepared the meal. There was a little jar of wild plum jelly that was like a garnet jewel in the center of the feast. Mr. Cloud refused to share the cheese and jelly, took only a small bit of biscuit and coffee.

He did not ask for any further explanations of my extremity, and I offered none. He passed along to me what news he had on the Texas rebellion. He said the war was actually in progress. It had opened at Gonzales on October second when the Texans refused to give up a cannon that the Mexican commandant at San Antonio had demanded of them. Mexican soldiers who came for the cannon were routed, and the Texas volunteers, a week later, rushed the fort of Goliad and seized for themselves much-needed military supplies that the Mexican government had stored there. Then about seven hundred Texans, having converged on Gonzales, had elected Mr. Austin their commander and marched on to San Antonio. Mr. Cloud said he had heard that the Mexican troops at San Antonio outnumbered the Texas volunteers more than two to one, but he didn't think this would stop them. And he thought it quite likely that my father, brother, and husband were among these volunteers. What the outcome would be, he could not predict, but he was certain that I wanted to get into Brazoria as soon as possible. He said if the good weather continued, he'd have wagons sent for me within three days. If more rain came, he'd send riders.

"I must hurry away," he said. "For the faster I ride, the sooner you can depart from this unhappy spot."

The children and I were reluctant to let him go. He was aware of this, as we made efforts to detain him.

I tried to express what we felt, "Mr. Cloud, your presence has strengthened us as much as Mrs. Abit's food."

"I am only a messenger," he said, "to come and go. The spirit of the Lord abides with you always. There is no wilderness lost to His presence, no situation beyond His awareness.

"*Whither shall I go from thy Spirit?*, the Psalmist sang unto his Lord, *or whither shall I flee from thy presence? If I ascend up into heaven, thou art there: if I make my bed in hell, behold, thou art there.*"

I felt myself trembling, as in a chill, and I wanted to be strong before this man.

He clasped both my hands in his and his eyes caught and held mine as he finished the quotation: "*If I take the wings of the morning, and dwell in the uttermost parts of the sea;/Even there shall thy hand lead me, and thy right hand shall hold me.*"

I became very still and was possessed by a most amazing serenity.

"I leave you in God's hands," he added.

My mother's own words! It seemed to me that my heart would overflow. God was being awfully generous with His reassurances on this day.

"I have been in God's hands," I said. "He kept us alive until you came."

"Two wagons will be sent for you," he said in further explanation as he departed, "to avoid heavy loading and miring down. The drivers will be Mr. Reckon and his boy Bud. I am to meet them in Brazoria tomorrow for supplies they have freighted in. Mr. Reckon is lame and looks like a pirate, but his nature is kindly and his dealings trustworthy."

"I can pay him in cash for his services."

"That will make him very happy for cash is hard to come by and he often takes payment in barter. Can you spare this money without depriving yourself and children?"

"Oh yes."

"It was a wise husband who left you thus provided for. When I tell Mr. Reckon he is to be paid in hard money, he will put the mules to a brisker trot."

I laughed with Mr. Cloud but not at the same point of humor. And I laughed also at the pure joy of deliverance. I let Joe wade to the bridge with Mr. Cloud, and held Ginny high to wave good-by.

Even with Mr. Cloud's warning, I was hardly prepared for Mr. Reckon's sinister appearance. His lameness caused him to lurch forward with every step as if about to pounce and stab. And if he had worn the black eye-patch I half expected, it would have been less disturbing than the drooped and motionless lid that hung in a half curtain over one eye as though he constantly contemplated mayhem. And when he smiled over black and broken teeth, it was much worse than when his face was in repose. But Mr. Reckon smiled often; his was a blithe spirit, and he wore his battered hat jauntily turned up in front with a turkey feather stuck in the band to proclaim his blitheness.

Bud was a big, obedient fellow, and the loading proceeded through and around Mr. Reckon's distorted movements and sharp commands with amazing rapidity. A straight chair and Virginia's crib were placed near the front of Mr. Reckon's wagon for Ginny and me. The bench was arranged to serve for a double seat on the other wagon for Bud and Joe Boy.

"Bud needs help drivin' that wagon, I reckon," the old man said to Joe, winking his good eye in a grotesque way that made me wonder why my child was not frightened out of his wits. But he smiled joyfully into the gruesome visage and held out his arms eagerly to be lifted to the place beside Bud.

Mr. Reckon, maneuvering himself into driver's position up over the wagon tongue and onto his bedroll so that his legs dangled over the front endgate, slapped the lines over the backs of his mule team and called out to them.

"Hist anchors and shake out yer canvas, ladies! Kate! Kristy!"

The tugging mules and rolling wheels brought to me a dizzying surge of relief. Moving! Moving away from the lonely little house . . . moving away from sorrow and despair. I kept looking back until I could see it no more and then settled into my chair with a sigh.

"Outta sight now?" Mr. Reckon inquired.

"Yes."

"Had a hard time back there, I reckon."

"Yes. Terrible."

"Well, ma'am, put it behind. Let it fade. Let it fade. Just like the cabin faded from your sight. If you chew on a sorrow like it was a cud, it gets bigger and bigger until it chokes ya. Best swallow it and take another big fresh bite of life."

"Is that the way you do?"

"Every time."

I thought Mr. Reckon looked more as if life had been taking big bites of him, but I only inquired politely, "Are you a happy man?"

"I reckon." Thoughtfully and forcefully he spat tobacco juice through the crevices of his teeth twice, smacking each of the mules on a rhythmical rump.

His name and his frequent use of the word "reckon" had me puzzled. So I asked him if I had his name right and if he spelled it "r-e-c-k-o-n."

"Yes, ma'am. Except there's more to it. 'I. Reckon.' "

"You mean the initial 'I'?"

"Yes, ma'am. And now I reckon you'll be wantin' to know what the 'I' stands for?"

I didn't know whether he was being serious or facetious, so I only smiled at him.

"You haven't been in Texas long enough to know some of the customs about names, I reckon."

I felt so happy and amused that I couldn't resist replying, "I reckon not."

"Nobody asks anybody questions about his name right out. That is, one man to another. You bein' a lady and a newcomer meant no harm, I reckon."

"Mr. Reckon, it doesn't matter a copper cent to me what your name is," I told him, "Jones, Brown, Smith, or Sneezebutton—just so you get me back to civilization."

He grinned delightedly. "But, ma'am, my name is not Jones, Brown, Smith, or Sneezebutton. My name is Reckon."

"That's perfectly agreeable with me."

"That is, it's my Texas name."

"What was your seafaring name, Mr. Reckon? When you were a

pirate, that is?" Provoked by his jovial pirate-face, this thoughtless repartee was uttered before I could stop it.

He jumped as if he'd been stung, jerked his head around to look up at me, and almost dropped the lines. I was seated to one side and slightly above him, my chair within easy reach of Ginny's cradle. His open eye was fixed on me with frightful surprise and the other rolled about wildly under the drooping lid. He tried to say something, choked on his tobacco, and went into a coughing spell.

I was very sorry to have upset him and said so.

"Damn yer questions, ma'am," he finally sputtered, "and beggin' yer pardon, but I swallered my chaw for the first time in twenty year—first time since I quit the ship, that is."

It was my turn to be startled. Perhaps Mr. Reckon had been a pirate, after all. There was no word between us for a while. He got out his tobacco plug and sat hunched over renewing and conditioning his quid. After several, forceful amber jets, his equanimity was restored.

He looked up at me, his good eye steady and serious, and said, "Golden Ears. That was it, *Golden Ears*."

Harriet stopped her writing and reflected. If I write out all the stories that were told to me in those times, I shall never be done. I must pass over irrelevant tales and "Golden Ears" is one of them.

But Golden Ears would not be by-passed. And though she refused to write it down, she felt the need to clear her memory path, and sent Marcus to fetch Tricky. It was bedtime and Marcus protested.

"That child already sound asleep in her bed. Been to Mr. E.Y.'s all day and come home frazzled."

"I want her to sleep with me tonight. Go get her." Harriet's commands for Tricky's presence were a special law in the household so Marcus shook his head and went along.

Tricky came hurriedly, in her long nightgown, carrying her clothes.

"Are you all right, Gram?"

"Certainly. Just wanted some company."

"Why aren't you in bed?"

"My mind is occupied with a story."

"What kind of story?"

"A pirate story!"

"Oh Gram, tell it to me!"

"Are you sure you aren't too sleepy? Shouldn't we be in bed?"

"Perhaps we should—but a *pirate* story——"

"That's the way I feel about it. Well, one time there was a little boy who was captured by pirates—taken from a plundered ship where no doubt his parents perished—although for the rest of his life he had no memory of the event except the din of battle, the rolling sea, and a pain of fire in his eye that seemed to burn out all thought. The boy's master was Admiral Aury, a rascally robber who raided coastal lands and was pirate to any vessel he could overhaul. But he liked slavers best—had a real buzzard's eye for them. He kept slave pens on Galveston Island and smuggled from there."

"I thought that was Lafitte, Gram."

"Aury was ahead of Lafitte . . . This little boy he snatched became his cabin boy and personal slave. Aury hung doubloons in the big ears of the boy and named him 'Golden Ears'—or just 'Ears' for short. Although Golden Ears couldn't remember his origins, he knew he didn't belong with the pirates and sometimes he'd beg Aury to tell him who he was.

"Aury was always angered by the request and would give the boy cruel answers.

" 'Well, now, Golden Ears,' " he'd say, " 'Ya might be highborn and ya might be lowborn. Ya might be a planter's fine son and ya might be jest a white nigger slave to a planter's son. But what difference what ya might be? What ya are is Golden Ears, cabin boy to Admiral Aury, the sea tiger. And lucky ya be, Ears, to be alive and fat on admiral's fare when you could be in a pen out there waitin' to be sold at a dollar a pound.'

"Then he'd threaten the poor boy. He'd look him up and down and say, 'If ya put on any more pounds, it might profit me to put you out there and grab me a leaner cabin boy somewheres.' "

"Oh, the poor boy," Tricky sympathized. "That was enough to scare him out of eating altogether."

"That's just about what happened. I can see him there, a scrawny hungry boy about your age with an injured eye and the gold coins in his ears, yearning for the rich food on the master's table—afraid to eat —the fear of the slave pens holding him back, even when the food was unwatched."

"He should have poisoned old Aury and escaped."

"There probably wasn't any poison handy, Tricky, and besides Golden Ears was not the type to poison people, even pirates."

Tricky was unabashed. "I'll bet he thought of it."

"I don't know about that. At any rate, Golden Ears continued to serve Aury until he was a grown young man.

"Then one time Aury's men got hold of a whole cargo of wines and other spirits and what happened on Galveston Island was a regular devil's jamboree."

"They all got drunk, I guess."

"Quite viciously drunk."

"Old Aury too, I suppose."

"Old Aury too. Drunker and meaner than he'd ever been. He wore heavy, metal-tipped boots. He kicked Golden Ears in the shins, and when the poor fellow fell to the floor in agony, Aury gave him a stomping. Stomped boyhood and servility completely out of him, I guess, for Ears rolled over, threw out his leg and tripped Aury, jerked his boots off, put them on himself, and gave Aury a bit of stomping before he ran."

"Oh, good for Golden Ears!"

"It was an ideal time for escape with everyone on the island busy guzzling the liquid loot, all except Golden Ears and one lonely unclaimed child—a boy who was a leftover from a group of wretched women who had been held on the island at one time."

"What do you mean 'leftover,' Gram?"

"His mother didn't want him, or died perhaps."

"I didn't know any mothers didn't want their babies."

"Let's stick to the story. Golden Ears decided to take this child with him lest he become another 'Ears' for Aury. So he found the boy, took him to a boat, and pulled out for the mainland."

"Nobody tried to stop them?"

"Not a soul."

"Did he find his way home?"

"Never in his life did Golden Ears know anything about a home except the one he made for himself and Bud in the Texas wilderness. When I knew him he was a freighter named Ittai Reckon and Bud was a big strong fellow who worked with him. Mr. Reckon looked exactly like a pirate, had the disposition of a songbird, and the heart of an angel."

"Oh, Gram, how sad that he never found his home and family."

"Yes, but Ittai Reckon attained a wealth of happiness when he came into his heritage of freedom. He knew its full meaning and worth. He slit his ears to remove the doubloons, and spent the rest of his life rejoicing."

"How did he ever get such a funny name as 'Ittai Reckon'?"

"That's another story for another time. Let's commit ourselves to the magic touch of the feather mattress. Will you bring me my nightgown, please—the rose one with the nightcap to match?"

When Mr. Reckon had finished telling me of his life as "Golden Ears," slave cabin boy to the pirate 'Admiral' Aury, I looked him full in the face and said, "I am honored that you told me your story, Mr. Reckon. I admire what you made of yourself. And what you did for Bud was a kindly, wonderful thing to do."

He was embarrassed by my compliment. "The boy was company . . . thank you, ma'am . . . never had a lady listener before." He reached into his pocket and brought out a small tin box. He handed it to me.

"Have one, ma'am, and give one to the little lamb there."

It was candied dates. Oh my, what a treat! I took out one for me and one for Ginny, then carefully replaced the lid and returned it to him. This was such a special delicacy that it did not occur to me to eat more than one, nor to him to offer me more.

He began to talk again. "As for my Texas name, that just sprouted on me I reckon. I finally hired me and Bud out to a trader deliverin' to Mexicans and Indians. He said, 'You got a name?' and I said, 'I reckon' and he said, 'I. Reckon—that's all right with me,' and seemed to enjoy hisself callin' me 'Mr. Reckon.' Never had no trouble, bein' unnamed, for nobody asks your name right out. Some feller'd say, 'Could Brown be your name? You remind me of an hombre I met somewhere named Brown.' And I'd answer him, 'Could be, I reckon.' First thing you know, I was bein' spoke to all over as 'Mr. I. Reckon.' And one time I met up with a travelin' Word-of-God man and we camped together, and he offered to teach me to write my name, and when I told him the 'I' didn't stand for anything, he said he'd fix me up with something special. He rhymed some 'I' names from the Good Book and let me take my pick:

"I-chabod and Issachar
Isaac and Ithiel
Ish-bosheth and Ithamar
And David's friend named Ittai
All begin with the letter 'I'

'Ittai' was the one I liked.

"So 'Ittai Reckon' is my name,
But I look like a pirate just the same."

He winked his good eye at me.

"You don't look like a pirate any more, Mr. Reckon," I said, quite honestly, for I was seeing the real person beneath the facial disfigurements. "Ittai Reckon is a most pleasant sounding name, carefree and singy."

"Thank you, ma'am."

Contentment settled over us, and thoughts became more enjoyable than words. Ittai sat, his back to me, hunched over the lines, almost dozing. The team kept pulling to the left, and he'd give the lines a tug without looking up. I sensed that the mules were disturbed and began to study a strip of brushy growth that lay on our right just beyond a stretch of tall prairie grass. And what I finally sighted was so surprising and alarming that I jumped to my feet and shook my shawl frantically.

"Scat! Scat! Get out of here!" I screamed.

Big Tom was following us!

The mules jumped and leaped ahead but were held back by the heavy load and Ittai's full strength on the lines.

"Kate! Kristy!" he commanded and jerked them about.

The wagon lurched and the load tipped to one side some. I was thrown back into my chair and grabbed on to the cradle. Virginia began to cry.

Big Tom, bereft of his charges, went bounding back along the trail he had come. And I grieved that I must frighten him away, that there was no way for me to express the gratitude and affection that would have brought forth his gusty purrs of pleasure.

Mr. Reckon was beside himself. "God's breath and the devil's tracks, ma'am! Why didn't ya tell me ya saw a painter and I could've got him? I been feelin' Kate and Kristy's worry in the lines. It's a mighty wonder we didn't capsize. What did ya have to scream like that fer?"

"It was Big Tom, following us."

"You mean that painter was——"

I felt a little ashamed and very sad. "A friend, Mr. Reckon. Big Tom was a friend and protector."

"I've heard of painters bein' friendly now and then, but—a little woman like you—not bein' afraid——"

"You won't shoot if he comes back again, will you?" I pleaded.

"Ma'am, I won't shoot yer friend as long as he keeps proper distance between us," he said, "I don't desire to stroke him, but unless he tries to make a meal of man or mule, he's safe as yer baby there."

I thanked him profusely.

He kept muttering, "A pet painter—a pet painter——. Well, skin me fer fine fur if ever I thought such a thing could really be. And a woman, such a little thing——" He'd fix a bright eye on me, and then turn away as if speaking to someone else.

"Well, there's some folks with power to turn wild things tame—and there's some with another kind that turns tame things wild. God, you made people so curious—includin' this woman——"

He expectorated in contemplative manner, then reached into his pocket and took out the tin of dates again. He examined the little box as if asking himself if it were a fitting offering, then handed it to me.

"Here, ma'am. Eat 'em all," he said. "Eat 'em ever God-blessed one!"

I found a cabin in Brazoria recently emptied by a family returning to the States, fearful of the war storm in Texas. It was much poorer shelter than the one on Austin Bayou—just one room with a dirt floor— but it was in sight of smoking chimneys and sounds of human activity and sweet refuge for me. Mr. Reckon protested at unloading here, saying it was no fit place for a lady and such nice belongings. He knew my father was Dr. Moore, and had assumed I was going back home. I told him simply that my mind was my own and fully made up. So to ease his concern, he made some repairs around the premises, sent Bud for fresh meat, and hauled in a supply of groceries.

After a few days, he pulled out with loaded wagons and came by to bid us farewell. He lurched around checking the cabin, and the well and the yard, cautioning me, agitating his quid, and rolling his eye.

But back on the wagon, he settled down to a happy take-off, turned the special radiance of his ugly smile upon us—waved his hat, then readjusted the turkey feather to a jauntier angle, and gave his merry commands.

"Kate! Kristy! Hist anchors! Roll!"

And above the grind of his wagons, we heard him on down the trail calling, "Shake out yer canvas, ladies, shake out yer canvas!"

The last we ever heard of Ittai Reckon.

8.

I didn't really settle into the little house in Brazoria until after Christmas of 1835. I got word to Sarah of my location, hoping father and John would eventually learn of my safety and whereabouts. Sarah sent one of my younger brothers for me, and I went to my father's house for a while, the sharp edges of my pride being worn down considerably since the day I had left with Solomon.

Late in December we got word of Old Ben Milam's victory in San Antonio—how he routed General Cos with a small band of Texas volunteers while the main Texas army was preparing to go into winter quarters. It was three hundred volunteers against a force of sixteen hundred Mexicans and only two Texans were killed, one of them, alas, poor old Milam himself. Cos agreed to escort the six hundred convicts among his troops back across the border, since this quartering of convict soldiers among them had been a big point of agitation with the Texans. But even though there wasn't a Mexican soldier on Texas soil by New Year's, 1836, there was anything but peace among the colonists. Citizens of various settlements, including Brazoria, had already declared in favor of independence. There were many rumors about Santa Anna's plans for retaliation, and the Texas provisional government organized with Henry Smith as governor and Sam Houston as commander in chief was in utter confusion. The army of volunteers did not consider themselves under the direction of the provisional government—they moved around on expeditions of their own, the most foolhardy being the Matamoro Expedition with grandiose plans for taking the war to Mexico by seizing the port there. Mr. Houston, meanwhile was pow-wowing through East Texas trying to keep the Cherokees quiet. John came home for a while to tell us all these things, but father remained at one of the camps where his services as a physician were much needed. John was gloomy about what would happen next, but there was one happy note in his visit. He brought Amy to us—his bride of several months. Her folks lived somewhere around Gonzales. He wanted to get her away from the conflict areas. We were not long in planning that she and I would live together in my little cabin in Brazoria. John saw us well settled and provisioned with a fine cow, some poultry, and garden seed, and then he pulled out to rejoin father a   be closer to whatever might happen when the Mexican forces recrossed the Rio Grande. He left us with the assurance that he would return home to care for us ahead of any war danger that might reach the Brazos.

Amy was a big turning point in my life. She transformed me from a city woman who knew fashions and business into a country woman who could set a hen and milk a cow. I marveled at these tasks and enjoyed them. We called our big roan cow Charity, and her young calf—an appealing little thing with a heart-shaped white marking in the middle of its forehead—we named Heartface.

It was quite an occasion the first time I undertook to milk Charity all alone. I sat on a milkstool we had improvised from a short section of log, my head pressed against the cow's flanks, milking thin streams into the waiting bucket. Eight anxious eyes were bent upon my efforts. Two belonged to Heartface who had been allowed a few sucks before being pulled off and tied. She stood with milky froth on her mouth, chiding me with pitiful half bleats. Amy, who, of course, could do the job much better, was giving me impatient scrutiny while she stroked the cow's neck as if to reassure her through a painful ordeal. Joe and Virginia stood at the other end of the cow, each with a cup in hand, looking uncertain about the prospects for having them filled. It was Amy's habit to fill their cups with a few quick squirts, leaving a high top of foam for them to plunge their faces into. I would have to get larger and more forceful streams from Charity before attempting this trick.

The calf kept distracting me. "I feel like the worse kind of robber," I said to Amy.

"Forget the calf," she said. "Charity won't stand forever. I'm always through by the time she finishes eating."

Charity punctuated Amy's statement with a harsh switch of her tail, wrapping the brushy end around my head and into my eye.

Amy extended me no sympathy. "You're hurting her some way," she told me. "Are you doing like I showed you: reaching up high to pull the milk down, then squeezing it out with your fingers? . . . Why have you stopped? Is she holding up her milk?"

"No, just contemplating it, I think. My fingers are cramping. I'm just resting my wrists."

"Let me finish," she insisted.

"No," I said firmly, "I like to finish what I start."

I decided that I was being squeamish and overly considerate of the cow, so I pulled and squeezed with my full strength, and, sure enough, the streams came larger and faster and began to make a satisfying rhythm in the bucket, almost like Amy's. The cow raised a hind foot off the ground a time or two and shifted about some.

"I don't think Charity likes the way you milk," Amy commented anxiously.

"Whether she likes it or not, I'm getting her milked," I bragged and gave an extra vigorous tug with both hands. She shifted again, lifted her foot, and this time set it down in the milk bucket.

I was stunned. Charity had never done such a thing before, and all that good milk ruined! And she just stubbornly stood there, her foot planted in the bucket. I groaned.

"Well, Jeruselum, Hatty! It's not the last milk in the world! She's got plenty more! Don't feel so bad. Back up, Charity."

Charity reluctantly took her foot out of the bucket, overturning it as she did so.

"She's such a peaceable cow, Hatty, you must have hurt her. Did you trim that long fingernail on your thimble finger?"

I hadn't.

"Well, that's it. You dug that nail into her. Now let me finish up."

"No," I said. "I'll go wash out the bucket and trim that nail. I'll be right back."

"But, Hatty, you like to keep that nail long for your sewing."

"It's more important to learn to milk properly, and I won't be talked out of it!"

When I got back, Charity had been given more feed, I suspected that Heartface had been allowed a pacifying tug or two, and the children both had telltale mustaches of milk foam.

I seated myself firmly, planked the bucket on the ground, and took hold. With a sharp swish of her tail, Charity flicked me painfully on the neck. This was just a further goad to my determination. I grabbed her tail and sat on the fringy end of it, then grabbed her milk faucets and turned them on full power. She began to chew in a sort of tempo with my tugs, and I could sense in the flow under my fingers that she had accepted me and we had become partners in the effort. I suddenly felt humbly grateful to Charity and deeply satisfied with my task. I settled my head more comfortably into her flank. The children moved closer in admiration of my achievement.

Joe said, "Mama, will you fill our cups?"

Amy was silent. I ignored their mustaches, milking each cup brimful, getting a special joy out of having the same trim of tall froth on the tops that Amy did.

I remember so well how happy we were that night around the supper table—how beautiful Amy looked to me—like Ceres, goddess of the fruitful earth—how contented the children were—how satisfying the bread and milk we ate together. Amy had a flashing abundance of red-gold hair that she wore stacked carelessly on top of her head. She was a creature who loved and laughed much, generously made in all respects. Her cheeks were pink and plump, her eyes a warm blue, and her pregnancy obvious. There were no secret channels in Amy's nature. She was as clear and sweet and giving as a mountain spring.

"Amy," I said to her, as I crumbled more cornbread into my bowl, "Amy, dear, you're the blessing of my life." She smiled and pushed the crock pitcher toward me. I refilled my bowl. I took a few bites of the soaked bread. It had a special sweetness that night. "Just think," I marveled, "I milked this myself!" Amy gave me another indulgent smile. I felt inclined to make a speech.

"Amy, I wish I could somehow convey to you how I feel about good food, nourishing food. It's all so beautiful. Everytime I skim the beautiful yellow cream off the clabber, every time I work the butter, gather the eggs, take a bite of bread or a swallow of milk, I want to say out loud, 'O God, thank you! thank you! thank you!' And when I hear the hens singing their scratchy songs, just before they go on their nests, I get so full of happiness I want to sing with them, and I feel like going out to the nests and stroking them and saying, 'Dear hens, dear food creatures. How wonderful you are!' "

Amy threw back her head and laughed so hard the big golden coil of hair loosened and fell to the back of her neck. "I don't mean to make fun, Hatty," she said, "but you do tickle me."

That night I lay wide awake and thinking while Amy lay breathing gently at my side. It had been over three months since my rescue and I hadn't received a word of news from or about Solomon. When John came home with Amy, I asked if he had heard anything of Solomon's whereabouts—he said he hadn't and hoped to God he never would. I had passed through so much since Solomon's departure that it seemed as if years lay between us, and when I let my mind dwell on him, I felt only a dull blankness, unrelieved by either anger or concern. If he should step back into my life again someday, what would I do or say?

Amy jerked in her sleep and awoke.

"Hatty my baby moved! Do you think it's all right?"

"Of course. You're far enough along for it to be stirring about some. You feel all right, don't you?"

"Yes, but——"

"What is it?"

"I wish John were here."

"Of course. So do I."

"It's been two months and no word."

"You know how hard it is to get personal messages across country when men and mounts are so much needed for other things. If there's danger of any kind, John will come and get us out."

"Sure. I know he will—if nothing happens to him first. It's not being afraid. I just want John."

"I know, Amy, I know."

"I guess you want your husband sometimes too, even if—even if——"

"No! I have no husband!" There. That would be my answer if Solomon ever dared face me again, ever returned, expecting me to live with him.

Amy was shocked. "Why, Hatty, you do too," she insisted. "Even if he's no good, you've got him . . . What do you aim to do when he comes back?"

"Maybe he won't come back."

"Hatty! I believe you want him to get killed. Oh, no, Hatty, that's sinful!"

"There was a time, Amy, when I said I wanted him to get shot, and I meant it. But now, I simply don't care what happens to him. I do hope and pray I never see him again. And I am resolved, so firmly that I'd take a Bible oath on it, that I'll never live with him again—never let him touch me again. The very idea makes me sick!"

"Why Hatty!"

"I don't want a man—don't need a man—don't ever expect to depend on a man again as long as I live!" I declared.

"Why Hatty," was all Amy could say.

"I can take care of myself very well," I added.

Amy thought this over. "Sure. But if you didn't have a husband any more—well, I just don't think, Hatty, that you'd be safe without a husband."

I was amused. Dear Amy. Dear innocent. "There are always dangers to be faced, Amy, with or without a husband. Just what do you mean?"

"I mean safe as a woman. Men always look at you so funny—like you were something special——"

"Men have always looked at women funny—like they were something special. You were just too young to notice or know what it meant until you got married. Usually, a woman is as safe as she wants to be."

"Yes, usually. But you're different."

"If not wanting, or having, or intending to have a man makes me different—so I am."

"Maybe you don't want anything. But you sort of give off sparks."

"You don't know what you're saying. Go on back to sleep." I wanted to laugh but was afraid she wouldn't understand.

She sighed, turned over, and was almost instantly asleep again.

It touched my vanity of course that Amy thought me so different, so dangerously desirable to men, but she couldn't realize how ironic was her tribute. She couldn't know as I did that this something special of mine when put to the test couldn't arouse as much desire in one man as a game of cards, nor influence another to lay aside the cautions of maturity. My answer to her had been an honest one. I had no yearnings, no desires. I tried to call into my mind the kind of man I could love—would want to be loved by—if Solomon were out of my life, and there was no image—nothing.

Work and weather kept Amy and me close to the cabin those winter weeks. We had no chance to get out and get acquainted, and few visitors came to our door. We didn't have proper clothing or footgear to venture far in cold and slush, and fortunately there was no need. We were a wee world, sufficient unto ourselves, wrapped in an atmosphere of tranquillity, entering that fateful month of March, 1836, with no awareness of the war tempest it ushered in. We were concerned only with nature's tempest, the freezing norther that blasted over Texas as we teamed our strength to keep the children and animals safe and warm. Now I can look back on that particular landscape of time, and I can see the momentous and calamitous events that paralleled the simple routine of our existence.

I can see the women of the western settlements in a panic of fear, grabbing up their children, leaving meals on the tables, calves in the pens, and fleeing with a single compulsion: to run faster than the Mexicans could march—for the Mexican army had swarmed back over the Rio Grande. General Urrea's forces were slaughtering the men of the Matamoros Expedition. General Santa Anna, who was commander in chief and determined to exterminate every white man in Texas, had San Antonio under seige.

While Amy and I kept a high fire in the fireplace and were amused at Joe and Ginny hovering over a box of baby chicks brought into the circle of warmth, delegates convening at the shanty and stump town of Washington-on-the-Brazos were assembled in a crude unfinished room intended for a blacksmith shop. Here, shivering and shouting, they declared independence from Mexico . . . received the desperate appeals for aid from Colonel Travis in the beseiged Alamo . . . watched the budding of personal enmity between Sam Houston and Robert Potter.

While Amy churned and I sewed, while mush bubbled in the kettle on the crane and the pleasant aroma of hot coffee filled our cabin, the men in the historic meeting up the river, reducing the freezing temperature in their little room with hot wrath and fiery opinion, heard Mr. Potter plead for adjournment and a rescue mission to the 182 liberty-or-death men holding the Alamo . . . heard Mr. Houston shout "folly and treason" and plead for the creation of a sound government on the spot.

And while we had a little winter party, eating frozen yellow cream sprinkled with sugar and nutmeg, and listened in contentment to the raging wind outside, these men warmed their hands around their pipes and cigars, drank whiskey and chewed tobacco, wept and worked on, midwifing a new republic from the womb of war. They re-elected Mr. Houston commander in chief (over Mr. Potter's opposition) and sent him directly to Gonzales where the army of defense was gathering . . . then pursued the task of writing a constitution and electing officers for the newborn *Republic of Texas*.

When the norther subsided and rains set in, Amy and I carefully planned a spring garden and worried some that Ginny didn't gain weight and no message came from John. But we had no intuitive uneasiness as the harassed patriots at Washington-on-the-Brazos received the couriers of defeat from the Texas-Mexican battlegrounds and hastily wound up their business to flee in all directions: "Some flew east, some flew west, and some flew home to the family nest!" The new officials (President Burnet, Vice President Zavalla, War Secretary Rusk, and Navy Secretary Potter) flew east to set up government headquarters out of the path of the Mexicans. Some flew west to join up with General Houston, and some flew to the rescue of their families.

A passer-by or so brought us vague rumors of Mexican victory, but we still relied on John's positive promise to come for us if danger threatened. Brazoria, lying so close to the coast and out of any likely line of army movement, was later than other settlements in feeling the panic. Most families fleeing from the west crossed the Brazos much further inland, so we almost missed being drawn into the famous "Runaway Scrape." Almost . . . if it hadn't been for Abe and Ada Gibson . . . or the drunken Mr. Norton . . . if they had passed us by . . . if we could have been left unnoticed and undisturbed only a little while longer, Amy would have had a longer life, and I certainly would have had a different one! That crazy Mr. Norton led me right into the adventure that led me right into the arms of—but I must not sidetrack into aimless supposition. Perhaps everything that happens to us is but a signpost toward the inevitable.

Abe and Ada Gibson were Amy's parents, and they did come—in a hysteria of distress. They came horseback and leading two horses, one of them loaded as a pack animal, the other saddled.

Mrs. Gibson announced their arrival with a distressed call to "Amy Girl!" and almost fell off her horse as Amy rushed out to meet her.

To the two women enfolded in each other's arms, Mr. Gibson shouted, "No time for that. Amy, git yer gear and make it a mighty small pack."

Amy said, "What's the matter, Pa? What's the matter?" He didn't notice her question. He strode up to me and the children at the cabin door. "And you, ma'am, ain't you got no men around?"

"No men," I said. "Just Amy and I."

"Any mounts?"

"No mounts. Just a cow and calf."

"Can't leave a woman and kids here to be butchered. You're not much size. You ride behind Amy. Ada and me'll carry the young 'uns. And take no belongin's—just a bag of food. Git a move on. I'll loosen the cow and calf. Don't want to leave nothin' penned up to starve or to feed those Mexican fiends."

Before I could stop him, he'd darted around the cabin, loosed Charity from her stake and Heartface from the pen and scared them off into the brush with his "huy-ya-huy-ya's!" He had also put the chickens into a squawking panic.

In the meantime, Amy's mother was pushing her toward the door urging her to come alive. "We got no time to lose. Gather up some necessaries, wrap 'em in a kivver, and let yore Pa tie 'em on."

But neither Amy nor I moved to obey her parents. We just stood looking at each other, stunned, amazed.

Mr. Gibson rushed back to us carrying three squawking hens and exclaimed, "Fer God's sake, are you fool women jest goin' to stand there and wait fer hell to come over the hill?"

"What are you going to do with those hens?" I asked. At the moment, I felt more resentment of Mr. Gibson than fear of the Mexicans.

It was his turn to be amazed. My question seemed to choke him up.

So I tried another question. "Why are you so frightened?"

His eyes grew big in surprise and anger. He walked up real close to Amy and me, exploded right in our faces.

"Why am I so frightened?" He mimicked me. "Because I got sense enough to be, that's why. The Meskins are after us—thousands and thousands of 'em—out to kill ever white man and take ever white woman this side of the Sabine! They killed ever man in the garrison at Santone—ever man, hear me!"

Amy gasped as if she'd been struck, and the hens squawked in pathetic punctuation.

"And thirty-two of 'em were men I knew personal—Gonzales men! And where's Sam Houston and that piddlin' army of his'n? Runnin' with the Meskins on their tails, that's where—or maybe cornered and killed by now! We're *all* runnin'—runnin' fer our lives!"

He paused in the agony of his thoughts to pant for breath. "— and the Meskins spreadin' out to cover the land like a plague. And a bloody plague on us it is—our sins comin' right down on our heads, that's what! Comin' in here to Meskin country, sayin' we'll be Catholics so's to git the land when we're no more Catholic than a Comanche —livin' lies and deceits—lettin' the priests remarry us like we'd been livin' in shame, bornin' our children in sin! That's why I'm sceered, sceered righteous! The fear of God is ridin' me—ridin' me hard! I don't want their infested land!"

His voice rose to a shout. "I don't want their priests!" He tried to shake his fists and the hens raised an awful din.

"All I want is to git me and mine outta here alive. Amy, if you ain't in that cabin and back out with yore things before I kin name the plagues of Egypt, I'm gonna lay hand on ya, so help me God! As for you, ma'am, I did my duty in askin' . . . you can do as you damned uppity please."

I didn't answer him. I was trying to think. The news he delivered was terrifying, if wholly true. But he was too overwrought to be capable of good judgment. My silence and inaction infuriated him.

"Maybe you ain't in such danger after all," he said. "You look enough like a Meskin, you could pass fer one and maybe fall in with 'em."

"Oh, Pa," Amy cried out, "Hatty's our kin. She's John's sister! Oh Pa, where is John?"

"How in God's name would I know where John is? Dead, most likely, or runnin' with Houston's bunch. Dead or alive, he ain't no help to you. I come to git ya, risked life and limb to git here, and I'm takin' no back talk!"

"I've got to wait here for John. He said he'd come."

"Well, if he comes, ye'll welcome a corpse or a deserter. Didn't ya hear me say, ever man in the Santone garrison was killed—and no breathin' bodies even got a chance to crawl away. That Santa Anna beast with his long tail and bloody jaws had 'em piled up and set fire to, like so much carrion—brush piled on 'em for a devil's bonfire! Now mind me, and move!"

He actually began reciting the plagues of Egypt:

"*And the waters—all the waters—of that land turned to blood!*"

I gently pulled Amy inside—told her I'd wait for John—that she'd better go with her parents—protect her child—John would want that.

"I don't want a child without John," she said.

"*And the frogs came up and covered the land of Egypt . . .*"

I spread a good quilt on the floor and began piling food and clothes essentials on it.

"*All the dust of the land became lice . . .*"

"Things may not be so bad, Amy. I just don't think John was at the Alamo."

"If he's dead, I want to die too. Pa can't make me go."

"*There came a grievous swarm of flies . . . the land was corrupted.* Jest five more, Amy. And if you ain't out here ready to ride when I finish, I'm comin' in for ya." He moved to the pack horse to check the gear and tie the chickens on top, and raised his voice to intone, "*And all the cattle of Egypt died.*"

Amy said, "I don't care about the old Mexicans. I'll just kill myself."

"*And the Lord sent thunder and hail and the fire ran along the ground . . .*"

"Amy, you don't know John is dead. Until we know for sure, we must act as if he were alive."

"If he's alive, I want to wait for him here."

"*And the locusts went up over all the land of Egypt . . .*"

Amy rushed to the door and screamed, "Shut up, Pa. I'm not comin'."

"*There was a thick darkness in all the land . . . they saw not one another.*"

I rolled the quilt and its contents into a tight pack and took it out to Mr. Gibson. Ada Gibson, with her arm firmly about Amy guided her to the horse.

Mr. Gibson, fittingly enough, completed his Biblical threat with, "*And it came to pass that the Lord smote all the firstborn in the land.*"

Amy began crying in open and utter despair. While doing what her mother and father guided her to do, she kept saying over and over, "I don't want to go. I want John. I don't want to go. I want John."

She paid no attention to me and the children and our farewells.

I had a final word with Mr. Gibson. "John may not be dead," I said to him. "Remember that. Amy is his wife and he left her with me. Where are you taking her?"

"I'm headin' for Opelousas. Aim to find work there. Later on, I'm goin' to git me back on the east side of the old Mississip and stay there."

"The Mexicans may not have it so easy as you think," I told him. "Sam Houston may lead them into some kind of trap. Numbers don't mean anything. Look what Ben Milam did. When this is over, Mr. Gibson, I think there'll still be some Moores around Brazoria. You can send word here as to Amy's whereabouts."

"That might be like sendin' word to a heap of ashes—like sendin' word to Gonzales."

"You will try to keep in touch though—for Amy's sake—and John's —won't you?"

I thought he nodded. He was absorbed in getting away. He gave Mrs. Gibson the pack animal to lead. He rode beside Amy's horse with a lead rope tied to the bit ring of her bridle. She made no effort to guide the horse herself.

As they rode out of sight, her voice was raised in a keen of sorrow that chilled my heart.

"I want John!" farther and farther away, with the feeble screeching of the hens a doleful accent to her lament.

Had I been a fool to stay behind, I wondered. That very day, I took the children with me and walked to the settlement trading post. As I made a few purchases, I inquired about the war. It was reassuring to learn that Houston wasn't retreating but was camped on the Colorado at Beason's Ferry, opposite Columbus, gathering an army —most of the able-bodied men of Brazoria had left to join him. The Alamo atrocity had inflamed the Texans, turning a political rebellion into a full-fledged war of vengeance. The rumor most disturbing to settlers was that Santa Anna had divided his forces and was sending them across Texas in many directions. But messengers could be expected well ahead of any advance upon the settlements, and aimless flight could be as disastrous as invasion. So I returned to the cabin with the decision not to flee from the fire until I knew the direction of the wind. With Amy gone, the little place that had been such a pleasant refuge seemed to become a haunted hovel. To make things worse, Charity and her calf couldn't be found. Mr. Gibson had done a very thorough job of saving them from the Mexicans.

For several days, I tried unsuccessfully to work off my feeling of lonely uneasiness, keeping busy in the garden Amy and I had started. I came to realize that I had delayed too long getting acquainted in the settlement. In spite of distances and muddy trails (my nearest neighbor was a mile away), I must make some neighborly calls, offer to help with sewing or some other friendly task. Since Amy and I had been without menfolks to get around in the settlement, we were relatively unknown in the neighborhood; at the same time, the weather and the demands of war had kept other women as confined as we were.

But before I had acted upon my resolution, I had a visitor. Mr. Norton. I had heard of Mr. Norton as a drunkard and a curiosity. The story was that no one ever saw him eat anything. He apparently lived on whiskey and nothing more. I almost believed it when I saw him.

A bearded, dirty, pitiable wreck of a man was Mr. Norton—trembling so that his teeth chattered and he could hardly speak—his eyes bloodshot, his hands clutching—clutching at nothing. I did not hear him approach. When I came in from the back door, I found him leaning against the front entrance, like he might topple in.

"Who are you?" I asked.

"N-n-norton," he stammered. "I—I—fer God's sake, ma'am, a sip of brandy fer a dyin' man!"

"I have nothing for you, Mr. Norton," I said firmly. "Nothing at all."

He fell on his knees before me. "I'm dyin', ma'am, dyin'—spare me just one little dram of yore brandy medicine. Everybody's got a bit of brandy fer bad times. I'll pay ya." Still on his knees, he rummaged in a jacket pocket and brought out several pieces of gold and held them before me, tempting, begging.

"You can have it all, ma'am, fer just a sip frum yer brandy bottle."

I shook my head.

"I could work fer ya, ma'am. You need some man-work done around here, don't ya?"

I was tempted to tell him if he'd find Charity and Heartface, I'd give him a drink. But I didn't. I just looked at him hard, trying to show no feeling.

His expression became sly and conspiring. "Maybe you need protectin'," he said. "Anybody botherin' ya, old Norton'd be glad to do some quiet killin' for ya." Then he became frantic again.

"Anything ya say, ma'am! Anything! Help me! Save me! I'm dyin'!"

He started on a rising scale and ended in a scream, "Dyin'! Dyin'! Dyin'! Dyin'!"

"Mr. Norton! Stop it!" I commanded, and stamped my foot.

He slumped. With his head bowed, he went into a rush of words like a delirium.

"Demon Rum's got me . . . got me in hell's torture . . . no whiskey in the settlement . . . all the men went to fight and took it with 'em . . . not a drop left . . . not a drop . . . tried ever place but here . . . you got some . . . you ain't said you ain't . . . you got to believe I'm a dyin' man . . . Satan a-flashin' his red eyes at me . . . his fires burnin' inside me!" He slumped down further, gasping, trying to clutch at the pangs inside him.

I went over to the fireplace where I had the coffeepot on a bed of coals. I filled a large cup with the strong black liquid and took it to him.

"Coffee for you, Mr. Norton."

He looked up at me, quieted, and reached for the cup. But his trembling hands couldn't hold it. So I guided the cup to his lips while he drank. When I refilled it for him, his trembling had abated and he could hold it for himself.

Finally, he was able to rise to his feet, though shaky and uncertain.

"Thank you kindly, ma'am," he muttered, now too ashamed to look at me.

He tried to hurry away, stumbling and staggering in an agony of sobriety.

Mr. Norton's visit prodded me right into action. I must go seeking some cheerful interests. And if I were going to call upon strangers, I must look my best. I dressed with care. I hadn't studied myself in the mirror so much in a long time. I realized that I didn't even know what the latest fashions were—that it had been a year since I'd had a fashion book to look into. But the women I would visit, I reasoned, had likely been as preoccupied with other things as I and wouldn't be too critical of my outmoded dress and bonnet.

I selected a black silk dress, something I hadn't worn since leaving New Orleans. It was above-ankle length and cut quite low over the shoulders to be worn with a white crepe shawl. My hat was black velvet with trimmings of white satin ribbon and a feather cluster in white and rich aqua blue. The shawl was held in place by a big glass pin the color of the blue feather. I dressed the children in their best too: Joe in black broadcloth with a white satin blouse, Ginny in ruffled velvet—her redbird dress.

It was ridiculous, putting on such finery for a long walk over muddy pathways to visit with we-didn't-know-who. But at the time, it just seemed a happy thing to do, and it did raise our spirits. The children became gay and excited for the first time since Amy's departure.

Before leaving, I took my reticule from the trunk and fastened it securely about my wrist. It contained all my money, carefully concealed in pockets and padding. I carried some needles and threads and a few other notions as possible gifts to my neighbors, and several biscuits and hard-boiled eggs for the children's refreshment along the way.

It was a sunny day, and we started happily down the trail. Joe said "Sing something, Mama," and I started out on "Sweet Laurie."

"Oh, Laurie was pretty,
"Oh, Laurie was sweet,
"With bows on her bonnet
"And slippers so neat . . ."

Then he said, "Stop, Mama, stop!" in a frightened way.

I broke off . . . and I heard what had frightened him.

There was a distant popping sound. And a sound much closer, someone running hard and fast.

Then Mr. Norton came into view. He ran past our cabin and on down the path toward us.

"Run," he panted, stopping for a moment beside us and gasping for breath. "Run fer yer life! The Meskins are comin'! Shootin'! Burnin' and killin'. You kin hear 'em. Listen!"

Yes, we heard. The faraway popping sounds. Gunshots surely.

"I've got to warn everybody. Got to tell 'em." He ran on ahead of us, calling back, "Come on! Run! They're comin' this way! Right behind ya!"

I picked Ginny up in my arms and ran as fast as I could. By the time I reached the settlement, Mr. Norton was racing around like a madman screaming his warnings.

People were leaving on foot, on horses, in carts and wagons. They were fully panicked, with all attention on self and family. There was no one to direct or command.

164

We had run so far already that Joe was exhausted.

He pleaded with me, "Mama, Mama, I can't run any more."

A man driving a wagon loaded with meat passed me. I called out to him.

"Mister, can my little boy ride with you?"

"If he can catch on behind. I'm not stoppin'."

Joe didn't have the strength to run and climb on. I caught him up with my free arm and kept pace with the wagon until he could clutch on to the load and crawl up on top. Then I walked behind the wagon carrying Virginia first on one arm, then on the other.

The prairie trail was muddy and I often sank in over my slipper tops. My black silk skirt became heavy with mud. Ginny tugged at my white shawl until it was up around my neck and clutched at my bonnet to keep her balance.

What a fashionable trio we were! Joe in his best broadcloth, sitting on a slab of salty meat, anxiously watching me as I trudged along in the slush, shoulders exposed and hat askew. Ginny, in her redbird dress, bewildered and uncomfortable, shifted this way and that, chewing my bonnet ribbons for consolation.

I expect we were the best-dressed family in the Runaway Scrape!

9.

Mile after mile I trudged after that wagon, not daring to pause and risk separation from Joe. Hour after hour I kept a firm hold on Ginny, my heart pounding, my arms aching with the load that grew heavier and heavier. I never let the thought enter my head that I would weaken and fall. The strength of extremity!

We had traveled nine painful miles toward doubtful safety when nightfall overtook us on Bailey's Prairie. We stopped at a campsite known as Camp Pollie and tried to get some rest. I was thankful for the bit of food in my recticule so casually included as a snack for the children.

Soon after we made our stop, several of the old men mounted on some mules announced they were going to go back and find out what the Mexicans were doing. One of them said, "Old Norton's disappeared. Maybe he was just having a crazy spell. Maybe we won't find any Mexicans a'tall."

Someone yelled out, "Then I was having a crazy spell too. I heard gunfire—no mistake about it!"

Others echoed that they had heard it.

Another mounted man said, "We're gonna make sure. Best not to pauper ourselves without looking back. Moon's in our favor. Just stay put till we get back."

"What if you don't get back?" A woman's voice made blunt inquiry.

"Give us till sunup."

"Then what?"

"Run for your lives and pray for a boat when you hit water."

In the dim light, people clustered in their own anxious little groups of relatives and close friends. I asked the grumpy driver of the meat wagon if we could rest under the protection of his vehicle. He gave a nod and went about unhitching. I noticed that he staked one animal very close to the wagon and knew he planned to make a quick getaway if the Mexicans came upon us. Then he climbed back upon the wagon and settled down without a word, apparently too absorbed in self-preservation to be aware of the woman and children under his wagon.

I knew there was only a scattering of menfolk left in the camp, and with the old men gone, no leadership. We must wait out the night without any plan of defense—without even the comfort of firelight. And the night itself offered no consolation with its veiled moonlight, damp chill, and the eerie nocturnal sounds of prairie life. But exhaustion dropped around me as thick as a log wall, sealing me off. I clutched the children tight in my arms, leaned back against the wagon wheel, and slept.

Our scouts returned before the morning light had fully aroused the camp. Their news brought some relief. The Mexicans weren't in Brazoria. Old Man Norton had spread a false alarm. The popping had been from a fire in the canebrakes, with the exploding reeds sounding like the discharge of horse pistols. The cane fires had been set by Negro slaves from a deserted outlying plantation—they were on a rampage of burning and destroying. Here was a new danger, for no one knew how many renegade slaves were loose in the area. Though some in the camp argued against returning to the settlement, it was generally agreed that this was the only thing to do. Before setting out, fires were built that people might chase the chill from their bodies and eat what could be found. The driver of the meat wagon refused to share his meat, saying that his load was commissioned to a ship's master at Velasco and not his to divide. He did let one piece go, however, to an angry fellow who threw a bowie knife so that it whizzed past the driver's shoulder and plunged neatly into a slab of meat.

"Sorry, mister," the man who threw the knife drawled. "My knife slipped. Good thing it missed you and landed in the meat." He went over to the wagon and picked up the knife with the hunk of meat suspended from it. "Guess I'll have to eat the meat off to get my knife back," he said as he walked away.

I took some money from my recticule and offered it to the driver if he would prepare a piece of meat at his campfire for me. I told him also that I could pay him well to give us a place on his wagon for the return trip.

"I'm headin' for Velasco," he said. But he did take my money for some meat which was not yet fully cooked when he hitched up and departed, carrying with him a half-raw piece on the end of a stick for his own breakfast.

As I fed the children and looked about me at the other campers, I began to realize how conspicuous I was in all my finery, and how people were staring at me. They were all strangers to me and no one made a move to make my acquaintance. The women about me were poorly clad, their dresses long and plain, and those with heads covered wore shawls or sunbonnets. Some still had on their kitchen aprons. It was only the purest accident that I was there decked out in silk and velvet, but they looked at me as if I had appeared thus on purpose and was somehow indecent. I had thought my dress out-dated when I put it on the day before—now I realized that here in this group it was an advance style that appeared bold and frivolous. No other woman in camp wore a dress above her ankles.

So I must stand there under their scrutiny feeling more and more undressed. You can't explain to a group of frontier women in the early morning out on the prairie that above-ankle lengths have been fashionable for several years now. And you cannot inform them that even house dresses are being cut to expose the shoulders. I rearranged my shawl for better concealment.

I tied my treasured velvet bonnet securely upon my head though at the time it made me feel like a freak in a sideshow. And I was fully aware too of the curiosity and suspicion that was focused on my recticule. Few men in Texas were able to carry coin money in their pockets these days; so a woman bringing out money to pay for meat was a most unusual sight.

Without speaking or asking my name, they passed judgment on me, subjected me to the indignity of their disapproval. I could not defend myself against an unspoken condemnation, and it was impossible to flee. So I just stood in silent misery, my cheeks burning, waiting for the procession to move out.

The sound of riders approaching broke the ugly spell, and attention shifted from me to watch five mounted men approach the camp. They were soon in our midst: Two were men of official bearing, and three— one a Negro—were attendants. Each rider was well armed. The leader of the group wore a sword as well as a pair of pistols, all beautiful weapons, apparently selected for adornment as well as protection. But he wore them with more confidence than vanity, and his whole appearance proclaimed him a man accustomed to public performance and command.

"I am Colonel Potter, Secretary of the Texas Navy," he announced to the gathering, "and by my side is Colonel Hall, Commandant of the Port of Velasco. We are here to advise all settlers in this region of the full gravity of the war situation and to make arrangements for you to flee to Galveston Island for safety. The new seat of government is at Harrisburg. At last reports, Sam Houston and his army were running from the Mexicans. I see you are in flight already. Prepare to move on to Velasco. We will lead you there."

While all the others moved about in excitement and hasty preparation, I stood quite still in my bewilderment. Could I walk all the way to Velasco, carrying Virginia? Could little Joe walk that far? Must I suffer the final indignity of tramping along behind these people?

There was some hope for me in the appearance of Colonel Hall, a man well known to my father. In fact, I had once been introduced to him at my father's house when he had made an overnight stop there. But he probably wouldn't recognize me from that one brief meeting. His glance roved over all the gathering, but he gave no sign of having seen me before. Did I dare approach him? To have him deny me would be a crowning embarrassment before the camp. He moved away to check on some of the vehicles.

Colonel Potter's black stallion pranced in impatience, showing the rider off to good advantage. I watched him still the beautiful beast with a soft-spoken command. Then when he looked up, his dark eyes roving restlessly over the camp, his glance met mine, and I gazed steadily back at him. His expression became quite grave. I thought for a moment he was going to address me, then abruptly he turned and rode over to Colonel Hall and engaged him in conversation.

They were discussing me—I knew that. Colonel Hall turned and looked at me, giving a sign of recognition that was like a flag of hope to me. I expected him to come directly to me, but instead he spoke something to Colonel Potter who nodded, immediately dismounted, and came toward me.

While we stood face to face, some special pleasure flowed between us, an excitement beyond his curiosity and my need. He had removed his hat, and his abundant black hair, fashionably styled, was shining in the sun. He was a slender man, handsomely clad. Though not tall, he stood well above me in height. To me his whole appearance was shining: his eyes glowed approval of me—his fitted coat so bright a blue—his polished boots so glossy black. With him, I was suddenly at ease in my silk dress and velvet bonnet, pleased that I was wearing them in fact.

When he spoke to me his voice was gentle and kind.

"Madam, may I beg to inquire if you are the daughter of Francis Moore of Brazoria?"

I assured him that I was, gave him my full name and presented the children. In an easy manner, he touched each of them, Joe on the shoulder and Virginia on the head.

"A beautiful pair," he said softly, "and no wonder!" He looked back at me so directly, I could not miss the personal meaning. Just three words, tenderly spoken, and I was trembling. I wish I could convey to you the magic quality of his voice. Here for the first time I was touched by the scepter of the Potter personality—a voice that could reach out and put a net over the senses. Of course, I was easy to enrapture that morning. A wounded vanity is a greedy one.

"Colonel Hall tells me that he knows your father well and that you are a lady into whose welfare we should inquire." Formal words but the sweet sound of them! If there was any boldness here, I was unable to resent it. Also unable at the moment to reply.

"Are you without escort?"

"The men of my family are in the war," I said. "I do not know even if they are alive."

"Surely you are not without conveyance?"

"Only my two feet."

"But among your friends here——"

"These people are all strangers to me. I had only recently settled in Brazoria."

He looked down at my mud-stained slippers and hemline.

"Madam! Am I to believe that you made your way here on foot?"

"I walked behind a wagonload of meat, carrying my baby. The driver allowed Joe Boy to ride."

"Allowed? Do you mean there is a man in this camp so brutish, so contemptible—where is he? Point him out to me!" Colonel Potter was actually in a rage on my behalf, and again my vanity feasted.

I explained that the old man had already departed for Velasco with his load. Then I told him briefly how I had been caught up in the Norton Panic to find myself stranded out here on the prairie and looked upon most critically by my companions as being improperly dressed for the occasion.

He gave me a merry smile at this detail and said, "Madam, from now on I shall try to make the occasion more worthy of your attire." He signaled to his servant, a robust Negro riding a big bay.

The Negro rode over and dismounted.

"Yassuh, Colonel."

"Mrs. Page and her two children are stranded without escort and will henceforth be under our protection."

"Yassuh." Jethro looked on us with obvious approval and waited for instructions.

"The children will ride with you—the boy behind and the little girl held carefully in front of you. Remount and we'll hand them up to you."

I realized that again I was the center of attention and people were staring. But I was no longer embarrassed. I was elated. Colonel Hall rode over and courtesies were exchanged. Colonel Potter inquired if I thought I could ride in comfort behind him.

I made no mention of my limited horseback-riding experience. I just assured him that I could.

"Gadolphin is lively but manageable," he said. "If you have no fear of him, he will soon accept you."

I was too thankful to be fearful, and told him so.

So he mounted first in order to get a firm rein on his steed. Then Colonel Hall assisted me with a foothold in his locked hands. I placed one hand on his shoulder, and when Colonel Potter reached down and took my other hand, I was neatly boosted into a side position on Gadolphin's sleek hips.

"Hold onto me!" Colonel Potter commanded, as the skittish stallion began to prance about, excited over his double load. So I clung to him tightly, while he guided his mount out into lead position on the trail.

The march to Velasco was begun. And a most eventful ride it turned out to be, changing the whole course of my life.

After a while, I was able to release my grip on the Colonel's waist and ride comfortably balanced and erect, my hands resting lightly on the back of the saddle.

What a reversal of fortunes this was! What an incredible adventure

—riding behind the Secretary of the Texas Navy on his grand horse! I felt exhilarated, rapturous, rescued in this storybook fashion—the hero so beguiling and attentive—so kind to my children.

Yesterday had been panic and mud and exhaustion. Tomorrow might be anything. But today was the gladdening sensation of motion on horseback, through fragrant air, over green earth, with romantic escort. I wondered if my delight in it all might not be wicked and so resolved to keep it well hidden.

When the colonel inquired, "Are you all right, Mrs. Page?" I wanted to reply "Wonderful! Wonderful!" but I said instead, "Quite all right, thank you."

Jethro, who rode behind us most of the time, came up to ride by our side for a while, and looking at us with lively interest, remarked, "You know what you all looks like. You looks like a runaway prince and princess, thas what!"

"You are a romantic fool, Jethro," the colonel replied with more pleasure than reproof.

"Yeah, sur!" Jethro agreed happily. "I is that very thing."

Then the trail narrowed and he dropped back.

"Prince and princess . . . knight and lady . . . poet and true love . . ." Colonel Potter mused in that beautiful voice of his. "The very pattern of romance . . . riding away together on a spirited black stallion . . . to an ever-ever land where they——" he paused significantly. "Do you know the end of the story, princess?" His voice was just a whisper. I was trembling again as I had when he first spoke to me. I held tight to the back of the saddle and leaned away from him as far as I could.

"Mrs. Page, have I offended you?"

I didn't answer.

"Forgive me, Mrs. Page. You see I am something of a poet as well as a statesman. And poets consider themselves privileged in the presence of beauty. But I will doff my poet's mantle," he gestured as if throwing off an imaginary cape, "and we will become properly acquainted."

He began to talk to me about himself, explaining that he was a man without family responsibility, lawyer by profession, and statesman by will of the people whom he had served in state and national legislative bodies. He had no sooner arrived in Texas, he said, than the people of Nacogdoches district had elected him to serve as their delegate to the recent convention at Washington-on-the-Brazos. There he had helped to write the Declaration of Independence and frame the Constitution of the Republic of Texas, and had been made a cabinet officer in the new government. And, he further confided, if war matters were resolved favorably, he expected to obtain large land holdings in a beautiful lake region of northeast Texas and continue a career of public service.

Then, in answer to his polite inquiry about my family and circumstances, I found myself telling him all about my trip to Texas and the trials I had been through. I didn't realize at the time that I was being adroitly and thoroughly questioned by a skillful lawyer. I even told him all about Solomon—about his gambling—how he had abandoned us in the wilderness—and that I never expected to see him again.

"A Mexican bullet is too good for him," the colonel commented. "There is other punishment more appropriate for his crime."

Neither of us discussed any further what might or should happen to Solomon. He was an unwelcome shadow.

For a while we rode in silence, absorbing what we had learned about each other.

Suddenly, Gadolphin shied, and I almost slipped off. I grabbed Colonel Potter around the waist, and as Gadolphin's prancing antics continued, the colonel's hand closed over mine, locking my arms around him. When the horse was calm again, and my hands were free, I could not help wondering if the colonel had provoked the little incident on purpose. But of course, I could not be sure. I could be sure of only one thing: I must be more wary of the colonel's nearness than Gadolphin's capers.

The progress on to Velasco was halting and slow as settlers along the line of travel were given the news of the exodus and advised to hurry on to the coast where the men were to help Colonel Hall fortify the town and women and children would be evacuated by boat. It was Colonel Potter who answered questions, sent and received messages, gave commands, for he was in charge of the whole plan. As our privacy diminished, we conversed only in formal phrases, but I must admit I was perfectly aware that my presence stimulated him to make all he did and said a performance to provoke my interest and admiration. And I was interested . . . and I did admire. I knew the other women looked upon me with envy and suspicion. And, at the moment, it bothered me not at all.

Early in the afternoon, a man on horseback joined our ranks. Casual in movement, bold in manner, he rode a dark chestnut horse that appeared better fed and groomed than its owner. He rode along, not far from us, and seemed in no hurry to make himself known to Colonel Potter. I began to be uncomfortably aware of him for he bent a steady gaze on me when the colonel's attention was elsewhere. He seemed determined that I should acknowledge his presence in some way, but I ignored him.

I did not like it when he approached the colonel on the side facing me, and after an insolent stare, lost to Colonel Potter, made soft-spoken comment in a voice unpleasantly intimate.

"Yo' hoss is favorin' the hind leg on this side, Colonel Potter. I'm something of a smithy. Want me to give a look before he goes lame?"

Colonel Potter was startled and plainly annoyed. He answered crisply, "I certainly hadn't noticed." He looked at the man and I felt an unspoken antagonism between them. Then he added, with studied mildness, "But perhaps it would be wise to look."

The stranger dismounted, touched Gadolphin with a certain skill along haunch and hock and lifted the foot for inspection.

"Anything wrong?"

The man didn't answer the colonel at once. He took out his knife, scraped around the shoe, chipped at the hoof here and there.

"Ragged job on the shoe. Just a spot needed clearin'."

As he released Gadolphin's foot, and the colonel turned away with a curt, "Thank you, smithy," I felt a sharp tug on my foot and my slipper dropped to the ground.

I called to the colonel to stop, that I had lost a slipper. I was startled at the man's action, but felt I must not arouse Colonel Potter against him. I brushed the matter aside by saying to Colonel Potter, "It was I who had the loose shoe and not Gadolphin."

But the stranger was not through with us. He quickly dismounted and recovered the shoe. The natural thing to do was hold out my foot and let him put it on for me. I looked at the colonel. He sensed my displeasure and as the man held my foot and put the slipper on with neat competence, the colonel's face flushed red. I felt a caressing finger against my ankle and gave an involuntary shiver at the man's audacity. Then with soft insolence he rounded out his insult.

"I guess I made a mistake, ma'am. It's you that could use a good smithy."

Colonel Potter's rage was instant and superb. His shiny pistol flashed, aimed at the stranger's heart.

"Tender your apologies to the lady on the instant," he demanded. "Or I shall be pleased to give your soul a lead ticket to hell!"

The man smiled, then composed his face into mock seriousness and said to me, "A poor jest, ma'am. No disrespect intended. Yo' servant, ma'am." He removed his big battered hat and bowed most gravely, but when his head came up, his eyes were hot on Colonel Potter and he replaced his hat with a tug of disrespect in the colonel's direction.

"Am I to be let off so easily—without a challenge from the *Honorable* Robert Potter of North Carolina?"

The heavy sarcasm in his rich southern accent carried most unpleasant implications. The exchange between him and the colonel became a dialogue of hate and caution with many unspoken meanings, understood by them alone.

Colonel Potter said, "Dueling is for the satisfaction of *gentlemen*."

"No so many *gentlemen* in Texas as in North Carolina, Mr. Potter."

"Obviously. Now get out. I am in command here and I want no more of your company."

"Nor I of yo's. I'll take my chances with Sam Houston."

"You'll find him running somewhere between the Colorado and the Brazos, Mr. Smithy."

"I'll wager he won't run so fast to get out of Texas as you did to get out of North Carolina, Mr. Potter."

"And I'll wager you're some sneaking varlet sent by Houston to spy on me and taunt me to rash action. You can tell that consort of savages that I know how to deal with knaves, fools, *and barbarians!*"

"And *preachers*, Mr. Potter?"

The shock and fury in Colonel Potter's face was awful to see. This mention of "preachers" for some reason turned on a force of violence within him that I could sense like a deadly palpitation.

He brought the gun in his hand to more meaningful aim. "I'll cripple you," he threatened fiercely. "I'll cut out your tongue."

"Quite a *cutter*, aren't you, Potter?" the man jibed, keeping his hands far away from his own gun, putting the colonel at disadvantage before witnesses—not only myself and Jethro, but others who were gathering around.

"If you aren't out of my sight by the count of ten, I'll kill you!"

This was no threat. It was implacable statement—and the colonel began to count.

"One——"

The stranger was like an actor in a role well rehearsed, performing with precision and delight.

"I'm quite sure that you would like to kill me, Mr. Potter."

"Two——"

"It would please me to give you satisfaction sometime, man to man——"

"Three——"

"*Knives!* No paces . . . no ladies present."

"Four——"

With a mocking smile for me, the daring fellow tipped his hat and bowed slightly in my direction——

"Five——"

Leaped into his saddle with sudden, easy grace——

"Six——"

Onto a horse trained to hit a dead run at such a mounting.

"Seven—eight—nine—ten!"

He was out of sight.

I gasped in relief.

Jethro who had been very near us, sitting his horse in a paralysis of fear and fascination, Ginny clutched protectively in his arms, slumped and muttered, "Satan been here sho'. And lef' his brimstony smell."

Colonel Potter holstered his gun and spoke to me with formal, easy grace.

"I deeply regret, Mrs. Page, that you have been subjected to the indignity of that ruffian's presence and the unpleasantness of our exchange."

For the crowd, he had only a cool glance of dismissal, and our journey was resumed.

I was disturbed that this dangerous episode had originated through me and at the same time deeply excited at Colonel Potter's fiery intervention in my behalf. It was months before I had occasion really to understand the stranger's antagonism toward the colonel and to realize that my part in this drama of insult had been a very minor one.

At the time it happened, I felt called upon to express to the colonel my regret that my presence had provoked such a scene and burdened him with my protection.

He hastened to reassure me with such a wonder of words, complimenting in meaning, caressing in tone, that I was led spellbound into an interpretation of the whole affair as brave-gentleman-protects-fair-lady. At the same time, he did not neglect to include the children in his tender regard. His concern for them during the whole journey was genuine and tinged with a wistfulness that touched my heart.

I could not help but contrast all this with Solomon's indifference. And Joe and Ginny, so unused to masculine attention, glowed with pleasure at his interest.

By the time we reached Velasco, I was won to full trust and loyalty. I tried to find proper words to express my gratitude, thinking that once the ride was ended, I might never get the chance to speak so privately to him again. I framed a little speech that started out, "I am deeply beholden to you, Colonel Potter——" but when I spoke it, the words came out with starched reserve.

Propriety had dominated my every gesture during the whole ride. I had not touched my escort except for balance and safety. Now Gadolphin's gait was as easy as velvet cushions, and there would be special meaning conveyed if——

I reached out and let my hand rest in the bend of his reining arm. Instantly his free hand closed over mine.

"Dear Lady, the reward far exceeds the service," he said, and his voice——

(Tricky, it may be that you will know a man sometime with a voice as magnetic as the Potter voice, so I must write this feeling out for you as clearly as I must record certain matter of events.)

. . . his voice embraced me. Indeed voice can command mind, and my unguarded imagination was wholly susceptible so that in his embrace I envisioned great new dimensions of happiness.

Which sense is the greater conjurer of love's sublimities, sight or sound? I know not. I only know that I was subject to each in turn. My first enchantment had come as I looked on Solomon Page and in his restless hands saw a beckoning toward woman's glory. Now it was a voice beckoning—the voice of Robert Potter.

10.

At Velasco, Colonel Potter ordered the wives and children of men fighting in the Texas cause to be taken aboard the armed schooner *Flash* anchored at the mouth of the Brazos. He continued to keep me and my children under his personal protection. We were the first to board the *Flash*, for on our arrival Captain Flavell sent a shoreboat to bring the Secretary of the Navy out to the schooner. Captain Flavell and his crew had been sworn into the service of the Texas Navy only a few weeks previous by Colonel Potter himself. They made every effort to provide for the Secretary and his party the accommodations and comforts befitting his rank. Thus, I was set apart from the other refugees, having a private cabin and being personally attended by Jethro, who had free run of the galley and the ship's stores to prepare our meals.

For several days, the *Flash* remained at anchor while Colonel Hall tried in vain to fortify the port and Colonel Potter issued directions that couldn't be carried out and received messengers reporting nothing but disaster—Mexican victories at Refugio, Goliad, and Victoria—Houston running to God-knows-where. The Palm Sunday slaughter of three hundred Texas prisoners at Goliad put the final touch of terror on all inhabitants. Colonel Hall gave up in despair the task of fortifying Velasco, for the people scattered like frightened quail. Some rushed into the canebrakes and hid—some grabbed boats with no attention to safety or ownership hoping to escape along the coastline to the United States—and still others attempted flight overland in spite of bogs and swamps.

One afternoon in early April, the bleak news reached Velasco of Houston's retreat up the Brazos, and Colonel Potter came to tell me of it. It seemed to clear his mind to think aloud in my presence. On this particular occasion, Jethro came in with him and he expounded to the four of us and yet seemed hardly aware of us.

"Now, at last, Houston is condemned by his own action to the ignominy he deserves. My courier has brought all the ghastly details. On March 27, the very day of the Goliad Massacre, Houston dragged his dreary rag of an army into camp at San Felipe de Austin, his force cut in half by desertions. Then he ordered further retreat *up* the Brazos, nothing but a hide-saving movement. San Felipe left in ashes! The Mexicans left a clear passage all the way across Texas! Clear passage for Santa Anna, who has already set out from San Antonio, his stomach full no doubt, his general's regalia glittering, his forces eager, equipped, and fast-moving. And what will this sleek he-wolf track down for his prize prey? Not the hungry, frightened crowds jamming the ferries—not the epidemic-ridden soggy camps along the river banks. But rather the officers of this new government whose creation is in defiance of his authority. He must seize them and make examples of them. And where is the most likely place for this inevitable final conflict?"

We knew he didn't expect an answer from children, servant, or mere woman.

"Galveston Bay! My ships will bring the officers from the mainland to Galveston Island. I will get word to them at Harrisburg. Santa Anna will be expecting supplies and transport ships in Galveston Harbor. Texas naval vessels have already done good service in seizing cargo destined for the Mexican army. The Texas Navy will be—shall be—the deciding factor in this whole revolution! Enough armed schooners under proper command at the right time in Galveston Bay can save the Republic! Chief Pow-wow Sam is on his way back to the Indian wigwams and what Robert Potter tried to tell the convention at Washington-on-the-Brazos is in the process of being demonstrated, engraved into history by the fumbling and cowardly Houston command. We will sail immediately for Galveston!"

He turned abruptly and left us.

"Ise proud to be that colonel's man!" Jethro said, and followed him.

And I was proud to be the colonel's audience, proud witness to the functioning of his gallant leadership.

It seemed only a matter of minutes until the ship sprang into life and movement, and as soon as we were well under way, the colonel returned to me and asked me to walk on deck with him and watch the ship's progress down the coast. Jethro would mind Joe and Ginny.

As we walked, his mind was much on the approaching crisis and upon himself as a participant. When I inquired how it had come about that he had been placed in charge of naval affairs for the Republic, he told me of his experience as a midshipman in the United States Navy.

"I spent the springtime of my life, six years from the age of sixteen, bearing the arms of my country in the Navy. When I went in, I reported to my boyhood hero, Captain Oliver Hazard Perry, commander of the USS *Java*. The glories of the War of 1812 were done. I had to be content with ship's lore and ship's service and constant drill in some of the manly arts: boxing, fencing, wrestling, and the general art of survival! I was impatient that there were no wars, but I learned many things about ships and about personal courage." I commented on how fortunate it was for the Texas cause that he had been so trained.

"I was the only one at the convention with such experience to back up my interest in naval affairs," he said. Then he added most gravely, "I feel we may be moving toward a naval encounter in the Gulf of Mexico as decisive, as significant in national history, as Captain Perry's exploit on Lake Erie. I hope we can cry in triumph as he did, 'We have met the enemy and they are ours!' "

I told him that I felt sure there was no one better equipped to follow the path of the great Perry to a similar glorious conclusion.

He looked at me as if to measure my sincerity, then he said, "It would be wonderful to walk a path of glory—with you."

I already felt that I was on such a path, moving on this ship up to the heart of conflict by his side. But I sought to evade personal discussion.

"Is your navy a large one?" I asked.

He chuckled. "Are you trying to puncture a dream, madam? No. I must say the Texas Navy is not a large one. Not many Texans even know of its existence. The act of the provisional government that authorized its establishment was put into execution only three months ago. Of the four schooners purchased and armed, the *Liberty* and the *Invincible* have already been harassing coastal shipping meant to strengthen and supply Santa Anna's forces. The *Brutus* and the *Independence* have just arrived in Texas waters, and I hope to find them in the harbor ready for action. The Republic doesn't own the *Flash*, but it is armed and crewed to function as a part of the Navy if we need it. So we have a total of five armed schooners in our present fleet. Also there are several merchant ships and steamboats plying our waters well armed against pirates. If the battle moves into the harbor, they will not hesitate to turn their guns to our defense. So I think my naval forces will be entirely adequate to protect Galveston Island and hold off any Mexican vessels from contact with Santa

Anna. Separate him from food and luxury, ammunition and sea passage home, and he'll be trapped too deep in Texas to pull out."

"You don't think there's any chance that Houston might stop Santa Anna before he reaches the coast?" I asked.

"I've never heard of one army stopping another by increasing the distance between them."

"But could the General's move up the river be some kind of trick? Just an appearance of retreat in preparation for a rear attack."

"A man with his followers deserting in droves, with no more morale and equipment than a herd of frightened beggars, is in no position to maneuver. Even the weather is against him—rivers flooded —lands mired. No, my dear, you overestimate the man. He has his tricks all right, and he wants a crown and a throne in this new country. He's been conniving to get Texas for his private domain for some time now. He has a monstrous power-madness for becoming Indian-chief Emperor. I've seen him strut in blankets and feathers, and I've seen him more recently strutting in a meaningless gaudy uniform got together by his own vanity. But he wears no fabric of bravery under his blankets and braids! By this time, I doubt he has an army. He's probably rejoined his brother savages, and I hope that someday his mangy scalp may serve as a ritual piece in their heathen celebrations!"

The colonel broke off in his tirade against Houston—abruptly changed his voice to a poetic flow. "The clean sound of wind and water, the beauty of the April sky, may soon be desecrated by roar of guns and battlesmoke, but now, let's pay them tribute, in a more secluded spot."

He led me aft along the starboard side to a spot where ship's paraphernalia stacked high formed a concealing bulwark between railing and main passageway. Here we stood and talked more personally than ever before—about inner things, our likes and dislikes, the beliefs we shared. Sometimes we stood near the rail and gazed upon the lively waters, sometimes we leaned in comfort against the stacks and looked at the sky, but we seldom looked at each other. The motions and sounds of sail and ship in union with water and wind were harmonious background for the mood we shared.

At last the blissful blue of the April sky began to bedeck itself in a thin garment of scattered gray clouds shot through with the gold of sunset. And, in our delightful seclusion, we found ourselves canopied by a vast coloring of blue and gray and gold that faded as the sun went down into star-studded blue-purple. And the blue and gold of sweet confidence changed into the blue-purple of enchantment and desire.

Colonel Potter quoted Shelley:

> "Nothing in the world is single,
> All things by a law divine
> In one spirit meet and mingle."

He moved closer to me and his arm touched mine. We both waited for composure after the touch, and then his hand grasped mine and held it tightly. And he spoke an urgent argument.

He said that any man whether facing actual battles of conquest or smaller battles of everyday life found the struggle without point or grace unless there was a woman standing by, his woman, spectator to his heart and deeds. He pointed out that our meeting had come about through events outside our control. We had not willed to come together, but we had. The attraction between us, he expounded, had not resulted from artifices of seduction on either side, but had been instant magnetism, as certain and undeniable as loadstone to iron.

He began to plead with me passionately. "Oh, my dear Harriet, you do share this ardor? I'm not alone in this consuming obsession? Am I? Answer me! Am I?"

I had to answer him. I had to assure him that he was not alone!

He was facing me now, holding both my hands, drawing me closer, his voice becoming triumphant, possessive, saying the things I had been trying to keep out of my thoughts.

"You do love me! And it's the first time you've ever loved so wholly, completely beyond reason or circumstance. You didn't intend to. You don't want to. But you do! I know it. Come into my arms. Tell me so!"

I pulled away from him, though not wanting to. And he let me go. I clinched my hands to keep from reaching out to him, and I spoke in a whispered jumble about how wonderful he'd been, how kind, how I'd never known anyone like him. I told him I wanted to help him, not injure him. That his position in the Republic—we must think of that. And my children, we must think of them. That in the eyes of the public our status was simply married woman and single man, and the gossips would not spare us—were not sparing us now.

He said, almost accusing, "You told me you never intended to live with Solomon Page again."

"I don't!"

"Then what will you do?"

"I'll go back to Kentucky and live with my grandmother."

"And leave me?"

"I have a duty to my children," I said.

"Don't you believe I could love your children—make them happy?"

"Yes," I said. "Oh, yes, you've shown that."

"You think my asking you to declare your love for me is a prologue to asking for something less than marriage—less than a permanent union?"

How could we have marriage? I was indignant at his inconsistency.

"Death is the only decent release from the marriage vow," I said. "You know that as well as I do. And you know too that in public scandals, a woman's infidelity is always given more shameful emphasis than a man's. Of course, I've heard how important people do manage legal releases from marriage, but I've never known anyone who did, and I'm not in the least important. Only the rich and famous can afford such things, and even they are tarnished, linked by the public with crime and scandal."

Colonel Potter became strangely silent, almost withdrawn.

I kept trying to explain. "I would not want such a thing for you and me. It does seem an injustice that I can't be rid of a husband who deserted me—a man I despise. But we must face the fact that I'm not rid of him, and people will scorn me as the faithless wife of a fighting man if I appear to place my affections elsewhere. And you will be injured by any such attachment—your reputation——"

He interrupted me. "Stop holding your hands so tightly! Give them to me!" He unclasped my hands and held them again.

"Can you deny the feeling between us?" he demanded.

I could not.

"Then I say we are deserving of a few moments of our very own snatched from eternity! Tell me this—I will not be denied: If you were free, would you say you loved me—would you marry me? Let me know at least how it might have been!" His hands now grasped my arms and he shook me gently. "Tell me!" he demanded. "Tell me!"

186

I obeyed him. I told him, "I would say 'I love you.' I would marry you."

His arms slid down around my waist and he drew me to him. I could not make even the smallest effort to resist him, "And I would love you," he said, "as no other man could possibly love you."

This seemed to be the ultimate truth of my life, with past, present, and future blended into a *now* that I could not deny.

The music in the waves that slapped the side of the ship was sweet and mad and wonderful. The wind that struck the sails was like a soft throb of drum in accompaniment. No sensation or experience, or thought of love, had prepared me for the tumult of the senses that I felt in this man's arms, his lips to mine.

The light of a ship's lantern in the hands of a boatswain touched us, dissolved our ardent embrace, restored us to partial awareness.

As we returned from our stroll, there were others about us in the dusk, also strolling or gathered in clusters, sharing their hopes and fears.

I felt as if insulated from reality . . . all my vision was a whirlpool of ecstatic color, all my sensation an artesian stream of delight flowing through my fingertips held in the bend of the colonel's arm.

I remember he said, "The evening's glow is kind to us, concealing the aura of joy in which we move."

Later, I realized this aura was not as invisible as we thought. And the boatswain was not a secretive fellow. Even on that sweet evening, the tongues of envy and sanctimony were forming the phrases, "illicit love . . . public scandal . . . Colonel Potter's paramour." Pharisaic whisperings that were magnified with repetition until they reached across time and space—across the Republic of Texas—across the years ahead.

(Surmise and Scandal were ever hearty collaborators, Tricky, and once these hounds are at your heels, there is no shaking them off. They follow with intent to wound and devour. If you choose not to be a docile prey, you can fight and tame them, and have respite from their pursuit now and then. These intangibles have a longevity beyond mortal span. They may come to lie on your grave and howl their maledictions to your memory, or worse still transfer their evil allegiance to a loved one among the living.

"Colonel Potter's paramour." It may be a phrase that will meet your eye on ancient court record or reach your ear through some unpredictable historical coincidence. With my story in your heart, you can further tame the hounds, perhaps even change their nature altogether until they can no longer be Surmise and Scandal. They will have become Adventure and Romance.)

Colonel Potter found the situation in Galveston Harbor even better than he had anticipated. The two naval vessels *Independence* and *Brutus* were on hand to make a gallant display of sails and Texas colors in recognition of the *Flash* and its distinguished passenger, the Secretary of the Navy. The Steamboat *Cayuga* was also in the harbor, and three merchant schooners lying nearby off Point Bolivar were loading refugee families. Then the appearance of the *Invincible* with a captive ship—the American brig *Pocket*—caused hope and jubilation to run high in Galveston Bay. The *Pocket* was a legitimate war prize since it was loaded with cargo for Santa Anna, purchased in New Orleans by his agent. Also, it carried crew members that were commissioned in the Mexican Navy, strategic maps for the Mexican campaign, and was intended for transport of Mexican troops upon their triumphant arrival at the coast.

I suppose there were celebrations on all the ships that night as there was aboard the *Flash*. But since Captain Jeremiah Brown of the *Invincible* brought both his reports and some choice wines to Secretary Potter, our celebration was longest and loudest. I say "our" only in the sense that I was on the boat, for it was strictly a masculine jubilee. But the women were certainly not excluded from the sound of it—could not escape the shouting of toasts, the yells and cheers that followed. Jethro was busy serving the colonel. I strolled the deck for a while, Joe at my side, Ginny in my arms, feeling both elation and anxiety, sharing the colonel's high spirits, yet disturbed that Ginny was restless and hot, unable to sleep.

And the lively toasting went on and on . . .

"To *The Texas Navy!* Wherever she goes—defense of her country —dread of her foes!"

"To *The Invincible*—her guns and her crew! Here's to you! And to you! And to you!"

"To *Captain Jeremiah Brown!* Wearing courage like a crown! Drink it down! Drink it down!"

On and on the toasts rang out: to the Republic of Texas, to its heroes known and unknown, to its cabinet members, one by one, its resources, large and small, its future, full of bigs, bests, and greats.

Virginia settled into quietness on my shoulder at last, but her body burned against me in feverish heat. I took her to the cabin and sat watching her as she slept. Her cheeks were very pink and her body wet with perspiration. I was deeply worried.

There was a gentle knock at my door. It was the colonel and I admitted him.

"When they started toasting other nations and their heroes, I slipped away," he said. "I brought this container of rare wine, a gift from Captain Brown's store on the *Pocket.* It's especially fine for toasting, my dear, since it was destined for Santa Anna's discriminating palate. I came to toast my fair lady and to suggest that she raise a glass to her new home."

"My new home?"

"Aboard the *Pocket.* I'm happy about the prize ship for many reasons—not the least of them that I can provide better for your safety and comfort. I'm moving you there. The other ladies will be moved too."

"That's kind of you, Colonel, very kind. Is there a doctor on the *Pocket?*"

"Why, some sort of ship's physician, I think. Is someone ill?"

"Ginny. She's feverish. I'm worried about her."

He went to the bunk where Ginny lay, touched her hot face in a gesture of affection and concern, hastened to reassure me.

"Probably some simple child's complaint. I've ordered the crew of the *Pocket* detained and something was reported about a physician from New Orleans among them. We'll command his services early tomorrow."

Just to know a doctor was available comforted me. "Oh, thank you for your blessed goodness to us, Colonel. You deserve all the good fortune that your approaching victory can bring you," I told him.

His reply was a soft inquiry, "Don't you think 'Colonel' rather a formal way to address me now?"

"It would not seem respectful to address you otherwise," I said.

"I like respect, my dear. But after holding you in my arms——"
his voice took on its bewitching quality, "any tender word or phrase
would rest so sweetly on my ears. My friends call me 'Rob.' My
beloved could make endless affectionate elaboration——"

"I am your friend—Rob—you know that. For always I'm your
friend! But I'm not—I mean I can't be—your——"

"Hush. I'll not allow you to say you're not my own, my ever-
beloved."

Virginia stirred and muttered. I stooped and soothed her brow.

Rob opened the bottle he had brought and poured wine into a
cup. I looked up and studied his countenance to see if the evening's
flow of spirits had altered him in any way, for his manner and speech
were natural enough. The spell of the grape, whether blatant or
subtle, usually leaves its mark. Was it in the witchery of his lips, so
oddly shaped, full and deeply indented, now appearing more boldly
outlined and puckishly enlarged? Or was it—his eyes met mine and
the special luster of them flashed out at me like a black blaze—yes, it
was in the eyes, always so bright, but not full of such dazzle and
glitter. And his words matched his eyes.

"I shall never give you up. You are to think—to know—that you
are mine. I will have you. It will be managed somehow—soon—
respectably. Don't fret. Just love me—be my love. I'll manage the
rest."

I didn't answer. I closed my eyes.

His voice changed to quiet solicitude. "Here take the cup and drink.
You are much too weary."

I took a sip and returned the cup to him.

"I am determined to have my little ceremonial," he said. "I'll
drink where your lips touched, love's seal on our avowal." He finished
what he had poured.

I had avowed nothing, but I didn't protest. He handed me the
bottle.

"A love potion for my beloved," he said. "Let its rarity and deep
flavor symbolize our attachment. And I could wish that each drop
symbolized you in my arms—to fulfillment."

"Thanks, Rob, for the wine—and the wishes," I said, accepting
the bottle, and turning away from him to put it carefully aside.

I sensed his disappointment, his displeasure almost to anger. My concern for Virginia was a barrier to his love-making, and I dreaded the attempts he would make to break through it. It was a feeling hard to explain—I loved him, but if he compelled my ardor, my motherhood would be shamed. He stepped nearer to me. I held my breath and my body tensed. But I tingled so at the expectancy of his touch that I was shamed already.

Then without touching me, he turned to the bedside where Virginia lay. He leaned over, kissed her tenderly on the cheek, picked up her hand and held it for a moment.

"Good night, my loves," he said, and without looking at me, quickly left the room.

The keenness of his perception, the beauty of his gesture, stunned me. I had been braced for the effects of wine and desire and I had been given the perfect tribute of understanding love.

I knelt beside Ginny and wept. I kissed her cheek as he had, kissed the hand he had held—and the tears I shed were tears of happiness that the love of Robert Potter had come my way.

11.

Aboard the *Pocket,* my own turmoil matched the agitations of war all around me. I had no thought or energy for living the roles of anxious refugee, deserted wife, or woman in love. I was simply a mother in despair.

Colonel Potter was much occupied serving the government at Harrisburg. He used the *Flash* to freight supplies from the *Pocket* to New Washington for delivery to President Burnet. The government did not want to flee to Galveston Island until they were certain that Santa Anna's penetration could really be accomplished.

The young physician to whom I turned with Ginny's illness was no comfort and little help to me. He had been engaged to attend the Mexican officers expected aboard the brig with Santa Anna's arrival. His cynicism, his vague diagnosis and limited medication, served only to alarm and anger me as Ginny's condition grew steadily worse.

I could finally restrain myself no longer. "Are you really a doctor," I asked, "or some charlatan in disguise?"

"Madam, it is my misfortune to be without disguise and my even greater misfortune to be aboard this cursed vessel."

"Do you know nothing of children's ailments?"

"I know about them, yes, but know very little to do about what I know. After all, it was expected that my services might be needed for bullet and sword wounds. I have an excellent reputation for digging out lead, binding up gashes, and removing a useless limb neatly and quickly."

"Don't you care that my child may be dying!"

"What good my caring when there is nothing I can do?"

"You know more than you're telling me! You believe my child is going to die! You're being so hateful because you're so helpless and useless!" I accused.

"How discerning you are, madam. For that you deserve the whole truth." His manner changed. The bitter tone was gone from his voice. He spoke with weary quietness. "War does not agree with children. Your baby has been subjected to exposure, to hunger, to fright, making her easier prey to illness. Her vitality is extremely low and fast burning out. For the comfort of your heart and my conscience, I venture to surmise that she is not in pain, and——," he sighed, "that she will not survive the night."

Our eyes met and I saw that he was as desolate in his inadequacy as I was in my loss. He turned around a time or two in aimless movement, glanced at Ginny, and then like a man with vision impaired bumped against several objects before making a stumbling exit.

I sat looking at Ginny where she lay so limp, breathing so lightly, no longer responsive to word or touch. I had the impulse to grab her up and run about over the ship asking everyone to tell me what to do for my child. I wanted to scream, "She's dying! Help me! Help me!" But reason told my heart that no one could help me. The doctor was right in the diagnosis I had forced from him. But he was wrong about the cause. Not war. Solomon Page. He had brought us to Texas. He had deserted us in the wilderness. Those weeks of hunger had robbed this tender child of strength to survive illness. With this realization, my hatred of Solomon returned with a great violent surge that almost smothered me. How I longed to accuse him, berate him, burn him with bitter reproaches! He should be dead—not this wee lamb—not this sweet innocent with the clinging arms and pretty ways.

My hate reverie was interrupted by a knock at the door. It was Colonel Potter.

"Oh, Rob, Rob! Ginny's dying," I cried, rushing into his arms.

He tried to soothe and calm me. "You should not be alone," he said. "Where's Jethro and Joe? Where's that doctor? Some arrangement should have been made for one of the ladies to sit with you."

I told him the doctor had advised that Jethro take Joe away. Then, not being able to bear his own helplessness, he too had left. And I told him I wanted no strange women about watching me curiously as I grieved.

Then I sobbed against him, pleading that he help me. The pain of such loss so near seemed too much to bear—too big—bigger than I was, tearing at me, pulling me apart. I had thought I knew something of the proportions of grief, but this was an entirely new equation.

"I can't give up my baby, Rob. She can't be taken from me!"

"You can if you have to, Hatty." He made the assertion as if he knew exactly how I felt.

"You don't know what you're saying! You've never had a child to lose! . . . Do you know what that doctor said? Exposure! Hunger! She's dying from a father's neglect. An innocent baby—ignored—deserted—while her father gambled her life away. He's the one who should die! He's the one to be stricken if there is such a thing as God's mercy or justice!"

"Hatty—Hatty—compose yourself. I've come to tell you that Solomon Page *is* dead."

"Dead?" It is one thing to wish something vindictive—it is quite different to be faced with the reality of that wish.

"I was informed so by a man who came aboard at New Washington. It was in the Grass Fight, in San Antonio, in November."

"Grass Fight?" I mumbled, not quite able to accept or comprehend.

He explained to me that the Grass Fight was an engagement that took place before Cos was routed from San Antonio.

"Some soldiers under Bowie attacked a detachment of Mexicans approaching the town with a large number of horses and mules. A scout had reported that the animals were loaded with bags full of money to pay the Mexican troops. The Texans won the skirmish but found the bags filled with grass to feed the starving military mounts in San Antonio. Grass! A grim and appropriate exit for a gambler. He fights for gold and gets grass!"

I could not speak. The tide of my feelings began an awful reversal: what had gone out as hate washed back over me as guilt. Solomon was dead—just as I had wished. He was beyond accusation—beyond responsibility. It was as if my desire for his death had actually destroyed him. My farewell to him had been a hope that the first bullet fired against him would find his heart. And he had fallen in what might have been his first battle. Now I would never know whether or not he intended to come back to us. And my feeling of guilt was accented by the love I had felt and declared for another man, aware that only Solomon's death could free me for this love.

My self-accusation mounted. Was I unworthy of this child?

Rob was saying to me, "Don't you understand, Hatty? You're free. I realize it's something you can take little comfort in at this tragic hour. But face it. The man was unworthy of you—unworthy of the two fine children you gave him. You surely feel no grief for him?"

"I do not feel grief," I said, and almost added: I feel guilt. But I wanted to avoid any justification he would put forth to comfort me. In self-condemnation I could push back the full agony of grief a little longer.

Rob held me in his arms, kissing my hair, murmuring caresses, wishing my burdens could be entirely his. I leaned against him, feeling withdrawn, unresponsive.

But he kept talking to me quietly, musically, telling me of his love, making avowals of his intent.

"We will not be parted now. You will not be away from me. I can rightfully and publicly claim you for my own from this moment forward. I will protect you. I will cherish you."

I felt comforted and relaxed against him. He held me more tightly.

"I love all of you, dear one," he declared. "All you are—all you've been—all you'll be—the children you've had—the children our love will bring."

A pang of grief, fully realized, clashed into my brain. I jerked away. "No! No! No! I want no other child! I want my Ginny!" I fell on my knees at her side, started to snatch her to me and then refrained from even touching her, for she appeared so utterly fragile, her breathing so very delicate that I knew the least disturbance might stop her faint heart altogether.

So I prayed, made all the pleas and promises that lie in a mother's breaking heart. Alternately prayed and wept. And after a while I knew Rob knelt by me. He was very still, saying no word, nor touching me.

I entreated him to pray with me. "You're a good man, Rob," I said. "You're full of kindness. Pray for me. Pray for Ginny." But there was no sound from him.

Even supplication comes to an end. Before I let my head fall on my arms in respite, I looked at Ginny and detected still the slight rise and fall of breathing. And then I glanced at Rob. He was looking out above Ginny at some point in his mind. And I was surprised at the strange mask of grief on his face. His lips were drawn in a tight line that might have been stubborn pride or bleak loss, and I knew quite well that his suffering was apart from mine, unrelated to the child by which he knelt. I was too immersed in my own sorrow to probe his. It is not an uncommon thing for a deathbed scene at hand to enliven the memory of one long past.

I closed my eyes from the face of death for a moment, or perhaps it was longer. I was next aware of Rob's touch on my shoulder.

"Harriet, my dear. Sweet Ginny is dead."

So I arose and faced death and moved about in the dark cloud as best I could, trying to be grateful for what was done, trying to hide my desire for what could not be done.

A child dead must be buried, and a mother bereft must be denied the comfort of ritual under the conditions in which we were stranded. At Colonel Potter's direction, men were sent ashore to dig a grave somewhere on the bleak and sandy desolation of Galveston Island. Others constructed the small wooden coffin and cross, crudely carving name and date that weather would soon erase—and the words "Of Such Is the Kingdom of Heaven."

Then I was taken in a boat, Joe's small cold hand in mine, the box beside us that held Ginny's stiffened form. I had done my best to make her final bed one of comfort and beauty, but all effort seemed so barren of what she deserved: no white satin for making a proper shroud for an angel—no choir for musical transport on her heavenward journey—no Mr. Cloud with the look of Christ on his face to commit the body with proper reverence and bring some spiritual wisdom to bear on the whole dreadful circumstance.

When the box was placed in the sandy hole and Jethro and another attendant were covering it, Colonel Potter said simply, "We commit you, sweet Ginny, with our love unto God's love, thy brief mortality to dust, thy immortal spirit to the celestial realm."

I said, "Jethro, Ginny loved you. Won't you say a prayer?" But his tears were flowing and choking him, and all he could say was, "Lawd—Lawd——"

My sorrow-fogged mind reached out to the only spiritual comforter I had known since coming to Texas—Mr. Cloud.

"Mr. Cloud should have been here," I said. "He would have said something about the Lord's presence. He would have quoted that scripture about the Lord being everywhere, whether you ascend up to heaven or make your bed in hell . . . My bed *is* in hell."

When I said this, I had a sudden illumination in my mind. It was as if I had been transported back into the scene with Mr. Cloud at the cabin on Austin Bayou. I could feel his hands holding mine, experience again the consolation of that long serene look from the depth of his blue eyes, hear clearly the concluding line of his quotation from the Psalmist: *"Even there shall thy hand lead, and thy right hand shall hold me."*

And I felt indeed as if the hand of God had reached out to sustain me, my mother's benediction with me still. I was in God's hands and Ginny was in His eternal Presence. My mother had entered the realm of the spirit with such confidence, could I not relinquish my little one into that same abiding faith? I was answered with a wondrous image of consolation: My mother, arms opened wide to enfold Ginny, heaven a more blissful place with the two of them together there.

"Take me away, Rob," I said. "Ginny is not here. She is in my mother's arms."

Jethro sobbed audibly.

I turned and thanked him for his love and kindness. "Don't cry, Jethro," I said. "Don't you know God is smiling, Jethro. Smiling at his beautiful new little angel."

(I have noticed how the years always bring eulogies and monuments to the heroic dead of a conflict, but no proud historic pages or tributes in bronze and marble for such as Virginia Page, innocent sacrifice to the dragon of war . . . I wonder what is the character of her resting place now? Are the sands no longer desolate? Do happy children play there and mortar their castles with her sweet dust? . . . If I could stand again on that spot that was her graveside, would I sight great spans of bridges? Would I be surrounded by the clean purposeful structures of progress and habitation? . . . Whatever of good for Texas is there, may be, after all, a more appropriate memorial than any statuary, dated and inscribed.)

Colonel Potter was right in his predictions about Santa Anna. He did not pursue Houston up the Brazos, nor turn aside to slaughter the settlers. When he reached San Felipe de Austin and found that the Texas army had moved out of his path, he felt so certain of conquest that he didn't even wait for his divided forces to gather but rushed on to Harrisburg with several hundred picked men, intent upon capturing the government itself. (He was also much concerned with a personal vengeance upon his personal enemy Lorenzo de Zavala, Vice-President of the new born Republic.) When he reached Harrisburg, however, he found the town deserted and burning. He tracked the fleeing government officials and refugee families to Morgan's Point at New Washington, arriving there just in time to see the *Flash* move out into Galveston Bay with President Burnet and more than a hundred other refugees aboard. This was a big triumph for Secretary of the Navy Potter, making possible this dramatic escape by a naval operation within sight of Santa Anna's army. President Burnet was so impressed that he made Rob "Commandant of the Post of Galveston and its Dependencies" and addressed him as "General."

Temporary quarters for the government of the Republic of Texas was set up on Galveston Island. All this new activity on the island actually made little change in my life aboard the *Pocket*, except that I saw less of Rob, engaged as he was in his multiple defense duties. As we waited for decisions and battles, Joe and I were much alone in our grief for Ginny. We saw little of Jethro since he was needed at General Potter's side. Occasionally he came aboard to deliver some message to the ship's officers concerning supplies or keeping the brig in readiness should it be needed for escape transportation. At such times, Jethro always brought some personal message to me from his general with specific remembrance of Joe. Gradually, I began to reflect more and more on the future—to dream what life would be like for Joe and me with Robert Potter. To divert Joe, and myself, I spoke of the beautiful lakeshore home we might have, the pony he would ride, the domestic animals we would acquire. In our fancy, we named the horses, the cows, the dogs, even a pet rooster—discussed their care, colors, and habits. And as we did so, I dreamed my silent dreams of being Mrs. Robert Potter, wife of General Potter, statesman, warrior, lawyer, poet. How strange it was that a woman as ordinary as I had captured his heart! How enchanting the thought that he might someday write a poem about our love.

These idle thoughts were a refuge not only from grief but also from the loneliness of my position as the woman under General Potter's protection. Captain Howes and his crew, being detained on the *Pocket*, were in a very unhappy frame of mind, and placed the whole blame for their plight on Captain Brown and Secretary Potter. In their idle state of imprisonment, I knew they spent much time denouncing the man of my dreams. I knew too that any sight of me always set off their malicious conjectures and jests. They gave me distant courtesy whenever necessary, but there was no respect in it, only fear of my protector.

As for the women, they became even more withdrawn after Ginny's death, as if in some way they blamed me for it. The only one that approached me with any degree of sympathy or friendly interest was a sprightly elderly lady who came aboard with some of the Harrisburg refugees. No doubt, she was hastily given a full briefing on the Page-Potter affair, but she was aroused more to understand than to scorn. She spoke to me very brightly and openly, and one day came to visit me in my cabin, which no other woman aboard had ever done. She had a delightful name, Mrs. Measure, and a warm forthright manner, bold but cheering. She first sympathized with me in the loss of my child and told me of similar losses she had endured as a young woman. After a while, she asked me if I understood why I was being so shunned by all the women. I told her I understood quite well.

"Then why have you made no effort to place yourself in a better light?" she inquired.

"I was condemned in their sight on my first appearance among them—by so simple a matter as being dressed differently," I said. "It is much more difficult to change an opinion from evil to good than from good to evil."

"Wisdom granted. But surely you knew that acquiring a gallant escort could not possibly improve your reputation."

I told her I had been more concerned with rescue than reputation.

"Romance emerges from rescue as naturally as a butterfly from a caterpillar," she said. "But if you had been sour-faced and plain, and his not such a princely mien, envy would have slept and gossip languished. But, oh my! Even my bones are not too old to grow warm at the blaze of your hero's charm! When he rescued us all from under the nose of that villain Santa Anna at Morgan's Point, he was knighthood in full flower. I can easily understand why a woman would exchange her reputation for his favor and feel that she had a bargain. But I do not understand your forfeit of respect and duty to husband and children. The word is out that your husband died in the Grass Fight at San Antonio and that you have shown no reverence, no grief, but continue keeping warm the bed of his successor. You are not a woman of callous character. I would vouch for that. I told them your husband was probably some worthless rambler not worth grieving for. Was I right?"

"I don't care to estimate his worth now, Mrs. Measure, either living or dead. If I pass along to you for distribution some sad tale of a no-good husband, it would not be accepted. They would only say that I am the more wicked for besmirching him to justify my attachment to another man."

"I like you, Mrs. Page, I like you. But I am an inquisitive witch, and I don't mind giving you a glimpse of my wicked curiosity. Are you really General Potter's paramour?"

I should have been furious, I suppose, but her geniality had been such a relief to me that I laughed.

"Mrs. Measure, you know quite well that I will not answer such a question. If I said 'no,' none of the women so eagerly awaiting your report would believe it for an instant. I even doubt that you would."

She herself laughed at this point.

"And if I said 'yes' they would scream in horror and say, 'The brazen hussy! She admits it!'"

She laughed again. "Dead center, my dear. But you do intend to marry the man, don't you?"

"Yes, I do."

"Has he asked you?"

"Do I appear to be a woman in pursuit of a man, Mrs. Measure?"

"No, you impress me as one who has caught and caged the prize. Do you know all about him—his past, I mean."

"I know enough."

"And I know enough to know you mean that you don't care to hear any tales that I might bear."

I didn't reply, just smiled at her.

"Well, I'll dispense with the rather sensational ones I'd like to pass along, but there is certain information I think you need. Watch out for this ship's crew—stay out of their sight, if possible. They hate General Potter. Truly, they carry a heavy grudge and nourish it constantly. They'd like nothing better than to get the news that he had been stabbed, shot, drowned, beheaded by the Mexicans or otherwise happily disposed of; they are irked not only by his authority over them but by his good fortune in having the company of a woman like you while they hunger. They have invented a card game called 'Potter's Privilege.' High man is supposed to have first chance at the 'little charmer' (that's you), in case the general should depart this world before they get into the next game."

"Thank you, Mrs. Measure. But I have no fear for General Potter, or, for myself."

"What makes you so brave, Mrs. Page?"

"Panther milk, Mrs. Measure."

She looked at me in astonishment, then broke into laughter loud enough to be heard all over the ship.

"You have outflanked me, Mrs. General. I retire." She got up to leave, still laughing. And as I thanked her for her visit, she just kept on laughing, calling out several good-bys to me through her laughter as she departed.

Even after she was out of my sight and I had closed the door, I heard the distant sounds of her mirth.

I have often wondered what she told the ladies who must have flocked to hear the account of her visit with General Potter's "paramour."

Rob was thirty-six years old when we met, ten years older than I. I was aware that I actually knew very little about his past, beyond what he had told me of his achievements in public life and a few scattered bits about his parents and other relatives. Mrs. Measure's hints about the tales she could tell did arouse my curiosity some, for I had detected in him at times a mood of burden unrelated to me or his present duties. It was most unusual, I had to admit, that a man of such charm had never married. He must have suffered some disappointment in love, some heartbreak, that had kept him a bachelor; this would only serve to make us mutually indebted for the love we now shared, I thought.

My musings had no anxiety in them until after Jethro's disturbing visit. He came to me in a most hesitant manner and without his usual message from Rob. He seemed so miserable, I was sure he brought bad news.

"Ah cum—Ah cum to tell ya—to tell ya——" he kept saying over and over without telling me anything.

"Has something happened to General Potter? Tell me!"

"No'um. I jist cum to—cum to——"

"Don't be so frightened. Tell your bad news. If I can help you in any way, Jethro——"

He turned away from me and mumbled, "Ise leavin'."

I was relieved that his news was no worse. "Oh, that is too bad,"

I said. "We'll miss you. Where is the general sending you, and when will you be back?"

"He sendin' me nowheres. Ise jist goin' and neber comin' back."

"You don't mean you're leaving the general's service? Running off?"

"Thas whut."

"But, Jethro, how can you?"

"Nobody own me. Ise free. General owe me some hire, but Ise not askin' it, so's he don' say Ise cheatin' or stealin' frum 'im effen I jist leaves."

"But that's not the way to do it, Jethro," I told him. "If you must go, tell him—be fair about it. And collect your wage—you'll probably need it."

"Ah neber wants to lay mah eyes on dat wicked man agin!"

"Jethro!" I was amazed. I wondered if Rob had lost his temper and mistreated this loyal attendant in some way. "You must remember that the general is under great strain in these critical times. He needs you. He didn't strike you, did he?"

"No'm."

"What did he say that hurt your feelings?"

"Did'n say nuthin'."

"Then what on earth has come over you?"

"Ise scaid, thas what! Da mark o' Satan's on dat man. Thas what I cum to tell ya, Miz Page. You oughta be scaid too—oughta git away frum 'im—da mark o' Satan on 'im sho'!"

Jethro's face was shiny and agonized. I stared at him, pitying his fear and ignorance, and spoke to him sternly.

"Jethro! You're mouthing a lot of foolishness. Speak sensibly. Tell me exactly what you mean."

He twisted his old hat in his hands. He moved around as if one part of his body then the other was in a dreadful cramp. He stammered. He tried to look at me and his eyes filled. Finally, he ducked his head and managed to say, "Ah heered men on dis ship talkin'—know da colonel-general way back—dey say—dey say—wicked words—lak I neber heered of—dey say—dey say——"

"Listen to me, Jethro." I began a patient explanation. "These men are General Potter's enemies. They hate him because he has caused them to lose a fortune that they expected to collect from Santa Anna.

They are the wicked ones—not General Potter. Whatever you heard was said out of their wickedness. Can't you understand that?"

He didn't answer me.

"What did they say to frighten you so?" I pressed him. "Tell me."

"Ah—ah couldn'—sech talk not fo' any lady."

"I see. Then you choose to heed the coarse guff of angered men rather than believe in the goodness and kindness of a man who has treated you well—has shown the heart and mind of a real gentleman—caring for the helpless, defending the weak, fighting for the cause of liberty and right! I am surprised at you, Jethro!" I began to plead with him. "Stay and defend the general against treachery and slander, Jethro. Help him instead of deserting him. I thought you loved and understood us all—Joe and me and the general—and Little Ginny."

I waited, but he would not answer or look at me. He moved a step or two away, but he found it hard to leave us, I knew.

Then I said, "I intend to marry the general, Jethro. You might as well know I will not tolerate even a breath of disloyalty toward him."

He accepted my declaration as one who has been condemned beyond recall. He was stricken—all huddled up, though standing. He still did not speak a word.

I wanted to comfort him. I wanted him to turn and say he had changed his mind—that he wasn't afraid of the general—that he'd made a mistake. I wanted to forgive him quickly and restore him to a happy trustful state.

Joe went over to him and tugged on his sleeve. "Don't go off, Jethro. We're gonna ride horseback together some more when we get off this old ship, ya know. 'Member you said we'd go get that big horse and ride and ride and ride. You said we'd see Indians and go to that big lake an——"

Jethro turned away from Joe as he had from me.

"You aren't really going away and leave us, are you, Jethro?" Joe pleaded.

Jethro started crying, as he had at Ginny's grave—jerked away from Joe and fled.

Joe loved Jethro. He stood quite still, uncomprehending, painfully absorbing the shock of this new loss.

12.

During those fateful April weeks of 1836, the express rider for the Texas cabinet could not locate General Houston and so had nothing to report of any land move against Santa Anna.

Rob assumed that Houston's military career was as lost as the army itself and was convinced that the whole defense of Texas depended on what would be done in Galveston Bay under his command. He and President Burnet were much in conference on possible naval strategy.

Then on April 25, four news bearers, exhausted with four days of hardship and rowing, brought their skiff alongside the schooner *Invincible* and broke the glad tidings of sudden victory for Texas—of Santa Anna's defeat and capture at a camp on the San Jacinto.

The freedom news fanned out to every vessel and group around the harbor and on the island. Commodore Hawkins fired thirteen guns from the flagship *Independence* and had a feast prepared for the half-starved hero-couriers. There was wild hurrahing and cannon salutes all over the bay.

The independence declared at Washington-on-the-Brazos was now an actuality! . . . Long live the *Republic of Texas!* Bright new nation on the map of the world! . . . Long live Sam Houston, Liberator! Heroic leader of the Texas Army!

But President Burnet did not join in these jubilations. He took offense and sulked because the messengers had come into his presence last of all, their story dulled with repetitions and so much food and drink piled on their exhaustion that all but one fell asleep as he questioned them. He notified his cabinet that they would all leave immediately on the steamboat *Yellowstone* for the San Jacinto battleground. And Rob came to bid me a hasty farewell.

"Now we are the officers of an established government," he said, "and we must hurry to the field of battle to see that proper steps are taken for the full security of our new country. We must make an example of that tyrant Santa Anna. We must not allow Houston to lord it around too long without governmental restraint. The report is that he lies wounded, but able to give orders. However, by the time we arrive, he may be unconscious, or dead and buried, and leadership problems rife."

There was in his voice a quality that let me know he hoped this would be so.

"Does this mean an end to flight—and waiting?" I asked.

"An end to flight—and only a little more waiting," he assured me. "Naval business will take me to New Orleans soon. Uniforms must be designed and ordered, more supplies procured, matters concerning the *Pocket* and its crew properly set in order with the United States. And something much more personal set in order: We'll be married. After that, a trip back to Nacogdoches, and on to the northeast region of the Republic, to the shore of our dreams in the Caddo Lake country."

"Make it happen soon!" I pleaded. "Soon! I long for a place of peace—ground under me—a home."

He took me in his arms and his flow of promises and phrases of love quieted the sorrow and anxiety in me, gave me a feeling of standing before the gates of our own lovely garden of life. The gates were ready to open to us. The rest of the waiting would be easy.

I could not explain this feeling in words, but when our lips met, he said, "You make me feel like a conqueror!"

Just as he was about to leave me, he inquired, "Where is Jethro? I want him with me."

"Jethro is gone," I said. "He ran away. He told me he was afraid of you."

"*Afraid?*"

"He heard some of the rough talk among the crew. You know how they are turned against you. I tried to reason with him, but he was too frightened to heed me."

"Did he say what the men said to scare him so?" Rob's voice took on a strange softness as if it tiptoed past some sleeping danger.

"There was some nonsense about the mark of Satan—no talk for a lady, he said. I scolded him soundly for being taken in by such treacherous slander. I pled for him not to desert you. He wouldn't answer me even—seemed completely bereft of his senses."

He pulled me close to him again, pressed my head against his shoulder and held me so that I could not possibly look into his face.

"I'm sorry to lose Jethro," he said. "I'll miss him. But I must be charitable toward his desertion. He's of a race excessively emotional and fearful. In my vanity, I assumed that his devotion was stronger than it turned out to be. How grateful I am for your defense of me! Your trust!"

He held me so tight against him, I could hardly breathe, and spoke with great intensity. "I must warn you such things may happen time and again. A man who elects to be a leader, to serve the people's cause in times like these, is laid open to attacks of all kinds—malicious attacks on his motives, his deeds, and even on his person."

"Be careful, Rob," I murmured against his neck. "Oh, promise me, you'll be careful!" He had infused me with an awareness of some dreadful threat to his very life. I wished I had been more persistent in questioning Jethro.

He was saying to me, "Wherever I go, I'll get back to you, always. Promise me that no matter what the future holds, you'll never fear me, never seek protection elsewhere, never desert me. Promise!"

He held me back from him now so that he could read my countenance. I was startled at the deep dark glow in his eyes. It was a look of haunted tragedy, something far deeper and older than his hurt over losing Jethro. I had a new realization of how much he needed me.

I poured out my promises in a stream of love that matched all he had pledged to me. I told him I couldn't possibly fear him ever, for I loved him too much. He held my face in his hands as I said these things. I told him what a wonderful person, what a great man he was, and how fortunate my lot to be loved and protected by him. His expression gradually changed. His eyes closed in relief, and when he opened them, there was the usual reflection of restless energy and possessive affection that was such a magnet to my nature.

We clasped each other in reluctant farewell, and he strode away, reassured and confident.

There was only one point on which I was not in harmony with Rob. I had many selfish reasons for feeling most grateful to General Houston for his triumph over the Mexican Army, and in my heart was a most earnest prayer for his survival.

While Rob was gone on the *Yellowstone*, I spent some time in his cabin going over his clothes. Since Jethro's departure, he missed the attentions to his clothes that kept him so well groomed. On this particular afternoon I was mending the ruff on one of his fine white shirts, when I heard a knock on my own door, down the passageway. I had left Joe Boy asleep and didn't want him aroused. I rushed out and shushed the figure that was standing there, back to me.

"My little boy is asleep in there. What is it you want?"

He turned and faced me, a man thin and stooped, sickly-looking, face unshaven, hair untrimmed. My mind for one awful moment strove to look upon him as a stranger, refused the reality of recognition. I felt as if I had swallowed a lump of iron, making a great pain in my chest, cutting off my breath. As he advanced toward me, I stepped backward into Rob's cabin, still holding the shirt, clutching it against me now, as if for protection. The ghastly apparition followed me in, closed the door, came near enough to touch me. There was about him the fetidness of a body fatigued and unclean, protesting bad food and strong drink.

I felt sick enough to retch and held onto the side of the bunk to steady myself.

He stared at the shirt I had been mending, then his eyes roved around the cabin as if identifying General Potter's possessions and associating them with me. Finally, he spoke.

"You made out all right I see."

Yes, this was Solomon, alive and speaking to me.

"I take it you hadn't been expecting me."

I managed to answer him. "I thought you were killed in the Grass Fight."

"Who brought you the news? Potter, the Great? He should have picked a different fight for me to be killed in. Nobody was killed in the Grass Fight—nobody but Mexicans."

"Why are you here?" I asked.

"Same as the others. To get my family. The war is over. It'll be safe in the settlement now."

The tone of his voice stunned me, even more than his appearance— it was quiet, tired, lonely, nearer to humbleness and appeal than I had ever heard from him. The emaciated appearance, soiled clothes, stooped shoulders, on one once so proud and dandy, were like buckets let down into the well of my pity. But neglect, hardship, and grief had left the well very shallow.

"Where have you been?" I asked, wondering how he had come to know of my whereabouts, wondering if he and General Potter had met, wondering if his appearance in Rob's absence had been accidental or intentional.

"With Sam Houston," he answered me.

"Did you fight in the battle on the San Jacinto?"

"I was left at the camp near Harrisburg to guard the baggage trains and look after the ones too weak and sick to fight. I've been sick myself."

He was making no show of bravery. He wanted me to feel sorry for him. It angered me that he almost succeeded.

"If you were so interested in your family, where were you in December when there wasn't a Mexican soldier left in Texas to fight—when other men went home to see after their families? And later on—you weren't with the regulars or the volunteers that got caught with Travis or Fannin or you wouldn't be here. Why didn't you try to find your family then? Did you just take it for granted that we had starved to death out on Austin Bayou and you were free of us?"

"I'm not that much of a brute, Hatty. I knew you'd make out somehow. I just had to get away that's all."

"You had to follow Lady Luck's siren call and ignore your own child's hunger cry."

"I intended to come back sooner but there wasn't any way to get back. I was with the volunteers at San Antonio for a while—then I drifted on to Gonzales and joined up with Houston there. I had no mount, no weapon, hardly enough to eat. The army wasn't able to furnish anything for a while—no clothes, no ammunition, no food."

"You did stay alive though, came nowhere near starving to death?"

"A bunch of men can manage better than one alone."

"And a gambler can manage better in a bunch of men."

"I'm through with that."

"I know what you mean."

"No, you don't. I'm different now. All the gamble has been walked out of me. I want to settle. We'll be entitled to bounty land. We'll start over."

"You got me out of New Orleans with that kind of talk and left me stranded with two helpless children. I told you not to come back. I meant it."

He didn't protest, just asked, "What do you intend to do?"

In my heart, I forlornly reviewed what I had intended to do before Solomon's appearance and what I must do now.

"I'll go back to Kentucky to grandmother."

"You're leaving me?"

"You left me—six months ago!"

"I went to war. Now it's all over. I want my wife."

We studied each other through a silence weighted with needs and uncertainties.

He took a stubborn stance, hands across his chest, looking at me in a way that left no doubt of his resolve to make me his wife again.

Although my love for him was a thing dead and buried, I dreaded the appeal of his weakness, the possibility that he could arouse me to feel duty bound by a need renewed—that I might respond to a plea for forgiveness. But when he spoke it was in accusation, words that turned the lock on my compassion.

"You don't have any intention of going back to Kentucky. You're causing a scandal all over the country. You've brought disgrace on your family. People are saying that you've run off with Potter, deserted your husband. Maybe you did think I was dead. Maybe you did think he'd marry you. But he's not the marrying kind, and he's so all-important now as the President's pet general that he wouldn't be tying up with a nobody like you even if you didn't have a husband. So if you have any idea of becoming a government man's fine lady, forget it. I'll take you back, for the children's sake. The disgrace will blow over. Get your things together. There's a boat waiting to take refugees back to shore. We'll go along with the others—be out of here before the *Yellowstone* gets back."

My fury choked me. I just stared at him.

He thought my silence was an admission. It pleased him somehow to think my disgrace placed him above me, obscured his own offenses. He tried to break through my silence by smiling at me.

"Let's let bygones be bygones, Hatty."

Then he tried teasing. "I stayed away too long. A man with a woman like you can expect poachers if he goes away and leaves the gate open. Well, now I'm back, barring the gate, claiming my own, prettiest woman and kids this side of New Orleans."

My delayed response made him uneasy.

"Where are the children, Hatty? I want to see the children."

"Do you indeed?" Now I could speak and there was venom in my heart and on my tongue.

"That's the first time since they were born that I've heard you say so. You're a little late. You have no children."

"What do you mean by that?"

"Virginia's dead—buried out there on the wastes of Galveston

Island—the tender baby—hardly weaned, living for weeks on haw
berries after you rode off and left her—left her to suffer exposure—
opened death's door with your neglect! And Joe! He's alive—but
you're dead to him, and not one tear shed for you!"

Now it was his turn to be shocked speechless. But not for long. It
amazed me that his sense of paternity, so long dormant, could be so
outraged.

"You talk about my neglect! What kind of a mother are you? She
died here, didn't she, where you brought her, dragging around after
that rotten rake of a Potter!"

We were committed to battle now, exchanging wound for wound.

"You dare to denounce the man who gave your children what they
never had from you: affection, food, protection!"

"He doubtless gave you something I never did too! So you like it
better being a fancy woman than a wife, do you? Well, I'll tell you how
I feel about it then." He was leaning toward me now, almost touching
me. "I'd rather have my child dead and buried out there than living
with an adulteress for her mother!"

"And I'll tell you something, Solomon Page, I could account to my
conscience better for living in adultery with Robert Potter than for
sharing the marriage bed with you—heartless father and husband that
you are!"

His denunciations became louder and more shameful. "What they
say is true, I can see that!" he shouted. "You're taking up for him and
denying your own husband. You belong to him! I see it all over you.
He's made a common trashy woman out of you, and you like it. He's
made a fool and cuckold out of me and you don't care—you're all for
the prancing general, that's it, isn't it?"

"You're right for once. I care more for his little finger than I do for
your whole rotten body. Now get out of my sight!"

Tears of rage and self-pity rolled down his cheeks as he continued
to berate me. "I'll go back and tell everyone I see that you're living
with him—that I tried to get you to come back and you wouldn't come.
I'll tell how I found you here in his cabin, mending his shirts, so bold
in your shame that you wouldn't deny it. I'll say everywhere I go in
Texas that it's all true—that you've turned hussy to a toad!"

"Say that to General Potter if you want a sword through your
liver!" I challenged, and this silenced him—in speech but not in weep-

ing, for he began a strained sobbing and his features were grimaced with inner torture.

In this tragic finale of antagonism, across this awful chasm of insult and loss, we were at last fully united in one respect—in misery!

When he had stumbled from my presence, and his jerky gasps of distress were out of my hearing, I knew no relief from his presence. The wretched odor of him seemed to surround me, making me physically ill. And for a bitter while all man-love and man-desire seemed a hateful thing to me. Simply to be a woman was to be desolation's handmaiden.

When Rob came back aboard the *Pocket,* he was in such a state of high excitement, so keyed up over the events of the trip to the battle-field, that I delayed telling him about Solomon. For a little while he was aware of me only as an audience, so eager he was to express his true feelings on the controversies that were raging around Houston and Santa Anna.

Rob thought the Mexican general and his officers should be hanged and the other prisoners condemned to servitude for life, and he declared that the name of Robert Potter would not be affixed to any treaty entered into with Santa Anna. Houston had betrayed the brave men slaughtered at Goliad and the Alamo, he said, by dealing with Santa Anna as a government head and vanquished general. And the Secretary of the Navy was not alone in his stand. Colonel Lamar, now Secretary of War, supported him in proclaiming that Santa Anna had forsaken civilized warfare and become a murderer.

He reported also, not without satisfaction, that General Houston had been thoroughly de-heroized by the visiting officials, and President Burnet was more ready to chastise than reward him. Houston's bargaining with Santa Anna and his actions in paying the troops with money taken from the Mexicans were considered presumptuous assumption of authority. The officials felt that the money should have been turned over to the impoverished government. There had even been a proposal before the cabinet to dismiss Houston from the Army. Whether or not Rob made the proposal, I do not know, but he did say that he boldly denounced Houston and but for General Rusk's spirited defense, would have been successful in getting him ousted.

General Rusk had been placed at the head of the army because

Houston was so severely wounded, having a shattered ankle and a leg full of lead. The army doctor reported that Houston must get to New Orleans for surgery and the arrangements for this brought on a lot more controversy. He was not offered passage on the *Yellowstone*, and when he asked to be taken aboard he was refused.

I told Rob I thought this was carrying personal antagonisms too far. As the daughter of a doctor, I felt that to thwart the prompt and proper care of the sick and wounded in any way was a despicable thing. I asked him who issued such an order. He said President Burnet . . . and added that if I knew the personal derision that Houston had heaped upon both him and Burnet in the past, I would understand their lack of sympathy.

But finally, Houston had been taken aboard the *Yellowstone*—the captain of the boat had refused to sail without him; moreover, the army doctor had defied Burnet's orders and accompanied Houston aboard and for this disobedience had been dismissed from the service.

"Where is General Houston now?" I asked.

"On the way to New Orleans aboard the *Flora*."

I had seen the *Flora*—a creeping, dirty old trading schooner!

"Why Rob, his wound will be a month old by the time that old boat drags into New Orleans! That's slow death!"

"Surely you wouldn't expect me to insist that he be taken in a ship under my command after the humiliation he subjected me to before the convention?" he countered indignantly. "He openly ridiculed my proposals for a Texas Navy—said it would take more than some tubs and a bogus sailor to win this war—and other things unfit for a lady's ears. It was actually President Burnet, not I, who denied him naval transportation, but I must say, I think the President acted more in expediency than spite for defense precautions are still necessary until the news of Santa Anna's capture and his order to suspend hostilities has reached all Mexican fighting units. I'm still commandant of the Port of Galveston and must keep every ship in readiness."

The other members of the cabinet, he explained, had proceeded on to the Port of Velasco with their important prisoner. There they would set up another temporary headquarters for the purpose of executing treaties—and he could depend on Colonel Lamar to keep the Potter-Lamar viewpoint on Santa Anna bristling at the conference table.

"My war talk has wearied you." His attention shifted wholly to me.

"You look sad. Wouldn't you like to walk on the deck? You need fresh air and happier conversation, some stargazing and love planning."

I told him I preferred not to walk. I had stayed very close to my cabin since Solomon's visit, knowing that I would be more conspicuous than ever. Though many of the women had returned to shore, there was still the crew, antagonistic and curious.

"Then for a small change of scenery come to my cabin for a sip of wine. I've opened a vintage mild and comforting. Joe won't mind being alone for a little while, will you, Joe? You're almost asleep anyway. While we visit a bit you can be dreaming about that pony you'll have when we're living on land again."

Rob tucked the covers around Joe, pushed the hair off his forehead in a gesture of affection. Joe was content, and I didn't protest our leaving him. I hadn't told him about his father's visit. I didn't want him overhearing what I must say to Rob.

When we were alone, he reached to take me in his arms, but I turned away.

"Rob, Solomon Page is not dead. He came here to this boat and tried to take me away."

"I don't believe it!"

"Ask anyone on the boat, except Joe. He was asleep."

He was dead silent for a moment, and then he exploded, "That perverted coward, sneaking in here while I'm gone! Now why should he be alive? Is there no more room left in hell?"

I didn't ask him if he had deceived me in reporting Solomon's death. It didn't seem to matter.

"Did he threaten you—mistreat you in any way?"

"He threatened me with disgrace—lashed me with insult. But he didn't touch me."

"Thank God, you stood firm, Hatty. Did you even consider going?"

"No."

"My darling!" He reached for me again. I deliberately avoided his embrace and moved to one side, seating myself upon a high stool.

"Hatty! This mustn't make any difference between us. Don't you know that if he'd taken you away, I'd have followed? I'd have challenged the wretch and disposed of him properly. If only I could've surprised him here!"

I was thankful that such a meeting had been averted. I was convinced that Rob would have killed Solomon to free me. (But now, as I reflect on it, I think his threats were just the male preening.)

"I'm going on to Kentucky, Rob, just as I planned in the first place."

He didn't answer me at once. He moved restlessly about the cabin, taking one stand and then another. Then he began to talk to me.

"Hatty, much of life is made up of accepting what we don't want and losing what we do want. Haven't you noticed?"

I nodded.

"Oftentimes, we accept what we should cast off, lose what we should hold on to, simply because we lack the courage to act outside of precedent. We must conform—do what is customary—we think."

I had no comment to make.

"We want each other, you and I. We must not lose each other," he insisted. Then he startled me by shifting to quick jealous inquiry.

"You didn't, by any chance, discover that you had some love left for your roving gambler? Why are you shutting me out with this shell-covered pose? Are you brooding over some lost-love dreams of the past, beggaring our true love now?"

Rob's poetic flow was melting my resolutions all around me, and when he put his hand under my chin and made me look into his eyes, he saw there the answer he wanted, so he shifted to eager decision.

"Hatty! We'll sail to some foreign shore! Get married! Build a new life together in another part of the world. Start over!"

My heart accepted, and, for a glowing moment, I envisioned all the wonder and delight of such a romantic adventure. But the glad answer never reached my lips. I think it was the expression "start over" that disenchanted me, for this had been the betrayal phrase in my life with Solomon.

"No," I said. "We could never sail so far that I wouldn't still be a bigamist, a woman with two husbands and the absent one Joe's father."

"I would be Joe's father. He would forget he ever had any other."

"Even so sometime I'd have to remind him of the truth. I love you and Joe too much to risk the confusion and shame that could overtake us all. If you gave up your public career in Texas and that wealth of lake property you can now secure for yourself just to enter into an irregular union with me, there might come a time when you'd consider the exchange a very poor bargain."

"I could face any loss easier than giving you up."

"Time will dilute our emotional distress."

"Quite the little female philosopher, aren't you? What do you know of emotional distress? Let me tell you that time and separation can widen purgatory and deepen hell!—I know! Don't leave me, Hatty!"

"If I'm ever free, you'll find me in Kentucky waiting for you."

"In Kentucky! In Kentucky! You say that like it was just a stroll over the hill! And you've been in the Texas wilderness. You know what travel and communication are like. Uncertainties! Delays! Disasters! If we don't stay together, we'll not get together again. I feel it! I know it! I'll not let you go! You'll stay near me until I find some legal way out of this stupid snare."

"Rob, I've given up a child to death. When you've done that, you know any kind of separation is bearable if it has to be. So you'll give me up—and—after a while—you'll find another woman to love—it won't be hard." But I found it was very hard to accept what I had just said.

"Find another woman! I wasn't hunting a woman when I found you. I never wanted another woman in my life as long as I lived! And then there you stood before me in your muddy skirts, your big black eyes fixed on me—and my fortress crumbled! With you I could shut out the past! . . . The past! . . . Oh God! . . . Haven't you ever wondered why I am reduced to playing politics on this barbaric frontier when I once strolled the high halls of honor in the Congress of the United States?"

Here was the hurt I had seen arise in him before. Now he was about to expose it to me—and I realized it was some tragedy beyond anything I had ever imagined for him. His anguish struck me like something tangible. I slid off the stool and went to him. His back was turned and he was as far from me as the small space allowed.

"Do you want to talk to me about it, Rob?"

He turned and faced me, his eyes burning into mine. And I waited for his rush of words. Then he flushed red. Sweat broke out on his face. He reached for his handkerchief and turned away from me again.

"Oh, no, Hatty! God, no! Never!"

I came to him and laid my hand on his arm. "Never mind, Rob. We both have much to forget. We can't find all the answers. We can't see ahead. We simply have to trust that we're in God's hands."

He whirled to face me again.

"God's hands! Spare me any religious prattle, Hatty. I'm no infidel, but if the God of the Universe can be interested in anything as puny as man, then it must be manifest through the man himself molding his own destiny with his own hands, his own mind."

"Then with your fine mind, and strong hands you should mold a great one, Rob, alone, if necessary."

He held his hands out, palms up, fingers spread. "You think I have good hands, Hatty?"

"You know I love your hands. They're so expressive, Rob—your constant gestures—they fascinate—you use them like someone always on the stage—like an accomplished actor. And they're nimble, skillful, like a surgeon's hands, or a musician's."

He chuckled in a most unnatural way and said, "Surgeon—well, not quite. Musician—almost. I played the violin some, Hatty. You didn't know that, did you? I played until—until——"

I watched some awful memory engulf him again. He slammed the side of the wall with his open hand. "Why did you start talking about hands, Hatty? Why? Why? Go away! Leave me! I want to drink my wine alone."

I had never seen Rob like this. I felt that I was failing him. I was leaving him exposed to a misery that my love and presence could heal. Heretofore, I had been the one in distress and he the comforter. Now he was slipping down into some abyss of woe.

I rushed to him. "Please don't despair, Rob, I love you—no matter what—I love you!"

His arms were instantly around me and he was holding me tightly, frantically against him. "Say that again, Hatty! Again and again!"

So I did, repeating over and over how much I loved him.

And I did shut out the past for him—I know that—for the present became all there was for both of us. Sympathy and sorrow so weighted the demands of love that I found myself pulled over the rim of reason into a whirlpool of passion where I could no longer speak and there was no thought at all . . . only the whirling walls of sensation . . . and his voice at the center. . . .

"Mine! Mine! You're mine, Hatty, and I'll keep you!"

. . . words tugging at me, pulling me deeper . . .

"Sweet Hatty! Foolish Hatty! To think you could get away from me!"

. . . words whirling me faster, faster . . .

"You'll never get away from me! You're mine! Mine! Mine!"

. . . a possessive chant wrapping around and around and around me . . . binding my whole body into taut helplessness. "Never get away! Mine! Mine! . . . Never get away! Mine! Mine!"

My heart pounded so heavily that it seemed actually to be making an audible knocking against my chest. And then Rob's lips were no longer at my ear, his voice no longer compelling me and I came to realize that there was actual knocking at the door of the cabin. It was like a hook thrown into the tug of the whirlpool, catching me, bringing me back. I struggled against Rob, begged him to release me.

The knock was repeated, sharp, insistent, and a youthful voice announced: "A message for General Potter, please."

"Leave it and go," Rob commanded harshly.

"It is a word-of-mouth message, sir. I am to deliver it in person." The voice was polite, determined.

"Come back later," Rob ordered.

"I cannot do that, sir. A boat is waiting for me."

"I don't give a damn. Get out!"

"My instructions are not to go until I've delivered my message. It's very important, sir."

"Rob, the message may be momentous. You must receive it," I said.

In a fury, cursing softly in tone and phrase I had never heard from him before, he let me go. In hasty, angry movements, he made himself presentable, buckled on his sword like a man expecting to use it, and moved threateningly to the door. He flung it open, making no effort to conceal my presence there.

His first soft-spoken words to the messenger escaped me but his voice carried a violence that chilled me. Then their dialogue clarified.

"Who sent you, boy? Out with it!"

"A friend of Sam Houston's, sir, a close friend—something of a smithy, I am to say, and a former resident of the state of North Carolina acquainted with your record there."

"If this is impudence, I'll have you flogged!"

219

The smithy who had insulted me! I was involved in this. I moved up close to Rob.

"I am a messenger, sir. I speak only what I am told. Have I your permission to deliver my message, sir?"

"Say it."

"Exodus, twenty-first chapter, verses twenty-three, four, and five. In order to escape retaliatory justice, a man living under the eunuch's curse should be exceedingly cautious in his choice of enemies. If General Sam Houston dies on the *Flora* for want of a surgeon, there will be performed in his name a surgery of vengeance upon another."

"That's a base and cowardly threat! I'll kill you for mouthing such words at me!" He slapped the young man viciously across the cheek and drew his sword.

I flung myself between them. "No, Rob, no!" I cried. "He's only a boy doing what he's told."

The messenger fled.

Rob looked insanely mad and wild. He was trembling violently.

"Oh, Rob, are you in danger? What was that about a curse?"

"Harriet," he spoke to me with difficulty, in a hoarse voice, trying to get control of himself. "I cannot talk now. It will be better—for us both—if you go—to your room—at once. Leave me alone. Leave me, I say!"

This time I obeyed, for his request was like the command of a stranger. He closed the door behind me, and I heard the lock slide into place.

I had gone only a few steps when I knew that he was unleashing a solitary rage. He was swishing and slashing at an imaginary opponent while his voice denounced and taunted. Finally I heard the sword clash as if it had been thrown on the floor. I crept back to the door to listen, fearful that he might have harmed himself in some way. What I heard was the sound of wine bottle against glass—even alone, Rob would not be drinking from the bottle. How long he would be wrestling with this evil mood, I could not tell.

So I went back to lie very still and wide awake in the deep dark, with the feeling of violence crouching on every hand, ready to pounce . . . realizing that my escape from an actual wilderness had led me into a wilderness of another kind. And though I was no longer surrounded by wild beasts or on the brink of starvation, still I could be preyed upon by wild passions in the jungle of life and must watch for precipices along the trails of mind and sensation—a kind of danger I had never before encountered.

But in my thoughts was no actual condemnation or fear of Robert Potter, only the travail of trying to understand. I must move along the way that seemed right in the light of what I knew, but, oh, I knew so little. I wished for a Bible that I might look up the threatening verses in Exodus. I thought about the phrase, "A man living under the eunuch's curse," and I wondered how I was going to come into the full knowledge of its significance in the life of this man I loved so much and must leave so soon.

13.

Rob remained in moody seclusion on the *Pocket* while treaty matters were being resolved at Velasco. He wrote protests to President Burnet about the negotiations, restating his convictions that Santa Anna should be hanged. It did not improve his mood when he received official notice soon after May fourteenth that President Burnet and Santa Anna had entered into a final treaty agreement on that date. Colonel Lamar had refused his signature but had agreed that it was a good treaty.

The war was truly at an end, with Santa Anna pledged to remove his troops beyond the Rio Grande and never again to take up arms against the Texans. In exchange for his safe return to Mexico, he made a secret agreement with his captors to use his influence with the Mexican Congress to recognize Texas independence and set the boundary at the Rio Grande. Rob labeled this the "finale of folly." He said no man had less influence in any country than a defeated general.

His attitude toward me during this last weary week before sailing was considerate aloofness, inquiring of my needs, keeping me informed, as though I were some impersonal duty. I accepted his withdrawal with both relief and loneliness.

Just before the *Pocket* was to get under sail to New Orleans, he brought on board a companion passenger for me, a thirteen-year-old girl named Martha Moore, whose parents were sending her to Kentucky to enter school. When he placed her under my care, I knew his explanation meant acceptance of our separation.

"Martha is going to Kentucky to be with her grandmother also," he said. "Her father is a friend of mine, and I have promised him to give her safe conduct and secure proper passage for her out of New Orleans. He was much reassured to know that she could travel the whole distance in the company of an older lady. Do you mind if she shares your cabin?"

I was relieved to have this break in my gloom. I realized the arrangement was a bulwark against any temptation to cling to the love we couldn't have. He could have refused to take her aboard; but, by doing so and assigning her to my cabin and custody, he was deliberately freeing me from the bondage of his need and the danger that seemed to be following him—at the same time using the girl's presence to signify publicly our detachment. Then, too, I felt it minimized his own danger in some way and was thankful for this.

Whatever the purpose, Martha and I got along well together. Though we bore the same family name, we could not figure out any kinship, but decided to pretend we were cousins "Hatty and Matty." Her happy chatter and confidences and her fascination for my knowledge of styles, hairdos, and needlework kept me much occupied during the trip to New Orleans, softened my sadness for the child I had buried and the love I had forfeited. I saw little of Rob. He stayed in his cabin and continued to brood.

The first big news we heard on arrival in New Orleans concerned Sam Houston: his safe arrival, his widespread public acclaim, the likelihood of his recovery.

This news transformed Rob, throwing him into a mood of excited satirical comment. As he drove Martha and me out to Camp Street, where we were to stay with a friend of mine while we waited for passage up the Mississippi, he talked of the Houston affair and his own plans as though a dam of restraint had broken.

"And you thought we had 'condemned' him to the *Flora*. What we did do, apparently, was prepare him for promotion from hero to god. I can see it all—the cheering throngs meeting the boat, full of worshipful sympathy for this suffering savior, his neglected wound a plea for their further adulation, putting a special gloss on his heroism, exciting angered loyalty. The key to any kingdom is forged with sentiment, shaped by emotion, so Mr. Houston now has the key to the Republic of Texas, every tear a vote-breeder, every cheer a tribal pact. He'll be president before the year is done. Hail and beat the tom-toms!"

I was very much aware of the current of relief under his sarcasm—relief that Houston was alive and a threatened vengeance thereby removed.

"Well, that empties my bucket of political luck, and the well is too polluted right now for a refill."

"You still have your important post as Secretary of the Texas Navy," I said.

"A bubble that has burst in my face," he quipped bitterly. "I have nothing but the ugly taste of soap on my lips."

"You have a fleet to command," I protested, "and all your wonderful plans for a proud navy."

"No commands from me could be heard above the Houston hurrah. And the wonderful plans you speak of will become no more than empty gestures. I'll authorize the overhauling of the *Liberty* and *Independence*, perhaps order uniforms—give my successor something to worry about, for there are no funds to pay for such things. Then I'll be about some business of my own much more opportune."

"In Texas?"

"Of course, in Texas. And the business will be land—property— choice property—in the northeast region. Land is a foundation from which a man can build a career with dignity and tenacity. An estate is becoming to a statesman. Given land, time, clients, and causes, I'll return to the well of Texas politics to dip and drink my fill!"

He spoke as if he had never included me in his plans. Not a glance or a tone or a touch to hint of the dreams we had shared. I began to feel resentment at his self-absorption. I had accepted his reserved manner since the night of the fateful message as special consideration for me and my wishes. Now I began to wonder if he might not be dismissing our romance along with the Texas Navy. I was miserable in this thought (strange inconsistency of woman, wanting to be wanted, even though she cannot give) and did not altogether conceal it in my reply.

"I'm sure you will, Colonel Potter, and I wish you a most pleasant drinking—and may you also fish and catch your fill in the lake of Texas romance!" I turned my head from him as I spoke.

"Thank you, Mrs. Page," he spoke quite formally, but I felt that he was amused. I did not look in his direction for the rest of the ride. Martha was seated between us, another prick to my resentment. Since we must part so soon, why had he denied us this brief consolation of nearness?

At our destination, he disposed of us with the impersonal courtesy of a hack driver, and said he would return when suitable passage on an upriver steamer could be arranged.

I thought it would be so good to be in a house again, enjoying the luxury of firm footing, feather bed, and friendly woman-talk. Instead, I felt restless and caged, baffled by Rob's treatment of me, hostile to my fate. I dreaded his return and the final strain of parting at the boat, yet I was constantly looking and listening for him.

After several long days, he arrived one morning quite early, prepared to take us to the docks in a fine open carriage. He was hurried and cheerful—happy to be getting us off his hands, I thought.

He took Joe and Martha out to the carriage ahead of me, seating Joe with the driver and Martha on the far side of the back seat. When he handed me in and then took his seat close beside me, my resolution for remaining impassive to his presence evaporated in the warmth and tremor that swept over me—the same engrossment of the senses I had experienced that morning on the prairie behind him on Gadolphin. As if he were aware of this, he accented my feelings by announcing matter-of-factly that he would be escorting us to journey's end in order to have no doubt about our comfortable passage and safe arrival.

I did not want to be as happy as I was over this arrangement. It resolved nothing—only delayed parting. But oh, what a beautiful morning in June it turned out to be! My mood seemed to have tentacles that reached out and touched the teeming life of the great city around us. I felt the excitement of its growth, sensed beauty and brutality, ugliness and lofty ambition intertwined. The air was laden with odors tantalizing, stimulating, repellant: fresh flowers, coffee brewing, breads baking—hides, fruits, fish—waste putrefications of exuberant growth and commerce. Gentle morning breezes blended everything, moving veils of fog here and there, playing a tag-game of revealing and concealing. I glimpsed a drunk in the gutter, ignored by the passers-by, and soon after a flower girl with a large flat basket of colorful offerings carried pridefully on her head.

I called to the others to look at the lovely flowers, for we could gaze right out upon the contents of the basket as we passed her. At my exclamation, they all turned to look and Rob commanded the driver to stop. To my astonishment, he called the girl over to the carriage. She came with a big smile and when he gave her a small gold coin, she protested, "It is too much—then you must take them all—all you want." She extended the basket.

Rob selected a large bouquet for me and one for Martha. As he filled my arms with vivid pink flowers, his hand hidden by the bouquet closed over mine and his shoulder pressed close against me. We were together again, lost in love's rapture, no word spoken, no word needed.

Flower fragrance, clatter of vehicles, fog against the face, pulse of love in heart and hand. I closed my eyes to live the beautiful moments more intensely.

In the late morning, the steamer on which we were passengers, left New Orleans, its wheels palpitating the waters like a giant heartbeat. I looked out over the gilded waves, watching the city until it was no more than a gray streak on the distant shore. New Orleans and Texas were behind me. I would miss the turmoil and challenges of these places. Kentucky was ahead and I had no visions, no anticipation with which to greet it. I had the sensation of being cut off from the past and the future. The present was a throbbing steamboat on the great Mississippi, and a vibrant consciousness of Robert Potter still at my side.

Rob spoke no personal word to me until finally we were apart from other strollers on the deck and Martha and Joe had joined some children in a game.

I gazed into the distance, apparently unaware of the absorbed attention, the steady look, he had focused upon me.

"Hatty, you haven't forgotten, have you?" he inquired.

"Forgotten what?"

"How much I love you."

I didn't answer.

"I thought for a while that I would make it easy for you to forget. But I've changed my mind. I'm going to make it hard for you to forget —impossible for you to forget."

As we stood there, apparently in casual converse, leaning over the rail, Rob began to woo me with a flow of poetic words beyond any love-making he had ever lavished on me. The tones of his voice were like strange music, soothing and possessing, exciting and consuming. And his genius for word power brought all the sights and sounds around us into the orchestration of his lover's rhapsody. He made me feel the beloved of the elements, the female of the universe, in response to the wind that tugged at my hair and pressed my skirts against me, to the spray that kissed my hand with stinging coolness, to the warm force of the sun on my face and arms, seeking, desiring my whole body. It was a most sensual ecstasy in which I felt no guilt, only the rapture of being a woman, comprehending the wonder of female-

227

ness in all creation. His beautiful play of words kept accenting the sensations until I was leaning dizzily on the railing.

"Hush, Rob, hush," I implored. "You'll have me so giddy that I'll go overboard."

"No danger," he said. "With a navy man so close beside you, you'd simply land in his arms."

He was silent for a while and I regained my composure. Later, he had a steward bring deck chairs for us and took up his refrain of adoration while I sat with my eyes closed absorbing it like reviving rain upon the drouth of my senses. Sometimes I seemed to drift off where there was no meaning to his words, only exotic sound—then again meaning would stream in and arouse me.

"Up the river and by a stream . . . not long, my love, not long . . .

Through the woods and to the lake . . . not long, my love, not long . . .

On an island from a dream . . . not long, my love, not long .

Lovers' treasure there to take . . . not long, my love, not long . . ."

Here was meaning that reached me clearly—it nullified any kind of parting—it promised fulfillment. And I resisted such self-deception.

"Rob, are you trying to bewitch me? All love and all poetry can't change the meaning of 'not long' for us."

"Poetic pretense, Hatty. Please pretend with me—that we're going to our promised land together—to the lakeshore we dreamed about."

"No, Rob, it's too hard to stop pretending."

"But, Hatty, just imagine what it would be like . . ."

So I let him continue to weave his magic spell of lakes and love and tried to stay on the edge of it, rather than in the center, tried to be observer rather than captive to it. But that evening as we walked under the stars, after Joe and Martha and most others aboard were fast asleep, I became so completely entangled in his artful mesh of pretense that I lost all awareness of our approaching separation.

"Hatty," he instructed me, just before our good night embrace, "Your last thought before you sleep and the first when you awaken will be of my lips on yours, of my arms about you." And it was so. My mind became vestal to his fire of love.

When I awoke the next morning, Martha was calling, "Mrs. Page!

Mrs. Page! Wake up and look at the river bank. It's so strange, like a wonderland."

Rob's lips on mine . . . Rob's arms around me . . . I was waking up in a wonderland, no doubt of it!

Drowsily I complied with Martha's insistence that I take a look from the porthole. I was amazed to behold a bank of tall green willows only a few yards from the side of the boat. The river water appeared green, then red, in hue and the reflections of the trees created a bewildering fantasy of sailing among the treetops.

"We are awake, aren't we, Cousin Matty?"

Martha laughed. "I believe so, for I've been looking out for a long time while you slept. I thought the Mississippi was a big river, Cousin Hatty—big all the way."

I thought so too, but I didn't say so. And other thoughts that came crowding in must not be uttered either. I told Martha we'd dress quickly and go investigate.

When we were up on deck, appearances were even more startling. The willow banks pressed in from both shores. The current was swift and curving and sometimes on the bends, the willows would appear to reach across from shore to shore and interlace their branches. And the alternate green and red coloring of the waters was no illusion.

I hid my concern from Martha, tried to arrive at some explanation as I appeared to be engrossed in the scenery. Martha kept chattering excitedly.

"Cousin Hatty, my father told me the Mississippi was a great wide river and that I was not to be frightened if the shore seemed awfully far away sometimes and waters as deep as the ocean. He said that was why it was called the 'Father of Waters.' This doesn't look like a 'Father of Waters,' Cousin Hatty. Do you think maybe we got on the wrong boat?" There was fright in her voice.

"Colonel Potter wouldn't make a mistake like that Martha," I said, and added to myself: unless he intended to. "Don't worry, there's some explanation. Perhaps this is a side trip up some tributary for passengers or goods. We'll go ask the colonel."

We found him engaged in conversation with some other passengers. He excused himself and joined us immediately, his manner cheerful and natural, or apparently so.

"I hoped you'd be out in time to join me for morning coffee. The steward is waiting. Come along." Before any questions could be asked, he had us seated in the pleasant compartment where meals were served and was giving detailed instructions for our breakfast and the serving of coffee which he had already ordered prepared according to special blend and strength.

Now that I was facing him, I was reluctant to ask my question. Intuitively, I felt that something was wrong and that he was no more eager to make the explanation than I to ask for it.

The coffee came and I sipped it. It was very bitter, or else my thoughts gave it that flavor.

"Mrs. Page, are you well?" he inquired solicitously. "Does river travel agree with you?"

Martha burst out, "Colonel Potter, is this the Mississippi River?"

"No, Martha, this is the Red River. We came into it during the night." Bare statement of fact, no more.

"Why are we on the Red River?" I asked and took a big drink of the bitter black coffee to fortify myself.

He delayed his answer while he sipped coffee. Then he said, slowly, carefully, "This was the last boat leaving New Orleans for a while. A yellow fever epidemic is expected in the city. I thought it best to hurry you and Martha and Joe away without alarming you unduly."

"Where will this boat take us?" I asked.

"To Texas, the far eastern part."

No epidemic, my reason flashed. Abduction by deceit. Back to Texas. Into an unlawful love. Not forced . . . tricked by love witchery. Tempted to accept what I had admitted wanting. A very neat net thrown over senses by depriving me of attentions, then intoxicating me with them.

While my conceit was feasting, my will had been violated.

"If I had my choice, I would rather be in an epidemic than in Texas," I said. "When we come to Alexandria, I will get off and find someone to take Martha and me across country. I'm sure my father and hers will take care of any expenses I cannot meet. You can go on to Texas without the burden of our company."

He answered me with quiet patience. "I can understand your indignation." (And I'm sure he did—every aspect of it) "And perhaps I erred in not informing you about the boat. Believe me, I was only trying to act in your best interest—and will continue to do so. If it is your desire to make the overland trip from Alexandria, I will make the arrangements and the expense will be mine, since I took it upon myself to act in this matter without consulting you."

His ready acceptance of my plan fostered a slight compunction. He turned to Martha.

"Miss Martha, don't you fret. Your father entrusted you to my care. I think he would have wanted you out of the city, no matter which direction we went. I shall, of course, advise him of the delay and the cause of it."

"Oh, that's all right, Colonel," Martha assured him with a bright smile. "I like traveling around and I thank you for getting us away from that awful yellow fever."

I resented her childish gratitude. She liked traveling around!

We weren't just traveling around! We were already deep in wilderness country where travel was wholly man's conquest and beskirted woman a helpless follower—and every turn of the wheel was taking us farther.

The Colonel graciously accepted Martha's tribute to his protection with a remark calculated to dilute my resentment. And it did.

"Those of us who have lived through the ravages of the fever, Miss Martha, forever after want to protect those we love from it, especially the young who have no growing strength to spare."

Ginny hadn't had the strength to spare! Joe might not! And what a dreadful thing to happen to sweet Martha away from home and kin. As he very well knew, I had had yellow fever, and but for the care of Dr. Anson Jones might not have been alive.

I began to feel ashamed, to struggle less against his solicitude.

He sent Martha to bring Joe to breakfast so that he could speak to me alone.

"Your tone and your eyes have censured me, Hatty, when all I am striving for is your welfare and happiness."

"Forgive me, but perhaps we have different ideas about my welfare."

"Hatty, you made me a promise of faith and love during our tribulations aboard the *Pocket*, remember? 'Never the breath of fear or distrust between us,' you said. Do you wish to withdraw that pledge?"

How could I—when my memory was so crowded with all his kindness and attentions? I wanted to trust him and had promised to do so, so I told him that the pledge would be kept. This meant that I must believe that there really was an epidemic in New Orleans and that this journey up the Red River was not a plan for luring me away from my own intent . . . It was a relief to be so committed. Love imposes a loyalty, and kindness an obligation, that gives little residence to reason.

At the flourishing town of Alexandria, Colonel Potter went ashore to investigate travel possibilities while we remained on board. Several hours later, he returned to report that any attempt at an overland journey to Kentucky from this point would be exceedingly dangerous. He would not want us subjected to the risks and hardships involved. But he had another plan that he hoped would work out to our satisfaction. There was a family, the Turners, who wished to return to their home in Colorado, Illinois. They were willing for us to travel with them to a point safely near our destination. He would bring them aboard and all would stay on the boat until Bennet's Bluff, near the Texas line. From there one of the main overland trails to the east could be reached and followed by comfortable wagon accommodation.

The Turners, he said, carried credentials that satisfied him they were trustworthy. He explained how supplies would be taken on at the Bennet's Bluff trading post.

"I'm informed that this place is now much more than a trading post. It is being called *Shreveport* and is a thriving town where all kinds of frontier supplies are procurable. We can get wagons there and the latest information on all roads that must be traveled. Then I can see you started homeward in this more secure fashion. Do you approve of the plan?"

I gave my approval.

"You don't suspect me of inventing these delays to keep you with me?" The inquiry was a teasing one.

"I trust you—remember?"

"I'm glad you do, Hatty—very glad indeed." His eyes were dancing, his tone mischievous. I was annoyed, and the look I gave him told him so.

He suddenly became quite grave and startled me with another impulsive proposal.

"All right, Hatty. Now that I've made all these gentlemanly preparations, I'm not going to sit passively by and let you slip away from me. Let's get married now—right here on this ship—the captain will read the ceremony—we'll go right on into Texas as man and wife, make our home in this far northeast river and lake land. In a frontier country, legalities don't matter. Texas is a new nation—laws on marriage and divorce don't even exist yet. It's vast and uncharted. Brazoria and Galveston are hundreds of wilderness miles from the Caddo lakes, regions apart. Laws will be fashioned from the people's needs—severing old ties, strengthening new ones. People will make their homes before they create their courts. Men and women will be joined in honest, natural union all over the land before there's judge or churchman to pronounce them man and wife or government clerks to record it. And I'll be there, in the congress—I swear it!—framing the laws that protect, abolishing restraints that hinder personal achievement and happiness. Can't you trust me a little further? I'm no idle speeler trying to seduce you. I'm a signer of the Declaration of Independence! I'm a framer of the very Constitution of the Republic of Texas! I'm one of the builders of this new nation—entitled to mold its laws and sanctions—I want you to share my new life there. It can be such glorious adventure, Hatty—it can be everything—everything you accepted in the castle of dreams we dwelt in yesterday—the actuality of it all. Hatty, let's build that castle—really build it! Let's put substance on that dream—now, this hour, erase these false barriers, really belong to each other!"

"Yesterday you said—'not long'—you meant this—you thought you could persuade me."

"I hoped, Hatty, I hoped! As I have hoped ever since your arms were around me on Gadolphin. I would have made this same proposal if we had been sailing right on up the Mississippi. I would have made it at the threshold of your grandmother's home on the hope that you would return with me!"

"What would we tell the captain?"

"Simply that you have no husband. This is more fact than falsehood. He deserted you under conditions of criminal neglect. In all good conscience, surely you can say, 'I have no husband.' "

"I don't believe I can."

"Then you put the final denial on our love. You kill it. Solomon Page will not accommodate us by dying and sending us a special notice

of release. Don't you know wastrels live forever? He'll probably outlive me by half a century! If your mind must travel such a technical
trail of morality, I ask you, is it any worse to pretend him dead than
wish him dead?"

"I can avoid the pretense and try to avoid the wish."

"You try my patience, Hatty. I know you have the fiber for frontier
living, the zest and the grace to give it a pristine joy that I covet for
us both. I would close my heart and mind against you if I could. And
I shall try. It is quite a blow to my self-esteem to realize that though
I may sway multitudes and found republics, one small woman remains
unmoved by my pleas, unswayed by my arguments, and cold marble
to the flame of my love."

He left me abruptly, and I stood at the ship's rail, pretending for
passers-by some interest in the water, trying to hold back my tears,
but in my heart feeling that I could cry the river into a flood.

At Shreveport, four wagons, teams, tools, ammunition, and camping supplies were bought—enough to outfit the whole party including the Turners and an old man named Hezekiah George, a sort of
general attendant and hired hand for Colonel Potter. The Turners
were a family of four: the man elderly and taciturn; his wife about
half his age, stolid and humble, more like a servant than a wife; and
two boys—one a grown stepson to Mrs. Turner and the silent pattern
of his father—the other a dumpy good-natured youngster about Martha's age.

Colonel Potter managed it all with a kindly paternalism that made
everyone comfortable except me, for I was given no more attention
than Mrs. Turner or Martha. When the pleasant little caravan got
under way, Joe rode in happy privilege at the colonel's side on his own
pony, Black Hawk, a gift from Rob in fulfillment of the promise made
on the *Pocket*. Martha and I rode in the wagon driven by Hezekiah.

The plan of travel, as he announced it to us all, was that we would
travel together along the main trail between Shreveport, Louisiana,
and Nacogdoches, Texas, until we reached the Sabine River. The
point at which this river crossed the trail was supposed to be some
twenty miles inside the Texas line. He explained that he had scouted
this area upon his entrance into Texas the previous summer and had
located an excellent campsite on a stream forking out of the Sabine

only a short distance upriver from the trail crossing. This would be the point of separation. The Turners would leave him at this campsite and proceed on to Nacogdoches, where they would turn eastward on the main overland trail back into the United States and take up the long journey to Kentucky and Illinois.

The Ferry and Sodo lakes region, which he had so often described to me, lay about forty miles distant from his campsite, and since the area was comparatively unsettled except for some Indian villages around the lakes, it was his intention to use his camp near the Shreveport-Nacogdoches trail as a base of exploration until he had selected the land he wanted to claim for permanent settlement.

My second entrance into Texas was as awesomely beautiful as the first, but here was no flower-carpeted prairie—here was the forest land, dominated by lofty and fragrant pines, but nurturing also the walnut and hickory tree, the white oak and red gum, the white ash and red birch, the sweet bay and winged elm, mulberry and persimmon, all in the generous green foliage of lush Junetime, greens of every hue and pattern. Hezekiah knew the trees and would pluck leaves for my study as we brushed the branches. I had never before been aware of the vast intricacies of leaf design or how they seem to symbolize certain emotions of the human heart, concepts of mind, or qualities of spirit. It presented me with a game to fill the moment, and developed into a pastime that I pursue to this day. Every leaf is like a cleverly designed puzzle. Let your whole mind become absorbed with the involved and enchanting pattern of it, and a most amazing pattern of related thought will be released, a sort of mental peep show into creation—its universal kinship. (If I were not so old, I would not be writing things so ridiculously personal—but since the aged are expected to be as daft as children, it doesn't matter.)

When we arrived at the designated spot for parting, Colonel Potter announced with good humor, "Ladies and gentlemen. This is Potter's Creek. Be my guests. I suggest we all take our ease in this beautiful spot for a few days—hunt, fish, and rest from travel. Hezekiah will be making a trip on to Nacogdoches for the purpose of freighting in here some possessions of mine stored there. He can get latest reports on trail conditions and activities of hostile Indians as further precautions for your trip. If you proceed uninformed, you might encounter delays less pleasant than this one. Is there any need for haste, Mr. Turner?"

"None a'tall. Me and the boys'll help you raise a cabin while we're hangin' around, if yer wantin' it. Kin have it up by the time yore man pulls that hunnered miles to Nacky and back."

"That would be a great service, Mr. Turner. I do need a cabin."

Then at last he turned to me, "I hope this further delay won't inconvenience you, Mrs. Page?"

"Though my grandmother is not expecting me, I do hope to arrive during her lifetime," I retorted.

He ignored my dart and addressed Martha.

"I will have a message sent to your family from Nacogdoches as to your whereabouts and other arrangements."

"That will be fine. I like it here, Colonel Potter."

Well, the truth of the matter was, we all liked it there. The delay was easily accepted, the surroundings entirely pleasant. Hezekiah set out for Nacogdoches with a wagon and several pack animals.

The Turners made their camp up the creek and out of sight. Martha and I shared a comfortable tent, and the wagon nearby served as sleeping quarters for Rob and Joe.

The cabin was begun and a garden patch set out.

When Hezekiah returned to report that hostile tribes were preying on small caravans along some sections of the trail we were to travel, the camp accepted the information as good news. Hezekiah said the only way to make the trip was with other wagons equipped to ward off such an attack. He had left word at Nacogdoches that a messenger would be paid well to bring word to Colonel Potter when his wagon could move with an escort of some kind.

I decided to wait a reasonable time before protesting and while I waited to be as helpful as possible to Colonel Potter, to repay in some measure his generosity to Joe and me. His house was soon completed—a large one-room structure with puncheon floor and rough spacious chimney. Hezekiah made shelves, benches, and other simple furnishings to supplement what he had brought from Nacogdoches. The colonel's desk and chair, a large bed, his trunk, a box of books, and a violin, made possible a room of comfort and charm—a civilized nook in a setting of wilderness beauty.

236

Other things procured in Nacogdoches gave us a camp stock almost luxurious. There were bolts of cloth, tea and coffee, brandy and wine, flour and sugar, and a variety of garden plants and cuttings.

It was good to be working again as I had with Amy—with the earth, with animals, preparing good meat, enjoying labor and abundance—the long days never quite long enough. I enjoyed keeping the big room shining clean, made beautiful and fragrant with the wild flower bouquets that I gathered every day.

Rob insisted that Martha and I occupy the house at night. He and Joe slept in the tent, and Hezekiah made one of the wagons his bunkhouse.

The colonel sent Hezekiah out to locate any settlers in the vicinity, and several times made a few excursions himself. One time they brought back some pigs—another time a small herd of cattle, including two milch cows.

In a few short weeks, the garden was rows of hearty green, and we were like a busy contented family in an enchanted forest not subject to violence or hardship.

The paleness was tanned out of Joe's cheeks—he was no longer thin and quiet. He was Rob's noisy energetic shadow. It puzzled me that Rob seemed to need him too. He bid for and enjoyed Joe's admiration, and I detected in his attitude an element of sadness. I could have believed that he was trying to hold me through Joe, but the need between them was too mutual for that, as if son sought father and father son. Poor Rob, dear Rob, I thought—such a man as you should have a true son—many sons of his own blood—and how I wish I could give them to you!

This was one of the many things working a steady erosion in my determination to get out of Texas and away from Robert Potter. I was daily becoming more familiar with the happy life I could lead as his wife here. I occupied his room, handled and cared for his clothes and his possessions, was enthralled with his reading aloud in the evening, learned all about his weapons—the several swords, the guns, pistols, and small cannon, how to care for them and how to load and discharge all the firearms—shared his interest and affection for horses—found the attraction between us in these natural peaceful surroundings even more compelling. There was no day passed in which he didn't say, "Why must you leave me, ever, Hatty?" or, perhaps,

"Must you close the door on paradise?" And he was a master at the art of pursuit by deferred desire. He never sought a kiss or an embrace except that I desired it already and could make no pretense of denying him.

Now I understood how Mr. Merrick had felt when he fled from me. The only resistance I had left was for running.

So I approached the subject at an angle one gentle after-supper evening as we walked out to inspect the garden.

"Rob, do you suppose something happened to the messenger who was to bring the travel information you requested?"

"No message, I presume."

"Surely there must have been travelers we could have joined before now."

"The main stream of travel is now westward. Only stragglers and failures turn eastward."

"Not very flattering to Mr. Turner and his passengers . . . But what of freighters? Why couldn't we go on to Nacogdoches and catch some of these caravans—travel east in their company?"

Rob sighed. Then he said, "I've been wanting to tell you something—rather difficult—and I suppose now is the time." He sighed again. "The Turners are not going to Illinois."

"Not going at all?"

"Not at all. Mr. Turner has decided that he likes it here on the Sabine. That he will stay and settle in this vicinity."

"Oh, no, Rob!"

"Please don't sound so trapped. I can get you back to Shreveport and arrange something from there. But you'll have to be patient. There'll be more waiting, and delays not of my contriving. Things can't be done in a hurry on a frontier."

"What of Martha? It isn't right to keep her away from family and school like this. I feel an uneasy responsibility. And her family may not understand, may censure——"

"I'm not worried about Martha's family." He spoke sharply. "And certainly you shouldn't be. They entrusted her to my care. And only rank ingratitude could provoke criticism of the care I have given her."

"You have been very good to all of us," was all I could say.

"And you've been good to me." His mood softened. "We've been like a happy family—no discord or contentions—a little interlude in life filled with beauty and harmony—lacking only one thing—the release of the love between us to grow and blossom and fruit as all nature does around us . . . In the end, Hatty, there is death and decay for us as for the peach and the rose. Allowing a true love to wither is wasting one of nature's greatest endowments, it seems to me."

It seemed so to me too in that moment. I didn't trust myself to speak, and I resented the inner discipline that kept me from speaking.

"Is my company getting to bore you?"

"You know how I feel."

"I'm not sure that I do. I haven't been reassured in a long time. Walk with me by the stream."

The long summer's day was not done. Martha and Joe were engrossed in Hezekiah's whittling some trinkets they had requested. It would be pleasant by the creek, welcoming the cool of twilight—alone together—undisturbed. I walked with him a little way. He helped me over a log and we strolled on to the water's edge, hand in hand. It was a night that beckoned, invited lovers, pressing in with warm scented breath and persuasive sounds of birds calling and water rippling. Where the creek narrowed, logs had been placed across for a low footbridge. The open bank was on the far side. Rob started across.

"No, Rob, no," I protested, realizing with sudden clarity that on the other side of the creek, there would be no cautions, no concern with anything but the love feast that waited there to satisfy the cravings that beseiged me. It was as though love and reason were actual creatures to be dealt with, love strutting and beckoning from the other bank, reason clutching for a frenzied hold on this side.

Rob knew this too. He held my hand tightly.

"Are you afraid that I might propose again and this time you might not have the heart to refuse me?" he queried—"that love might at last prevail against you—that we might walk to a spot so prepared for lovers—a time so right—that for a perfect while, nothing else could exist—just the two of us completely encased in love's cocoon?"

I let go a trembling breath but made no other answer.

"Or perhaps you're thinking I might suggest some pagan ritual of love. That's about the only kind of proposal I haven't made. Would you be more yielding under the enchantment of wood and stream—

under the spell of the moon's rays? See—it's peeping through the trees now—one of summer's biggest and best."

I looked at the curve of the moon through a frame of foliage and the appeal of it was so poignant that I could not endure merely to observe it. I must become a part of it or hide from it.

I jerked my hand from Rob's and fled to the house. I looked frantically for a place to hide—away from Colonel Potter—away from the things that belonged to him, the things he handled and lived with. Across one corner of the room a blanket was hung to protect my things and Martha's—clothes on pegs and shelves. I went behind this curtain, seated myself on the floor in a little huddle, grasped my knees tightly, hid my face, and abandoned myself to misery, accepting the inner curling pain of denial that moved through my body.

When Martha came in and looked behind the curtain for her nightclothes, she cried out in fright. I muttered something about a pin I had dropped and was ashamed before myself that I had retreated to a position that was like an effort to escape from life—folding myself like the unborn. To be seeking sanctuary of the womb was certainly not a healthy state of mind.

From the doorway, I could distinguish Rob in the moonlight across the creek, seated against a tree trunk in the posture of deep thought. Martha was in bed, and I seated myself where I could watch without being seen. When he finally came in, he walked fast, and right up to the cabin, as though he considered coming in. Then he paced up and down a while, stopping now and then as if to call out, then changing his mind. Finally, he went to his tent. I gave him plenty of time to get settled for the night. And then I slipped out—down to the creek—defiantly crossed the bridge and went along the bank to a pool I knew well for bathing. I removed my clothes and stepped in. I was learning to swim, in my own way, and tried this for a while. I lay on my back floating about. I lay on the creek bed at a shallow place and let the ripples race over me. I felt the harmless pricks of water life against my body. Finally, I just sat where the water moved around me, swaying me, almost lifting me, and I clasped my knees again, but not in agony, just in a response of balance. I lifted my face to the moon, leaned with the water, until only my head was free of it, gave myself to the beauty of the night and achieved a physical serenity that left me barely enough energy to dress and return to my bed for the bliss of deep untroubled slumber.

I awoke much later than usual and then only at Martha's insistence. I was amazed to see that she had on her bonnet.

"Hezekiah is taking Joe and me fishing. We're having breakfast at the creek. Good-by."

She was almost gone before I could respond.

"Wait a minute. Where's Colonel Potter?"

"Hunting. Said he'd be back for coffee later."

Was this some sort of plot, I wondered. I hastily dressed, made fresh, strong coffee, and took care of the milk Hezekiah had left in the doorway. The day seemed full of hidden excitement. I made the bed and straightened the room with special attention. As I worked, I missed something from the room. Finally, I stood and studied the walls, and located the vacant spot: The low peg near Rob's desk, on which his violin case hung, was empty. The violin was gone! He must have taken it somewhere to practice out of our hearing. What could have happened to him, I wondered, to awaken his desire to play the instrument that had been cased and silent for so long?

This discovery accented the excitement I could not yet identify. Startled at some slight sound, I turned to face the doorway and there he stood holding a bouquet of long-stemmed bluebells. He knew full well how the beauty of these flowers stirred me—each like a fairy chalice filled with delicate ambrosial fragrance. For some reason, no greeting passed between us. We just met in the middle of the room and I took the bluebells in my arms and buried my face in them for a moment, and then our eyes locked in a long exploratory gaze before I moved to the table to arrange them. We were seated at the table sipping our coffee in an unexplained mood of high anticipation before he spoke.

"Harriet . . . I have some questions to ask you . . . about your past . . . some questions very important to our happiness. Have I your permission to do this . . . probe into certain facts about your marriage to Solomon Page?"

His courtroom gravity and courtesy awed me.

"Yes. You have my permission."

"You will answer clearly, thoughtfully, and with utmost gravity?"

Something momentous was about to happen to us! Something that hinged on my answers.

"Yes, I will."

"Was your marriage to Solomon Page a Catholic one, solemnized by a priest?"

"No. I was married at my father's home in Nashville by a clergyman."

"When did you come to Texas?"

"In the spring of 1835."

"Did you know that your marriage was not legal in Texas at that time—that the colonization law of Mexico required of its immigrant settlers that they profess Catholicism and be remarried by a priest?"

"Yes. I knew something about this. I remember my father saying that non-Catholic settlers had to be married again by the priest before they could get land."

"Then, since you knew of this requirement, were you remarried according to the law of the land?"

"Why, no. We made no application for land. We came to Texas for that. But we did nothing about it. Just mistakes, quarrels, suffering from the time we got off the boat."

"Harriet! Do you know what you've just told me?" He pounded the table with both fists, shoved back his chair and stood up, leaning over the table toward me. "Your marriage to Page was not legal, not valid in Texas without the Catholic commitment! And you're still in Texas, not in the United States!"

"But aren't things different now, Rob, with independence and all?" My pulse was racing, but I tried not to be overwhelmed with his dramatic pronouncements.

"The new machinery has not been set functioning yet. You came to Texas in 1835 before independence. Those are the laws by which your marital status can be determined, and I say by the laws of Texas that you are just as free as you would be if you never had married!"

"Does that make Joe illegitimate in Texas?"

This question startled him. I'm sure he hadn't expected it. But he found a satisfactory answer.

"No. Joe was born in the United States under its laws—if he had been born after you came to Texas, he would be."

"Laws are confusing, aren't they? They don't always make sense."

"That's the job of the legal profession—to make sense out of them. And I'm a lawyer. I say you are free. Don't you believe me?"

"Why, yes, I believe you, Rob," I heard myself say while still finding it difficult to believe. "I'm surprised, that's all."

"You know what this means, don't you? We're free to be married."

"I suppose so."

"It's not supposition! It's reality! We can belong to each other, legally. Isn't that what we've been waiting on—hoping for?"

"Yes. Yes, Rob, and the idea makes me very happy, I just can't get used to it so suddenly. When did the possibilities of this odd legal angle come to you?"

"Last night, as I sat against the tree, watching the moon—love's desperation, I suppose, at your flight from me."

"What would we do with Martha?"

"Martha is my problem, as I've said before. I'll send word to her family. They can come after her. Think about us—not about Martha!"

"How would we be married?"

"By bond—a statement properly witnessed—that's a quite valid procedure in our circumstances—judges being not yet in office, and only a few roving clergymen. I'll write out the bond myself and we'll have three signatures. Not the Turners—I doubt any of them can write. And not Hezekiah—we want the occasion to be a bit festive, not commonplace. On my last scouting excursion, I met three men in camp about twenty miles from here, map makers of civilized demeanor prospecting the country. They would welcome such a diversion—their company would be pleasant, I'm sure."

"When would you want this bond ceremony to take place, Rob?" I could tell that my questions and composure annoyed him. He wanted a complete and elated capitulation, at once.

"I'll let you decide. I could send Hezekiah with the invitation and have the witnesses here by tomorrow night, but will not impose my haste upon you."

I did not want to appear wary about accepting the happiness that now seemed so easy and right, but he was sensitive to my hesitation.

"I think you want to be alone. I'll leave you for a while, Harriet. When I come back, I want you to tell me if you'll marry me and when—tomorrow, I hope. I shall not propose to you again. I must have you or be rid of you. Both my devotion and my endurance have been put to the test."

"My mind will be made up, Rob. I promise you."

He left me at once and I sat in quiet thought, wondering why I had not snatched greedily at what I had so long desired—had not been swept up in a great wave of relief at this solution to all the difficulties and uncertainties I had been facing. Perhaps it was just that I wanted to savor the intermission of freedom—a little space of time and thought all my own—to enjoy being unbound before being bound again . . . chains of duty severed . . . shackles of love to be put on. Woman could linger happily in such an inbetweenness if—if she were not woman.

I looked at the bluebells, reached for them and buried my face in their cool delicacy a second time, and it was as if I breathed in an elation, an intoxicant that filled my mind with a dancing happiness and my limbs with a sweet ache for the fetters of connubial intimacy. Suddenly it was important that I look as beautiful as possible. I rushed to the corner and checked my skimpy wardrobe—some rather drab things made on the *Pocket* from materials Jethro had brought aboard for me at Velasco—some skirts my friend in New Orleans had given me—and one spot of gay color, a garment I had recently put together from a piece of rose cloth Rob had brought from his trunk, so bright I'm sure he intended it for an Indian trading piece.

Since my sewing supplies were so limited, it was more draped than fitted, with as little cutting and seaming as possible. I had hesitated to wear it, for when I had it on, I felt like a character in a pageant for the ancients. But this was no day for grays and browns and blacks. I quickly changed into the rose, using a girdle of the same material to adjust blousing and length. Then I spent a long time before the little hand mirror that Rob had propped on a shelf near his desk, arranging my hair in a high knot of curls with a few ringlets at the forehead. Finally, there was the matter of shoes. How I longed for a pair of pretty new shoes! At Shreveport, I had procured ankle-boots for out of doors, and this was all I had except the rather bedraggled slippers of the Runaway Scrape. I had purchased nothing in New Orleans, under the necessity of holding to what little money I had until I reached my grandmother. I sat down and pulled off the sturdy shoes and thick stockings. I still had a mended pair of white stockings for my slippers. How plain and unromantic was my grooming! Then the bluebells met my eyes and the thought came to me that plainness was as often lack of ideas as lack of materials. I ran for my precious scissors and began to snip insertion holes in the neck and shoulder lines of my dress. When I was done, I selected the choicest of the tuliplike blossoms from the bluebell bouquet, snapped the clean brittle stems at the lengths I desired and worked them into a neckfront trim, more lovely than jewels or lace. Humming to myself in happy preoccupation, I went to the mirror and fastened others in my hair. I was so pleased with my reflection that I entered into mock dialogue with it.

"Oh, so you are Mrs. Potter," I said, "Colonel Robert Potter's wife. A charming man, the colonel. It must be fascinating, being the wife of such a gentleman."

"It is wonderful indeed," the reflection admitted. "I am fortunate to be so cherished by a man of such talent and accomplishment. We love each other excessively!"

"You are a lucky woman, Mrs. Potter, a very lucky woman!"

There was a hearty laugh behind me and I turned to see Rob standing in the doorway. I flushed rosier than the dress I wore, I'm sure, so embarrassed was I to be caught barefoot reciting such nonsense to the mirror. But he was delighted.

"The colonel is a lucky man, beautiful Mrs. Potter, a very lucky man indeed! Please don't run for your slippers, Hatty. Just let me look at you in that startled Diana pose. You don't realize I suppose that you have put a new glory on the Greek chiton with that costume. I propose to a pretty little lady of the frontier, and find I have won a Grecian goddess!"

No man ever praised woman with more poetic genius than Robert Potter.

"Are goddesses capable of flesh and blood love, or will you vanish in my arms? I want to know—right now!" He came toward me, arms outstretched, and I rushed into them. I was very much flesh and blood! The crushed bluebells were a love incense between us.

"Tomorrow is not soon enough," he said.

"Not soon enough!" I echoed.

14.

The bond of our marriage was signed in the evening of September 5, 1836, first by Rob, then by me, and after us by the three witnesses Rob had selected: Joe Miller, George Davis Torents, and Paddy Roling. Rob wrote out the document himself. I do not have it to quote from but remember well the statement that we bound ourselves together as man and wife through mutual agreement and personal devotion, and in the absence of proscribed legal instrument and proper civil authority to attest same, we did declare before witnesses that it was our honest intent and purpose to consider this ceremony by bond as conferring upon us from this date forward a permanent and binding state of wedlock—that this written testimony was to stand as a valid contract of marriage.

Martha and Hezekiah were busy putting the finishing touches on a big supper while the signing and the toasting of bride and groom were in progress. The wedding supper was a lavish meal by any standard. There were six varieties of meat, fresh vegetables from the garden, mounds of butter and cheese, sweets and pastries from our limited valuable stock of sugar and flour, an abundance of wild honey, wine, and coffee, and for the men, after-dinner luxuries of brandy and tobacco.

When the table had been cleared, I came to sit in the presence of the four men and their attention and conversation was all turned in my direction. The visitors' pleasure in my company was obvious—so much so that I began to sense Rob's irritation in their reluctance to take their leave. He moved to prevent a prolonged evening visit by presenting each of them with a bottle of his choice brandy for their services while explaining that sleeping quarters had been prepared for them in the tent. Beds had been made down in the two wagons to accommodate Martha, Hezekiah, and Joe.

The men had planned an early morning departure—so they spoke their farewells, taking much more time than was necessary, being rather openly amused at the colonel's impatience with them, expressing at length their gratitude for food and drink and pleasant company and their many good wishes for our happiness.

"Infernal bores," Rob muttered, when they were out of hearing. "They should have enough sensitivity to know we want to be alone."

"They knew it quite well. But they've been lonely, and they enjoyed teasing us besides."

"They enjoyed looking at a pretty woman!"

"Thank you, sir! Now let's see if all goes well with our household."

"Your servant, Mrs. Potter." Hand in hand we strolled out into the deep dusk together and spoke our good nights to Joe and Martha and Hezekiah and returned to sit in the doorway, my head on his shoulder, his arm about my waist.

"It's hard to realize that you're mine at last, Hatty. Let the moon rise and confirm it—that we are sitting here together—on our own doorstep—surrounded by this vast serenity, with our love a priceless jewel at the center of it."

"Like a world of our own—a beautiful wonderful world to be explored together."

"Are you afraid—of anything that might be experienced—or discovered?"

"Afraid? Of what could I possibly be afraid? It's not my nature to be fearful, Rob. You know that. And your love makes me feel extra strong, extra brave!"

I snuggled against him but didn't receive the response I expected.

He tensed and said, "I wonder what those fools are up to?"

Our wedding guests were emerging from their tent and the three indistinct figures were moving toward the cabin. He had his answer when they stopped and sang out in serenade:

> Will you come to the bower I have shaded for you?
> I have decked it with roses all spangled with dew.

Rob was vastly displeased. "I don't like it, and I think I'll tell them so," he said.

I protested. " 'Will You Come to the Bower?' is rather sweet for a wedding night and they sing it very well."

> There beneath this glad bower on roses you'll rest
> While a smile lights the eyes of the girl I love best.

"I heard too much of that song in the aftermath of San Jacinto," Rob said. "It brings back the stench of dead Mexicans and some of the barbaric revelry of the undisciplined soldiery still howling it days after the battle, because they had been singing it when they made the attack."

The serenaders continued, all unaware of their offense.

248

But the roses so fair will not rival your cheek,
Nor the dew be so sweet as the vows we shall speak.

"Forget war scenes," I begged. "That's a love song for us. Whoever started singing it on the battlefield must have been in love and using the sentiment to rout his fears as well as his foes."

We shall swear 'mid the roses we never shall part,
O thou fairest of roses, thou queen of my heart.

"They're finished, Rob. Shouldn't we thank them?"
"No. They'd be encouraged to continue."
They needed no encouragement. They were enjoying themselves. They launched into a robust toast song.

Here's to the bride!
Here's to the groom!
Here's to the happy bride and groom!

Here's to the man!
Here's to the wife!
Here's to a long and happy life!

Here's to your love!
Here's to your kiss!
Here's to each night of nuptial bliss!

To daughters fair!
Sons two or three!
Here's to a happy family!

Happy bride and groom!
Love is in the bloom!
The vows are done
And the twain are one
Blending love so true
Here's to you! And you!
Happy bride and groom.

"That's nice. We should applaud," I insisted.
"If we do, they'll sing all night."
There was a pause and we thought they were done. Then we heard

the clink of bottles and knew they had only taken an intermission to drink a few of the toasts just sung.

The moon rose higher as if spotlighting our romantic scene and cuing the serenaders into an exuberant love song. It started solo, became duet, and developed into triumphant trio, carrying both singers and listeners away and away, high on the wings of love!

> Love is a bird.
> Hadn't you heard?
>
> Love puts you on wings,
> Your heart sings and sings,
> Your song soars so high
> It brushes the sky!
>
> Oh, Love is a bird.
> Hadn't you heard?
>
> It's a bluebird of promise,
> Redbird of desire,
> Love puts you on wings
> Takes you higher and higher!
>
> The canyon wren's rapture,
> The solace of dove,
> The lilt of the lark,
> A bird is your love.
>
> The yearning you have
> Is a whippoorwill's cry
> That tells you to love
> And love till you die!
>
> The way of true love
> Is a song with a thrill
> The sweet fire that burns
> In a mockingbird's trill.
>
> Oh, love is a bird.
> Hadn't you heard?
>> Love puts you on wings—the lightest of wings!
>> Your heart sings and sings—it sings and it sings!

Your song soars so high—so heavenly high!
It brushes the sky—the faraway sky!

There was a short silence on both sides when the beauty of the song was done and the joy of it seemed to linger in the air between us. Then Rob called out to them.

"If you men can survey as well as you can sing, your fortunes are made."

The one named Paddy Roling answered. "Whatever our good fortune, it cannot match yours of this day"—then added meaningfully —"and this night."

Hastily he said, "Good night, Colonel. Goodnight ma'am," and moved back toward the tent as if fearing he had spoken too boldly. The others followed him.

"Rob, it's customary to treat the serenaders."

"I have treated them to expensive brandy already."

"That was for the signing, not the singing. They should have some of the sweets I prepared. Some of the pound cake and molasses candy to take back with them."

"All right. Get it and we'll carry it out to them. I am grateful for that last song. I'll recapture it for you on the violin."

Another cup of happiness! Somehow this represented to me a triumph over the old sorrow that had plagued him so, separating him from the music of his violin.

George Torents was singing a lonely ballad about a sweetheart left behind as we approached the tent, so the men had no idea we were nearby. When he had finished singing, he remarked gloomily, "Why are men always wanderin' off without their women to places where there aren't any women?"

I was startled to hear Paddy Roling say, "That woman out there followed her man to the rough places."

Rob tightened his grip on my arm to signal that I keep still.

"She's a special kind of woman," Roling continued. "Knows how to fix things up, make a log cabin into a banquet hall."

"It takes more than a woman's touch to be able to pass out stuff like this," Joe Miller said, slapping the bottle he evidently was drinking from. "That Colonel Potter is a good provider."

"Well, she can't have it too easy," my champion Mr. Roling was insisting. "If she was out for provender, she could have it grand in the city—with her looks and ways she could be a rich man's darling and travel on plush. I still say some women have the strength and spirit to go anywhere with their men. Why, look at the Indian women—it's really wonderful the way they follow their men around and do all the work besides!"

"Yeah, it's wonderful," Miller conceded, "but who wants an Indian woman?"

"I do," said Torents.

"I want another drink," Roling said, and took it. Then he commented, "This is a stout brew. I guess the colonel knew we'd need it after looking in on his luck. Here's to the little woman out there!" His bottle gurgled again.

"Any woman!" said Torents, and there was a duet of gurgling sounds.

"All women!" said Miller making a trio of emptying bottles.

Rob took the treats from me, slipped them under the edge of the tent without being discovered, and we hurried away.

It was amusing to him to be so envied by the men in the tent. I felt a pang of sadness that they must be so lonely.

But this night was ours—ours alone—and we shut out all else—claiming all love, all moonglow—taking possession of the night as we took possession of each other.

I remember that the wind began to make music in the treetops as we went in. "Now the pines are singing," I said.

"Sweet accompaniment for nuptial surrender, my darling," he replied as he took me into his arms and on into a night of love where desire, at last released from bondage, was free to run its rhapsodical course through mind and body.

(Tricky, if the whole happiness of life or comprehension of its meaning were bound up in the exquisite demands of mating—nothing more—and if all character could be analyzed and goodness estimated by what happens on the marriage bed—or on couches of lesser prerogative, for that matter—then the whole process of living and understanding would be simplified. The gentle and articulate lover would be the strong character, faithful and true. The transport that well-matched lovers achieve in the union of their bodies would be a yardstick for all mutualities . . . and right and wrong would be as simple as desire and repulsion. But the life balance is not achieved by such a standard. The procreative force is not the only poise along the scalebeam of existence—only a small fraction of man's whole self is revealed in his execution of the mating duty nature imposes upon him. He may exhibit grace or greed. He may stalk and ravish only in hunger, or beguile and hold only in pleasure. He may not pursue at all, only offer a yearning need that woman-nature will reach for. Or, he may make pursuit such excitement of desire and capture such beauty of fulfillment that romance and reality are for a time completely unjointed. And this was the effect that Robert Potter had upon me. In the enchantment of our physical union, I thought I was being fused into the whole character and career of the man. As I now unravel the details of this romantic error, I want you to become concerned with the importance of exploring by our own good light the self-house that a man inhabits before you decide to marry him. I want you to have at marriageable age a protective judgment that I lacked when I was twenty-six years old, marrying for the second time. What I knew about Rob's inner life, before our marriage by bond, had been learned by the wavering light of his own purposes directed only to what he wanted me to see. If I had dared to light a lamp of reality and gaze boldly upon the inner man before he lighted the candle of privilege for amorous gaze upon my body during our wedding night, the echoes of the personal chaos provoked by our union would not be sounding in my deaf ears fifty-four years later.)

I awoke early the next morning in astonished delight to behold Rob standing at the foot of the bed, clad only in his trousers, playing his violin with joyous abandon, improvising, blending gay tunes and love songs that seemed to bring the world awake around our cabin —his violin calling up the glorious colors of sunrise and arousing the birds to join him in lover's exultation. He captured the "Love Is A Bird" melody of our wedding night serenade for a more personal serenade to the morning of our married life.

> Love puts you on wings,
> Your heart sings and sings,

Your song soars so high
It brushes the sky!

And for that day and through some jeweled ones thereafter my love flew high, my heart sang and sang a song that brushed the sky to its heights and horizons. It seemed to me that man and woman had not had such idyllic surroundings in which to live and love since the Garden of Eden, and I achieved a heightened sensitivity to it all. Garden crops and domestic animals commanded closer scrutiny and more intimate understanding. There were new marvels to be sensed in the shape of a leaf or the composition of a stone.

I would call to Rob to look again at the lush and lovely melons or consider the shape of an oak leaf, its suggestion of love and happiness—and couldn't he write a poem about it? I would inquire if he didn't suspect some secret consciousness of life in the very soil or hidden movement in the stone?

He would reply in affectionate amusement, "I thought I married a woman of fashion who might long for trips to the city and stylish gowns, and behold I am wedded to a naturalist . . . Why write a poem when we can live it? . . . I am no geologist, Mrs. Potter. Do not expect a statesman to instruct you in the life cycle of a stone!"

We had been married about a month when Rob proposed to make a trip to the lakes and select a site for our permanent home there. He explained to me that his purpose for settling in far northeast Texas involved more than securing choice land. In sparsely settled Red River County, he could become a man of influence as the population increased—and this would happen rapidly now that Mexican restrictions had been removed. With his legal experience he could serve the people in capacities that would soon make him a logical candidate for the Congress of the Republic. Although the first popular elections held September first had brought Sam Houston to the presidency, and he promptly appointed S. Rhoads Fisher Secretary of the Navy, Rob had no intention of remaining in obscurity.

We were agreed that I should remain at our location on Potter's Creek while he made this trip into Red River County, getting acquainted with settlers in the region as he went, and making arrangements for the construction of proper buildings at a point on the lakes where supplies could be brought in by boat from Shreveport, as these lakes were connected with the great Red River waterway.

Although I did not like this separation from Rob, I was proud of our possessions and knew that I must remain to tend crops and cattle and guard the cabin. I knew Rob would need Hezekiah on the trip and insisted that he go along. There was nothing about the place that Martha and Joe and I couldn't do.

"Won't you be fearful if I take Hezekiah with me?"

"Why should I be?" I wanted to know. "This room is strong as a fort. I have all kinds of weapons and you've taught me how to use them. Mount the cannon on the table near the door. If I'm threatened, I'll show it, and no one will dare molest me. Please take Hezekiah. You'll be able to accomplish more and can return to me sooner. You'll be safer too. I don't like to think of you traveling in the wilderness alone."

He studied me to make certain I was not pretending and then told me he had never known a woman so fearless and that he was very proud of me.

"Still I don't feel easy about leaving you," he said. "You may have Indian visitors. The Cherokee crossing isn't too far from here. The Caddoes are drifting back into Texas from Louisiana, and there are some Coushatta villages in the region, though none close by. Roving bands, moving or hunting, might wander this way."

"What of it? They're all friendly tribes, aren't they?"

"Well, at least they're seldom aggressive unless opposed, and most of them speak a little English which makes it easier to deal with them. When more settlers move in, they'll have to move on and there'll be trouble, but right now they're not being crowded."

"I can understand how they might consider us a threat," I said, "intruders on their beautiful forest lands, the hunting grounds they've been free to roam and call their own."

"Don't waste your sentiments on them. They own nothing. They've wandered around and warred among themselves for centuries. Barbarians. The land belongs to the civilized."

"Maybe they think they're the civilized ones."

"I doubt they do any thinking."

The discussion ended there. Rob agreed to take Hezekiah. I would have no help from the Turners. They had already moved on. But

Rob made arrangements with a Mr. Wells to come by every few days and give me any assistance necessary. Mr. Wells was our nearest neighbor. He had settled about six miles up the creek.

"I'll miss my sweet lady," he said, as he held me close in farewell. "I'm tempted to take you up behind me and ride away as we did on our first meeting. But we've collected these possessions that now command our attention. And Martha. Someone may come for her any day now."

"I hope not before your return. It would be lonely with you both gone. But don't worry. I won't be in the least afraid. I've known nothing but peace and happiness here in our very own Garden of Eden. No serpent. No forbidden fruit. I'll be saddened when it comes time to move away."

"My dear Harriet," he addressed me gravely and his dark eyes clouded in moody sadness, "no lovers' paradise remains long inviolate. The serpent always makes an entrance. The forbidden fruit is always there. It is outside my power or that of any other man to perpetuate happiness, you know."

"I am no innocent," I declared. "I know that. Life pours a cup of sorrow, then a cup of joy. When you've drunk deep of sorrow, happiness tastes all the sweeter. And when you've drunk deep of happiness, the next cup of sorrow doesn't taste quite so bitter."

"A right agreeable philosophy, Mrs. Potter," he said as he lifted me playfully off my feet to kiss me good-by. "Stick to it, and during my absence see that you have no careless conversations with serpents!"

His admonition was more fitting than I knew, for actually this spot that seemed such paradise was located on the very edge of a serpent's nest. Not far eastward, along the Sabine, was the old Neutral Strip, the Badlands.

I have come to know the history of that outlaws' haven—that breeding ground of nefarious activities created thirty years before I settled with Robert Potter on the fringe of it—and will set down certain factual matter concerning it in order that you may realize how close I walked along the precipice of danger in those days after Rob left me.

There had been boundary struggles involving French, Spanish, and American claims in the Sabine area for about a hundred and fifty years before the founding of the Republic of Texas. The Indians,

256

bewildered over the many intrusions and conflicts, alternated between submission, evasion, and resistance.

It was near the end of the seventeenth century when the hostility of distant monarchs first reached these woods and a country named *Texas* came into existence as a barrier province created by Spain in answer to French encroachment westward from the Mississippi. Friendly Indian tribes between the Trinity and Red rivers, mostly of the Caddo confederacy, used the word *"tejas"*—meaning friends or allies—so frequently that early Spanish explorers called them the *Tejas Indians*. Thus the land they occupied came to be called the "province of friends" . . . Tejas . . . Texas . . . where some of the most involved enmities of the frontier flourished for generations.

When the United States purchased Louisiana in 1803, century-old French and Spanish claims were still undefined and little wars continued to be waged along the great curve of the Sabine. President Jefferson thought the purchase from France should extend to the Rio Grande. The outraged Spanish contended that their boundary was east of the Sabine, although they had forsaken their East Texas missions and their province capital at Los Adaes thirty years before. In 1805, they sent General Herrera to refortify their old Presidio Adaes. The American outpost, meanwhile, was only a short distance away at Natchitoches on the Red River. General Wilkerson ordered General Herrera back across the Sabine and set up a neutral-ground barrier over which neither country would have jurisdiction: a poorly defined strip of land with a little stream between Adaes and Natchitoches—the *Arroyo Hondo*—as the eastern limit and the Sabine the western line. This makeshift agreement between two generals uncertain about what they should fight for, straightway became frontier headquarters for organized crime. Here a robber organization flourished with stations throughout the lower Mississippi Valley for passing along stolen goods, especially slaves and horses.

While I was still a child, there was a treaty negotiated (1819, I think it was) to abolish the Neutral Strip, but this treaty was not put into effect until 1832, and even then the actual boundary line was not surveyed between the United States and Mexico.

So the depredators so long nurtured by neutrality had not ceased to hound the honest and slay the innocent when Rob brought me into the area soon to be designated Shelby County and camped within the shadow of their domain. But on that bright October day in 1836 as I watched him ride away with Hezekiah at his side, I was burdened with no protective knowledge of my perilous surroundings or of his sinister past.

Again I was standing alone in a cabin doorway in a wilderness, left with two children to care for, but there was no desperation or resentment as there had been on Austin Bayou. This time I was well fortified with provisions, weapons, and a happy heart.

"The forest is a friendly place," I told Martha and Joe, trying to erase the uneasiness that seemed to envelop them after our menfolks were gone. But they would not be cheered. They must have had some instinctive awareness of Ed Creuber's approach. There was certainly nothing cheerful or friendly about Ed Crueber.

He arrived three days after Rob's departure. He rode up to the cabin in the early morning, leading two horses: one carrying a side-saddle, the other a pack animal.

When I came to the door, he gruffly inquired, "Are you that Page woman?"

"I am Mrs. Potter," I answered, angered and on guard. "The wife of Colonel Robert Potter. Who are you and what business have you here?"

He ignored my question. "Marty!" he yelled. "Marty, are you here?"

Martha moved into view behind me. "Yes, Ed, I'm here."

"Git out here where I can see you. Are you all right?"

Martha slid around me and advanced timidly toward the visitor. He dismounted and stood looking at her as if he were reluctant to admit that she was all right.

"Sure they ain't done you no harm?"

"No, Ed, no." She was pitifully frightened.

I was incensed. "Martha, who is this man?"

"My sister's husband, Ed."

"Ed who?"

"Ed Crueber."

"Mr. Crueber, will you stop acting like you've found Martha in some criminal hideout."

"I don't know a better name than that for it, Miz Page. You and Potter ought to prosper in this cutthroat country—a woman like you ought to be a big help to a badland settler. Horse stealing, nigger stealing, wife stealing, same shades of business. Is Potter gonna jine 'em or lawyer for 'em when courts come to these parts, Miz Page?"

"Address me as Mrs. Potter, you insolent bully!"

"Down our way, you're still Miz Page, that woman who run off with Potter—and down our way a decent woman is still limited to one man."

I was seized with a rigor of fury. I stood clutching my skirts, striving for control, and Martha began to weep. Pity for her stilled me and I could speak.

"If Colonel Potter were here, you would not speak to me in this abusive manner."

"If Marty wasn't here, I wouldn't bother speakin' to you a'tall. Or if I did, I wouldn't bother to clean it up so much. Well, anyway," he looked at me with bold insult, "I'm glad I got here before she was put to tendin' a bastard."

"If you are anything besides a brutish lout, and you care at all for Martha's feelings, spare her now. You've come to take her away, I suppose."

"'Deed I have. Git yer things, Marty."

Thankful for a chance to escape, Martha ran into the house and darted about in a panic of embarrassment and fear, stuffing her possessions into the two carpet bags that were her luggage.

In spite of my burning anger with Ed Crueber, I realized that he must have carried with him on his long, hard trip, the indignation and anxiety of Martha's whole family. I longed for some way to find out what kind of message Rob had sent to them, but I was too proud to inquire. He had doubtless mentioned something about Martha being in my company and referred to me as Mrs. Page. At the same time, Solomon and the refugee women from the *Flash* and the *Pocket* must have done a thorough job of making my name a scandal in southeast Texas. Ed Crueber's contempt was understandable and I tried to lessen the animosity between us.

"Martha and I have been as close as sisters for six months. We are fond of each other. You have no cause to be so hostile."

"I guess you ain't the kind to care about all the trouble you cause. You wouldn't think about her folks worryin' to death, not knowin' if she was dead or alive and somethin' worse maybe—while you drag her around with you learnin' yer sinful ways."

"Mr. Crueber! Martha was placed in Colonel Potter's care by her own father! I had nothing to do with the arrangement!"

"Her Pa's an ignorant man, and Potter's a smooth-tongued rakehell, but she'd a got to her school if you hadn't sidetracked the whole thing—you that was goin' to Kentucky to live with yer grandma!"

Certain that this man had talked to Solomon, I struck back.

"You must be well acquainted with Solomon Page, a certain gambling man of sterling character."

His eyes shifted in a way that let me know I had hit the mark.

"You must have a lot in common," I continued. "If you are ever in a friendly little game with him, Ed Crueber, and he should happen to be the winner, will you pass along my suggestion that he buy a tombstone to mark his daughter's grave on Galveston Island—the child he left to starve—the child that died because of his neglect. Then after that, continue your defamation of Robert Potter who fed and sheltered his children, and of me who cared for a strange young girl whom I never knew or saw until she was brought on the boat at Galveston, and I was asked to share my cabin and watch over her while I grieved for my own dead child."

Martha called out, her voice a purposeful and tearful interruption, "Mrs. Page, I can't find my blue cape!" Martha hadn't grown accustomed to calling me "Mrs. Potter."

"Miz Page," Crueber echoed tauntingly, trying to cover up the sense of guilt that must have been creeping into his mind as he thought of his games and gossip with Solomon.

I turned my back on him and rushed to Martha who was weeping so that she could not finish her packing.

"I hate Ed! I hate him!" She whispered against my neck as she clung to me and cried.

"He doesn't understand, Matty dear." I tried to comfort her. "You must go now. I'm sure your parents have been distressed about you and they'll be so happy to have you safely home. Forget about the words between your brother-in-law and me. Just remember the happy times we've had together and be sure to tell them of Colonel Potter's kindness to you."

I did not accompany Martha outside. It seemed best that I remain out of Ed Crueber's sight while he secured Martha's bags to the pack-horse and Joe sorrowfully stood nearby. It would be futile to exchange more bitter words with the man—only add to Martha's pain.

I heard her saying defiantly, "Mrs. Potter has been good to me. I will not! I like Mrs. Potter!" and calling out, "Good-by, Mrs. Potter."

I went to the door then. Crueber was riding away and Martha was lagging behind.

"Good-by, Martha, good-by," I answered, trying to sound cheerful. "Have a good trip!"

"Good-by, Martha. Come back to see us sometime!" Joe added. She waved to us and rode away weeping.

I had the impulse to sit down on the steps and weep wildly, but I didn't. I just took a deep breath and let out a long sigh.

"We're all by ourselves, Mama." Joe stated with sad matter-of-factness.

"Yes, we are."

"I wish Ginger was here, don't you?"

This startled me. It was the first time Joe had mentioned his sister in a long, long time. The other times we had been left alone, after Solomon's departure, and after Amy had been taken away, Virginia had been with us.

I admitted that I too felt especially lonely for her. I suggested that we go out to the melon patch and pull out every weed. The melons were looking very nice. They'd soon be ripe.

Hand in hand, we went to the garden.

As we worked, Joe asked me, "Mama, when will Colonel be back?"

"I don't know, Joe. He's making arrangements for a beautiful home for us by a lovely lake. That will take a little time, you know."

"When will Mr. Wells come to see us?"

"Soon, I imagine. Tomorrow perhaps." Joe was missing the man-company he found so satisfying.

We bent over the lush melon vines that shaded the large green melons, carefully clearing out every weed, but I couldn't banish the thoughts that Ed Crueber's accusations had conjured up. Now, for the first time, I began to realize the possible proportions of the scandal my actions had set off. In the stories about me, there would be no account of my marriage to the Colonel and how it had come about. I was simply the woman who had run away from her husband to live with another man. I hoped Father and John weren't too ashamed. Knowing Solomon, they would believe the best of me.

I pulled my bonnet low over my eyes and allowed myself the luxury of a few tears, letting them fall as I bent over, hoping Joe wouldn't notice. I pulled back a vine, and my tears splashed on a big melon.

"Don't cry, Mama," Joe said with adult composure. "We got plenty to eat. We got a cannon. And Colonel loves us."

15.

Mr. Wells was a jolly man. He came by to see us every three days and his visits became pleasant breaks in our isolation. He would bring fresh meat on every trip—a deer or a turkey—and one time a bear, thinking I might be in need of the oil. I told him I thought the big creature looked pathetically human and I hadn't the remotest idea what to do with it. So, he delighted in demonstrating the whole process of skinning, preserving the hide, trimming up the meat, and rendering out the grease, while he described the multiple uses for this valuable fat—culinary, medicinal, and tonsorial!

"There's no meat in the woods as fine as bear meat," he said. "The fat through the meat makes it juicy, not dry like venison or beef. Bear meat and wild honey with heavy sweet bread from new corn— that's a feast you don't forget! . . . And good clear bear oil is a fine drink—better'n milk—just as tasty, twice as healthy! It's good to cook in and burn in a lamp . . . And a little rectified bear oil, perfumed with this or that, how it would make that black hair of yours shine! . . . Yes, ma'am, bear oil you should never be without!"

I told him I didn't expect ever to be without it again after finding containers for the twenty-five gallons we rendered from this one bear. We even filled several deerskin bags.

Mr. Wells made a routine of checking the livestock and the wood-pile, letting Joe ride his horse, and consuming with gusto and lavish compliment the big meals I prepared for him. But he never spoke about himself or any family he might have. In the hope of finding the companionship of a woman neighbor, I inquired if he had a wife. He said he had.

"Please bring her to see me the next time you come," I eagerly invited. "I'm so lonely for woman company."

He hesitated and then began a careful explanation.

"I'm afraid my woman wouldn't be proper company for you, ma'am. She's a Mex-Indian—that is, her pa was a Mexican and her ma a Caddo. Her pa and some more of the family live with us—or, I guess it's closer to the truth to say we live with them. They settled on the land a long time ago. I drifted in. They don't speak English. Ma'am, as far as I know, you're the only white woman right around here. There's some newcomers named Slidell settled about fifteen miles from here. I was there once and can tell you how to go. To my notion, Mrs. Slidell would be mighty glad to see you, and maybe she'd be company for you too, though she hasn't got your looks and ways. She's soured, and bitter lonesome. But she's from the Southern States—speaks pretty English."

"Thank you for telling me, Mr. Wells, but fifteen miles is too far to go to hear pretty English."

He laughed, and we spoke no more of family or neighbors.

One bright afternoon, several weeks after Colonel Potter's departure, Joe rushed in to announce, "Mama, a band of Indians is coming up to the house!"

"How many, Joe?"

"A big bunch!"

"Walking?"

"Yessum."

"Any guns?"

"I didn't see any."

"Have a light ready if I need to set the cannon. We may have to frighten them when they find out we're all alone."

"Yessum."

I grabbed a pistol from Rob's desk and slipped it into a dress pocket under my apron. I checked to see that the loaded gun was propped against the door in its usual place. I stood near the door, close to the large table where the cannon was securely tied, and watched the Indians approaching. I counted them as they came toward me. Thirteen. An old man and a dozen younger ones, hardly more than boys. They carried no weapons that I could see. They eyed my garden where the ripening melons tempted and invited, their green sides glistening among the vines. They advanced to the open door as if they would all come right on inside. I motioned them back and shook my head.

"No. Do not come in."

The old Indian waved the others back and stepped forward to stand almost in the doorway, close enough to reach out and touch me.

"Tejas," he said. "Friends. See your man."

He held up a piece of paper that looked like a letter.

"My man is not here." I said. "You may hand me the paper."

When he stepped toward me, I moved back to put the table between us and he handed me the paper. The young Indians kept turning about to look at my melon patch.

The note was addressed to Colonel Robert Potter. It read: "Chief Tasha-bahat (River Wolf) had a herd of horses stolen from him. The robbery put most of the outfit on foot. I told him you were a man of law and importance and might give him some help. Don't ever say I didn't send you any clients!" It was signed "Paddy Roling."

I was relieved. I said to Tasha-bahat, "I am sorry you have lost your horses, Chief. If my man were here, he would go with you, but since he is not, you will have to go without him."

Chief Tasha-bahat looked at me as though I were a great curiosity. He made an ugly grimace, which I supposed he meant for a smile.

"You not big woman," he said.

I didn't answer him. He stared at me with a brazen scrutiny, and his big ugly smile evolved into a hoarse chuckle.

"You act brave like big woman."

I gave him a level look and still did not comment.

He pointed at the cannon. "What for?"

"To kill anyone who pesters me," I answered promptly.

Chief Tasha-bahat laughed, big and loud, and spoke one word that sounded like *kishi*.

The Indian boys, thinking their chief was settling down to a visit, turned and ran for the melon patch. I was horrified to see them trampling underfoot the vines I had tended so carefully.

"Chief River Wolf," I addressed him firmly, "if you let those young Indians get my melons, we will not be friends. Do something!" I motioned to the raiders.

He looked at me—looked at the cannon—laughed his big guttural laugh again. The sound of it was sinister, as if he meant to imply, "I'd certainly like to know what you'd do to stop them," but he resisted the temptation to find out.

"Kishi-woman," he said. And I did not know whether it was an insult or a salute of respect. Then he turned away and called out gruff orders to the boys. They left the patch with sulky reluctance, and River Wolf led them away without so much as a backward glance in my direction. I realized he had shown me great consideration in doing this, and it came to me how hungry and thirsty they must have been after their long walking. I think we parted in mutual wonderment: What would I have done if he hadn't ordered the boys away?

At supper that evening, Joe said, "Mama, if you'll let me tell Colonel about the Indians, I'll let you tell Mr. Wells when he comes tomorrow."

I told him that he could have the pleasure of telling them both and that I was very proud of the way he had stood by ready to help me.

"That old chief looked so fierce that I thought of crawling under the bed," he admitted.

"But you didn't," I pointed out, "and that's what counts."

"Why weren't you afraid, Mama?" he asked.

"I was thinking what to do next and getting mad about the melons."

Long after we had gone to bed, we continued to talk over the details of our first meeting with the Indians. Finally, Joe fell asleep and I lay awake for a while dwelling pleasantly on the thought of Rob's return. I was looking for him to return any day now and I went to sleep trying to imagine what our home on the lake would be like. I slept soundly and awoke at dawn. I was drowsy and comfortable and decided to rest a while longer. I had no more than dozed off, it seemed, when I awoke screaming, giving Joe a terrible fright.

I sat on the edge of the bed panting and rubbing my wrists.

"Nothing is really the matter, Joe Boy . . . just a dream . . . a horrible nightmare."

I got up at once, poured water into the washpan, and bathed my face and hands. But the agony of pain persisted in my wrists. I kept rubbing them and groaning.

"Are you sick, Mama?" Joe asked me.

I told him I was, a little, and went about getting breakfast for Joe. I couldn't eat and drank only a little coffee.

"Are you afraid of something, Mama?" Joe asked me, as I examined the guns and the fastenings on the door and cautioned him that he must stay close to me until Mr. Wells came.

"It's a feeling I have after my bad dream," I tried to explain. But you don't tell a child about the sick fog of horror after the terrors of a nightmare. You make a supreme effort to discredit the awful things so vividly experienced outside the world of the waking senses—you hesitate to acknowledge the premonition of danger close and real. I was given neither to nightmares nor to fear, but I could no more resist the conviction that my dream was a positive warning about which I must take positive action than I could ignore the table and the cannon before me and Joe's dependence upon me.

So I stayed close in the house until Mr. Wells arrived. His cheerful presence served to dispel the horror of my nightmare and as the details of the dream receded, I changed my mind about mentioning it. It would sound very gruesome and crazy. He'd think I was addled indeed if I admitted that I was preparing for the terror to materialize on my doorstep. I decided that since I'd gone this far on my own, I'd continue that way. Rob and Hezekiah would arrive any time. I'd be all right.

With Mr. Wells there, I felt free to work out of doors, and by noontime was refreshed and hungry. Since I'd eaten no breakfast, I piled my plate nearly as high as Mr. Wells', and we were all eating quietly when he put down his fork and spoke to me.

"Mrs. Potter, I want to ask you to help me remember something while I'm thinking of it. I brought my ax over here a week ago to grind it on that good stone Colonel Potter has in the shed out there, and I keep forgetting it. Remind me, will you, to grind it and take it home with me today? My woman don't like me to use her ax. She says if I come home one more time without mine she's going to give me hers for keeps—right between my chin and my shoulders." He laughed heartily. "She can say some funny things, that woman!"

"Oh no . . . oh no . . ." I shoved my chair back, and rushed to the doorway to look out . . . the dream so close to me again . . . the mention of the ax was like a word of black magic filling the room with horror. I stood leaning against the doorsill in dizzy sickness . . . oh, so deathly sick!

Joe and Mr. Wells rushed to me.

"What did I say wrong, Mrs. Potter? What ails you?"

"I just became ill—suddenly," I evaded.

I asked for a cup of water and Joe brought it to me. I took it and then dropped it in horror. It looked like a cup of blood!

Mr. Wells insisted that I lie down and I let him lead me to the bed. He brought brandy and I took a few sips. And then I rested a while.

I knew I must tell Mr. Wells about the dream. When I felt I could talk, I sent Joe out to fill the wash pot and build a fire around it for scrubbing water. I told him I was feeling better now and we must get the house in readiness for the colonel's return. When he was out of hearing, I spoke to Mr. Wells.

"You must try not to think me demented or hysterical. I feel this way because of a dream that I cannot put from me. In this awful vision, I see a huge black man in desperate circumstances. He is here . . . to murder me . . . and get the firearms in this house. He carries an ax with which to do this awful deed . . . He wears a frayed dirty hat, pointed in shape . . . death in a duncecap. There's madness in his eyes . . . no other expression . . . just a determined madness. I'm in the house . . . alone . . . when he appears. He fills the doorway. I reach for the gun, and he strikes out with the ax . . . to my neck . . . to sever my head. I feel the blow, but my hands are all right and my hands keep reaching for the gun. I must get the gun in my hands! The ax strikes me again and again! My hands are cut off! Still I struggle toward the gun . . . and the ax . . . comes down again . . . and again! Mr. Wells, it's so real . . . so real . . . I can hardly keep from screaming again. I woke up screaming." I began to moan with the very real agony that attacked my wrists again.

"That's too bad, Mrs. Potter," he tried to console me. "And too bad I happened to mention that ax in just that way to remind you. But don't let a dream upset you. Just a dream—that's all it was. You're getting a little jumpy being here all alone—that's all."

"But, Mr. Wells, I'm not the jumpy type. I'm not given to foolish fancies and fears. I've never known what it was like to be really afraid of anything—that is, something real that I can use wits and gumption on. But this—this stuns me. I feel stricken with it—that I must accept the warning of it or be doomed to exactly what I saw in the dream."

"Mrs. Potter, my wife's pa hollers and takes on in his sleep like the fiends got him on a fork, and nothing bad ever happens to him. He's got good health and no scars."

"I knew you'd feel that way, and I hadn't intended to tell you. But it's too much for me. If you can't believe there is such a danger to me, then just humor me in my fancied plight. Please stay here with me and Joe until Colonel Potter comes, or until the sickness of this dream leaves me. Will you do that?"

"Why, yes, Mrs. Potter, I'll stay around. I wouldn't want to leave you by yourself and sick like this." He was still refusing to attach any significance to the dream. "I'll stay tonight. I won't be missed— sometimes stay out on a hunt a day or so. If you aren't any better in the morning, I'll go home and get my wife's sister to help you out. She won't know what you say to her, but she'll know what's wrong with you. She's good with the sick."

Wearily I thought: He doesn't believe I've been warned. He thinks it's woman weakness of some kind. I don't care what he thinks as long as he stays.

I drifted off to sleep and when I awoke, I felt restored and strong. Joe and Mr. Wells seemed vastly relieved with my normalcy and when I got up to go about my scrubbing, they went out to the shed together. Joe liked to turn the grindstone.

I dipped up scrub water from the pot and set to work cleaning house. Now and then I could hear the sound of steel on grindstone. Mr. Wells was sharpening his ax.

I was down on my knees wiping the legs on the table when I heard a slight sound at the door. I looked up, and there he was! The huge, shabby, black man, filling the doorway, his look surly and threatening. The dream is upon me again, I thought. I must overcome it—hold it off—exercise my strength of mind, or lose it altogether. I shook my head in a daze, closed my eyes, caught onto the edge of the table and pulled myself to my feet. I stood facing the door and opened my eyes wide upon the world I knew was there. The Negro was still before me, and I realized his actuality, I think, only because he did not carry the ax as in my dream; he carried instead a large heavy stick. Perhaps it had been in his plan to steal an ax before coming to the door. But this was still my dream in its full horror. I stared in terrible fascination at his dirty old hat for it was the fantastic pointed headpiece of my nightmare! My heart began to pound so fast, I thought I would choke.

Mr. Wells didn't know. The grindstone was going—Joe was spinning it fast and steel was singing. My murderous intruder must have watched them go out to the shed, and then planned to kill me and seize the firearms. That way he would be equipped to slay them too if they interfered with his deadly plan. I wondered if they could hear me if I screamed. But this would invite his violence. He would not have to raise his crude club to strike me—it was already poised, held ready on his shoulder.

My eyes remained glued on his duncelike headpiece—because it was such unmistakable identification from the dream, I suppose—while my mind cried out to God for help.

Then I heard myself say (it was as if listening to myself from a distance), "How dare you come to a gentleman's house and not take your hat off!" My voice was sharp and reproving.

He was startled from his intent for a moment. He had been ready for scream or movement, not reprimand. He looked stupified, his face twisted in trying to force a meaningless smile, his hand moved as if to reach for his hat. Then his need and purpose repossessed him—he gripped the stick more firmly—madness filled his eyes.

The gun was just out of my reach and I'd have to move toward the doorway to get it. I knew I must not make that move! I had been shown the dreadful consequences much too vividly!

The small whirring sound in the shed had stopped. I realized the Negro wasn't aware of this and it dawned on me that he hadn't heard the grindstone—that he probably thought I was alone—that he couldn't hear very well. I spoke out very loud.

"You are very much mistaken if you think there are no menfolks around. I am not alone. Go find the men. They are at the shed."

A crafty look came into his face. He thought I was trying to trick him. He raised the stick, opened his mouth to speak, but before a word was out, an angry voice behind him jerked him around.

"Hey, you! Turn around here! Get away from that door before I put an ax through your back! What do you want?"

Mr. Wells was standing with his sharpened ax raised.

Down went the stick—off came the battered pointed hat.

"Hungry, boss man, dreadful hungry I is," his voice was a deep rumble. "And Ise huntin' fo' da road—got clean off the trail, I did. Wanna git me to dat Red River and boat job. Maybe you'se got some job, boss man, 'round heah I could do fo' some grub. Then I gits outta yo way."

"See that corn patch out there. The fodder's cut. Pile it up and we'll feed you," I was surprised to hear Mr. Wells say.

The Negro went out to the corn patch in a loping gait.

"That's a runaway nigger," Mr. Wells said, as soon as the man was out of hearing. "You can tell the look of them every time. When he comes back to be fed, we'll capture him. I'll take him to Nacogdoches and find out who he belongs to. If nobody claims him and offers reward, I'll sell him. A big nigger like him is worth a thousand dollars if he's worth two bits!"

"Mr. Wells, we will do nothing of the kind." The idea horrified me.

"I'll give you half of what I make, reward or sale. You're a brave little woman and we're partners in this."

"No. Mr. Wells, no. That would be wrong. It would be dangerous. You can't possibly be certain that man is a fugitive."

"I have yet to meet up with a free nigger in these parts. There's only two kinds: bought slaves, or stolen ones. He could be either one."

"Regardless of what he is, he's dangerous. If you'd looked into his eyes as I have, you'd know he could not be captured. He intended to get firearms at this house, and would have killed for them."

"But he's not armed. We could both hold a gun on him."

"He'd attack us still. We'd all be murdered unless he was killed stone dead with the first shot. Please, Mr. Wells, don't try to capture him, and don't ask me to help you."

Mr. Wells did not easily give up his plan. I pled with him.

"Let's pretend to believe his story. I'll prepare some food for him, and you can watch him while he eats, and then direct him on his way."

"What makes you think he won't come back and try to kill us all, or that he won't kill someone else to get a gun?"

"Better to risk letting him go than to invite killing or being killed."

Mr. Wells couldn't believe I really meant this. "You mean if we send him on his way, you'll be willing for me to go on home and you'll stay here alone?"

"Yes, I mean exactly that. The time he would have killed me is passed if we leave him alone. If we arouse him to defend himself in any way, he'll get possession of your ax and slay us all." I felt very certain that I spoke the truth.

"You're a peculiar woman," he said, and grudgingly let me have my way.

When it came time to feed our nightmare guest, we had made every preparation for defense should he attempt to harm us. But he made no hostile move. He wolfed the food set before him, listened carefully to Mr. Wells' directions for getting to Shreveport, thanked him humbly, and was quick to disappear on the trail eastward.

"I'm going to wait around," Mr. Wells said uneasily. "Maybe Colonel Potter will get in. I don't like this."

I went back to my housework, though I felt tired enough to have been at hard labor all day. Mr. Wells sat outside smoking, disgruntled that he had let my will prevail. It was still his notion that the Negro should have been captured or killed.

Sometime later, he jumped to his feet and listened intently. Then he came to the door and announced grimly, "I heard two pistol shots quite a piece to the east. I'm going to ride over and investigate. Your 'free' nigger has likely met up with somebody. You might be prepared to dress wounds, or a corpse, just in case."

He left me and was gone until after sundown. When he got back, he brought no dead or dying, but he had a story to tell, and he told it with a certain amount of satisfaction.

"It was Mr. Bolwear on his way to Shreveport."

"Rob knows Mr. Bolwear well. Oh, I hope he came to no harm."

Mr. Wells refused to be rushed ahead in his story and enjoyed my anxiety.

"Bolwear met up with this runaway, recognized him, knew where he belonged, ordered him home."

"He didn't obey, did he?"

"He just stood there—said nothing a'tall, waited for Bolwear to pass on by. Bolwear ordered him again and this time leveled a pistol at him to start him moving."

"Oh, why didn't he leave him alone?" I protested, already sensing the outcome. "It wasn't any of his business!"

"Mrs. Potter, ma'am," he reproved me, "a runaway is anybody's business. This wild brute leaped like a tiger at Mr. Bolwear, big enough he was to give a tussel to horse and rider both, aiming to get that pistol. The gun went off. That was the first shot I heard. It didn't hit anything, but the black got dislodged and Bolwear drew his other pistol and shot him."

"Killed him?"

"Dead by the time I got there. But he told Bolwear something before he died."

"What?" My heart thumped heavily. I knew what his answer would be.

"Said he came here to kill you and get guns—said if he had, it would've been the other way 'round. He'd have got Bolwear."

I couldn't answer for a while. Finally I said, "I'm sorry he had to be killed."

"Me too. Dead he's not worth a centavo to anybody. We could've captured him," he reminded me accusingly.

"No, Mr. Wells, I think not."

"You thought not about him being a runaway slave too, but I knew better. He was a property just like I said."

"But he died with his freedom, didn't he?"

"I guess you could say he did."

"Did you and Mr. Bolwear bury him?"

"Bury him?" He looked at me to see if I was serious. "Why, no, ma'am, we didn't. Our fingernails was a little short for grave digging. So we drug him off the trail into a holler and left him lying there with it."

"With what?"

"His freedom," he said in sour mockery.

Two days later, Rob returned. The travel had been good for him. He looked rested, vigorous, bronzed, and to me had never appeared more romantic, more the ideal of a woman's heart than during the moments of sighting and greeting after the longest separation since we had met.

His magnetic black eyes caught and held me even before his arms were around me. His kiss communicated his eagerness for the time of love the night would bring.

It put me in a happy haze of anticipation that relegated everything that had happened during his absence into unimportant background —my mind filled, my body tuned for the blissful hours just ahead.

I let Joe do most of the talking about the visit of the Indians, the slave's fate, and Martha's departure. I was relieved that the insulting details of Ed Crueber's visit had left little impression on him, and I resolved to remain silent about it myself. It would be sacrilege before this love now so potent between us to enter upon a discussion of the scandal that vicious gossip had made of it. I was content to fill my thoughts with my husband's sweet praise and pride in my actions.

"I am quite certain that I'm married to the bravest little woman in the whole Republic of Texas!" he told me. "I wish I could pin a diamond-studded medal on her lovely bosom. I wish I could take her into a grand shop and buy her any gift her heart desired."

"Your safe return is gift enough for me," I assured him.

"That statement, my dear, makes you doubly worthy of the gift I have brought," he replied and led me out of the house and around to the pens beyond the shed—and there, waiting for me, was a little gray mare of bluish sheen bearing a sidesaddle with gay blanket and fancy bridle.

"This is Sukey Blueskin, Mrs. Potter. Sukey, meet your mistress!"

Oh what a beauty! How I loved her at first sight! I began to besiege Rob with questions about her, where he got her, how he had concealed her before arrival.

"Just consider me a miracle man," he answered me, "and ask no questions. Do you think you'll like her?"

"I love her! You know I do! I can hardly wait to ride her."

"Try her now."

He assisted me to mount and then watched as we became acquainted with each other.

"Well matched," he called out.

Sukey carried me as if she was accustomed to a woman rider about my size. She was well mannered, beautifully gaited, and yet spirited and prideful.

My first horse. I longed to be off somewhere, on a long ride, a pleasure trip.

"Oh, Rob, we must go somewhere—visit somebody. Sukey Blueskin and I must get a chance to know each other better, and real soon! This is not enough—just to ride around in circles."

"We'll do just that. You deserve an outing. Let me rest a little first, then we'll take a journey somewhere together, perhaps tomorrow or the next day."

As I lay beside my husband that night, in the time of repose after love, I was wakeful with my deep content, reluctant to slip away into slumber. I could tell by Rob's breathing that he was fast asleep. He lay on his back, his arms outflung. I lay on my side, turned away from him. We touched only where my cheek lay against his hand. Though he slept, his fingers moved in a slight caress and I kissed them—a touch of adoration I had never before given him.

How expressive his hands were of his nature, I thought—so sure, so tender—hands quick of movement, eloquent in gesture—hands not large, not delicate—hands of many strengths and skills: palms broad, fingers almost stubby with a sparse coating of fine black hair on the second joints—hands seldom still and never spread out wide in relaxation, fingers in repose turning inward, nearly clinched as I felt them against my cheek.

One by one, I straightened out the fingers, brushing them with my lips and amused that they curled back into the characteristic closed position as I released them. My feeling for my husband at that moment was near to worship.

But this was to be the only night in which I ever paid him the lover's homage of reverence of the shape and worth of his hands.

The next day Rob sent Hezekiah to inquire of Mr. Wells where the Slidells lived, and from there he was to go to the Slidells with a message: Colonel Potter had just learned of their settlement in this part of the country. He sent neighborly greetings and this bottle of good Cuban wine with his compliments. He and Mrs. Potter would call around midday of the day following.

Rob decided on this visit after I had passed along Mr. Wells' comment that Mrs. Slidell and I might be company for each other. This should be just the outing I needed, he said, and an opportunity for trying out Sukey Blueskin. Also, it was his intent to make the acquaintance of every settler in the region. Although we would soon be moving forty miles away, he expected his law business and political support to extend over this area.

So, very early on the second morning after his return, we were riding side by side through the forest. Joe had been left behind with Hezekiah. It was a pleasant journeying, full of contentment in each other's company, the delights of woodland scenes, and the good gaits of our horses. Rob was riding a young red-roan stallion that he had purchased from Mr. Bolwear and named "Shakespeare," a pretty contrast to my little blueskin mare.

When I met Mrs. Slidell, I was reminded of Mr. Wells' expression "sour and bitter lonesome." It seemed extremely difficult for her to pull up the corners of her long thin mouth into a smile of greeting. But there was no doubt of her excitement and keen pleasure in having visitors. Her hands trembled and her voice was unsteady as she greeted us. Her protruding light blue eyes, set in shallow sockets, seemed about to pop from her head with the effort of saying and doing the proper things. The wrinkled face was given a young-old look by a hair style that was little-girlish and unbecoming—curl clusters behind each ear. She did speak "pretty English," as Mr. Wells had said, and indicated a background of education beyond what I had known. But I felt no envy, only pity for the beauty and happiness so plainly lost.

Mr. Slidell was a tall spare man who had very little to say beyond the necessary amenities. He was not awkward, but withdrawn, and preferred not to look directly at anyone, turning a quick glance into a faraway gaze. The few words he did speak came out in a time-consuming deliberate drawl in startling contrast to the nervous rush of words his wife turned off and on.

There were similar contrasts in the way they lived. The house was rough and sparsely furnished as if set up for temporary quarters, but three Negroes—man, woman, and boy—waited upon the Slidells and their guests as if the visit were taking place in a much grander setting. Mrs. Slidell was dressed in a blue poplin gown, very well made, but of a style about four years old. They spoke of no family, had no children to present.

The food set before us was excellent and I was enjoying the association, strange as it was. Rob did most of the talking and I was very proud of him. He seemed to consider it his social duty to put these people at ease who seemed so awed at his presence. I noticed Mrs. Slidell's hands continued to tremble as she ate, and that she would stare in fascination first at the Colonel, then at me.

Poor thing, I thought. She is much lonelier and more miserable than I've ever been—except out on Austin Bayou. I got the feeling that she hated being where she was, and I wished she didn't stare quite so steadily. It was most discomfiting after a while. I was glad Rob handled such things with so much ease.

When the meal was done, Mr. Slidell invited Rob to a game of cards and Mrs. Slidell suggested that she and I take a stroll. The house was located, as ours was, near a running stream. We walked along a clear hard path toward a small waterfall.

I had an uncomfortable feeling of being watched. I searched the woods along the opposite bank and located a boy, standing like a deer in a disguise of stillness and staring at me. Mrs. Slidell stopped, and, following my attention, located him too. Aware of our discovery, he stepped out into full view. He carried a gun as long as he was tall, and, he had evidently been on a most successful hunt, for he carried in his right hand a huge upside-down bouquet of dead squirrels. He looked exactly like Mr. Slidell half size. Why hadn't they mentioned a son? I wondered. His stare stuck to me like a big burr while he moved on down stream in a sort of sidewise saunter.

As we resumed our stroll, Mrs. Slidell, who hadn't exchanged so much as a nod with the boy, explained with bitter brevity: "Saddled with orphan kin. On my husband's side. His kid brother."

When we came to the waterfall, there was a pleasant secluded nook back from the bank, and in it a rude bench which had evidently had much use—Mrs. Slidell's private brooding bench, I surmised. A large white cat that had followed us leaped into her lap, and she began to stroke it with nervous gestures.

"Sinner and I come here often," she said, smiling her twisted drooping smile. "It is our retreat. Sinner is good company. He is an attentive listener and appreciative of my affection. Nowhere else about me do I have such an audience, such response. Mrs. Potter——" The woman was wanting desperately to say something to me that she hardly dared to say. I thought she wanted to confide some personal distress, and waited, ready to listen, and, if possible, comfort.

She made a strangling sound, and then said in a rush, "Weren't you afraid to marry that—that man?"

I was startled. "You mean Colonel Potter?"

"Yes—yes—the notorious Colonel Potter. I just can't understand how you could bear to—well, I just never could have married such a man. You seem—you seem—oh, I just don't see how you could!"

I was tempted to say: From all appearances you have done much worse. But I simply asked sharply, "Why do you say such a thing?"

In a rush, placing her shaking hand on my arm, she said, "Don't you know how he treated his first wife?"

"His first wife!" The exclamation was out before I could stop it, releasing my whole ignorance in just three words. But I could conceal my feelings, and there was plenty to conceal! Surprise—disbelief—anger—jealousy—alarm—and a stunned sense of being forced to confront something I had long hoped to avoid, and that Rob had hoped to keep from me. Well, I had had a husband before him. I would not let any facts about a previous marriage of his hurt or shock me. But I had told him of my marriage, and he had posed as a bachelor. I saw no reason for pretending otherwise to Mrs. Slidell.

"I did not know that Colonel Potter was married before," I said, looking her candidly in the eye. "He always told me he was a bachelor."

"God pity you, woman," Mrs. Slidell exclaimed, stroking Sinner more rapidly. "You're married to a criminal—an insane man!"

"Let me be the judge of that!" I felt such a fierce anger that I wanted to reach out and strike her across her big twitching mouth. "Tell me what you're so eager to tell me," I commanded.

She was frightened at my reaction and quite obviously frightened by the enormity of what she was about to reveal and the consequences to follow. She slid away from me to the very end of the bench and gulped and panted a few times before she became vocal.

"He——. It was——. I don't know how to tell you! Woman's tongue should never be soiled with such a story."

"I think yours is well adapted to it, whatever it is," I said acidly. "Get on with it."

"He cut—mutilated—he castrated two men, one of them a preacher, and his wife's cousin."

With that statement out before us, we sat in an awful silence until Mrs. Slidell could stand it no longer.

"You know what castrated means, don't you?" she inquired huskily.

"I certainly do," I told her bluntly. "Bull, steer. Stallion, gelding. Man, eunuch." As I said the word *eunuch*, memories hit me like sharp pains. The insulting man on the dark chestnut: *You're quite a cutter, aren't you, Mr. Potter?* The boy with the message to *a man living under the eunuch's curse.* Jethro, good, kind Jethro: *Da mark of Satan is on 'im.*

I was able to hide my anguish from Mrs. Slidell. "Now finish the ghastly discussion you've begun," I said to her.

She resented my composure. Her fingers tightened convulsively on Sinner, and he snarled and scratched at her. Her strokes became even and gentle again and the cat began purring and digging his claws with a rhythmical brittle sound into the stiff fabric of her blue dress.

"He was a U.S. Congressman from Granville, North Carolina, when it happened. He was married to a good woman——"

"How do you know she was good? Were you acquainted with her?"

"No, I wasn't, but folks said she was. She was religious and respected and from a good family. They had two children, a girl and a boy."

I thought: That's why he yearned over my children—cared for them so devotedly.

"The little boy was an idiot child—born so."

"How do you know?"

"That's what folks say. And some had it that Mr. Potter stirred up all the disgrace because he didn't want to claim his dim-witted son. Anyway, he accused his wife of being a whore. He said she confessed to him that she had carried on with this preacher, Louis Taylor, who was her second cousin, and with a young man named Wiley—just seventeen years old, also some family connection. So Mr. Potter went to Taylor's house, pounced on him like a wild beast, beat him insensible and operated on him. Then he went after the boy, found him in the woods near his home, tied him up and used the knife on him in the same fiendish way. He said they all confessed their guilt, but the truth of the matter is that he simply scared them crazy."

"What makes you think that? I can't imagine what manner of wife he had to say she was guilty when she wasn't—who would name her paramours when she had none."

"To pacify him. He was mad with jealous rage, threatening her in horrible ways, I'm sure."

"Pacify him! By confessing other men had defiled his marriage bed? She would be the crazy one to do such a thing!"

"He was insanely jealous, I tell you. He never claimed to have actually caught her in the act of infidelity. There'd been a revival going on and she'd been converted, or repentant, or something. Anyway, this Taylor had spent some time praying with her, the way I heard it. Mr. Potter's evil nature was aroused to place the wrong light on her actions."

"Where did this supposed prayer-session take place?"

"Why, in the home, I think it was."

"Whose home?"

"The Potters' . . . you see that was perfectly natural . . . he was kin . . ."

"Cousins marry."

"I know—but——"

"I suppose the prayers were in the bedroom—just for the convenience of kneeling by the bed."

"I've neither heard nor read all there is to know about it, and I've never set eyes on him till this day. But I can see in him some power of darkness. He can put a person under a spell—make you say or believe anything. Haven't you ever been frightened of him?"

"What nonsense! Never! Continue your ridiculous story." My attitude was bravado, but my mind was thumping: *part of this is true— true—true*.

"He was put in jail. Mobs surrounded the place and he made wild speeches through the bars."

"I'm sure he did! Why were the mobs there—to listen or to lynch?"

"That's the strange part—they were his followers. He claimed his being in jail without bail was a trick of his political enemies. He's a rabble rouser—a mob leader. They had to move him out of the county, to another jail, where he wasn't known. He got a sentence of two years in prison and a big fine. Of course, he lost his seat in congress. The North Carolina legislature granted his wife a divorce and gave his children a different name, her mother's maiden name, I think it was. His victims recovered. I mean they didn't die. It was a dreadful thing, that young man having his manhood taken, wasn't it? It would have been more merciful to have shot him . . . Where do you suppose Mr. Potter learned to perform an operation like that? He must have planned it all carefully—studied up for it."

I had heard enough. I started to get up. She hastened on.

"That wasn't all. He wrote things while he was imprisoned—got them published—tried to justify his vile crimes. The legislature passed a new law just to fit his crime—such a thing had never been heard of before—at least, not in North Carolina. So he got off light. But such an infamous crime will be punished hereafter in that state by hanging without benefit of clergy. It was a pity he was let loose. No telling what he'll do, left free to mix among people."

"Possibly as long as I remain faithful to him, he'll be harmless," I said, but my irony was lost on Mrs. Slidell.

"Now that I've seen him, looked into those black electric eyes of his, heard the magic of his voice that makes you listen for more and more, I understand how he got such a hold over the people of Granville, filled their ears with his beautiful lies and compelled them to vote for him after he got out of jail."

Re-elected after he got out of jail! I was ready to hear more! "You mean he ran for public office in his home town after his offense?"

"I mean he ran for the state assembly and got elected! Straight from the jailhouse to the legislature! To become a member of the very body that had enacted a law making his crime punishable by death!"

"Then he could not have been altogether in the wrong—not such a monster as you seem to think."

"I think any man who commits such an act, whatever the provocation, is a monster, his nature lower than animal, his mind deranged!"

I tried to protest, but she rushed on.

"He didn't last long in the assembly. He got in a fight over a card game. His fellow members expelled him on the grounds that his personal character was degrading to the body. It was after that he came to Texas. It was a wonder that he got out of the state alive. His wife's brother fired at him once in court and missed. Men hate him, and you can understand why."

"Do the women vote in North Carolina?" I asked.

"Certainly not!"

"Then it must have been the men who returned him to public office," I pointed out.

"They were bewitched by the words he wrote and spoke. He has a godly gift of words but puts them to Satan's uses. He had been elected to the assembly twice before he went to congress. If his unnatural deeds hadn't exposed his true nature, he might have gone on and deluded voters into electing him president of the United States some day. Then I suppose he would have made eunuchs out of his political as well as his personal enemies—made the act of *potterizing* legal and fashionable."

"Made what legal?"

"*Potterizing*. It's a new word, coined in North Carolina—the modern synonym for castration." Mrs. Slidell was pleased with this intellectual twist to her narration.

I sat very still and quiet for a bit—just thinking.

Mrs. Slidell shifted uncertainly, finally stood up. "We better get back to the house. I told Mr. Slidell he ought not to invite Colonel

Potter into a game of cards, considering his temper and all, no telling what might happen. My husband is a good player. If Mr. Potter should be losing——"

The fuse on my fury had burned short by this time and I exploded, "Mr. Slidell might be getting 'potterized!' By all means, let us hurry!"

I jumped up and went past her up the trail, but my indignation burned so that I had to turn on her with another blast.

"On second thought, Mrs. Slidell, from observing your husband's appearance and disposition, I feel inclined to ask, are you sure he hasn't already been?"

Her prominent eyes stood out so far, I thought surely they must slide down upon her face, and the wide mouth seemed stretched from ear to ear in a thin tight line of rage.

We did not exchange another word until the murmured inconsequential farewells in the presence of the men a short while later. I took Rob's arm as we walked from the house to the horses, spoke a few soft words to Sukey Blueskin before I mounted, and graciously accepted Rob's attentions in seeing me comfortably settled on my horse. I made every movement a studied air of dignity and composure calculated to agitate and mystify Mrs. Slidell.

When we were out of sight, Rob remarked, "Deadly company, weren't they? And I wanted you to have a good time. Well, anyway they set out an excellent meal and I won a few banknotes off that dull fellow—not enough to foster ill will—just enough to promote his respect for my wits."

I couldn't think of anything to say—just sighed.

"A sigh of relief if I ever heard it!" Rob chuckled. "They were an odd pair of plebes. That woman had the face of a hungry frog. What did she talk about when you went for a stroll?"

"Very unpleasant things," I said.

"Well, forget them. It's a beautiful afternoon. Let's not mar the pleasure of a good ride with ugly thoughts."

He sensed nothing strange in my silence. He thought I was absorbed in sights and sounds along the trail, and he himself kept scanning the forest on his left.

When we were about a mile away from the Slidell cabin, he remarked, "There's another trail over there. I want to investigate something. Wait here for me."

He was gone so long that I became uneasy and had just made up my mind to follow him when he reappeared. He looked tousled and angered.

"I am tempted to go back and flog that scoundrel out of the country! Do you know what I found—a counterfeiter's hideout! That damned traitor. The very money he gave me in that game was counterfeit. There's no court to take him to. But I'd like to show him he can't ply his nefarious trade in these parts—wormwood in the economy of the Republic!"

"No, Rob. No! Let's don't go back. You'd be risking your life and you could do no more than chase him into another part of the woods. You may be in danger anyway if he knows you've spied on his den."

"He won't know I've been there. I was careful—walked part of the way. But he's not so dangerous—a slow-turned weasel. I could handle him well."

"No, Rob."

"What's the matter? You're so fearless in my absence. Are you less brave in my presence?"

"I simpy want to go on home. I've had enough of the Slidells for one day."

"All right. Have your way. But I'll not countenance criminals on my very doorsteps, nor be hoodwinked like a nincompoop into taking spurious currency. I'll settle with Slidell, but not on this trip—not in your presence."

We rode on ahead, now holding mutual grudges against the Slidells, Rob planning to punish the counterfeiter while I absorbed the full shock of all I had heard and was preoccupied with what my course of action should be.

16.

"Rob, Mrs. Slidell told me that you had a wife and family in North Carolina—and a tragedy separated you from them. Is this true?"

We were at the cabin. We had finished supper and I sat across the table from him.

His body jerked as if he had been struck suddenly across the shoulders very hard, and then his eyes met mine directly and he said, "It is true, yes."

"Why didn't you tell me?"

"I did not think it necessary to our welfare or happiness that you know."

"But you told me you were a bachelor without family."

"I am the equivalent of that. I was legally deprived of my family— my name taken from my child, another substituted."

"Mrs. Slidell told me you had two children, a girl and a boy."

"The boy was not mine. What else did she tell you?"

I gave him a full account of Mrs. Slidell's disclosure.

"Some of the facts are there," he said when I was done. "But the old wag's version is highly colored."

He got up from the table and went to the tin-covered, chest-shaped trunk, and brought forth a small book. After carefully relocking the trunk, he brought the book over to me.

"This will tell you the whole story," he said. He turned and left the room, walking out into the dusk of late twilight.

I leafed through the book.

(I have it by me now as I write this—its yellowed, crumbling pages a fragile record—and as I review my first reading, I'll copy certain pertinent passages that you may grasp the full effect of this revelation upon me and consider his defense as he himself set it down. It is eighty-six pages of fine print, a careless printing job, done up in pamphlet style, titled, *Address to the People of Granville County*. On the end page it is signed "Robert Potter, Hillsborough Prison, 1832," and a printer's apology follows, explaining that "The execution of the work in as short a time as possible was earnestly desired by the author.")

My mind felt weary and reluctant to approach the contents of this booklet presented to me at the end of a day already so burdened with disillusionment. I read the first few pages without moving from the supper table or adjusting the dim candlelight before me. The language was such pure Potter eloquence that the phrases seemed to dance around me and have actual substance.

FELLOW CITIZENS:

The manner in which I have been treated—the reckless and exterminating fury with which I have been trampled down—has determined me, at times, to maintain perpetual silence; . . . but I cannot thus abandon my reputation. No—though all mankind desert me, yet, by the blessing of God, I have not deserted myself. And perhaps at a time when the world combines to bear me down with injustice, there is the more reason I should be true to myself.

I speak to you, therefore, not to invoke compassion, for I need it not; . . . it is not for the purpose of entreaty or complaint that I address you; but it is to expose the designs of those who have misled you—who have taken advantage of the excitement which blinded you and prevented you from seeing into their motives . . .

With straining eyes I read through his denunciation of his political enemies for foul play, envy, calumny. Finally, the print became so blurred in the glimmer before me that I got up and lighted a fresh candle and moved over to his desk. There I sat and read on, putting my mind into his mind as I read, willing to understand every fact and feeling he had set forth.

I set out the *remarkable* fact that the *only persons* who had an *opportunity* of forming an opinion *upon evidence,* were satisfied, *beyond all doubt,* that the individuals I had punished *were guilty.*

Dr. Taylor, the physician who examined the wounded men, Colonel Guilliam, a family friend, and Richard Taylor, Mrs. Potter's brother, were according to the explanation Rob had set down, the only persons who, *before* his imprisonment, had seen and conversed with all the guilty parties.

. . . *and all of them were perfectly satisfied* that they had been *justly dealt with.* It was not until *after* my imprisonment that they *changed* their minds. It was then that the people . . . were roused against me by every species of falsehood. Yes: *It was the refusal to allow me bail,* to which the supreme law of the land entitled me, which turned the tide against me, by depriving me of all opportunity of *confronting* my enemies *before the people* . . . And while I could neither be seen nor heard in my own defense, my imprisonment was the signal for the poisoned tongue of envy to commence the work of detraction and death . . . those who had always envied me the favor of the people set themselves to work . . . their success depended upon keeping me out of sight. The people at large have no conception of the *foul game* which was played against me, in order to effect this object.

Word by word, I carefully read Rob's classic outline of the "foul game" played against him and was warmed to pure sympathy, sharing his indignation against the "wire-workers" so determined to hold him in jail until a trial took place, keep him out of sight so the people would hear only one side of the case. He had thought he could get bail when Wiley was pronounced in fit condition to be brought into court as a witness, for the physician had already told him [Rob] that Louis Taylor "was in no sort of danger." But the doctor expressed a different opinion to the court: Louis Taylor was in serious danger. So the application for bail was denied, and Rob could not carry any personal explanation to the public, as he yearned to do. I could imagine how crazed he must have been at this denial. He got some of this feeling into his printed word.

The Doctor seems to be, in morals, what Mimick was in the circus—a perfect tumbler . . . by this miserable jugglery, I was cut off from all opportunity of defending my cause before the people, while others were at liberty to pour into their ears a thousand lies, and excite them to madness against me . . . in the storm of passion . . . it were vain to expect that the voice of reason or justice would be heard. To consummate their frenzy, Wiley, in this wounded and prostrate condition, was paraded among them . . . A herd of cattle will be driven mad by smelling the blood of one of their number. And a community of men may be rendered furious by the sight of the blood of their fellow man. Let me not be understood as rebuking this principle. It is a noble instinct . . . deeply planted in the source of my feelings . . . and standing as I do before the world on a charge of cruelty, I may be excused for offering some specification of the proof.

A dramatic account of a duel with a fellow officer in the Navy followed, a duel in which Rob deliberately threw away his own fire and received the ball of his antagonist because he wanted to avoid shedding the blood of another.

No individual on earth can contemplate, with more pain than myself, the *necessity* of violence towards his fellow man. But what then? Is there nothing about a man more valuable than his blood? Do I, indeed live in a community which places a higher value upon the *blood*, than upon the *sacred honour* of a citizen?—which places a higher estimate upon the *carcass* of a man, than upon *the purity of the marriage bed?* Good God! Do I talk to men? Do I talk to human beings, and find it necessary to use words—to employ language to *describe* my wrongs . . . ? Why, if I could make myself intelligible to brutish beasts . . . they would gather around me, to justify and defend me against men more cruel than themselves! Such is the universal law of God upon the subject, that the verriest brutes of the earth revenge with death, an invasion of their marriage rights—yet I am treated like a wild beast by my fellow citizens, because I could not submit to a condition which even a wild beast would scorn to occupy! . . . I have before me a case which has occurred in Kentucky since my own . . .

Here Rob quoted a Kentucky newspaper report on "The Case of Dr. Pierce," a member of the state's assembly who after killing his wife's lover had been released to resume his honorable place in the legislature.

Though he slew the man that had wronged him, in the actual presence of the court, magistrates bailed him, and the grand jury refused even to find a bill against him. Such were the exalted feelings of the *people of Kentucky* that they held even life as nothing, *when compared with the purity of the marriage bed;* but *here in North Carolina,* your records shall tell that a citizen of the county of Granville, for punishing two miscreants, who though they were the near connexions of his family, had violated the sanctuary of his honor—had actually defiled his bed—*that for this* he was sent to jail—shut up with thieves and vagabonds, and filthy runaway slaves . . .

If the people of Granville think proper to *sacrifice* one of their citizens for *punishing an invasion of his bed*—if they will *suffer* me to be sacrificed for *this*—the disgrace and shame of the transaction be upon their own heads. I take no portion of it to myself. No, not a jot! Not a jot! If my cause was weak—if there was the slightest shadow of doubt upon my mind as to its justice—if I did not *know* that the individuals I have punished were *guilty* —*then, indeed,* I should be as feeble and helpless as a child, but armed as I am, in the truth and justice of my cause, they will find me invincible. They may torture and kill my body—they may bury me in a dungeon, till my eyes can no longer bear the light, till my limbs lose their strength, and my frame perishes with pain—but they never will subdue the independence of my mind. In the last convulsions of expiring nature—alone in the darkness and silence of a dungeon—still defying the power that oppressed me—I would appeal from the tyranny of man to the justice of God.

I paused in my reading to press my fingers against my eyes, and get some movement into my neck and back, stiff and aching with strain. It was a chill November night but my forehead was damp. As I read Rob's writing with all the italicized emphasis, as I felt his presence somewhere out there in the night waiting for my fuller knowledge and judgment, it was as if he spoke the words aloud to me. The impact was weakening, devastating. I was compelled to believe everything he wrote as I read it. And if I had been one of his constituents, I think I too would have been screaming for his release and eager to reinstate him in public trust and office.

I have no feeling of hostility toward the community . . . In the midst of the oppression by which they are seeking to grind me to death, my feelings are as warm towards the people of Granville, as when I held, by their consent, the first place among them: and these feelings will be the last to leave my heart. They will linger there until it is as cold as death can make it.

It would be a triumph indeed, to those who enjoy my perse-cution, if they could bring me into conflict with the people . . . But this is a spectacle they will never behold. They may make the people hate me; but they never can make me hate the people. They may deceive the people; but they cannot deceive me. I understand them perfectly well: and despise them as they deserve.

The men in the community who were using the "blood cry" as a pretext to degrade him before the people and destroy him politically were divided into two sets, he explained. One, the "would-be-great-men-and-can't-be-gentlemen" who were motivated by envy; the other, the "bank gentry" motivated by revenge. These latter had much good reason for feeling safer with Robert Potter behind bars, for his election to both the assembly and the congress had been made on a destruction-of-banks platform. While people went hungry in the de-pression of 1828 and watched their farms sold for indebtedness, it was Representative Potter from Granville County who cried out their dis-tress in high places, calling the twelve-per-cent-interest bankers "plunderers" and the attorneys charging fees above those proscribed by state law "extortioners." It was Representative Potter who fright-ened the "bank gentry" into a panic of their own when his legislative indictment which would have revoked their charters failed to pass by only one vote, fifty-nine to fifty-eight. They in turn cried out that here was a violent and turbulent man threatening chaotic ruin to the country's economy.

Now, he pointed out, in the fine pamphlet print, they were calling him violent again:

They would persuade you I am a violent man; and Mr. Justice Strange, who is certainly a strange Mr. Justice—yes, Mr. Justice Strange, in speaking of my case, said, that 'men of turbulent passions must suffer the consequence of their turbulence.' Was ever such a scene exhibited before, in any society having the slightest pretension to honor? A man pronounced *turbulent*, and treated as a fit subject for extermination, *because he would not suffer other men to go to bed to his wife!* Why, if I could be driven from my opinions, the treatment I have received would certainly have made me believe that it was entirely wrong for

one man to disturb another who should be in bed with his wife—
that I had acted very improperly—nay, very profanely indeed, in
interrupting the gallantry of Mr. Louis K. Wiley, and *the Rever-
end* Mr. Taylor.

The business of fornication seems to be a most respectable
employment in the eyes of the political and pharisaical *gentry*
of Oxford. They have countenanced and condoled with Wiley
and Taylor. Nay, the *interesting* and *romantic* Mr. Wiley has
been quite a favorite gallant with *the religious ladies* of Oxford;
while the man whose wife he defiled has been shut up in a
dungeon, for presuming to intermeddle with him in his gallant
avocation . . .

I assure them, with the most perfect sincerity that where Louis
Taylor is allowed to *preach,* and Louis K. Wiley to *gallant,*
Robert Potter will consider himself as occupying an *honorable
retirement in prison.*

But think of it, ye men of Granville, that the *gentry* of Oxford should openly countenance fornication to your teeth, for
the purpose of *putting down* the man you had put up— But
what! the political and pharisaical gentry of Oxford countenance
fornication!! Why they will rail against it at the top of their
lungs. They will abuse it in *theory;* and some of them will *pray*
against it in church. Yes, but in society, they uphold it in the
most barefaced manner, by inducing their wives and daughters
to dally with the castrated rascal that has been punished for it.

Let it not be supposed, for a moment, that, in exposing the
pharisaical gentry of Oxford, I mean to cast the slightest disrespect on religion. May my tongue cleave to the roof of my mouth
before it utters such folly—no—I love religion; and I love religious men—I have, during my confinement, attentively examined the principles and doctrines of Christ; and, in all sincerity,
can declare that I reverence them from the very bottom of my
heart.

Ten whole pages of the pamphlet were devoted to a discussion of
religion, creed, and certain Biblical quotations. As I read, I marveled
at the alternate wide vision and narrow selfishness of his views—at his
great spiritual concepts as related to all mankind and his restricted

interpretations as applied to his own actions. Had my husband ever enjoyed this religious feeling which he referred to as "wide as the universe," I wondered? Had his heart ever really warmed to all mankind? I believed him capable of such an experience, and yet he had shown himself completely unfit to practice sublime principle and holy charity in personal crisis—had pronounced merciless judgment and executed harsh unnatural punishment.

My emotions soared and sank as I read on: from pride and sympathy to heartache and sickness, from understanding to bafflement, as the language of the man I loved and wanted to respect carried me from one to another extreme of feeling.

In his most vitriolic style he described how everybody was free to discuss his case, present all viewpoints, while his own voice was throttled.

> My condition was that of a man under the agonies of moral suffocation—I had been buried more than six months in a dungeon—my case in the meantime had employed every tongue. Yet when after all this, I came into court, *where alone* I could be heard in my defense, the *judge* had the brutishness to deprive me of *liberty of speech*. He tied down my hands when battling for life—he stifled my voice when pleading for moral existence. He seemed quite anxious to protect everybody but me. I was in *his custody*—yet he even permitted me to be *dogged in his presence*; and though a pistol was fired, in the scuffle, *under his nose*, he took *no notice* of it. Yet he was so zealous to enforce the law *against me*, that, after sentencing me to two years imprisonment, he ordered that, at the end of that time, I should give *security for keeping the peace*.

Judge Strange and Prosecutor Seawell, he accused, were taking their revenge for his legislative exposures of corruption and fraud which had so offended and frightened them. He had heretofore branded Seawell "a villian, to his teeth" and the attorney had submitted like "a chastened hound," but now with Rob safely in prison, Seawell was traveling around over the district "like a moral dungcart, carrying the filth of his calumny at every step . . . "

As I read on through Rob's scorching indictment, I could well understand why Mr. Seawell might be as interested in protecting himself as in vindicating Taylor and Wiley. And by having Rob removed from the Oxford jail in Granville County to the Hillsborough prison in Orange County, there was little doubt that the main intent was to render his "word power" less effective by placing him among strangers.

> The real motives of the movement were carefully concealed . . . They were afraid if I remained in Granville, I should have opportunities, occasionally, of seeing the people and explaining myself to them, and thus they might be brought to their senses and petition the Governor for my release.

Members of the grand jury had also been visiting Rob at the Oxford jail and he had hoped to convince them that Seawell should be indicted on a charge of extortion and expelled from the bar.

> He got the judge to transport me out of the county, under the pretence that it was to keep me safe; when, *in fact*, it was to keep *him* safe.

Finally finished with the verbal slaughter of his persecutors, Rob set down in the last twenty pages of his booklet the fuller story of his crime.

> Taylor and Wiley were punished about the middle of the day. That night, her brother Richard Taylor and her cousin John C. Taylor, came to my house. It was late when they arrived. *She* lay in a remote and private part of the house. I invited them to go in and see her. Her brother Richard went in and had a long *private* conversation . . . he came out . . . and expressed himself *perfectly satisfied*. Richard and John then sat down and ate supper, and soon after rode off together, parting with me on the most friendly terms. . . .
> . . . Dr. Taylor and Colonel Guilliam came to my house the morning after Louis Taylor and Wiley had been punished. After punishing Louis Taylor, it being several miles from his house, and he unable to travel, I carried him to my house to prevent, *if possible*, the thing from getting out. He was there when Dr. Taylor came. The doctor went in to examine him . . . he came out and said to me, "Don't be at all uneasy

sir, for Taylor is in no sort of danger, and I have already heard enough from Wiley to save you in his case." The doctor and Colonel Guilliam were then invited by me to go in and see *her*. They did so. I was not present. After being with her a while they came out and told me she freely and penitentially acknowledged to them *that she was guilty*. Dr. Taylor seemed to evince all the enthusiasm of the most devoted friendship. He repeatedly declared to me, with the emphasis of his hand upon my shoulder, "Potter, your friends will stand by you." He said the husbands and fathers of the community, who had wives and daughters to protect, would justify and defend what I had done. He *enjoined* me to institute, forthwith, a proceeding for a divorce. He denounced Louis Taylor for a hoary-headed traitor, who had received no more than he deserved. The *only* part of my proceeding which he did not *entirely* approve was, the *manner* of Wiley's punishment. He said he could wish, on account of Wiley's youth, that, instead of the punishment I had inflicted, I had tied him up given him a hundred lashes.

I paused here to wonder: Were these men (the doctor, the colonel, the brother, the cousin) sincere in their expression of friendship and approval to Rob, or were they dealing with him as a madman, pacifying him, fearing him, until they could get him behind bars? Was Rob inventing these declarations, lying outright, as he was later accused of doing? And if so, why did he add the doctor's statement that was so critical of him for dealing with Wiley as he had. In these words Rob lamented and derided the turn-about actions of the doctor who:

> . . . the moment he saw how the wind set, turned somersault and lit right in the midst of my enemies; where he plied his legs, arms, and tongue against me, with all the nimbleness of a *Limber Jack*, though he had just before clapped me on the shoulder and ejaculated, "Potter, your friends will stand by you."

The doctor was responsible for Colonel Guilliam's change also, Rob accused, for the colonel had assured him after coming out of Mrs. Potter's room, "When this is known, sir, you will have thousands of friends where you have none now."

The friendly relation between the three, Rob recounted, continued until he was seized and jailed.

After this conversation between Dr. Taylor, Colonel Guilliam and myself, we all departed from my house, leaving *her* there alone. Dr. Taylor attended Louis Taylor home; and Colonel Guilliam and myself rode familiarly on to Oxford. . . . The morning after I went to jail the different parties fell to work, each acting his own appropriate part. Her relations, who, *the day before* had acknowledged her guilt and given up her case, now plucked up fresh courage, when they heard I was in jail, and bustled about to get certificates for her; which, when they had got them, they were afraid to publish.

Rob protested that Judge Strange on the initial booking would not allow him to question Dr. Taylor on the absurdity of a virtuous woman admitting she was a whore.

They *pretend* to believe she confessed her guilt to me, *in order to secure my confidence.* Are you men? Are you reasonable beings? Are you *human* beings and swallow such stuff as this? A woman confess herself a *whore,* to secure *her husband's* confidence!!! But then, how can they account for her confessions to Dr. Taylor, to Colonel Guilliam, to her own brother? If she had confessed herself guilty to me, *merely* to secure my confidence, *why* make the same confessions to *them,* after the matter had become public?

They never have attempted to account for this; and they never can, upon any *rational* supposition, compatible with her innocence. There is however, a more obvious and natural solution of the matter, upon one of the plainest and strongest principles of the human heart. The most hardened villain is unable to persist in denying, when actually detected in guilt. *Confession* flows as naturally from *detection,* as water from the clouds: and *her guilt* had been brought home to her, in a *manner* that rendered denial absolutely impossible.

Having had many indirect proofs of her guilt, I at length made an opportunity, and *heard it with my own ears.*

What had he *heard,* I kept asking myself, that he could consider such positive *proof* of her infidelity? He recorded nothing of anything *seen.* If his account were pure invention, then he would have gone ahead and invented what it was he heard and set it down. And if what he actually heard was anything he could have told with words and be convincing, I could not imagine his leaving it untold. The thought came to me that this might tie in some way with Mrs. Slidell's story of the revival, of Rob's wife and the preacher praying together over the condition of her soul, mixing personal intrigue and religion in a way he dared not publish. He referred in a later paragraph to "detail too shocking to be repeated."

I read on through toward the dreadful climax . . .

> I spread the evidence before her—*she saw that I knew it,* and this it was that brought forth *her confession.* She had seen before, from my deportment, that I suspected what was passing, but this full explanation never took place until a few days before the punishment of her paramours . . . Having confessed, she went on to tell me the commencement of her criminal conduct— how often she had sinned—with whom—and where. She even confessed to me that Louis Taylor was the father of her youngest child.
>
> At times I have thought I would publish every particular to the world; but the detail is too shocking to be repeated. In all this there was no violence, nor offer of violence on my part, nor the least apprehension of it on hers. Nor has she or her friends *ever pretended* there was. I proceeded with her in a very different way. I simply "held the mirror up to nature," and showed her her own image there, until she grew sick and confounded at the sight. No heart, retaining one single element of truth, could have resisted the probe which I applied to hers. The consequence, was a full, free, and circumstantial confession of her guilt.
>
> Here in the presence of God, whose judgement we all must soon abide, with uplifted hands, I swear, *that this is true;* and if it be not, than fall the wrath of heaven on my soul.
>
> . . . I understand when she was *first* asked, why, if *innocent,* she should have selected Taylor and Wiley as the individuals to confess herself guilty with? She replied, it was because I had selected them. But she *now* mentions some twenty or thirty more, whom she says I also charged. Why, then, according to her own

account, did she not confess herself guilty *with them also*, since she says her confession was merely to satisfy me?

Rob described the struggle he had with himself long before his wife's confession or his acts of punishment took place.

My heart was worn out and exhausted in the struggle. The aspirations of fame—even my love for my country, could no longer sustain me in the midst of this damnable disgrace . . . wherever I turned *disgrace, disgrace,* rose up before me, and haunted me like a specter. No exorcism could drive away the apparition but the punishment of those who had conjured it up . . . Yet . . . I resolved to take *the last chance* of saving the community the *shock,* and myself the *pain,* of *publishing* their punishment, and the *cause* that made it necessary. Hence *the mode* of punishment I adopted, and which in fact was attended with no more *cruelty* than should enter into the conduct of an officer while executing the behests of the law. It has been said that I ought rather to have killed them. That, of course, was thought of, but I could not think, even with such justification as mine, of killing a man, without letting the public know it; and *publicity* was the thing, which, of all others, I wished to avoid; and which I had submitted to such sacrifices to avoid.

This was my reason for punishing them in the manner I did. I intended to run the risk of being assassinated by them. I intended to submit to the cruel hardship of living with that woman, covered over as she was with crimes as black as hell . . .

Here ends my case . . . It is to the *people*—the people of Granville, that I speak—and if, even now, they will do me and themselves justice, and no longer submit to be brow-beaten and gulled by the villains who have transported me from among them, I will forget all that is past. I will return to them again with the same affection, and devote myself to their welfare with the same zeal, that has ever animated me in their service.

I do not wish to leave them. I was born among them, as my forefathers have been for a hundred years . . . All my hopes of usefulness are connected with them; and as God shall judge me at my dying hour, I swear I would rather remain among the people of Granville, if I could have their confidence and the happiness of serving them, though in utter poverty myself, than to leave them and go into a land of strangers, though I might there command all the treasures of the earth.

The selfish and the thoughtless may deem this sentiment extravagant, but it is twisted with the chords of my heart, and forms a part of my very existence. What are we? mere shadows, that dwell for a moment on earth, then disappear forever. And shall the brief interval of time, which fills up the measure of man's life, be spent in *selfish* pursuits? If it be gratifying to a generous mind to render assistance to a single individual, how much more exalted the gratification of serving your whole country?—of standing up in defence of truth and justice—that practical truth and justice, on which the dignity and happiness of your fellow men depends. This is my view of life; and such has ever been—such will be to the last—the unconquerable purpose of my soul. *

The address closed with his signature and the prison dateline.

I sat thinking for a while, the book clasped tightly in my hands, the candle flickering low. I knew from Mrs. Slidell's account that the *people* Rob addressed had responded to his appeal—had vindicated him with election to the state assembly as soon as the prison doors opened on him. For a moment I shared the satisfaction he must have felt in this triumph—realized the full measure of his power and was proud of him. But he had been expelled from that high body. Had his conduct really been ungentlemanly, degrading? Or, had his political enemies been too strong, prejudice against him for his crime too great?

I was ineffably weary. I felt no fear of Rob, no horror. Though he was ten years my senior, I felt older, stronger than he, and more aware of the conflicts in his character. There were penalties for such savage temper and sore pride as he carried, and a talent for deception could be soul-poisoning.

He had deliberately deceived me in posing as a bachelor, withholding all of his past except the parts that placed him in favorable or heroic light. This was easy to forgive. I could understand that he

* The pamphlet quotations used in this chapter are verbatim excerpts taken directly from a full copy of Robert Potter's *Address to the People of Granville County*, 1832.

Love is a Wild Assault

could hardly have said to me, a love so newly found and claimed: "I have maimed two men—many think unjustly and cruelly. I have served two years in prison. I have been brought low from a high place and forced into exile."

But wasn't it possible that his indulgence in deceit extended beyond this on into the corrosive practice of deceiving himself? Was this publication I held in my hand simply a superb example of self-deceit? Or, was it truly the impassioned protest of an outraged husband? Whichever it was, I was convinced that he truly believed himself wronged, his actions justified. He never would say, even to his most secret self, "I was wrong. I did a vile thing."

I could carry no comfort in my heart for either myself or Rob where the first Mrs. Potter was concerned. I could never be certain of her guilt or innocence. I could be certain of only one thing: the relationship between them had been pitifully, dreadfully lacking in some way. No such disaster could have befallen such a love as Rob and I shared. This was my reassurance.

As for the crime itself, it must simply be placed in the category of unexplainable brutal things men were constantly doing to each other: the approved rapacious slaughter and mutilation in battle—the legitimate duels in which men killed, wounded, maimed over trivialities—the so-called contests of honor in which sword or knife slashed, ripped, and stabbed at the body with no respect for its godly endowments—the beatings and lashings that lacerated, mangled, and disfigured.

The bitterest disillusionment lay in accepting Rob's capacity for brutality. However great the provocation, or momentarily insane the impulse, his mind had willed and his hand executed an act that profaned intelligence and humanity . . . the same mind that could flame to high purpose and poetic expression . . . the same hands that were so inexpressibly gentle and persuasive in love. Heaven knows I had not thought him perfect. I had observed his temper, his rash impulses, his tendency to be selfish and arrogant at times, but for all this there was ample compensation in his great capacity for kindness and affection and in his brilliant accomplishments. As lover and husband he had brought to my senses a whole new realization of beauty that gave him poetic and heroic stature in my eyes.

This contrast of beauty and brutality I had often observed in nature: the impersonal havoc of storm and flood . . . a snake under a clump of bright blossoms feeding on a bed of baby rabbits so young their eyes are still sealed . . . a mother bird impaled on a long thorn by some freak motion of wind or wing in the very sight of her nestlings waiting to be fed. Wasn't it possible that the nature of man and woman was a part of the same opposing forces? I could think of no place or way to live apart from this struggle.

I realized that if I were free to walk out the door and never see Rob again—if it could be made easy to forsake him because of his crime—I would not do so. I made up my mind that there would be no forfeit of my loyalty—or my love—through the knowledge that this day had brought. Rob wanted my affection and confidence. I liked the directness with which he had answered me, then given me the book and withdrawn.

I arose and moved stiffly about the room, feeling an aching soreness throughout my body. I carefully turned down the bed. I went to the door and breathed deeply of the sharpness in the night breeze, trying to recapture some of the strength that had drained from me. Finally I walked out into the night, down to the stream, for I knew somehow that Rob was sitting by the tree on the far side—the meditation trunk we called it, where he had sat the night he figured out how we could be married. I called to him.

"Come on in, Rob. You're probably chilled to the marrow."

I turned and walked back to the house and he followed me in. He saw that the bed was turned down. I moved to my side and started undressing. He moved to his side and stooped to pull off his boots. When he lay down on the bed and pulled up the covers, I went to the fireplace and brought back a warm stone to place at his feet.

"Thank you, Hatty," he said from a deep weariness.

I retired at his side. We did not touch—did not speak. We were neither alien nor close. We were exhausted and relieved that nothing more was demanded of this night.

Before I slept, I resolved not to tell him for some time yet that I was going to have a child.

17.

We put the ordeal of revelation behind us with hurried preparations for the move from Potter's Creek to Ferry Lake. We were silently agreed that hard work and planning ahead were the best antidotes for the poisoned past.

Rob was relieved that I knew and grateful that I did not reproach or condemn. There was an added kindness in his attentions and a new quietness in our affection . . . but no longer a rainbow of romance linking us together.

Rainbows are capricious, appearing sometimes in dim segments, at other times in whole and fully arched intensity of color—and even in double radiance—never lasting long, vanishing and reforming according to mood of climate and whim of weather. So it might be with the rainbow of our romance.

In the busy time of harvesting, preserving, and packing, Rob put our love to no test of intimacy that might reveal what had been lost. He was often in deep thought which I did not intrude upon or expect to share, and he spent many late hours at his desk reading and writing long after I had retired.

The main topic of conversation between us was our new home on the lake, and the discourse was mostly on his side, describing the scenic wonders that would surround us there. So my mind arrived at Lake Ferry ahead of my body, and in the word picture he painted, I was very much aware that he was sketching in a rainbow so bright that he hoped to banish the shadows that had fallen across our love.

(There was something of high dramatic finesse in the way Rob plotted and played out the scenes in his own drama of life. Through the lens of years gone by I can see so plainly how he loved the subtlety of contrivance, how devoted he was to artifice and strategem, and how he applied it to all his personal as well as public life. And I can see too how such a constant exercise of cunning, however refined it may be, builds character into an edifice that can house only tragedy. But half a century ago I was no critic of his drama, I was playing in it, cast in the role opposite him and wholly absorbed in my part.)

The move to Ferry Lake was accomplished during a mild sunny week of December, and the journey with two wagons and the livestock took five days. Hezekiah drove one wagon and Mr. Wells was hired to drive the other. Rob and Joe and I rode horseback, herding the cattle and hogs. Some of the stock had been left behind to be moved at a later date.

After two days of slow travel, the crossing on Cypress Bayou was reached. Here wagons had to be unloaded, wheels removed, and the wagon beds laid across dugouts lashed together. By paddling this improvised ferry, the loads were carried to the other side. Hogs and cattle were made to swim across, and the journey continued. Bogs could not be avoided—the wagons stuck and had to be laboriously pried out. Rob would ride on ahead picking out the best way for the vehicles to go, for after crossing the bayou, they were making their own trail.

Three days beyond the bayou, in the late afternoon, we arrived at *Potter's Point*. The house stood upon the farthest edge of a promontory that jutted out into the lake about three and a half miles with an average width of two and a half miles. The face of the promontory was a two-hundred-foot cliff, and the new log structures stood like a small novel ornament affixed rakishly at the hairline of abundant timber.

The place was approached through a level stretch of forest land, but the promontory itself reached back into a hill that lifted up its majestic timber growth for a backdrop of natural grandeur. From the front door of the house, there was an eight-mile view out across sparkling lake water that washed onto a white beach at the foot of the cliff.

The lake view gave an impression of being extravagantly landscaped with islands in lavish growth of tree and vine. Some of the tall old trees, seasoned by the centuries, spoke eloquently of a time before the rising of the lake waters around their roots. Noble oaks that doubtless started their growth in well drained soil still endured beside the water-loving cypress, the rank cottonwood, and fancy willow.

"What do you think of it?" Rob asked me, as we stood side by side in the doorway of our new home. I was gazing intently through the spy glasses he had adjusted for me.

"I never dreamed that any scene on earth could be as lovely as this," I told him. "It would be easy to believe that the islands out there are enchanted."

"Evidently some of the early explorers thought so," he said. "I saw a map of this area while I was in Shreveport, shown to me by a trader named Ames, and he had these waters labeled 'Fairy' Lake instead of 'Ferry.' "

"I can certainly understand why."

"That might be just a spelling error. Either name applies, one for the scenery, the other for the purpose. A few traders have already used it to ferry supplies this far in for distribution on the frontier. I believe as the country settles up, this lake will come alive with a big business in ferrying."

"Perhaps you're right," I said, "but I think it should be called *Fairy Lake*. Certainly it casts a wondrous spell on everything around it. Just look at the flowers! It's December, and yet flowers are blooming all around us. Am I dreaming?"

"Of course not. This is a special season, just for you. Doubtless the Spirit of the Lake knew you were coming and how much you loved flowers. You will recall that spring came late this year, and we have had a long and bountiful fall, very little frost."

I finally brought my enraptured gaze from the lake to study the flowers near at hand. Patches of lavender and white, of pink and yellow, of blue and orange dotted the grasses and reached back into the forest—not with the rank profusion of spring, but with the restraints and deeper colorings of the fall season. There were strips of blue mist flower. There were occasional clusters of white Indian tobacco blossom and bright pink spikes of smartweed. There were asters that showed daring purple instead of shy lavender, and scatterings of spring flowers, deceived by the warmth of the earth, awakening too early.

"This is more beautiful than spring," I told Rob. "Like an unexpected gift from Nature."

"I have more wonders to show you from my lake lookout," he boasted.

"You mean there is some point from which we can see more?"

"Not in distance, but in detail. Here we look down on the lake—there we are a part of it—a more intimate view."

"Where is this place?"

"Out in the lake, on that island there, the one nearest the shore. My private observation tower is located in the biggest and tallest tree."

"I wish we could go today." I studied the islands more intently through the glasses.

"It's too late. I can't show you everything in one day."

"I've located the tree. A huge cypress, isn't it?"

"Yes. With a little sandy beach at the foot of it."

"And some kind of shelter."

"I spent several nights out there and threw up a poled protection—two sides and roof using the tree trunk for a back wall. It fronts on an excellent swimming place."

"I wish I could swim as well as you."

"A few more lessons and I honestly believe you can. My dear, you leave me little to excel in. You shoot like a warrior, ride like a ranger, and will not be content until you swim like a sailor. You're invading the field of manly arts."

"Not arts, Rob. Modes of survival." I continued to peer through the glasses, studying the big tree but couldn't locate the platform in its branches.

"I didn't construct it to be obvious," Rob explained. "It's a rather difficult spot to climb to. I'm not sure I should take you up. You might get hurt."

"What's so hazardous about tree climbing?"

"Nothing at all for a wood nymph like you, I suppose. Sorry I lapsed for a moment and addressed you like an ordinary mortal."

I put aside the glasses. "You're teasing me because I love to be out-of-doors so much, because I get a little giddy sometimes with natural wonders—with the beauty and discoveries and mysteries around us in this wilderness! Such things affect you, too. I know they do!"

"Certainly. But I reach the saturation point. You never seem to. There are times when I would like to switch from forest to concert hall, from my solitary desk to senate chamber, from the rude table where we sit down merely to eat to a banquet board where lively converse makes dull food into festive fare."

"To me all food is festive fare, no matter how plain it is or how rude the table it's served upon." I said in a tone of reproof and created a strained silence between us until I added, "We're a long way from the things that mean most to you, aren't we, Rob? Do we have any neighbors at all except the Indians?"

"The Indians will make the best of neighbors," he said with forced lightness. "At least they don't carry gossip. There's a Coushatta village three miles away, and a few miles beyond that, a Caddo one."

"But no settlers nearby?"

"None yet. But it won't be long until they start coming. Many of them will land right here on this point, either to settle in this region or push on further into Texas."

"We'll need neighbors." I was thinking of Rob's gregarious nature —of his need for attention, discussion, causes. And I was also thinking of my special need, for within six months I would be delivered of a child and wanted to know that a woman would be near to attend me.

"We'll have them," Rob assured me. "I'll be making trips to Shreveport rather frequently and I'll interest some desirable families in coming here."

Several days later, Rob told me to prepare for an excursion to the observation island. Our boat was a dugout canoe made from a cypress log. We climbed into it during the calm and warmth of noonday. The lake reflected a blue blue sky and scudding puffs of white white clouds. I helped with the rowing. I wore an outdoor outfit of my own invention, made from dressed deerskins—a commodity Rob always had on hand from Indian trading. The skirt was short, some six inches above the ankle, and with it I wore fitted leggings laced protectively from moccasin top to kneecap. A long-sleeved jacket was low cut, laced tightly across the bosom, and left loose to hip length.

Noticing that Rob was studying me intently as we rowed along, I inquired, "Do I look too much like an Indian?"

"You look the woodswoman perfect—jewel of the forest—gem upon the lake."

"Would you like me better in an imported gown? You have never seen me dressed in high fashion, you know, except for the clothes I wore when I fled from Brazoria. And that was not really high fashion. I have never owned a fancy ball and dinner gown like the ladies you have seen and mixed with in state functions."

"You shall have one some day," he promised instantly. "In my mind I have often pictured you in court styles and have fallen in love with you all over again."

Somehow this statement left me with a feeling of inadequacy—of being a very ordinary woman. I had never moved in high society. When Rob returned to public life, how well could I fulfill the duties of social grace and ornament? I wanted him to reassure me that he was wholly satisfied with me just as I was—that he preferred me in this setting, in this costume, to anything he could imagine.

He is dreaming and planning for something entirely different from all this, I thought, as we set to rowing vigorously and left off words. This is only respite for him—sanctuary. He is not here by choice. He will tire of it—and perhaps of me.

These small remarks had revealed a cleavage in our compatibility that I had not faced before. I could be forever content with country life, plain fare, simple clothes. Although I had enough feminine pride and vanity, and talent for styling, to be interested in my appearance, I could find more honest pleasure in communing with nature than in competing with proud ladies of fashion. A sunset in rich profusion of color was more exciting than the most lavish gown in the same tones could be. A bright red flower peeping in shy triumph from beneath a brown golden-streaked stone was more breath-taking than anything I could design to wear in the same colors.

But this bit of disquiet evaporated as we beached on the beautiful isle that was our destination. This spot allowed only for the perfect present. Loveliness so filled the senses that there was no room for consciousness of past error or future uncertainty.

I began immediately to explore. "Why, Rob, you've been here already today. Here's a bed of coals. And what's all this inside the shelter?"

"Supplies. I thought we might want a quick fire and food. The late afternoon is chilly. I want you to see the sunset on the lake. I brought over the buffalo robe and a few other things we might need."

I was deeply pleased with his thoughtfulness. I had supposed we were merely taking a boat ride and would climb up in the big cypress for a view of the lake. He was making it a very special occasion.

The island was very small with little to explore in its tangled growth. Soon we were making a slow ascent into the browning ferny foliage of the cypress. Its total height must have been seventy feet and its amplitudes began some ten feet off the ground. We reached the first limb by climbing up two long notched poles leaning like a ladder against it. The way up to the platform resembled a crude circular staircase. With some trimming and notching, the main branches around the tree served as the uneven steps, and the foliage where the trimming left off resembled a sidewall or bannister. Some sixty feet above the ground, the platform was set off from the side of the central trunk so that the outer edge of it faced west with a limb reaching protectively across to serve as railing. The floor was ingeniously constructed of small limbs and trimmings cut from the tree. One large limb and a multiplicity of branches growing out from it provided ample support for the flooring.

We climbed with leisurely enjoyment, pausing to catch some special sight through the branches, watching a squirrel skitter away, leaping with winged-like certainty from limb to limb, waiting for a lizard that contested the trail with us by sticking persistently to one of the hand holds until prodded out of the way.

I was climbing ahead of Rob. My arm reached out onto the platform before my head was high enough to see over it. I jumped back in alarm and nearly lost my footing. "Rob! Move quickly. There's an animal up there. Feels like a bear."

He didn't move—just broke into laughter.

"What's so funny? Get out of my way!"

"There is a bear up there." He laughed some more. "But it isn't alive."

"For heaven's sake! Why didn't you tell me?"

"I forgot about it. I brought it up there this morning. I got the skin from the Indians the other day. The flooring was very rough and I didn't want to bring tools up here to finish it off."

Soon we were standing together, hand in hand turning in wordless wonder from one view to another. The opening on the west presented the broadest view, but careful thinning had made several windows of whimsical framework, each outlining its special picture of lake water and shoreline, of island magic and ever-changing sky. The cypress held its topmost tender branches over our heads, a feathered canopy through which the sunlight filtered in gay distortions. A light playful wind moved the branches around us and gave the great tree a gentle swaying motion. It was as if the cypress held us aloft with delight and pride that we might take a good look at the wondrous things it lived with, including the fascinating reflection of itself in the lake waters.

We sat for a while, comfortable with the bearskin under us, watching the clouds flirt with the sun in its gradual dip to the horizon—following bird flights to and from our own domain and out across the lake waters before us—occasionally taking up the spyglasses for a far off view—following the course of three Indians on a boat journey around the point—letting the imagination flow into the wonder-world of reflections cast by the growth on this and nearby islands.

It was utterly restful—a suspended, removed restfulness. Lulled by the rocking motion of the tree and the fair vistas from its height, the mind closed to cares and cautions, doubts and troubles, while the heart opened to unexplainable feelings of vastness and goodness.

Finally, with a sigh of blissful appreciation, I lay back and closed my eyes.

After a while, Rob inquired, "Asleep, Hatty?"

"No, I'm simply absorbing—and thinking," I said.

"Tell me—what are you feeling? What are you thinking?"

"It's a feeling words can hardly express—a feeling of being a part of all the earth and all the earth a part of me. I feel clean and glad and grateful."

"Grateful for what, Hatty?"

"For all the beauty around us—for life and love—and——" I opened my eyes and looked directly into his, "and you."

"Hatty, I've written a poem for you. Would you like to hear it?"

What a romantic contrivance! Love poem in a treetop! I was completely vulnerable. I told him I thought it the perfect time to hear it. The fact that I knew he had planned it so carefully made it no less perfect.

So he leaned over me, one hand on my upflung arm, the other free for gesture and touch, and the mellifluence with which he delivered his poem was the sweet drug to my senses that he had intended it to be.

> Ah, here on the lakeshore—beautiful lake!——
> Here on the lakeshore, my love, we will dwell——
> Ah, here with my lady love, beautiful Ann,
> Captured, enraptured by love's mighty spell:
>
> Love blue and deep as the waters at noonday,
> Love burning gold as the waves in the twilight,
> Love fierce and wild as the lake under storm clouds,
> Love silver ecstasy, ripples in moon-night.
>
> Here on this lake in the legend of Caddo,
> Here on this lake the beginning of man,

> Oh, come to my arms, my beautiful true love,
> I christen thee here, "My Lady Lakeann."

When he finished, the tree was very still as if it too were subject to the spell of Robert Potter's voice . . . and a while later there was a tremor through its branches like a shared ecstasy with the lovers in its embrace.

"Lakeann . . . Lakeann . . . my dear love . . ." Rob continued to murmur. He had made of my second name a poetic endearment.

"Thank you, my lover, for such a sweet name."

"Love-name for the sweetest of loves."

"I think it belongs more rightly to a lovely little girl, playing along the white sands of the lake shore."

"Is she ours?"

"Of course."

"Then we will give her your love-name when she comes."

"She may be on the way here now."

"Oh. Reality or romance, Hatty?"

"Reality. She should arrive in June."

"She might be delayed. She might send a brother on before her."

"Yes, she might. But from this day on I'll be wanting Lakeann. I'll be expecting her. My heart will carry a very clear picture of her. I will not be denied this darling . . . Lakeann."

"Hatty, that's strange talk, as if I might at will allow you a certain child or forbid it. Is having a child an ordeal for you?"

"To carry a child makes me feel stronger and more useful——"

"And more loving and loveable, I do hereby certify." He pulled me close to him again and I spoke my answer to his questions through his caresses "I want to be a part of all life . . . I like being fruitful. . . . I even—I do believe I enjoy the pain of childbirth—it is a part of the pain of love."

"Bless you. We'll populate these isles with beautiful offspring."

"Today—right now—I feel that I must bear multitudes of children for you—for me—for the earth. I should not feel like this I know. Life is too short to live out such a feeling. Why do I have it? Is it wrong? . . ."

"No more wrong than the responsive rhythm of the waves to the wind out there on the lake—no more wrong than the gracious growth of this tree."

"I must try not to love Lakeann the most," I mused dreamily.

"You're confused, my darling. Right now Lakeann is you, my lady of the lake, my treetop love——"

The tree was swaying gently again.

Love time is fast time. Too soon a sharp current of air shook the tree and penetrated the foliage, rattling some of the brown dead twigs over us, rousing us, moving us—first to look on the gold and crimson of sunset skies and the lake waters rippling with rainbow hues—then to seek the surer footing of earth, for the tree seemed done with its cradling of mortal love and threatening to shake us from our bower.

"I guess the tree is wanting privacy for her evening affair with the wind," I surmised fancifully as we clambered down the unsteady poles from the lowest branch.

"It's all right with me," Rob said. "I'm ready for fire and food, aren't you?"

"We shouldn't have stayed so long. Hezekiah and Joe will be worried."

"No, they won't be. I provided for that."

"How?"

"Follow me, and I'll show you."

He went into the shelter, brought out the buffalo robe and unrolled it to display provisions for a campfire supper. "Hezekiah and Joe were in on the secret."

"So I've been tricked."

"Don't you like being tricked—like this?"

"Thus far. What happens next?"

"You'll find how adequate I am when I travel alone."

"That could make me feel that I'm not very necessary to you."

"To make my bed and prepare my food, no. To love me forever as you have today, yes."

He spread out the buffalo robe. "Sit here and watch the sunset."

So I sat there, very quiet, utterly happy, while he dug sweet potatoes from the ashes and rebuilt the fire, went to a net in the edge of the water and got out fresh fish which he cleaned and cooked—then made coffee. When I moved once to come and help him, he shook his head, motioned me back. His waiting upon me in this manner was a love tribute to treasure, more especially since I had always accepted the credo that it was woman's place to give such service to a man. This had never happened to me before in my whole life.

When he brought the food to me and sat with me eating it, I inquired: "Is this dull food or festive fare?"

He gave me a quick penetrating look.

"The gods never feasted on better fare," he replied, "nor shared it with a fairer companion." It was proper reassurance for the time and place.

He watched the twilight place its last golden touch on the waves and the stars sprinkle their reflections in the darkness left behind. We waited for the late moon, and when it came it seemed more silvery than in its fullness and gave the illusion of shining for the lake alone, its radiance creating a blue-white glow on the water around us.

"Love silver ecstasy, ripples in moon-night."

Wrapped in the warm buffalo robe, enfolded in my husband's arms, I went to sleep, the sounds of the island and the lake mixing in irrelevant harmony with the words of the love poem he had written for me.

Early in June, Joe and I watched a large flatboat being poled away from the point at dawn and headed down the lake toward Shreveport. The boat was loaded with produce of field and forest to be sold and traded. Rob and Hezekiah, with several hired hands, were aboard; the Negroes were help that Rob had hired from their owners on a previous trip to Shreveport—and there were two white men besides, drifters, woodsmen who had come in traders' boats, willing to hire out for a while in field or construction work, for hunting and trapping.

It was an important business trip for Rob, and of special importance to me too, for he was to bring back a servant woman who could attend me through childbirth, now only a few weeks off, and also give me garden and household help and be company during his absences. I was also anticipating some mail from my family. I had written my father several months previously, anxious to know what had become of John and Amy, urging that they come and settle at the point.

The trip would be a quick one, Rob promised. He had intended to go several weeks earlier—not so close to my time of delivery—but there had been rains and other delays. He would be back before a week had passed, he said. I felt no particular alarm, only a flicker of aloneness as I watched the boat disappear beyond a far island.

As yet, my only woman acquaintance was an Indian squaw at the Coushatta village—I had not seen a white woman in the six months since I had come to the lake. But I was well satisfied with the beautiful surroundings in which I lived, excited and pleased with the improvements we had made around our home and my part in it all. I knew that other families would be settling in the country soon—that isolation and loneliness were only temporary.

There was nothing to fear. The nearby Indians had shown themselves friendly enough and must be watched only where the horses were concerned.

And how could one be really lonely or fearful with all the gentle animals for company and a strong house full of firearms which I could now load as quickly and fire as accurately as Rob or Hezekiah? Then there were the dogs—Domino and Dusty—always on guard. The poultry made serene and comfortable sounds. There was a new colt that Joe had named "Little Virginia," the adored pet of the place. There were two cows with young calves, and the milking and tending were tasks that I loved. The horses all wore bells and the sounds they made as they grazed were cheerful companionable sounds—unless they were disturbed. We kept saddle horses tied near the back steps throughout the day, ready for instant mounting, in case the horses should need attention, for Rob's fine mares were his prize possessions. Every evening Joe and I rode out together for the horses, bringing them up to the stables to be penned for the night.

Our cluster of log structures and fences presented an appearance of permanence, orderliness, and a natural sort of prosperity that was very satisfying. The original thirty-by-twenty foot pine log building with its great fireplace, spacious attic for extra sleeping quarters, and puncheon floor, was complimented with outside kitchen and shed, corncribs, stables, lots, and shelters, and several cabins to accommodate hired help or give overnight lodging to boaters, traders, and wilderness travelers who were discovering Potter's Point as a convenient landing spot for entering Texas and taking off on explorations to the west and north. A rail fence protected the main house and its backyard buildings. The corncribs and stables could be quickly and conveniently

314

reached by the use of a stile built over the fence. On the opposite side of the yard lay the garden, enclosed, and also reached by stile.

Down a steep bank beyond the stables a spring of crystal clear water gushed out and fell into a natural basin of rock from which it rippled down into a small branch that wound in and out until it found the lake. Rob had steps cut out down to the spring. At the foot of the steps grew three magnificent cypress trees, and the beach of white sand that reached under the cliff and out to the lake began here. This was the secluded beauty spot of the place and for several months, until the well was dug and a water supply found near the kitchen door, water for the household had been carried up the steps from the spring. It was still the favorite spot for bathing.

Several days after Rob's departure, I went down to the spring for a late afternoon bath. Joe had been allowed to ride out alone after the horses since their bells indicated they were close by. The day had been hot, and I was oppressed with an unnatural fatigue that I felt only the cool waters of the spring could alleviate.

Barefooted and wearing a single loose garment of bright blue that I had fashioned for my pregnancy, I went down the steps carrying the gun that I made it a practice to have with me at all times. I left garment and gun within easy reach and slipped into the rock basin that formed a smooth tublike depression at the foot of the springs to enjoy the luxury of heavenly cleanness and coolness. After a while, I felt so comfortable and relaxed that I closed my eyes and lay back on the rock for pleasant day-dreaming about the child that would soon be in my arms—Lakeann—surely it would be Lakeann—child of love and beauty.

I was rudely aroused from my dreams by the sound of Joe's pony running and his calling for me in loud alarm. In an instant I had thrown on my dress, grabbed the gun, and was rushing up the steps two at a time. Near the top, my foot, slick and wet, struck some loose clay and I lost my balance completely, tumbling back to the bottom and into the rock basin.

I lay there for a bit, stunned and wet, until I heard Joe call again, quite near and very distressed. I managed to answer him, and he came rushing down the steps to my aid.

My whole body was ravaged by one intense pain. I thought: I'm about to have my baby, and I must not. Joe must be spared somehow. God give me strength. What's wrong with Joe anyway?

"Pick up the gun," I told Joe. I had flung it far out at the foot of the cypress. "I fell down trying to get to you. What was wrong up there?"

"The bay mare is having a colt, Mama. I couldn't drive her up. What do you suppose will happen to her all night out there away from the stables? And the colt, when it comes, something might hurt it, or eat it maybe. She oughta be in the stable. What'll we do, Mama?"

The mare is not the only one in trouble, I thought grimly.

"Put the other horses up, Joe. She'll have her colt and lead it up to the stable, don't worry. It would be better if we had her in, but it's too late now."

I kept talking, putting off climbing the steps. I simply couldn't climb them, that was all—either with or without Joe's help. He was too small to carry much of my weight and I might topple bringing us both down. I could crawl up them perhaps, but that would frighten Joe. I sat down on the bottom step, doubling over in pain.

"Did you bring the other horses in and pen them, Joe?"

"No, ma'am."

"Then go do that. And see about the mare. By now, the colt may have been born. It may be standing up. If it is, she won't let anything harm it now. I want to rest for a while."

"Are you hurt bad, Mama?"

"Just kind of knocked out. I'll be all right. As soon as I rest a bit, I'll come on up to the house. You go ahead. And take the gun with you. Be careful with it. Set it by the fireplace. I'll put it on the rack."

Joe gave me a worried look and went on up the steps to do as he was told.

When I heard his pony gallop away, I allowed myself to answer the pain with a deep groan, and then on hands and knees began the slow climb to the top, each movement made in defiance of the stabbing, grabbing pain.

Somehow, in a blur of agony, I made a few crude preparations for my ordeal—knife, string, padding—finding it difficult to plan what must be done for myself—and got into bed.

In a prone position, I found the pain subsiding a little. I was able to give Joe instructions for his supper; had him arrange candles and drinking water at my bedside, secure the doors, and climb the ladder to his attic bed, reassured that I would be all right by morning.

After I knew he slept, my will released my body and the final relentless pains of childbirth were upon me.

Later . . . much later . . . consciousness ebbed as the struggle diminished, and I was left in some vast stillness where I waited for my child to cry and announce its arrival . . . waited for kindly hands to take it from me and separate it from my inertness . . . waited for the strength that must come before I could move so much as a finger. As the candle by my bed flickered out, I was pulled into heavy dark oblivion.

I awoke to the awful reality of my condition as daylight filtered into the room and I heard Joe stirring overhead. With great difficulty, I raised myself up, propped on my hands, and looked upon my son who had lived to struggle forward a bit and die at my feet. Not the little girl . . . not Lakeann, the child of my imagination . . . but a boy child, born clean and perfectly formed, in Rob's image. I felt a double grief. I had neither the daughter nor the son. So I wept for both.

I pulled the covers well over the bed and around me in such a manner as to conceal my condition and the dead baby from Joe. When he came down, I sent him directly to the kitchen to build up the fire, heat water, and make coffee. I rested and made my plans until he brought me coffee and cold bread to eat. Then I had him bring other things to the bed, explaining that I had been very ill during the night and must remain in bed for a while. I had him place a large iron pot on the hook in the fireplace across from me—then fill it with water and build a fire under it. After that, I sent him outside to do the chores, and told him not to come back into the house until I called him.

Slowly and cautiously I did all that must be done in caring for myself and the lifeless baby. After I was cleansed and bound, I separated the baby from the placenta and bathed the tiny form, caressing the soft abundance of black hair, kissing the cool mouth bud that my heavy breasts ached for. I had no baby clothes. Rob would be bringing the materials too late. From our supply of dressed deerskins, I selected the softest and whitest, and wrapped our baby in his shroud.

317

How would I bury the infant? I had no strength left for digging a grave. I bundled up the bed clothes in a special way to conceal the evidence of birth, spread out fresh covers and went back to bed, taking the baby with me until I could decide what to do. When Joe came in, I told him I must rest a while longer and that I would depend upon him and Dusty and Domino to let me know if anyone came. In final extremity, I could have Joe ride to the Indian village and bring back my squaw friend and ask her to bury the baby. Perhaps a traveler would happen by. But for a while I must yield to exhaustion and sleep.

"Mama! Mama!" Joe was calling me. The dogs were barking. "A boat has come! A trader man. He's coming up the trail to the house."

I prayed that this stranger might not be as uncouth and unwashed as many of our wilderness visitors were. I could not give my newborn dead into hands that were not clean and kind.

I heard Joe say without preliminary and in great relief, "My mama's sick. I'm glad you came."

And then there was Charles Ames, standing at the threshold of the room . . . on the threshold of my life . . . and a shock of recognition passed between us though we'd never met . . . a shared premonition of destinies interlocked. For me, it brought instant relief and trust.

It is not easy to describe Charles Ames—the inner man shines so much brighter than the outer. (You see, my account lapses into the present tense. That is because since his appearance in the doorway that day, he has always been with me, a presence not at all dependent on bodily substance.)

His eyes were a steady searching gray, reflecting neither guile nor gullibility. He was of medium height and bare-headed, his light brown hair in careless disarray, his face clean shaven. He was wearing the casual garb of a true woodsman that day, comfortable and protective. There was a quality of buoyancy in his bearing (I almost looked for wings on his feet) and an unstudied charm that vaunted neither wisdom nor strength while suggesting both.

I spoke first. "I'm Mrs. Potter. I'm sorry that I'm too ill to welcome you properly."

"I'm Charles Ames, ma'am, and I bring you word from your husband. He's well and doing good business in Shreveport. He'll rejoin you in a few days."

"That is good word, but I need better—I need him now! I had an accident yesterday. I fell down the steps to the spring."

"Were you seriously hurt, ma'am? Are you well attended?"

"There was no one here but my son Joe. He's done very well."

He showed his astonishment that we were all alone.

"Joe and I are old-timers in the wilderness," I told him. "We're seasoned woodsmen and don't mind being alone. This is not our first tight spot or timely rescue. Joe, will you go grind some coffee and make a fresh pot for Mr. Ames?"

As soon as Joe was out of hearing, I spoke in haste to Mr. Ames. "I must quickly ask a very personal favor of you. A baby was born to me last night and with no one to care for us, it died. It's here beside me. Joe knows nothing of it. Take it quickly from me—you'll find digging tools in the shed—do not take time for a coffin—just use pine boughs for lining and cover—in the timber—on the hillside—you select the spot. I'll keep Joe with me. Hurry!"

He came to the bedside. I uncovered the bundle and handed it to him. A long strengthening look of understanding passed between us. He held the bundle tenderly in his arms.

"I'll be back to tell you exactly how I did it and where."

I looked at the large kind hands holding my dead baby, and said, "I'm glad a good man came to bury my baby boy."

He couldn't speak. His arms tightened around the bundle and his eyes filled with tears.

"Hurry!" I urged, putting out a hand to touch the bundle and giving him a gentle push.

He left me quickly, but the solace of his presence stayed beside me.

18.

Charles Ames was a searcher—his whole attitude toward life a great search into which he threw the resources of mind and body: searching through the wonders and mysteries of nature, searching through the aspirations and bafflements of the human heart. For this reason he had forsaken the trade of trunk maker and wood carver to which he had been apprenticed in Massachusetts—for this reason he had come to the Texas country, almost a decade before we met at Potter's Point, and released his searching mind and active body to a trader's life on the Mexican-Indian frontier.

I often suspected there might be a strain of Indian blood somewhere in his family line, accounting for his delicate attunement with all natural elements. On the other hand, perhaps this quality is creative intent for all mankind, realized sometimes by individuals, sometimes by a whole race. Perhaps it is the universal achievement of such harmony that the Prophet Isaiah envisioned when he spoke of every man sitting under his vine and his fig tree at peace with every other man, and the animal kingdom the same: wolf and lamb, leopard and kid, calf and young lion, with a little child their playmate.

We were touched by such a harmony there at Potter's Point for a while—Charles Ames, Joe and I. He would help me to a chair in the doorway where I could sit and look out upon the lake. And when he and Joe were through with working about the place, they would join me, sitting on the doorsteps at my feet.

One afternoon as we were gathered here in charmed contentment watching the quiet drama of changing beauty in the lake scene before us, Joe made a bid for attention.

"When I die, I want to turn into a dog and go to dog heaven." He was sitting on the bottom step, Dusty and Domino on each side of him, already in dog heaven with the petting he dealt out to them impartially. "Dogs are so happy," he added.

"Especially your dogs," Charles said. "You'd make a good Caddo, Joe. Caddo boys are taught that kindness to dogs is a virtue. When they are given instruction (usually by a grandmother) on the dangers to be encountered along the road to the spirit-land, they are always warned about the place of the dogs."

"Tell me about the place of the dogs," Joe demanded.

"If a Caddo boy is cruel to a dog, he will have a very hard time getting to heaven, he is told. The mistreated dog, when it dies, goes to its people and tells what it has suffered. Then the chief of dogs goes and waits beside the road to heaven until the offender comes by. He's stopped and asked to look for fleas on the chief dog's head. When he finds one, he's told to bite it. When he does, he turns into a dog. Then he's taken to the place of the dogs and there receives the kind of treatment he gave the dog on earth."

"You mean he's got to stay there forever and ever?"

"He is never allowed to get away."

"Maybe he was just a little bit mean to a dog and was sorry."

"Well there was one way to get by the place of the dogs if he hadn't been too mean."

"How was that?"

"If someone who loved him very much would place a bead on his little finger when he died, he could bite on the bead instead of the flea and thus escape going to the dogs."

Joe was thoughtful. "I wouldn't mind stopping with the dogs for a while—just for a kind of visit. They wouldn't mistreat me, I guess." He stroked Domino's head, tugged gently on Dusty's ears.

"I'm sure they'd bark joyfully and crowd around to lick your hand," Charles assured him.

"What are some of the other dangerous places on the Caddo boy's journey to the spirit-land?" Joe pursued.

"Well, there's one especially dangerous to slow pokes. If a boy has learned to do quickly the things he's told in this world, he finds that he can easily jump over a certain stream that must be crossed. But if he's been a lazybones, the banks will seem far apart and he won't be able to leap to the other side."

"What would happen to him?"

"Can't you guess?"

"He falls in and turns to a fish."

"Exactly. But even if he's a quick fellow and makes it over the stream, his difficulties may not yet be over. He may land among the persimmon trees and never be able to leave them!"

"What's wrong with the persimmon trees?"

"Nothing wrong with the trees. The fruit on them is perfectly lusciously ripe, sweet and fragrant. It's the boy himself that makes the place dangerous. If he's been greedy all his life, wanting all he sees, he'll wander around from tree to tree, gathering a persimmon here and another over there until he's completely lost—off the good road for good."

"I guess he turns into a persimmon tree."

"No, you turn into a tree for talking about people unkindly, for gossip and mockery. For greed, you become a raccoon and live forever in a persimmon tree."

"I expect a raccoon would like to live forever in a persimmon tree."

"Sure. Heaven for a raccoon, but not for an Indian boy."

"What kind of heaven does an Indian boy have, Mr. Ames?"

"A place where there's plenty of everything that has made him happy in life and none of the hardships."

"What kind of heaven would you like, Mr. Ames?"

Charles didn't answer Joe at once. He looked out over the lake, his eyes squinting, his wide mouth tightened in a manner I had learned to relate to deep emotion held in check. Then he gestured out over the scene before us.

"Something like this." The late afternoon sun, hidden behind rolling banks of puffy clouds, was sending out lavish reflection of pink and gold, spreading a gorgeous unreality all around us. "The richest colors of sunset splashed over nature's greens and blues, waters and forests blending their splendor—this looks like heaven to me—and feels like heaven."

Joe was looking at him with such gravity that he felt compelled, I think, to lighten his mood. "Anything missing there, Joe? A pink and gold afternoon, peace around, and happy company."

"And dogs," Joe added positively.

"Of course. They're a part of the company."

Joe was suddenly done with seriousness. Something in the cool fragrant air seemed to prick him. He jumped up and the dogs leaped on each side of him, ready for a romp. But he made a final pronouncement before giving full attention to Dusty and Domino.

"I'll tell you what. If I can't take my dogs to my heaven, I'll just go where they go. Even if I have to bite a flea!"

Charles glanced at me to see if I were offended at the irreverent climax to his storytelling. I broke into hearty laughter, and he joined me. It was the first time either of us had heard the other laugh . . . and laughing together, we shared an unexpected irrational happiness— heaven's own touch on this pink-tinted golden day.

Ordinarily, I would have met Rob on the lake shore—would have been waiting when he stepped off the boat. But this time he must come to me. I could have managed the walk with Charles helping me, but I was embarrassed at my uncertain gait and preferred to stand in the doorway, using the spyglass to watch the approach and landing.

The easy healing mood I had enjoyed with Charles deserted me when he and Joe went to the landing and I was left alone to dwell on the sad news I must break to Rob. I thought of the other son—the son of tragedy—that he could not or would not claim for his own. Now I must tell him that our first child, true son of our love, sweet-formed, black-haired babe, was dead—nothing to show him but an infant's grave. He would be bringing the servant woman in happy anticipation of the child's birth. My grief over the loss came back to me with more sharpness than on the bleak morning when I first saw it dead. Then I had grieved simply for my own loss—now I grieved for us both.

I focused the glasses on the scene at the shore—watched Rob giving orders, vivacious and well-groomed, managing everything, crew and servants, in lordly and efficient manner. Watched the little tableau of greeting as he and Charles shook hands, while his other arm was around Joe pressed up close against him—knew the instant he inquired of me, looking about and up the trail, "Where's my lady?" he would be asking. Joe looked up at him with some word of explanation, then Rob asked something of Charles, looked startled, turned and called to someone on the boat, then hurried up the trail alone toward me. I waved and he waved back, coming almost in a run. Charles went to the boat and helped a woman off with some bundles and she trailed after Rob. Charles had evidently offered to direct the unloading. He joined the boatmen, and went to work furiously lifting and heaving among the boxes and barrels when all he needed to do was instruct the Negro help.

It would be a few minutes before Rob reached me. As he disappeared from view behind the cliff, I continued to watch Charles. He was working like a man possessed—handing the loads to the hired help rather than waiting for them to pick up the stuff, getting them started up the trail with their burdens only a short way behind Rob. Then he began carrying things from the boat himself and stacking them on shore. A boatman tapped him on the shoulder, holding up a jug, inviting him to stop and take a drink. Charles looked up at him, and his features were clear in my sight—too revealingly, painfully clear. Perspiration stood out all over his face and dripped from his chin. He shook his head at the boatman and then stood looking out over the lake, squinting. He raised his arm in an absent-minded gesture to wipe the drops from his chin and his eyes. The unhappy thought struck me that some of the moisture on his face might be tears. I put the glasses aside, wishing I had done so sooner, and wondering at the same time how much Charles knew of Rob's past.

In the next moment, Rob was there to monopolize all thought and emotion, saying and doing all the right things to make me happy in his return, whispering, "No tears for the babe, Hatty. There can be another—but never another you. How I've missed my Lakeann! You are all right, aren't you?" Then presenting Delia, a slender mulatto woman who was to serve me.

After that, the whole house, the whole place, became the bustle of activity that Rob always ushered in . . . getting his Negro help quartered and assigned to jobs while I got the quick-moving Delia located and busy with preparing the big meal at which the boatmen would be our hearty guests. Rob always invited them to lay over, and they seldom refused.

Rob was always a brilliant host. He excelled that day, addressing much of his conversation to Charles, who gave him grave attention but said little. I was convinced that Charles was controlling a deep agitation of some kind, for he consistently avoided my glances, and as soon as the meal was done announced to Rob that he had employed the boatmen to take him around the point to the Coushatta village that very day. Rob protested most earnestly, and it was quite evident that he enjoyed the audience Charles gave him and wanted him to remain for a while. But Charles firmly declined all invitations, explaining that he must soon get on down the river to New Orleans for a whole new pack of goods that couldn't be procured in Shreveport or Natchitoches. He wanted to load on what the Coushattas and Caddoes had to send out from the point and be on his way.

His farewell to Joe and me was hasty, almost abrupt. Only in the firm friendly pressure of his hands, holding mine an instant, was there any recognition of what we had shared.

I watched Charles and Rob walk down to the shore together, converse for a bit and speak their farewells. As I relive that scene in the light of my later knowledge, I am two selves—my young self and my old self—standing there in the doorway, my thoughts reaching out to Charles Ames and Robert Potter.

Rob, standing by to watch the boat depart, as a good friend does, waves a final good-by to Charles and turns back up the trail, meandering along in deeply contemplative mood. He stops once to gaze toward the spot on the hillside where his infant son lies buried.

Charles, his face still toward shore, watches Rob's retreating figure. The casual ease of movement so characteristic of him is not in evidence. His posture is stiff and strained. My selves both observe that he is hurrying away only because he wants so much to remain.

My young self observes further that Charles, though only twenty-nine, seems in many ways her husband's senior, and that his unstudied charm of exploring mind and open heart is a great contrast to the self-willed Potter magnetism. He has a capacity, she thinks, for friendship with a woman without desiring her—and this is what their relationship must be, affection without attachment. Her life is so full of love and attention, she wishes her friend might have the same. But he doesn't. She knows that. Unmarried and unattached, it would be easy for him to love her too much and be hurt. This, she fervently hopes, will not come to pass.

. . . Surveying her husband, my young self surmises that he is steeped in sadness, dwelling on the son lost, a grief he thinks it best to conceal from her. She wishes he would hurry on. She wants to comfort him with her love.

My old self views my young self in helpless self-pity for the old mind *knows* the trend of thought in the minds of the men down there—the one moving away from her on the boat and the one coming toward her on the trail.

Poor Charles. The old self is provoked to an aching sympathy. Poor, dear Charles. He wants his every thought and action to be right and just, and what turmoil is upon him that he must leave me— must face the full reality of what it means to him that I am the wife of Robert Potter!

He has heard many stories of Rob's brilliant mind and turbulent nature. His own meetings with Rob in Shreveport have been pleasant and friendly with Rob bidding in very positive manner for friendship.

Since it is not Charles' way to pass hasty judgment on hearsay, he has allowed a fellowship to develop between them that he wishes could be dissolved. What is this man really like, he wonders—this man to whom my life and love is entrusted? He reviews all he has ever heard of Robert Potter: great legislative battles for the common people (for the people actually? Or for ballot patronage?); the castration crime (could such a man be wholly sane? Where would his violence break forth next?); expulsion from the North Carolina assembly after a card game fracas (had he really gone into a frenzy at being stripped by a fellow-legislator, accused his opponent of cheating and at the point of a gun made off with all the money? Or, was this simply political ambush?). There's no way for Charles to find answers to these questions. And he can't trust himself to pass any kind of judgment on the man whose wife he loves. Still he can't trust Rob—can't believe that my welfare isn't threatened. That's why he stands there so stiff—so tense—watching Rob go back up the trail, knowing that I am waiting for him. It is the purest anguish to him that he must leave me in Rob's keeping—that he has no right to watch over me. He finally turns on himself and concludes that he is thinking like an envious, jealous fool—that he must continue his friendship with Rob along the course it has begun and keep his regard for me within the bounds of that friendship. This will be his outer discipline. What he feels in his heart of hearts is another matter.

My old self considers Rob now, strolling along down there . . . Is it my own gusty sighs or the lake wind shaking the trees around the doorway as I come to dwell on the thoughts wheeling around in Robert Potter's brain? . . . I glance at my eager young self standing there so erect with the wind holding back her skirt and her hair, a special radiance on her face, anticipating her husband's approach, her love thoughts like winged things pulsing about us. And my sighs mix with the wind again.

Robert Potter's thoughts do not touch Charles Ames, nor is he grieving for a son lost. His concerns at the moment are altogether legal, and he is trying to plot a course of action from a tangle of laws and lies affecting marriage and land—the marriage he has invented and the land he has staked out. At Shreveport he was able to procure a copy of the laws just enacted by the Congress of the

Republic of Texas. * He has memorized the single sentence in the code that is now foremost in his mind:

> Be it further enacted that all persons who have married agree-ably to the customs of the country having another wife or hus-band living and should continue to live together as man and wife sixty days after the passage of this law shall be considered guilty of the offense of bigamy and shall upon conviction be punished as such.

This means that in sixty days, by the law of the land, I will be a bigamist and subject to punishment! But unless the bond ceremony is recorded, there can be no proof that I have married and no con-viction of bigamy. Yet without the bond marriage we are living out of wedlock and I have no legal status whatsoever—not even a common-law wife. He has to admit that the argument with which he persuaded me to marry him would be about as acceptable in court now as a Greek myth. Catholic restrictions were abolished by the provisional government of Texas even before the Declaration of Independence! He concludes that for the present the marriage contract between us must not be recorded.

The other horn of the dilemma—the land laws—brings up the necessity of claiming me and Joe as family if he is to get his full head-of-family quota of land. As a single man he can get only 1,476 acres—as a family head he would be entitled to almost three times that much: a "league and a labor," 4,605 acres. The damned legal web, he is thinking, has certainly got him tied hand and foot—his Carolina family cut off from him by legislative divorce and his Texas family denied him by these fool marriage restrictions in the new code. There's another technicality that he must watch on land law: The Constitution of the Republic plainly states that this "league and labor" is for all heads of families in Texas *before March 2, 1836.* He had been in Texas on that date all right, but the divorce was several years behind him and he hadn't even met me until later in that month.

---

* Although Shreveport was a Louisiana settlement about thirty-five miles from Potter's Point, it was just the right distance from Clarksville, Texas, on the north and Shelbyville, Texas, on the south, to serve as news, mail, and trade center for a central section of the new republic's northeastern settlers.

And what of the land claims of Solomon Page? Wasn't it altogether likely that Page would file for his full head-of-family bonus, claiming Joe and me as he was legally entitled to do?

He looks toward the spot where his son lies buried. He feels a bit wistful and sad but decides with the marriage tangle as it is, the child is better off in its grave.

No direct legal solution of his problem, and mine, is possible—he must admit. Therefore, he will rely on bluffing, confusion, distance, luck, and the general instability of law interpretation and enforcement on a frontier. He has no intention of giving me up. He needs me personally as mate, publicly as family declaration. He is reasonably sure that no one, not even I, can assemble all the facts on his private life and confront him with them. But he can't delay any longer about getting into Congress. For only there can laws be made and unmade. He has no doubt that he can be elected. Hasn't he always been? And once there, he'll clear a path through the maze of marriage and land laws that will satisfactorily clear all the titles and names that concern him. This conclusion satisfies and relieves him. He looks up at me— quickens his pace.

The tempo of pulsing love thoughts around my eager young self increases to such a rate that the old self is absorbed into them and I rush out, my whole, happy self, to meet him and be clasped in his arms.

"Rob, I watched you gazing up there—toward the little grave."

"Yes, dearest."

"You were grieving. Oh, Rob, I wish you could have seen him—so little but so much like you—his hair so black—his mouth shaped just like yours."

He planted a long, sweet kiss on my lips before answering.

"I am not grieving so much, Hatty. I didn't see him, you know. I'm grieved most that you had such an ordeal alone." His arms tightened. "I promise you solemnly, as I live, there will never be another chance that you will be left alone without the best of care, the most loving attentions."

"You make me very happy."

With our arms around each other, we walked up the steps together, then turned to look out upon the lake. I leaned against him contentedly. "The lake poem you wrote for me, Rob. Remember?"

329

"Ah, here on the lakeshore—beautiful lake!——

"Here on the lakeshore, my love, we will dwell——"

He quoted the whole poem for me, his voice the purest love-making.

We had an audience of one, I realized during the reading. Some little sound like a small moan came to me, and I looked over Rob's shoulder. Delia stood just inside the backdoor, listening, spellbound. She was literally entranced, her eyes closed, her head thrown back, her arms at her sides with hands tightly clenched.

When Rob had finished, he pulled me to him again, the hunger of absence in his kiss, I heard the small moan again and knew that Delia had fled.

In New Orleans that summer, Charles Ames wrote more into his small, hide-bound account book than lists of goods bought and sold. "Profit and Loss on Love," he called it. Caring naught for legibility, he wrote over a used portion of the book, across columns of figures and around the edges of the pages. Many years later, my eyes, with the assistance of my heart, made treasured reading of it. Some parts of it seem to have been written for this place in my account.

"Toil and trade, toil and trade, all the way down the Miss, but can't change love, can't subtract anything from it—keep adding and adding until the sum makes me ill—feel too empty to live. Other times strange new elations come over me and am thankful simply to know that you exist. Always I carry the ache to share thoughts and experiences—can no longer feel or know anything just for myself and be content. Thought when I got to N.O. I could find substitute equations for love and companionship. Other women are shadows until some tone of voice resembles yours, some flash of dark eyes, or black curl on smooth skin—then an instant of delirious joy just as instantly dispelled when I realize the whole dear one is far away. . . .

"Even here in a wholesale house on Chartres Street, I feel your presence, as I do everywhere. Why do you follow me—give me no rest—no release? I almost address you aloud . . . So it is true that a man can go mad for love. But I must not go stumbling about, blind and babbling like a fool. I'll write it out instead . . .

"I'm constantly going down corridors of my imagination seeking some escape from you. But at the end of every one there you are beckoning me with greater appeal each time. Your hands are held out to me. Your eyes look clearly and directly into mine. Your mind reaches out to me with an electric attraction I am powerless to resist. There is such a vibrancy between our minds—it is as if countless sparks flicked from countless poles within the orbit of your personality and I felt the sting of each one. I want to get away and I want to come closer. I cannot come closer, so I must try harder to get away—run down another corridor—run—run—run—O God, there you are again! Your voice this time: it strikes me like a sound I cannot live without. A sound that I absorb as thirsty sand absorbs rain. But there is so much sand—so little rain—I retreat from my great thirst. I listen to other sounds: night sounds, day sounds, forest sounds, people sounds. There. You are silent for a while. And I am in the corridor of work— the long soothing corridor of work—no end to that—you can't come there—no intrusion there . . . I should have known better. There is no protection in the normal senses, nor in time, nor in space. For you can come on new paths to me—through any barrier. You can simply be with me, and I must stop and recognize your voice—feel your hand in mine—share your mood—be absorbed into the personality of you—in some unfathomable way so much a part of me that I could peel the skin from my body easier than I could separate my spirit from your spirit . . . I must resign myself to meeting you in every corridor of my existence. . . .

"I have just reread what I have written and think I must consider myself dedicated, committed—and through with running. I will see you again—be certain of your welfare and happiness—anything that I can do through another to add to your pleasure or happiness, I will do. My love is a good love and forever a part of me. The burden is secrecy, not shame. The torture is restraint, not regret.

"So I hereby accept the love inevitable, with its touch of glory and its prod of pain. . . ."

19.

Troubles erupted like a pox upon the land of northeast Texas in 1838.

Troubles with the Indians . . . *Run 'em out!* the settlers cried.

Troubles over the land . . . *Grab it!* was the general policy.

Troubles with the outlaws . . . *String 'em up!* was the practice.

And my tempestuous husband, with his learning and his eloquence, his ambitions and deceptions, added overtones to it all.

Potter's Point—also called Potter's Bluff and Potter's Landing—was becoming geographically important, and Rob was fast emerging as a political influence. Our residence, which we designated as Mulberry Shore, was a place of romantic interest to traders and travelers and inspired the invention of many fantastic tales concerning a "remote lakeshore paradise." In later years, I was astounded to learn how widespread was the publication of these tales. In some of these I figured as a sultry Mexican beauty, in others as a luscious New Orleans quadroon.

Rob's absences were frequent as he became more and more involved with his profession as a lawyer and his plans to win a seat in the Senate of the Texas Congress. I often had to deal with rough-spoken boatmen and taciturn Indians when he was not around to receive them. I never made any attempt to pretend he was nearby. I could handle a gun as well as any of them, and this fact was well known. They gave me a special kind of respect for being a woman unafraid.

Prowling Bear, chief of the Coushatta village nearby, was well named, for he was always prowling about the premises. Rob despised him, but I always considered him more inquisitive than dangerous. His squaw, Tall Flower, was the only woman visitor that I had for over a year!

The Indians gave Rob none of the regard they were willing to bestow on me. They were aware, I'm sure, of his opposition to Houston's policy of protection. Rob never missed an opportunity to express himself either publicly or privately on this subject. The Indians were intruders, depredators, thieves, he said. If the land was to be properly settled, developed by a desirable class of citizens, the Indians must be routed, cleared from the forests like obnoxious weeds from a corn patch. Sam Houston's red-brother attitude was revolting, he insisted, and an insult to every civilized man and woman in Texas.

In February, there was a public meeting at Wray's Bluff on the problem of the Louisiana Caddoes removal into Texas, and here Rob reached new heights of denunciation.

He often went into a great ecstasy of recitation at home in preparation for public addresses. For the speech he was to make at Wray's Bluff, I heard him shouting: "Where is your *hero* of San Jacinto now? Where is your big *general*? Where is the mighty *president* of this bruised and bleeding republic? I'll tell you! Your president is the *friend*—your general is the *ally*—your hero is the *brother* of the red-skinned devils who are depredating our frontiers—and right now he's luxuriating in a breech-clout, spreeing on headbust whiskey, feasted by their warriors, embraced by their squaws—while they plot to steal our herds, lay waste our fields—murder us—scalp us—dance on our graves!"

He spoke these things with such excitement, such passionate intonation, that even one who believed the opposite could not help sharing the excitement and becoming highly aroused until the blast had cooled and reason returned. I thought he was much too harsh on both the Indians and Mr. Houston, but would no more have interrupted his inspired frenzies than I would have struck a match to a powder horn.

I kept my knowledge of Indians and Indian problems to myself for my interests and sympathies would only have increased his antagonisms. Charles loved the Caddoes and had entertained Joe and me for many pleasant hours with tales of Caddo life and origin. He was much disturbed over the United States treaty with the Caddoes made in 1835 while the Texans were fighting for their independence. It was a virtual death warrant for the Caddoes because they gave up all claim to any land in the United States and agreed to remove themselves peaceably within a year's time, simply for the payment of eighty-thousand dollars in goods, horses, and money. Most of their settlements were in western Louisiana so there was no place for them to go except across the boundary into East Texas, and they couldn't go far because their payment was to be made in five annual installments through their agent at Shreveport.

These were "Tejas" Indians, not wild denizens of the plains. They loved their fields and villages. They were custodians of the sacred fire, smokers of the friendship pipe, planters of food seed. For Rob to speak of them as scalp-greedy warriors was fantastic nonsense.

Charles had explained to me how the Caddoes considered Ina, the earth, as their sacred mother. I can understand very well this consciousness of being spiritually nurtured by the earth. It is not a feeling confined to Indians. I have had it too. Sometimes I felt as if I was trespassing on sacred ground around the lakes. In one of their religious myths, the Caddoes claimed that they emerged from their original home under the earth (where men and animals were all brothers) at some point near Sodo Lake. They built a village called Sha-childi-ni (Timber Hill) and from there spread out in all directions, carrying with them what the first man and woman had brought into the world: fire and a pipe and a drum in the hands of the man, pumpkin seed and corn in the hands of the woman. Now they were being forced back into the cradle of their origins and were most unwelcome there. If they could have found the mythical opening by which they had come to the surface, they would no doubt have returned to their unmolested existence at Ina's heart.

Rob's speech at Wray's Bluff aroused the settlers gathered there to such an extent that plans were made to raise a company and attack the Caddoes on their way back from Shreveport where they had gone for their annuity. But Rob did not stay to participate. I do not know whether he was avoiding the fight he sought to promote or whether he was avoiding political involvement. Anyway, he was much disgusted when he learned that a young frontiersman, John Salmon Ford, who had been elected the company's first lieutenant because of his fighting ability, had turned diplomat and persuaded the would-be Indian fighters to call off the attack lest they start a cruel war on a defenseless frontier. Then Thomas Rusk, Secretary of War and Houston's close friend, showed up on the border to deal with the Caddoes. The Indians surrendered their arms to him in return for his promise that the government of Texas would support them. Then Mr. Rusk sent the arms back to the agent at Shreveport who had issued them as part of the payment in goods. It was a very mixed up arrangement and left the unarmed Indians at the mercy of the settlers.

Anyway, Rob left off promotion of war on the Caddoes and gave his attention to the more personal problem of securing a land certificate to cover the large acreage in the Lake Ferry location that he had selected for his headright.

He made his application to the Board of Land Commissioners of Red River County in March of the year 1838 for a certificate covering the 4,605 acres due a family man. He appeared in person before the board, taking the required oath about citizenship and family status, and his application was promptly approved. The certificate was issued at Clarksville; and, shortly thereafter, jubilant with his success, he set off on a spring jaunt to Shreveport for supplies now necessary in the further development of our Mulberry Shore estate.

As usual he must take the hired help for all the loading and unload-ing involved. I now had Delia to stay with me when he was gone. She was a good servant but little company to me as a woman. I knew from the quality of her French dialect that she had once lived in New Orleans but she revealed nothing about her past to me. Rob did not own her—her owner lived in Shreveport. Rob did legal service for the man and took payment in the labor of certain slave property for a period of time.

While he was gone on this particular trip, his Indian policy began to pay off.

It was a very rainy day and the horses had not been long out of the stables when I heard the bells jingling alarmingly.

"Delia! Joe! Come here!" We all stood at the back door listening to the sounds, muffled by the rain and growing more distant all the time.

"Dey're run-neeg, madam," Delia said.

"All together, Mama. Like somebody's drivin' 'em."

"It's the Indians. The horses are headed in the direction of the village."

"Dey know our man ees gone."

"And they know they couldn't trick me except in weather like this. They knew we didn't have our horses saddled, Joe. They must have been spying and saw us let Sukey and Black Hawk out with the others."

"I thought Prowling Bear and Tall Flower were our friends, Mama."

"So did I. They've left the horses alone for more than a year now. I'd grown to trust them. Well, there's nothing we can do on foot. But

336

one thing we can be sure of: Prowling Bear will be around before the day's out. His curiosity will drive him as certainly as he drove off those horses."

"Wat weel we do weet dee Prowleeng Bear?" Delia inquired.

"Try to persuade or frighten him into bringing the horses back."

"Two rabbeets an' dee Bunnee frighten dee Bear?"

"We are not rabbits, Delia," I snapped. "We are a couple of smart she-foxes with a clever pup. You're not afraid, are you?"

"Not weet you, madam. Alone, I be dee rabbeet. Weet you I be dee fox. Dee Ker-naw tell me long ago dees place ees wild, hees lady ees brave. Dee Ker-naw ees so right, but I could not know den. I just come."

Delia had a soft padded tone of speech that sometimes irritated me. It was as if she dared not express a single bit of her real thought. I felt this now, but I said briskly, "I'm glad you came. I'll try to see that no harm befalls you. Let's get busy. Idleness won't make us any braver or wiser."

It was late evening before Prowling Bear fulfilled my prediction. The rain had stopped and the sun had shone briefly on a bejewelled landscape before retreating behind a western cloud bank to create borders and fans of golden light. Joe was on watch and he went to meet Prowling Bear as I had instructed him to do.

"Hello, Prowling Bear. My Mama was hoping you would come to see us. She will be glad to see you."

Joe and his dogs ran along beside the big Indian, the dogs sniffing and skeptical, Joe apparently very friendly and happy. Prowling Bear gave them an indifferent glance and walked on to the door in silence.

I was standing at the door, "Good evening, Prowling Bear." I addressed him politely. "We have had a beautiful rain today." I gestured to the drenched landscape. He looked around as if he did not understand, and then nodded slightly.

I stepped aside and invited him in. He had not been in our house before. He entered boldly and stood staring around the room. I motioned to a chair and asked him to be seated. He hesitated so that I would not think him too obedient and then sat.

We stared at each other. His eyes wavered first and he looked up at the ceiling.

I spoke to him with deliberate emphasis. "Prowling Bear, a very bad thing has happened to me. I have lost my horses. They were driven off this morning in the rain. Some of your bad boys did this to me. I know you are a good Indian, and I know your squaw, Tall Flower, is a good Indian. You are my friends. You would not steal from me. As you know, my man is gone. I must depend on you to go back to the village and make those boys turn my horses loose. Do you understand me?"

Prowling Bear pretended that he did not understand. His eyes were veiled, his face impassive, and he made no sound or movement.

I jumped to my feet to startle him. "You do understand me!" I accused. "But I'll make it plainer!" I whirled around and went to the fireplace. He was on his feet too, watching me. Standing on tiptoe, I took the double-barreled shotgun from the rack and turned to face him, not in a threatening manner, but holding it like a staff at my side. The gun was nearly as long as I was. Grasping the barrel and jouncing it on the floor significantly, I made him another speech.

"If the horses are not home when my man gets back, he will be very angry! He will take this gun and cause much much trouble! He will kill to get his horses back. I like you and I like your squaw. I wish you no harm. But those bad boys in your village must not steal. You, Prowling Bear, must make them do right. Make them bring horses back here—tomorrow. Delia!"

Delia appeared instantly at the back door.

"Bring some salt and some flour as presents to Prowling Bear."

Delia had the sacks within arm's reach. She walked into the room calmly and slowly, placed the bags on the table near Prowling Bear, looked at him fearlessly, bowed a small polite bow and left the room with easy grace.

I stood where I was by the fireplace, holding the gun at my side.

"Take these gifts to Tall Flower," I instructed him. "Tell her I like her very much, and when my man comes home, she must come and eat dinner with me. Tell her to bring the little girl, Clear Water. My husband will bring some nice things from Shreveport, and I will share them with her."

He still didn't answer me. I was not sure how well he understood. I had never before talked to him at such length. Tall Flower usually came alone—sometimes brought her daughter. In his prowling about the place, it was usually Hezekiah that greeted him and dickered with him in matters of trade.

I grew impatient with his dumbness and his reluctance to pick up the sacks and leave.

"Do you understand what I have said?"

He surprised me by saying simply, "Yes."

"You will do what I ask about the horses?"

His eyes grew bright and warm. His face lost the stony look and he smiled at me, a wistful sort of smile, inviting, intimate. My skin prickled in warning. Now it was I who stood very still, my eyes cold, my expression blank.

"I spend night here first," he said. It was more statement than question.

I tried with all my might to understand his thinking. This was not a threat. I must not take it as such. Nor did I believe it was intended for an insult. I did not know the Coushatta code on man and woman relationships. I would have to assume there was some resemblance between their rules of conduct and my own. In this crisis, it seemed safer to assume that we were simply man and woman, not Indian and white woman.

"You let me stay?" My silence meant to him that I was considering the idea. "The trail gets dark," he added, indicating the dusk outside, giving me an excuse for accepting him in case I was being shy about it.

"No, Prowling Bear," I said firmly and quietly. "I cannot let you stay. You must go home. At once."

His face clouded. "You like Prowling Bear?"

"Yes, I like you. We are friends."

"You good woman with no-good man. I stay."

"My husband is good to me, Prowling Bear. I want no other man. Tall Flower is good to you. She waits for you now. Go."

He studied my face in gloomy disappointment. "Too much your friend," he finally pronounced.

"I will know how much you are my friend when you are gone from my house and my horses are back in their stalls."

We gazed at each other quite steadily, my demand meeting his defiance, until he broke the visual duel with a sweeping gesture of dismissal, picked up the two bags and left without speaking or turning back.

As I replaced the shotgun, I heard Delia laughing.

"Dee beeg rambleeng Bear like dee she-foxes' den, eh?" She laughed some more with an abandon that set my nerves on edge. "But dee horses—weel dey be back?"

"Indeed they will!"

"Weetout dee trade?"

With an effort I held my temper and ignored the implication of her remark. But I gave her a hard, angry look. "Go get supper," I ordered her. "I'm starved."

Her face took on a sober expression. "Yes, madam. Don' be mad for my laugheeng, madam. Eet ees just I am ahp-pee dee Bear ees not een dees house weet us."

She went on to the kitchen, but I was made more uncomfortable by hearing her laughter again.

The next morning before we had breakfast, I heard the horses coming down the trail from the Indian village. I sent Delia to let down the bars and rushed out to count and check them as they came in. All were there and unharmed. I could not resist giving Delia a triumphant look.

"I told you they'd be back, didn't I? All right, let's get busy and feed them. They're staying right here in this lot until the Colonel gets home."

In order to be perfectly satisfied that Prowling Bear had initiated both the taking and the returning, Joe and I rode out later in the morning and followed the horse tracks back almost to the village. I was quite aware that the horses had been returned neither in guilt nor in fear, but simply to prove a true regard for me. I knew too that in doing this he had made a sacrifice of prestige and personal gain in my behalf. How much of evil and how much of good was there in such a man, I wondered. So relieved and grateful was I that I was ready to believe that more good had been required to return the horses than evil to take them.

When Rob returned and I reported the attempt to steal the horses, he was furious, but I persuaded him that it was best to ignore the incident and keep the Coushatta on friendly terms with occasional gifts. I related nothing of the personal danger I had faced, only that I had been careful to blame the bad boys of the village and not Prowling Bear himself and that I talked of friendship and gifts.

"That will have to do for now, I suppose, but there'll come a time——" Yes, there would come a time, I knew, when friendship, false or true, would be at an end.

Only a few days after Rob's arrival home, Tall Flower came with Clear Water and I carried through on my promise with careful formality. I had Delia serve a long and lavish meal. I gave Clear Water a string of bright blue glass beads and Tall Flower a good length of bright yellow cloth as well as sugar, salt, flour, and tobacco.

After a few weeks, Rob and I felt secure enough from Indian depredation to plan a trip on horseback to our old camp on the Sabine to gather up the stock we had left behind. It was a fine April morning when we started out and we rode along feeling happily possessive of the land's richness and promise. All the beauty and bounty was our very own. Rob anticipated no trouble in securing full title to his headright as soon as exact location could be set forth and patent issued from the General Land Office. That morning he talked vivaciously of his ambitions for bringing in more settlers to Potter's Point, helping them to get land titles, building up legal trade and political influence, with his land as his central interest and security.

"It's one of the most important pieces of land in the whole Republic, Hatty. It will bring us prosperity. You'll see."

"I don't know how important it is, but it's beautiful, and I love it."

"I couldn't have picked a better spot for everything I want to accomplish."

"It's ideal, Rob."

"There's so much to do. Indians must go. Settlers must come. Fine herds for my pastures, more fields for crops, more labor—we need some blacks of our very own—not just hired help—that must be our next investment. Do you want me to buy Delia? We will have to return her in July or buy her outright. I wanted this to be a trial period. I figured she might become an exceptionally good and faithful servant or she might become a nuisance. How do you like her by now?"

"Her quick mind and lively movement suit me exactly and we work together well. But she is strange in some way I can't define, and sometimes I feel I'd rather not have her around. Let me think about it."

We rode for a while in silence. Just before we came to the forks of the road where we would turn left toward the Sabine, we heard a horse approaching at a hard gallop, and in a few moments the sweat-soaked animal, carrying a desperately frightened young man, was at our side.

"Colonel Potter, sir?"

"Why yes, what is it?"

"I'm Jim Cage. I've come after you. They're about to hang my father!"

"Who's hanging him, and what for?"

"It's just a bunch of lynchers taking the law into their own hands. They say my father killed a man. But he's innocent, Colonel Potter, I swear it! You met my father one time—he told us about it. Do you think he's a killer—that he'd shoot a man in cold blood, like they say?"

"No. Your father impressed me as a law-abiding citizen. Does he know who did do the killing?"

"The Indians. My dad and this man Boxer went on a hunt. They jumped some Indians and a fight broke out. They ran in different directions to divide the Indians. My dad got away, but Boxer was bad wounded and died. Some men from Clarksville found him, and he kept muttering my dad's name, they said. Since we came here from Shelby County, they think my dad's in that ring over there, that he killed Boxer for finding out something about the counterfeiters over that way—my dad had some counterfeit money on him—that made it look bad. For God's sake, Colonel Potter, try to save him!"

"Was there a trial of any kind?"

"No trial—no trial at all! They just came and got him and took him off to Clarksville—and next thing I know they've set a date for his hanging, tomorrow at sundown!"

"What about the authorities—what has the sheriff done?"

"The sheriff says to me, 'Sorry, son, too many good men with good guns in charge.' They want to make an example—a show of it—let people gather from all around and look on! O God, if they got to kill him, why didn't they just shoot him?" He turned his face away and wept.

"What do you think I should do about this, Hatty?"

"Do you think the man might be innocent?"

"Yes, I do, but he should have a trial regardless. The men who hang him will be committing a crime equally as bad as any killing Cage might have done. We should not allow such lawless behavior to get a start in Red River County, or there'll be no safety for anyone."

"It's a long, hard ride to Clarksville, Rob, nearly a hundred miles.

The men may do violence to you for interfering. You might get hanged along with Cage. I can't say that I want you to go. Yet, if you could save an innocent man—and you are very persuasive."

"Please, ma'am, Mrs. Potter, say for him to go. You can stay with my mother at our house and be safe there. It's hardly more'n half way. You won't have to go on to Clarksville. Please come! Please hurry!"

He turned his horse about and we followed him, though still undecided.

"I can turn back and go home, Rob, if you feel that you must go on to Clarksville."

"I won't have you riding alone, Hatty. If I go, you'll stay with Mrs. Cage until I return for you. We'll decide by the time we reach the forks of the road." He rode along with his head bowed, deeply concentrating.

"We seem so uncertain about our duty, let's put it up to the horses," I said. "See which road they choose at the forks and let that decide the matter."

The Cage boy had ridden on ahead of us in fretful haste.

The horses, reins loose on their necks, took the righthand turn, paying no attention at all to the lefthand trail. Rob raised his head and smiled at me. It was the decision we both had made.

"Your mind was made up back there, Hatty. You felt I should try to save Cage. You knew our mounts would follow the boy's horse to the right."

"And how about you—with the bowed head? Weren't you already making up your speech to sway the mob in his defense?"

"As a matter of fact, I was."

"I'm proud of you. I'm glad you want to help people in distress. Tell me, Rob, what did the boy mean when he talked about 'that ring' in Shelby County? Are the outlaws in control down there?"

Rob explained to me how the criminal element from the Neutral Strip, spilling over into East Texas, often pretended respectability (like the Slidells) while acting as receivers of stolen goods and offering hideouts for robbers and killers. In Shelby County they had gone further: disguised as honest voters, they had managed to gain control of local elections and placed their fellow outlaws in office to persecute the innocent and release the guilty. This had made for lynch law in several forms. The honest minority, to circumvent the lawless law, resorted

343

to personal vengeance for depredations. The well-organized criminal element, to confuse matters more, sometimes acted the part of outraged citizens and staged lynchings of their own—the victim some wandering horse thief, some newcomer to crime not wanted or needed in the ring.

I expressed my relief that we had removed to a location well out of that area, but I wondered how far this criminal influence might spread before the Republic would be strong enough to suppress it. Were we not even now in this Cage case feeling its malign presence?

We rode on at a steady gait, with only one brief stop to rest the horses before we reached the Cage home and the weeping family who waited there. Mrs. Cage was quieted and reassured by Rob's promise to do all in his power to get a lawful trial for her husband. It was too dark to ride on toward Clarksville that night, but Rob and Jim were back on the road at the first faint signal of dawnlight. I stayed behind to share the awful wait with Mrs. Cage.

Throughout this fateful day, the woman said little, found much to do in house and garden. When we talked together, it was of inconsequentials. Near sundown, Mrs. Cage sat down and tried to calm herself enough to nurse her fretting baby, a child about two years old. The child took a few swallows of its mother's milk and burst into tears.

"My milk's soured," Mrs. Cage said. "I got to git out of the house." She handed the baby to me. "I'm choking." Realizing the implication of her remark, she groaned deeply and rushed out. She grabbed a hoe and with long strides went to a nearby cornpatch. I handed the baby over to an older child and followed.

With vicious strokes of the hoe, Mrs. Cage chopped out more corn than weeds. I went along with her, not far behind, pulling weeds carefully from the next row. The sun sank lower and lower. There were no clouds to beautify its descent, and a haze in the air gave it the appearance of a great blood-red brooding star. Mrs. Cage stopped hoeing and watched.

When the last rim of redness seemed to make a visible movement and disappear, Mrs. Cage threw the hoe from her, raised her hands above her head, gave a wild scream, and fell face down across the young and tender corn. Her hands reached out and pulled up the plants under them before she relaxed into insensibility.

The two older children had come running at their mother's cry.

Together we carried her into the house and put her in bed. She did not rouse until the next day.

It was no shock to any of us when Jim Cage rode in to tell us that his father had died at sundown. I was concerned that he was alone.

Sitting by his mother's bedside, he told us the story in a voice strident with grief, breaking with weariness.

"We got there in time—we thought. Colonel Potter shoved through the crowd—it was a horrible big crowd and making terrible noises. I didn't think he could do it. He held me by the hand and took me through. It wasn't like feeling people around you, touching you . . . it was like a big slimy animal of some kind. They let him pass. He yelled at 'em, commanded 'em in the name of God and justice and common decency to make a path for us—give him a chance to speak— until by the time we got to the wagon, they were all quiet and ready to listen. The wagon was surrounded by armed men looking stubborn and mean. They didn't like letting Mr. Potter up on the wagon, but he ignored them and no gun was raised against him. Dad was standing there, his hands tied, the noose hanging right by his head, but he wasn't whimpering or afraid. He was glad to see me, and I stood up close to him while Mr. Potter talked. I'll remember that speech as long as I live—it was powerful—like a preacher with the spirit on 'im— and I thought for sure he had the crowd turned. He talked about the law and justice and a man being innocent until proved guilty. He talked about it being better on a man's conscience to risk being killed by outlaws than taking the blood of innocent men. He said Dad couldn't be blamed for the counterfeit money—that he himself had been tricked into taking some one time. He told about the awful things Indians were doing and how horrible it was that a white man should die for an Indian killing. The crowd was with him there at the last—I know they were. And when he talked about the family—what it meant to you and me and the kids—what this was doing to us all—folks wept out loud, and some of the men around the wagon started softening up. But the leader whispered something to his men while Mr. Potter was finishing up—gave them some orders—and when Mr. Potter paused to get his breath for his final appeal (he was wet with sweat and his voice was breaking), the man pounced on him with questions.

" 'Potter, can you prove the Indians killed Boxer?'

"And Mr. Potter said, 'No, not at this moment, but I'd like to have a chance to try before a court of law.'

"And the lynch leader said, 'We are a court of law, Mr. Potter. We heard the testimony of a dying man and we found the evidence of bad money, Shelby County counterfeit. This is a Shelby ruffian and we want the ring over there to know how we deal with the badland breed. Or, do you want them to settle up this part of the country, Mr. Potter, and be the law you think is so high and mighty?'

" 'The law is not perfect,' Mr. Potter said, 'but it serves justice better than unbridled passion.'

" 'You're a newcomer, Mr. Potter. You mean well, but you've got a lot to learn about dealing with killers. We know our business. We're gonna do what we come here for and no amount of your fine talk can stop us.'

" 'If you hang this man without trial, you're killers yourselves. This procedure is savage and godless—degrading to mankind!' Mr. Potter stormed.

"The leader didn't answer him back right off. He looked off to the west and the crowd looked with him. The sun looked like a big ball of flame about to touch the edge of the world. Then the man said, not to the crowd but to Mr. Potter, 'What right have you to discuss proper punishment for crime, Robert Potter of North Carolina? *You* should know well enough that the law don't always fit the crime.'

"The fight seemed to go out of Mr. Potter, but he pleaded 'In the name of God, let the law take its course!'

"And the man yelled, 'The law *is* taking its course! It's sundown!'

"And before we knew what was happening, he had given the signals: one man was holding me, one was holding Mr. Potter, the noose was over Dad's neck, and the wagon driven out from under him. I fought, but they got me down and held me on the floor of the wagon. The crowd went wild with hollering and crying. The lynchers held them off with guns until—until Dad was dead.

"Next thing I knew, Mr. Potter and four other men were taking me away. . . . They buried him, Mom, buried him decent. It was too far to bring him back. He looked peaceful."

The story was done and none of us spoke for a while. Mrs. Cage finally looked at me and said, "Thank you kindly, Mrs. Potter, for all you've done. And thank your man for me—for speakin' for my man—

for gettin' my son through to him so he had some family company—for buryin' him right."

I felt sick to my soul with the boy's story. "Where is Colonel Potter now?" I asked Jim.

"It'll be several days before he joins you, ma'am. He said to tell you that he was going back to Potter's Point by the shorter trail and four men going with him on some business about land and boating, I think, and one of the men wanted to buy a horse from Colonel Potter. He said he'd be by for you as soon as possible. These men were in a big hurry."

"Who were they?"

"Three fellows from Illinois, named Farris, Mead, and Johnson. And then there was a captain from Florida—I don't remember his name—an Indian fighter. They're all just prospecting around in these parts, I think."

I was distressed at being left with the Cage family. I felt like an intruder and knew I could be of little comfort and help from now on. I would be a constant reminder of my husband's failure to save her husband. I must get away! But if I rode back to Mulberry Shore there was a chance of missing Rob and causing trouble and anxiety.

"Where is the Douglas place from here?" I inquired. I remembered that Mrs. Douglas had sent me a gift one time. Rob had stopped overnight at the Douglas place one time. The gift had been a length of lovely satin ribbon—wide and rich red. Mrs. Douglas had sent word with her gift that I must come and visit her sometime. Perhaps I could go there now.

"About eight miles on up the trail," Mrs. Cage told me.

"I think I'll ride over there tomorrow for a visit with Mrs. Douglas. When Colonel Potter comes, you can tell him to call for me there."

"You're welcome to stay here as long as you like, Mrs. Potter," Mrs. Cage told me, "but if you want to go to the Douglas place, Jim will ride along with you."

"Jim's had enough hard riding for a while. I ride much alone. The trail is plain enough, isn't it? I'll be riding in the early morning."

"I guess it's safe enough, ma'am. But will Colonel Potter approve?"

"The Colonel is accustomed to my independent action."

Wanting to be alone with their grief, the Cages did not protest further.

So I rode away the next morning, Sukey Blueskin lively under me, and it was an immense relief to be alone with my thoughts and the healing interests of the out-of-doors.

Sally Douglas and I were friends from the moment of greeting. Sally was a large woman, standing head and shoulders above me. Her abundant brown hair, full of golden glints, was tightly braided and wound into a halo of neatness around her head. She moved and spoke with calmness, and her flecked hazel eyes gave direct and careful appraisal. She was older than me by ten years or more, but none of our differences seemed to matter. We could be friends, honest and outspoken, and knew it instantly. We needed to waste no precious visiting time in deceptions or restraints.

Sally's husband and young son were doing field work, so the day's long visit between us was hardly interrupted. I had not enjoyed such an exchange of confidences since my visit with Mrs. Abit on the journey to Austin Bayou. I talked freely of my life with Colonel Potter and expressed the only uneasiness I had ever spoken aloud about the possibility of Solomon interfering in my life again, making some trouble that might invalidate my marriage to Rob. I told her about the baby I had lost and my recent certainty that I was to have another.

"I had no doubts at all at the time of the bond ceremony that Rob could make everything all right legally," I said to Sally. "But now that I have borne and buried a son and my heart is so ready for Lakeann and possibly others, I want some further reassurance that in the eyes of the world I am his wife."

"That feeling is a proper warning that you should take steps—speak to the Colonel, discuss the matter with him. Has your marriage ever been recorded in any way on public records?"

"No."

"That should be done. Do you have the bond paper?"

"No. It's in Rob's trunk, I believe."

"We face many hazards on the frontier, Hatty. Your house could burn, your husband be killed and you left with a nameless child. I do not mean to be grim—only practical. I find it hard to believe the Catholic law will have any effect on the legality of your first marriage since neither you nor Solomon Page were Catholics. The Texans have ignored that requirement for years and banished it by legal proclamations before you ever met Robert Potter. You've told me of other deceptions he apparently used to get you to think Page was dead—and to get you back to Texas. Granted they were made for love and are forgivable, you've more at stake now than the love between you—there's home and property and children."

"I know, Sally, I know. But I couldn't leave him now, even if I found out that marriage paper was no good."

"Of course not. There are all kinds of irregular marriage arrangements being practiced on this wild frontier that will be given the legal nod later on. I didn't mean you'd have to leave him. Surely, there's an open-minded judge in this region somewhere who'll write out some kind of release—who'll believe what you have to tell about Page's neglect and desertion—and record your marriage to Colonel Potter or do it over as it should be done."

"After all, Rob got his land certificate on the basis of being a family man. That should give me some rights."

"Did Solomon Page do the same?"

"He might have—I don't know."

"Of course he has. He has every legal right to." Sally laughed. "The men get the land . . . three times as much as either deserves, all because of you. And what do you get? Love and babies!"

"Perhaps my investment may yield the most in the long run."

"The most pain, if you aren't careful."

"Sally, should one look for great weaknesses in a man of great talents?"

"One should look, yes. For greatness is in no way an exemption from fault, sometimes enlarges it even. But what you find may depend on circumstances and pressures. How do we know but that the lowest and highest attributes of the human race lie dormant in every man—and woman?"

For two days we visited thus, from one glad hour to the next, rejoicing in the good fortune of our meeting in this man's land where women were so scarce and close friendship between them such a seldom thing.

On the afternoon of the second day, I was helping her with some sewing, and while we talked of romance, I was dwelling again on Rob's many talents. I told her of the love poem he had written for me and she asked me to quote it.

As I was doing so, she got up and went to the door. I thought she was checking on her men folks for the well pully was squeaking. I continued quoting . . .

"*Love fierce and wild as the lake under storm clouds* . . ." and on to the end.

She turned to me, her voice very quiet . . . very calm . . .

"It's lovely, Hatty dear. I must say you're wedded to romance as truly as anything ever recorded in profane or sacred history—but you're just as truly wedded to danger. Here comes your man of tumult and talent with a bandaged head."

20.

While Sally and I applied fresh bandages to his head wound and set food and drink before him, Rob told us of a fight in which Mead and Johnson were killed and he and Farris wounded.

When he had arrived home and taken the men out to look over the horses, there were no horses. The Indians had stolen them, he concluded. So they went to the village to see what they could find out. There were no men in the village, only women and children. He had questioned Tall Flower and she refused to give him any information. He had taken her prisoner and tried to frighten her into a confession. He kept her locked in one of the cabins. She was very stubborn. The next morning he let her go, and went out with the men again to search for the horses. They met up with thirteen Indians, hideously painted and armed with guns. There were six white men—a boater had joined them that morning. The Florida captain who knew Indian warfare said, "That's war paint and they're in a frenzy. We've got to kill 'em or outrun 'em."

"I told him we couldn't run that fast or far," Rob related. "We'd have to fight them or get shot in the back. So I gave the command and we charged. I aimed for the chief, that old dog Prowling Bear, and took him with the first blast. The captain killed the son of Prowling Bear. That took the fire out of them. We brought down five more before they scattered—seven in all. But Mead and Johnson were dead. O God, it was a bitter task, burying them out there!"

"Rob! What about Joe and Delia? Are they in any danger?"

"Joe and Delia are safely on their way to Shreveport."

"Shreveport!"

"That's what I said. I sent our clothes and other portable possessions along with them, and we'll be on our way there as soon as I rest a little. We'll take the trail that branches out of this one a few miles back—the one to the northeast of the lakes."

"Not go back home?"

"Certainly not. Our lives would be in grave danger. Those savages will be vengeful. I killed their chief."

"But just to leave everything——"

"When you're dead, you leave everything! I'd rather leave alive."

"But nobody there to see after anything—my chickens——"

"Good God, Hatty! You talk about chickens when I've just missed death literally by a hair's breath!"

I saw Sally turn toward the fireplace to hide a smile.

"You know how glad I am that you're alive, Rob. But to abandon our beautiful home—the improvements—your fine stock—those things mean so much."

"They mean nothing! And my horses are gone. To hell with it all!" He groaned and held his head.

I said nothing further. I sat down facing him and waited for his agitation to subside. After a while he started talking again in quiet weariness.

"Hezekiah is there if that gives you any peace. The Negroes, everybody else, left on the boat. Farris got a bad wound and the boater was nicked. Hezekiah, the old fool, said he'd just as soon take his chances with the cannon. Says he thinks he knows where the Indians took the horses and he'll hunt for them if I'll give him those matched bay mares. I told him he was welcome to them. Easy to give away something you don't have. He thinks the Indians may move out—not try anything more. I think he's crazy. O God, my head!"

"Lie down, Rob, and we'll put some hot compresses on it."

Before long, he slept, but it was not restful slumber. He groaned and turned and muttered throughout the waning afternoon and night. Though he admitted to throbbing pain when he awoke, and his cheeks were flushed with fever, he would not delay riding on to Shreveport. Sally and I did not embrace and weep as we parted—we looked at each other with understanding and affection and said a simple good-by with no word about another meeting.

Rob recovered from his wound in Shreveport and we stayed on there for six months before repossessing Mulberry Shore. This time in Shreveport was not a happy one for me. I missed my lakeside home and fretted over the fate of all the domestic animals I loved. I dwelt with sadness on Prowling Bear and Tall Flower—felt deep regret at the abuse and killing he had considered so necessary. Hezekiah sent word that he had found the horses and the Indians had given no more trouble. Of course, the Indians had stolen the horses—or—had they? A highly inaccurate account of the fight, published in a Houston newspaper, did not make me rest any easier. It concluded with this indictment of Rob:

The horses which he lost were afterwards discovered in the range near his settlement; they had only strayed a short distance from their ordinary pasture grounds. What must be the reflections of this individual, who has thus rashly imbrued his hands with the blood of innocent and unoffending men, and possibly plunged his countrymen into all the horrors of a murderous Indian war!

". . . the blood of innocent and unoffending men . . . " The reference, I concluded, was to Mead and Johnson. It wasn't likely that any newspaper in Texas would refer to Indians as "unoffending men."

Rob himself, highly incensed, labeled the accusation "malicious political slander" aimed at the influence he was gaining in Red River County. Meanwhile, he worked diligently at getting settlers lined up to take into the area with him on his return to Potter's Point.

That we were going back was my greatest consolation—going back in time for Lakeann to be born at Mulberry Shore. And there would be Hannah to care for me. Hannah was another comfort. Rob had taken this slave, an elderly Negro woman, in payment for a legal service and given her to me. Her presence was cheerful, and she tended me with affection.

The house we occupied in Shreveport held no interest for me. It was overly large and like an aloof stranger. Its owner, who operated a prosperous sawmill business, had taken his family on an extended trip to New York State and left Rob and me in charge of house and grounds. Delia was a part of this household—she and a two-year-old daughter Matilda that had been left behind when Rob first brought her to Mulberry Shore. In all that time, she had never mentioned this child to me. And then George and Mary, half-grown grandchildren to Hannah, were also left in the house to serve us. Other servants had been hired out during their owner's absence.

Deprived of all house and yard tasks, with no animals to care for, no forest trails to ride, I had only my sewing with which to combat restlessness and homesickness. Actually, I needed to do the sewing; my family was in tatters and Rob cheerfully supplied the materials I requested. I made clothes for Joe and myself and a supply of fancy shirts for Rob, but the most enjoyable of all my work was a small chest full of baby clothes for Lakeann . . . weeks of delicate stitching and fancy work . . . the most elaborate preparations I had ever made for a baby.

It was during this time that I got in touch with my family again. I finally received an answer to a letter I had written John. He was all right, and so were others in my father's family, but Amy was dead. There had been no baby. She had died in the Runaway Scrape before her folks got out of Texas—at one of the river camps where sickness raged at the clogged ferry. He hadn't married again—didn't think he ever would. Rob suggested that I write John to come and live with us at Potter's Point—said he would give John a hundred acres out of the Potter headright if he'd come to the lakes to live. I wrote back in eager haste—it would be so good to have John close by.

Another decision Rob made did not please me so much, however. I talked to him about our marriage and the recording of it, as Sally had advised. He told me with brisk impatience that I was not to bother about it—just leave it all in his hands—he'd know best when it should be done. We must wait on several things, he said. Wait on Solomon to make some moves and mistakes. Wait for more amplification of law, sounder establishment of courts. It was a delicate matter that required careful timing, he said, and I must trust him and let it go at that.

This discussion left me in a depressed state of mind. It was about midway in our exile—we had been gone from Mulberry Shore for three months—and summer heat was at its peak. I decided that I must get out of the house and walk somewhere, regardless of the heat. I yearned for a cool bath in a spring, a lake view, a forest shade.

I walked rapidly down a path that led to the river. Somehow I must escape the sickness and sadness that was enveloping me. The sight of water would help, I thought. But the Red River looked hot and sluggish—no lake island enchantment—no sheet of sparkling coolness— no friendly breeze to stir about. The heat of the sun seemed to intensify, and I began to feel quite dizzy. I stopped in the sparse shade of a young live oak, leaned against the little tree and closed my eyes. I was aware of no presence until a surprised voice called to me.

"Harriet! Mrs. Potter!"

I opened my eyes and there was Charles Ames.

I could hardly believe it. I reached out a hand to him and he grasped it tightly. Then, to my embarrassment, my eyes were brimming with tears.

"What's the matter? Have I startled you, troubled you some way?"

"Oh no," I protested. "I'm simply so glad to see you. And so very homesick. Seeing you brings back to me the lovely scene from the doorway—it was so utterly peaceful there—with you telling Indian stories to Joe. And—I'm just childishly homesick, that's all. You know why we are here?"

"Yes, I've heard of the trouble. I'm going to the lakes and thought I might be of some service to you and Colonel Potter."

"Oh, Mr. Ames, bless you! Bless you! Do you mean that you can stop at Mulberry Shore and see about things and perhaps tell us all about it when you come back down river?"

"Exactly. That was my intention."

"Oh, how can I ever thank you enough? I think it may be several months yet before Rob is ready to go back and I want to know so many things. Hezekiah only sent word about the horses. See if Domino and Dusty are all right. Joe worries about them so. See if Hezekiah is feeding Sukey Blueskin the corn she should have and keeping her well brushed. And the filly "Little Virginia"—you remember, perhaps, she was just a colt when you were there—the pet that followed Joe and me around. And the cows—I always cared for them—Hezekiah hated to milk—for me it was a joy—if only I had a cow to milk here! But Rob says it wouldn't be proper." I rushed on and on, hardly able to stop talking.

Charles just stood, quiet and attentive, so calm and comforting, his eyes so infinitely kind. And, I found when I came to a stopping place in my eager flow of words that I no longer felt sick or depressed, and all agitation and intensity had drained out of me. We smiled at each other.

"Anything else you would like to know about?"

"Oh, yes. Socrates. I'd like to know about him."

Charles was baffled that I had switched so suddenly from pets to philosophers. But he tried to follow.

"So would I, but I've had little time for such study."

I laughed at him—my first good laugh in a long time.

"Socrates is my pet rooster. You know Rob so often quotes from his copy of Plato's *Dialogues*. I get weary of so much wisdom sometimes.

My rooster looked out on his world with such curiosity that I named him Socrates, that's all. And to prove his feathered wisdom, I taught him tricks. When I take him a tidbit to eat and say to him, 'Crow, Socrates!' he rares back and crows, regardless of time or weather. I do hope he's managed to stay out of the clutches of the coons. I lost a good many chickens to the coons."

"If he's as wise as you say, he's probably survived. I'll look up your poultry philosopher and bring back a full report."

"And now you must come up to the house with me and wait for Rob. You were on your way to see us?"

"Yes, I was. Where is Colonel Potter?"

"He rode out to visit on a nearby plantation—some matters about seeds and crops. He'll be back by evening. You must have dinner with us."

A whole afternoon to visit with Charles. How wonderful, I thought. But then I realized that he was hesitating—wasn't accepting—was avoiding my eyes.

"I can't stay that long. I'm sorry. My boat is tied up at the river and waiting. I had only intended a very short stop—to pay my respects—offer my services. I regret my haste, but I must go."

"Then I'll walk down to the river with you."

It was hard for me to hide my disappointment that he could not stay on for a visit. And oh, how I envied him the journey up river, and on to the blessed lakes.

"You can't imagine how much I wish I were going with you, Mr. Ames," I said.

My statement seemed to distress him.

"I must hurry along now, Mrs. Potter. The path is too steep for you here. Good-by. My respects to Colonel Potter."

He left me so abruptly that I was surprised to find him gone. He had not touched my hand or smiled even. I wanted to protest—call out to him—but I didn't.

I strolled back to the live oak shade where we had stood and talked. Some quality of his presence seemed still to be there, consoling me, making me stronger. The shade of the live oak even seemed more generous, and the heat of the sun milder, more benevolent.

Charles did not return to visit us in Shreveport as he had said he would. Instead, he wrote a letter that was delivered by another trader with a down-river cargo. Rob gave me the letter to read, and I didn't try to conceal my disappointment.

"Oh, Rob, this tells us so little and I wanted to know so much about things at Mulberry Shore. I was looking forward so much to his visit! I had so many questions to ask! He assured me he'd be back—and—oh dear——" I crumpled the letter and was ready to cry.

"Hatty, I've never seen you act so childish over anything as all this whining about being away from home. We'll go back just as soon as it's safe to go back—as soon as I get sufficient settlers to go in with us. I'm doing well here—getting acquainted with many of the Red River County people who come here to trade, making money with legal services. We should stay here until the child is born——"

"Oh, no, Rob, I've told you, Lakeann must be born at the lake, and Hannah is all the attention I need."

"That's just a romantic notion. We may have another son."

"No. This is Lakeann. I'm sure."

Rob turned away in impatience. I couldn't stop talking about the letter.

"I can't understand why he writes in such a flat and lifeless manner. He's a person of great warmth. He's our friend. Why doesn't he write as he is?"

"Ames is a businessman whose interests are confined chiefly to trade and geography. Certainly you've observed that both his appearance and conversation show no talent for ornamentation."

"He has a very special charm and wisdom where natural wonders are concerned," I defended.

"Oh yes, I'll grant you he excels as a woodsman. Ah, there I detect a wide streak of compatibility between you two—a couple of nature lovers."

He gave me a speculative and teasing look, but I had no response for it. I began to straighten out the letter and reread it, wanting to be quite sure that I hadn't missed something.

"He says the Indians are gone . . . 'hope you may soon return' . . . oh, why did he have to be so brief and formal?"

"Self-conscious about my learning and position perhaps—didn't want to make any *faux pas.*"

"Oh, rot! Charles Ames isn't like that."

358

"Find your own reasons then." Rob went back to work at the papers on his desk. I left the room, taking the letter with me, brooding on every sentence . . . "Your man Hezekiah has attended well to all your interests . . . Assure Mrs. Potter that no harm has befallen any of the farm pets . . . Joe's dogs are lively as ever . . . The Indian village nearby is deserted." I let my imagination fill in between the lines. I knew that he had brushed Sukey Blueskin . . . that Little Virginia had followed him around . . . that he had tested Socrates with the bread crumbs, and Socrates had crowed for him . . . that he had sat in the doorway, appreciating the beauty, patting Dusty and Domino, gently pulling their ears, lonely for the company he had enjoyed there, lonely for the tejas of the deserted Indian village.

The birth of Lakeann at Mulberry Shore on a sunny January day in 1839 was for me an event that could be labeled one of life's perfect gifts—dreams given substance—love made visible in fragile sweetness and pink delicate flesh. Black-eyed, adorable perfection of features, my Lakeann in my arms, at my breast after an ordeal so brief that it carried no remembered pain. For this birth, I had all the attentions and comforts, was surrounded by all the kindness and elations of a whole household that had been missing when my other children were born.

Rob was the first to hold the child after Hannah's ministrations, and as he placed her back at my side he was murmuring,"My little Lake. My little elfin angel."

And Joe, at my bedside, wide-eyed and happy, was telling me, "I'm glad for a little sister, Mama. She's not like Ginger, but that's all right. Do you think she's big enough?"

The servants tiptoed past, greeting me, taking a look at the new baby.

"Lawdy, ma'am, she got 'mos as much black hair as Colonel," George said.

"She pretty as a velvet kitten, mistress," Mary whispered.

Delia held Matilda up, showing a sort of defiant pride in her own golden child (and Tildy was beautiful). "Teeldy, madam geev you leetle meestress. You like?" Tildy nodded obediently.

Delia continued staring at Lakeann. "Dees babee ees a soon-spirit,"she said.

"I suppose that is something extra good, being a soon-spirit," I replied.

She nodded vaguely and went on out.

Hezekiah came in last and addressed his compliment with awkward embarrassment to Rob. "A princess, Colonel, a regular little princess."

This pleased Rob, for indeed he was feeling rather kingly. Things were going exceedingly well for him, and I sensed that he felt himself on the threshold of a new life. Prosperity gives a man that kingly feeling, and Rob was prospering: his headright of land uncontested, a good set of buildings for frontier living, and rich corn land cleared and soon to be turned in the spring ploughing. Servants give a man that kingly feeling too, and Rob was getting quite a collection. He now owned Hannah, George, Mary and Matilda: they were paid for, plus three years hire of Delia, all through legal services to their owner; and there were always at least three field hands around in addition to Hezekiah.

After this household viewing of Lakeann, Rob told them all, even Hannah, that he wanted to be left alone with us for a while. Then he walked around the room in restless elation, stood before the crackling fire for a while, then came back to look at Lakeann, slumbering sweetly, such a doll-baby in her long lovely first-dress. I had never seen Rob in the throes of paternal passion before, and it gave me a deep satisfaction.

"My little Lake," he murmured huskily, over and over, "my precious little Lake."

He went to his desk and took out a cherished bottle of rare wine and a small silver goblet. He filled it and came to stand at the bedside. "To my Lakeanns," he toasted, "love's own royalty!"

Then he began to pace back and forth across the room from bedside to fireplace, talking, to me and to himself, in one of his rare moods of confidence and revelation. He talked of his law business—how well he had done in Shreveport—how he must begin to branch out to the Texas towns even though they were more distant: to Dangerfield, Boston, Clarksville. He spoke of the new settlement on Big Cypress Bayou, called Jefferson. He was convinced that Jefferson was located at the right place to become a town of consequence, offering a wealth of legal business as navigation through the lakes expanded to make it a logical transport head. He even dreamed of another town, on Ferry Lake, called Mulberry Shore with Robert Potter its original settler and owner of townsite. He enumerated the families he had already persuaded to come and settle in the neighborhood—people he could help and trust and influence—like Stephen Peters and Sandy Miller. And John—how nice it would be to have John on the place, a man of responsibility to take care of things in his frequent absences.

He exclaimed at the blessed relief of having the Indians gone from the lake, and of having his friend Lamar the new president of the Republic. He thought this deserved a toast too—Lamar had just recently been inaugurated. So he drank to President Lamar, "Culture's champion and the redman's foe!"

Then he launched into a discussion of his own political aspirations. In a year's time, he said, he would be ready to represent the district of Red River and Fannin counties in the Texas Congress—as Senator. He confessed to the vanity of wanting the title of "Senator."

"You know, Hatty, there was one time in my life when I was only one political mile-stone from the United States Senate—only a short time-distance from being Senator Potter of North Carolina. But the past shall not haunt me! I'm going to team my energies with the future of this new republic, and I'm going to be *Senator Potter*. Before Princess Lakeann is two years old, she shall be calling me 'Papa Senator.' How does that strike you?"

"It strikes me that she will say it very sweetly, and we both will be very proud of you."

He returned to the bedside. Lakeann opened her eyes. They seemed to be staring at each other. Then he said to her, "Your Senator Papa will amend laws and make laws until you're Lakeann Potter as much by law as by love. I swear it!"

He kissed her and then me. It must have been reassurance for us both. We closed our eyes in contentment and slept.

Lakeann grew and flourished like an eager flower in the rich earth of parental adoration. Rob continued her devout worshiper, and she was in every way a happy, winsome child, rosy-cheeked, raven-haired, and quite clever in her accomplishments. Before she was two years old, in the summer of 1840, two things happened that paved the way for her father's fulfillment of his vow to her.

Solomon Page sought and secured a divorce in order to remarry. Robert Potter became "*Senator* Potter from Red River."

When Rob, returning from one of his frequent trips to Shreveport, informed me that he had received papers to the effect that Solomon desired to remarry, was suing for a divorce in Harris County, and that I was being duly notified, I felt a great relief—also a great curiosity about the details of the proceedings.

"Why notify me and sue for a divorce?" I asked. "Wasn't he as free to marry again as I was?"

"According to the old laws, yes. But there's some recent legislation on marriage ceremonies—the laws not yet properly tested and clarified by the courts. Some Harris County judge undoubtedly demanded that Page secure this release from you before being granted a marriage license."

"After all, I suppose neither Solomon nor the judge could know for certain that I had married again, could they, since our ceremony isn't recorded anywhere, and we had no license, nothing published or announced?"

"Give yourself no trouble," he told me. "Feel no concern. I will attend to the whole matter quietly, shield you from any possible embarrassment."

"You'll send proper legal notice of our marriage, won't you? That should be release enough. And then we'll need to do something ourselves to conform to the new laws, won't we?—go through another ceremony perhaps?—publish our marriage bond paper—something like that?"

"At the proper time and place, I'll do what needs to be done, Hatty."

"We must have everything clear and straight," I insisted, "for the sake of our children."

"Children? Why the plural, my dear? Conception?"

"Yes."

"You took our treetop agreement to populate the lakeshores seriously, didn't you?"

"I like having children. Are you displeased?"

"Certainly not! Let's have a son again, to make up for the one we lost."

He could say this to me, knowing that by the prevailing law I was either bigamist or paramour and our children illegitimate! He could say this to me, while representing me as Harriet *Page* in the divorce suit! He could say this to me and feel that he was doing me no injury, because he was so confident that with Solomon remarried and the senatorial mantle about his own shoulders, he could manipulate a happy solution. Knowing none of this, but aware that things were not as they should be, I shared his confidence. His constant expressions of devotion and his excessive adoration of Lakeann seemed security enough for a lifetime of happiness.

His election to the Senate was such a stimulant to his personal happiness that everyone at Mulberry Shore was caught up in a whirl of exuberance and excitement when he was at home. But violence was a dark angel always hovering over Rob. Even his triumphs stemmed from outrage. It was his plea for Cage that made his election so easy—the people impressed by his oratory applauded with their votes. Though they had let Cage be hanged, they felt his defender should be rewarded for the courage and judicial erudition he displayed.

And it must have been Rob's dark angel that personally escorted Captain William Pinkney Rose into the community about this time. The Captain located with his family of grown children, his Negroes, and his particular brand of violence in the section known as Caddo Bend just east of the Jefferson settlement and some ten miles from Mulberry Shore. He was a fierce and roaring old man who soon became known as *Old Rose, the Lion of the Lakes.*

Old Rose considered himself a sort of anointed warrior to rid the lake region of outlaws and any other element that he considered undesirable. There was an ever-increasing menace in this border area from criminals fleeing the United States, as well as an infiltration of the lawless breed from Shelby County. The arm of the law of the Republic of Texas was not yet long enough to reach into the far northeast, nor dexterous enough to comb the unpopulated wilderness. So the honest citizen was forced to be alert in his own defense. The most humble-looking immigrant might turn out to be a brazen thief or killer, a peddler of fraudulent land certificates or a counterfeiter.

Captain Rose, taking the bullet and the bullwhip as his insignia, appointed himself to annihilate and terrorize these unwelcome wanderers until lake shores and forests were clear of all except such as he himself judged to be honest men. So the shrieks of his victims under lash or death sentence became as characteristic of the region as the bellowing of the alligators in the bayous or the fearful outcries of forest creatures. His vigilance by violence brought loyal support from some, loud protest from others; but there was complete agreement in one respect: He *was* "The Lion of the Lakes!"

It was inevitable that Rob and Old Rose should clash. I don't imagine lions and peacocks are compatible in nature. I'm sure their counterparts in human nature are not. Rob with his stunning brilliance of oratory, his strutting and preening of person and intellect, long-spurred and dangerous at times, with a power of satirical denunciation as frightening as a peacock's scream, might just as appropriately have been called the "Peacock of the Pines" as Rose the "Lion of the Lake."

Up to the time that Rob went to the new capitol at Austin in November of 1840 to take his seat in Congress, there had been no indication, however, that peacock and lion found each other's demonstrations of leadership offensive. On the contrary, there had been some exchange of neighborly accommodations.

Through the months of Rob's absence in Austin during the 1840–41 session of the Fifth Congress, I was busily engaged in the management of affairs at Mulberry Shore and preparations for the arrival of my next child. My responsibilities kept me close at home, and for more than a month I had no menfolks to help with farm chores or business— only George, the Negro boy, and Joe, for Hezekiah had accompanied Rob as servingman. But in December I had a happy surprise when my younger brother, Abraham Moore, arrived and asked to make his home with me for a while.

I had anticipated another helper who didn't arrive as expected: Davis Torents, one of the men who four years before had signed our marriage bond. Torents had become a frequent visitor as he followed map making and surveying interests in the area. He had promised to headquarter at Mulberry Shore during Rob's three or four months in Austin and give me whatever assistance I needed in the management of Rob's various enterprises, but he had not appeared—so I felt doubly grateful for Abraham's company though he was hardly a grown man.

Delia was still my chief household servant. Hannah gave most of her time to the care of Lakeann, except for the few tasks that were her special pride—like soapmaking. Mary had been hired out. Matilda was a happy playmate for Lakeann.

I received long affectionate letters from Rob to brighten the winter days. He penned glowing descriptions of Austin, which he considered a lovely place of sublime scenery, gave exciting accounts of his speeches and the legislation which he favored or fought. These letters always carried expressions of love and concern for me and Lakeann and Joe. He found it much easier to send letters to me than I to him. I was dependent on visitors or boaters who would carry my letters to Shreveport where a mail service, unreliable and irregular, made connections with the Texas capitol. Rob, on the other hand, met many people of many interests traveling to the northeast, willing couriers.

It was in the latter part of January, 1841, that I received a letter containing the usual amount of comment on his work, affection, and instructions, plus an unexpected and pleasant arrangement in my behalf.

Austin, January 18, 1841

My dear Harriet,

I wrote you some ten days since by Colonel Frazier in reply to the only letter I have received from you since I left home. I send you now a paper containing the law which has passed to quiet the land titles of our people and protect them in the enjoyment of their homes. I send you also a pamphlet containing the evidence collected by the Committee on Public Lands which alone enabled us to get the bill through Congress. I drew the bill myself and it passed as it was at first presented with the exception of the clause which relates to the seventeenth and part of the sixteenth ranges. The law gives complete and effectual protection to our people, and I know it will make you happy to learn that I have accomplished so much good for them. Yet in the midst of this brilliant success for the people, I feel uneasy about my own private affairs at home, which I fear have suffered and are suffering by my absence. I know you will do everything in your power to keep things straight, but things which I could manage with perfect ease if I were present may embarrass you very much. Yet, let matters go as they may, you may be assurred I will approve everything you do. I was exceedingly glad to hear that Abraham was with you, he is a fine youth and I am satisfied will do all he can for your comfort. I sincerely hope that Davis has joined you, he is a man of the world and in his judgement and capacity for business I have unbounded confidence. If you had him with you I should feel that my affairs were in safe hands, indeed you may well conceive how anxious I am to get home again and once more behold you and my dear Joe and my little Lake but it is impossible for me to leave Congress yet, without endangering the rights and interests of the people confided to my care. I have therefore employed Mr. Ames to go on and aid in preparing the farm for a crop, the season for planting is fast approaching and no time is to be lost in clearing up the field and preparing to plant. I have written to Captain Rose to hire a hand if he can spare one, if he cannot Mr. Ames must do the best he he can with George and such assistance as Abraham can render him until I return when I will show you that I know how to plough as well as legislate. My friend Mr. Morrill will accompany Mr. Ames, he lives in Clarksville and is much my friend, he goes with Ames at my request to aid in getting safe home a couple of horses and a mule I have bought of Ames. You must have my horse stabled constantly and fed what he can eat; do not let him run out with the other stock at all, the horses should be fed eight "years" of corn a piece a day, if any of them are worked they should be well fed. I should be glad if stables could be put up for each of them, so as to keep them separate when they are eating and prevent them from fighting each other, which in their present condition might be dangerous to them. The hogs you say in your letter were turned in the field. I fear Abraham could not find them at all, they should be particularly attended to, and frequently seen—especially the young ones, or they will go wild and be of course lost—however to all these matters I will furnish Mr. Ames with a letter of instructions and Abraham I am sure will cheerfully aid him in carrying them

into effect—I think we can get off in eight or ten days and you
may be well assured I shall lose no time in getting home—

yrs affectionately,
Dear Harriet
Rob Potter

N.B. *I requested you in my letter by Colonel Frazier not to*
sell any corn for less than two dollars a bushel except enough
to raise three or four hundred dollars, that is still my wish as
corn is going to command a high price.

Endorsed: To Mrs. Harriet A. Potter
   Mulberry Shore
   Red River County, Texas*

This letter was delivered to me by a boater named Bruton. I didn't
like or trust this man. He had a gruesome trade: he robbed Indian
graves and traded the trinkets found there to other Indians for hides
and other negotiable stuff. His traffic was well known and the subject
of rough jesting. He was nicknamed "Grave." He had a disagreeable
way, almost insulting, of making himself too much at home when
he stopped to deliver mail or supplies, especially if Rob were absent.
But I was so elated at the news about Charles that I had a big meal
set out for "Grave" and took no offense at his coarse manners and
elephantine appetite.

The letter had traveled slowly. The two men, Charles and Mr.
Morrill, might arrive at any time. I made haste to instruct and assist
Delia and Hannah in preparing the guest cabin for occupancy,
having the boys lay wood for a fire, getting the bed in fresh readiness,
and putting into the oven a new supply of breads, meats, and pastries.

And all the time my happy thoughts were singing: Charles is coming! Charles is coming!

* Verbatim transcription from manuscript record, Supreme Court
of Texas Archives

21.

I think it is time to mention a man by the name of "Snake" Seecher. For two reasons: One—Snake Seecher, not Rob, was responsible for Charles coming to Mulberry Shore. Two—Snake Seecher paid me a personal call that shall be a treasured memory as long as I live.

Charles' meeting with Snake Seecher on a trip through southeast Texas was the beginning. To relate this event, I will rely on my own memory of Snake Seecher, the things Charles later told me, and some matter he set down in his little trade book under the title "kishi-woman."

Charles and I hadn't seen each other since our meeting in Sheveport. He and Rob kept up a friendly association through chance meetings, but otherwise I had no word of him. With him, it was quite different. Along the trails he traveled in the lower part of Texas, at boarding houses and trading posts, a new round of stories had been set off by the Page divorce. And Charles walked out on many a lurid tale about Rob and me—stories embellished with five years of distribution and the perennially sensational nature of the North Carolina tragedy. In the meantime, the first Mrs. Potter had died and Rob was given full blame for that too. Charles was disturbed by all this gossip but not genuinely alarmed for my welfare—not until he met the peddler Snake Seecher.

This peddler was a craftsman with snake hides, and he presented an amazing exhibition of his wares with generous trim of coral and copperhead on all he wore. His enormous teeth were his most startling feature and a few long drooping mustache whiskers made a comical line around his big mouth. In speech and ancestry he was a mixture that only the Texas wilderness could have provided. He described himself with garrulous pride as "some kinds of white man and many kinds of Indian." Abundant friendliness was his trademark and his mixed-language speech was musical with the word "friend". His dog was Ami-tasha, friend-wolf; his mount Amigo-macho, friend-he-mule; and his pack animals, two small white mules, were Amis-doble, his twin friends.

In early January of 1841, he and Charles were traveling together from Brazoria to San Felipe. Charles, riding a handsome bay he called Garnet, had with him his pack mule and a team of matched mares he planned to sell in Austin. Seecher, looking like a long loose-jointed clown, rode bareback on his big frisky mule, followed by faithful dog

and docile pack animals. At their last campfire, Snake took from one
of his packs a leather pouch and brought it into the firelight. From
the pouch he brought forth an exquisite piece of handwork in reptile
—a lady's pocket book in variegated greens. Charles wrote thus about
the discussion that followed:

> I examined the beautiful piece and asked him how he ever
> expected to get proper payment for an object requiring so much
> labor and skill. He told me it was not a thing to be sold—it
> was for giving.
>
> "Mr. Ames, sar, this thing's for a sartain woman—not a buyer-
> woman, not a lover-woman. For a stranger woman known only
> to my ears and my heart. But under the moons of this year I
> travel to the Rio Rojo and the lakes of the Caddo, and then my
> eyes will know the senora brava—so brave, sar, that you may tan
> my hide for muleshoes if she aren't the bravest in the whole
> spread-eagle Republic of Texas! Yea sar! Dee-wah!"
>
> I was amazed that he had made this fine gift for someone he
> had never seen—a worship-piece, I guess you'd call it.
>
> "Who is this senora brava?" I inquired. "Or, do I intrude
> too much on your privacy?"
>
> He made big comedy of my question.
>
> "Amigo Ames, does my sister Haowida, the wind, blow in
> private? Keep her whispers and roars a secret from open ears?
> *Mon Dieu, non!* It is the same with me. *Esta bien.* I will tell you
> who is this woman. I will tell you much more than a name.
> Are there webs in your ears? Dust on your heart? Brush them
> to clearness and heed!"
>
> I solemnly made gestures with open palms by my ears and
> over my heart. Seecher was pleased and aroused to speak in a
> form of rude balladry.
>
> "*Bien!* From the praise words and the poison words, I sift,
> and *Dieu merci,* what do I find? *La Belle! La Courageuse!* forest
> woman . . . lake woman . . . kishi-woman *sans peur!* Dee
> wah!"
>
> "*Válgame Dios!*" I muttered, thinking this description fitted
> a certain one much too well.
>
> "Ay! *Valgate Dios!*" Seecher responded, and continued.

"Came the gambler-pelado! Ay!
Wagered her coin and her comfort.
Wagered her love and her life.
Left her to wilderness captive!
                    Ay Dios mio!"
I changed my position before the campfire and averted my face. No doubt now about the identity of the kishi-woman he was describing.
"*Peur Y que?* Mira! Caddi-Ayo awoke!
Sent fruit of the hawthorne for food.
Sent Kishi the panther for friend.
Sent Niko with high smoke for rescue.
                    Dee-wah!"
He paused, and then brought his declamation to a climax.
"Came war thunder to her ears,
Come love thunder to her heart,
Came riding to her side the lawmaker—
The sword-flasher, the eunuch-maker—
Craving bride or paramour
                    Por Dios! . . . Asi!
To her he is Suko the sun . . .
                    She is blinded . . .
                    C'est la vie!"
I carefully concealed my knowledge and my pain.
"*Mais oui, c'est la vie,*" I agreed. "Such is life, amigo."
After he had carefully repacked his gift and was back at the campfire I reminded him that he had spoken no name.
"Well, sar, some name her first wife of the gambler, Solomon Page. Some name her second wife to the senator, Robert Potter. Some name her no wife at all. I call her Brave Woman. She will call me friend, *mediate Dios!*"
"Do you think she is in need of friends?" I asked.
"*Quién sabe. Es posible,*" he evaded.
"I have heard some of the stories," I told him. "I too call her Brave Woman and would be her friend. I heard it in the Red River country that she is the lawful wife of the Senator, recognized as such through the headright of land located on Lake Ferry."

"Caramba! The gambler-pelado was ahead of him there."

"You mean he proved up a headright too—got a league and a labor?"

"And why not, *mon ami?* The man was in our republic's army of independence. He was a man of family. He was entitled. The law does not look into the heart."

"Where is the Page land located?"

"No location."

"You mean he sold the headright certificate?"

"*Verdad.* The same month of the getting—for two thousand dollars."

"Do you know this for sure?"

"I saw the dollars. In the month of February, three years past to next month."

I did some fast thinking, and some alarming facts emerged. That would be February, 1838 when Solomon Page secured and sold his land certificate. Robert Potter's certificate was issued in March of the same year—very clear in my memory was our meeting in Shreveport right afterwards and his eager recital of the news. And Page did not seek his divorce until two years after selling his land certificate. No doubt about the family he claimed and his legal rights in that direction. So the two men, claiming the same family had been issued headrights within a month of each other! And now the Traveling Board of Land Commissioners were out on the road, sent out by appointment of the Fourth Congress to examine the certifications in every county and reject for patent any land fraudulently obtained. They had made a big stir in Shelby County and would be in Red River County before long. What then? What of the Potter land? What of the Potter marriage?

I was so absorbed in the implication of what I had just learned that it didn't occur to me that Seecher's story was not yet complete.

He roused me by saying, "Amigo Ames, there is more."

I invited him to speak on.

"Comes a tale to me all the way from Washington of the United States. I do not beat the truth drum when I tell it. *Quién sabe?* It may be a tale from the heart of caddaja, made of sea fog.

Pues sí. It has had more tellings than the stars we see. But this is its shape: There was a woman of riches and a young lawmaker. They loved and would wed. *Por Dios! No es posible!* In the distant home of his state, his wife waits with his son and his daughter. *Mon Dieu!* How to be rid of them? . . . Caddaja-diablo! He must prove faithless the woman he would cast off. Ya! Ya!

I stopped him, I knew the sordid story too well.

"You're trying to tell me that Senator Potter when in the Congress of the United States became attached to a wealthy woman and resorted to criminal action in an effort to get free of his wife. It could just as easily be true that his wife was wantonly unfaithful to him, that he found consolation in a new love, and that he became distraught and violent in the wreckage of his home."

"You would be friend to the eunuch-maker," Seecher replied. "I would be friend to the brave woman. *Esta Bien.* You heard me say, sar, I do not beat the truth drum with this story. But it is plain before us that the lawmaker now serves at another capitol, and far away another family waits. What else waits? Is it wicked to be wise and watch?"

"No," I assured him, "it is not wicked. The brave woman is fortunate to have you for a friend."

I wanted to say: *Gracias,* tejas. You've just given the spur to another friend who'll see her before you do and will do some watching of his own.

Just now I have begun to wonder: Could Snake Seecher have been deliberately informing me? Did we travel together by chance? Was he endowed with some super-sensitivity for detecting the secret locked in my heart? This possibility makes my mission seem even more urgent.

Charles arrived at Mulberry Shore in late January, bringing the matched mares and the mule Rob had bought.

Joe and I were not at the house to greet him. There had been a sunny break in the dull cast of the day and we had gone for a horse-back ride. Hannah was constantly scolding me for riding so close to my time, but Sukey Blueskin was as gentle in gait as a rocking chair and offered much better scenery with the rocking!

When we got back to the house, I saw the new horses already penned. Hannah was outside to help me dismount.

"Dat nice Mr. Ames done come all by heself. An' he pacin' up and down 'fo' da fireplace fitten ta weah da floor right down ta da groun'."

"How do I look, Hannah?"

"Lak Little Green Ridin'hood! When ya gits inta dat habit and hood-cape ah wonduh effen ya didn' hide da baby somewhuhs. Couldn' be on ya!"

Hannah and I laughed at each other, both knowing how I enjoyed her compliments.

I rushed in to Charles, thinking how wonderful to greet him in good health and happiness rather than with a dismal scene such as he had encountered the first time he entered this same room.

My first sight of him disturbed me. He was much thinner, and more intense. My entrance seemed to startle him in some way, shatter his composure for an instant.

"How happy I am to see you!" I exclaimed, as we met in the middle of the room and I gave him my hand.

"I'm glad to find you so well, Mrs. Potter." His voice was so quiet, his feelings so absent from it, that I wondered if he might be holding back bad news.

"Is there anything wrong, Mr. Ames? Where is Mr. Morrill?"

"We parted at the Sabine crossing. I needed no further assistance with the stock and we thought there was little danger of encountering horse thieves on this end of the trail. So I insisted he go ahead to Clarksville since urgent business awaited his attention there."

Joe had followed me in, and Charles had a warm greeting for him. We sat visiting for a while. I felt extremely stimulated and excited, almost tearful with the joy of having good company. I asked many, many questions about events at Austin and Rob's part in them. I noticed that Charles answered with a kind of caution not like the quick open appraisals I remembered. I thought perhaps he was weary from his journey and would be more like his old self after a good rest.

After a while, Lakeann came in carrying a small bouquet of white flowers, closely followed by Hannah. She wore a rosy pink dress and her black curls were held back on each side with small pink bows. She came directly to my chair, and showing the flowers said, "Pitty, pitty, Mama."

"I found the flowers for her this afternoon on my ride," I explained to Charles. "In a sunny secluded spot where the first ones always appear. She loves white flowers . . . Lakeann, this gentleman is our friend, Mr. Ames."

Lakeann gave our guest big-eyed and shy attention. He smiled encouragingly, spoke a gentle direct greeting. She left me and moved toward him, holding out to him a single flower from her bouquet.

"Pitty fower, suh, pitty fower."

"Indeed it is," Charles agreed, "but not nearly so lovely as the little flower presenting it."

Lakeann demurely studied the toe of her wee moccasin and fluttered her long eyelashes in coy appreciation of the compliment.

Charles was obviously fascinated with her. When she came closer to look up at him in wistful scrutiny, he reached out and drew her into the circle of his arm, but not insistently lest he alarm her.

She was easily won. She leaned against his knee and held up the whole bouquet. "Pitty fowers, suh!"

He recognized this as a bid for wholehearted attention. He lifted her to his knee.

"Thank you, Lakeann. But your mother intended the pretty flowers for you. Perhaps Hannah will put them in water so they will live for a while to be beautiful for us a little longer."

She looked at him, then Hannah, and rejected the idea of leaving the position she had attained on his knee. She held out the bouquet to Hannah.

"Pwease, 'anna, fowers firsty."

Hannah chuckled at the maneuver, took the bouquet, and went to get water.

Lakeann snuggled up close to Charles and played with his watch fob, a silver Mexican ornament set with a blue stone.

I was pleased and amused at this sudden mutual friendship. "Lake misses her Papa very much," I said. "He gives her much attention and romps with her when he's home."

"Pa-pa Sen-tur," she interrupted, as if explaining to Charles.

"She seems to think she deserves the same kind of attention from other gentlemen," I finished.

"I see no reason why she shouldn't have it," Charles said, in a tone that left no doubt in my mind that she would have it as long as he was there.

And it turned out that way. Throughout his stay at Mulberry Shore, it was Lakeann, not I, who set the pattern of his days. The daylight hours were filled with field work and care of the livestock. He was with the family only at mealtime, retiring early in the evening to his cabin. After noon and evening meals, he gave Lakeann the full attention and romp she loved, and at nighttime a special delight which was new to her—a simple little story about some forest animal before Hannah took her off to bed. Thus he established a bond of affection with her that belonged to just those two, entirely apart from family ties.

There was little occasion for private conversation between us, and since he sought no such opportunity, I made none. He worked very hard but did not eat like a working man. One noontime I remarked, "Mr. Ames, you work too hard and eat too little."

He answered lightly, "An Indian friend of mine, noted for his widsom, told me one time that, 'He who eats too well and sleeps too much endangers long life.'"

Mr. Torents was at the table. He had arrived a few days behind Charles, was sharing his cabin, and helping with the farm work.

He spoke up, chidingly, "I think you took that tejas too seriously, Ames. I'm sure he didn't mean that by not eating or sleeping at all you could prolong life indefinitely. I don't know when you sleep. When I turn in, you're sitting there staring at the fire—when I get up you're doing the same thing . . . I don't know whether he sits there all night or is just an early riser. I'll tell you, Mrs. Potter, I haven't had such good food and comfortable quarters since I last touched these shores. Please pass the danger, Ames." He indicated a big bowl of buttered sweet potatoes at Charles' elbow and there was laughter around the table.

Rob returned to Mulberry Shore the middle of February. His arrival as usual put fresh excitement into the whole atmosphere and he became the animated center of all that was said and done. The household echoed with laughter, high voices, and gleeful sounds from Lakeann. The servants either hovered around, raptly attentive, or raced about at twice their usual speed.

On his second night home, he invited Charles and Mr. Torents into the main room for an evening's visiting. I sat with them, for Rob was to review the work they had done for him and discuss some of his future business and political plans.

He gave us a brilliant account of his sojourn in Austin and spoke of his plans for re-election. The voting would be in the fall, for elections were annually, and he expected to have some opposition. His campaigning and his legal business would keep him much on the road, he lamented. He spoke like a man happily harassed by too much to do. With great pride he told us of the law partnership he had formed with a young legislator from Harrison County, Isaac Van Zandt: *Potter and Van Zandt, Attorneys-at-law,* to be in attendance at all district court sessions in East Texas.

Van Zandt was a leading voice in the House, Rob explained, and the two of them stood together on a number of vital issues. He appreciated Van Zandt's zealous defense of the Texas Navy against spiteful attacks in the House, as well as his support of bonuses for all who had served in the Navy. He had invited Van Zandt into partnership after his brilliant and successful opposition to Sam Houston's efforts in behalf of the Cherokees—Houston was now a congressman in the lower chamber.

He also held forth on land fraud problems of the Republic and explained some of the protective legislation he had presented and supported along this line. With a vanity pardonable among close friends and family, he let us know that he was now considered an authority on land matters in the Congress and was in line for chairmanship of the Committee of Public Lands when he was returned to the Senate.

Charles injected a casual question into the discussion.

"Colonel, what is the Traveling Board of Land Commissioners accomplishing? Do you approve of their work?"

Rob was extravagant in his praise of this board's investigation. They were out to put an end to the forging of land certificates and restore the vanishing virtue of the county officials mainly responsible of the wholesale graft, he explained.

Why, in Shelby County alone, there were enough fraudulent certificates issued to absorb the public domain!" he said. "Those greedy villains were making land transactions absolutely worthless. Van Zandt told me that he had seen certificates pawned for drinks in grogshops, not worth a sup of sour ale per acre! . . . And when the board refused to recommend for patent a whole basketful of certificates, a fantastic process of bloodletting was set off. Murder and counter-murder! A deadly purging! The rascals are killing each other off fast in those parts now—their first genuine service to the Republic! How I congratulate myself that I removed from that infested area before this feudal warfare broke out."

Before saying good night to the men, Rob reminded them that his absences might mean that he would need their help again soon. He expected to be home only a few weeks. Neither man expressed any eagerness to accommodate him, though both were polite.

"Where will you be going from here, Ames?" he inquired.

"I'm leaving for Clarksville tomorrow," Charles said. "I plan to start a furniture business there. I've had some experience with wood carving, trunk making, and such."

"I thought you were a trader, Ames—that you liked to roam the forests with only occasional turns at agriculture such as I can offer you here."

"I was a trader. I'm through," Charles said rather abruptly. "I'm settling."

"Oh. You've found some fair companion that requires this settling, I presume?"

Charles flushed and said simply, "No."

"Shouldn't try to settle until you get a woman," Torents said as though in bitter jest. "Don't count on me, Colonel. I may not be back."

"Not be back! Davis! You've been such a regular caller and able assistant around here the last year or so that I've grown to depend on you. What's taking you away?"

He and Rob stood looking at each other as if communicating something silently.

"Just decided to pick up my pencils and go the other way, Colonel. Tired of this half-breed world. That's all."

"Now, Davis, don't be a cynic. You know there's a big demand for maps of this region."

"Big demands for other things too. No, Colonel. You can have it."

"I don't want it all, Davis. Only my share. Plenty for everyone. No matter where else you go, you'll miss a lot of things we have to offer here. But I won't argue. Maybe you'll change your mind. After a good night's sleep."

After the door was closed behind them, Rob muttered, "I'll be damned!" I couldn't tell if he was amused or annoyed and he didn't enlighten me. He went out for a while and when he came back in to go to bed, he said, "I feel like serenading the world! Did you know it's full moon tonight! A chilling brilliance over everything!"

"I wish we could walk together on the lake shore."

"Too near your appointed hour for that. Get in bed. I'll put the buffalo robe over you so you won't chill. Then I'll open the door so you can see the splendor of the night. And I'll give a concert. The mood and the night compel me."

He got his violin and stood in the door playing with a force and quality that amazed me. The music of the single violin seemed to swell and dominate the night air like an orchestration on the theme of love with all its yearnings and excitements woven into the vast mysteries of the night. The wind that swept across the lake brought in the damp fragrances of the islands to mix with the fresh plowed earth odors from the fields. The whole effect was intoxicating—and my senses were simply swimming about in the ecstasy of it.

From what Hannah had to tell me the next day, however, the effects on others who listened were in a different extreme. I think Rob knew this. When I told him my supreme delight in his playing, and what a treat it was for all who heard, he made an odd reply.

"That depends on what they have and what they want. Music that is one person's delight may be another's madness."

And madness it must have been on the shores of the lake that strange night . . .

Hannah was very weary the next morning.

"Didn' git ta sleep till dat crazy ol' moon quit spreadin' hits witchin' light an' dat fiddle music Colonel Potter conjure up git time ta weah off."

"Music is such a rarity around here, Hannah, I thought it would make everybody happy."

"Ones Ise watchin' ack mo' lak da debbil grab a-hol' dey hawts an' squeezin' de blood out!"

"That's a ghastly expression."

"Yassum. Fus', Delia cum ta mah doo', an' she say, 'See 'bout Tildy.' Den she run off down taw'ads de lake, moanin' lak she do when she feel a wailin' spree comin' on."

"I've never heard her wail."

"She be roun' heah long nuff, ya will. She go plum wil'. Ennyways, ah goes outta Delia's cabin to see 'bout Tildy. An' dat Mr. Torens, he standin' in de doo' hiz cabin, listenin' an' talkin' 'bout haow he ain' heahed Colonel Potter play lak dat since de dawn aftuh yo' weddin' night. Low an' behol'! dat Mr. Ames come at 'im frum behin', shove 'im outta dat doo', an' whizz pas' lak heel flies on 'im an' he rushin' to wawtuh. Yassum, he hed fo' de lake sho' same as Delia."

"How strange, Hannah!"

"Yassum. Dat music sho' nuff chasin' 'em roun' en a debbil's frolic."

"What did Mr. Torents do?"

"Jes stan' dere, damnin' evuh thing cum ta hiz min'. Ah goes on in ta min' Tildy. Sweet chile, she a-sleepin'. Jes lak little Lake— she nevuh whimpuh all night. Effen dem two heahs enny music, hit jes lullaby ta dey angul souls. Wallum, whiles Ise peepin' at Tildy, cum a soun' at da doo'. An' who ya 'spose standin' dere? Dat Mr. Torens! Ah reckons he watchin' me cum ovah, an' he wantin' sum coffee er kivver—so ah asks 'im iz he wantin' sech, an' he laughs jes lak a maniac—yassum, he sho do! An' he answer me jes lak one. He tryin' ta fin' hiz way outta hell, he say, an' effen ah knows de road out, pleasta giv' 'im directions. Ah tol' 'im hit wuz jes a crazy night an' go on bak ta bed."

"I didn't realize Davis was so unhappy."

"Dat man way down pas' unhappy an' diggin' deepuh fas'. He pay me no min' 'bout goin' bak ta bed. Dat fiddle git mo' loud, an' he damn sum mo' lak he talkin' bak, den he go same way Delia an' Mr. Ames. Ah gits wurrisome 'bout 'em all outten dat chill aih'thout dey wraps."

"So you go to the bluff to see what you can see?"

"Haow 'ya know dat missus? Yo'all watchin' too?"

"Heavens no! I was cozy under the buffalo robe, enjoying the concert."

"Dat sho' yo' hawt content, missus . . . wallum, whut ah sees do mak me shivuh, hit sholy do! Way out yonduh on de lake in dat little ol' canoey, 'bout outta sight, iz dat Mr. Ames. Win' so high an' chill, sho' Gawd's wonduh he don' drown. An' out dere on de beach, somethin' thrashin' roun' . . . hit's Delia sho' . . . she allus claw and roll round' lak dat when she wailin'. Sho' nuff dat Mr. Torens fin' 'ur dere. He pulls 'ur up an' dey gits in a tuseel o' sum kin' . . . Don' know whethuh he tryin' ta hep 'ur, tryin' ta take 'ur, uh tryin' to kill 'ur—an' ah don' much cauh which hit iz . . . dey rassels bak untuh de cliff outah mah sight. So ah cums on bak ta de cabin an' jes sets up wif dat crazy ol' moon till hit ready ta go down an' folks iz unwitched. . . . Don' git fretted, missus. Dey al cum bak frum de debbil's dance in human fawm. Delia—she got no mo' to say den a swunk mummy head, and rat naow she all bus' out wif a rash an wawk down to de wash shed. An' de gennemen, dey bof packin' lak dey long time gone."

22.

I had a special reason for being heart-content the night Rob played his violin with such abandon on Mulberry Shore. It was much more than sentimental memory of our wedding night and yet tied in with it. I was thinking of the good news he had brought me from Austin—something for my ears alone. During our first moments of privacy after his arrival, with Lakeann held on one arm and his other around me, he had spoken it.

"My dear Lady Lakeann, I have some very special news for you. Through a petition which I originated, all such marriages as ours are now recognized as legal by a special act of Congress. The act passed the Congress the third of this month. So you need never worry about that any more."

"Oh, Rob, I'm so glad. There's nothing more we have to do?"

"Nothing whatsoever. It's right there on the statute books, made to order. It supersedes the 1837 law that had put a false interpretation on unlicensed frontier ceremonies. I'm proud of the job I did on it—no opposition to speak of. I'll read it to you later."

We spoke of it no more until the day our son was born (February 26, 1841) and then because of a quarrel.

Rob had been home about a week, and it was a very busy time. We'd hardly spoken of the child to come and were both surprised when he made such a sudden and undisturbing appearance. We had enjoyed a time together over the noontime meal, and then Rob had gone out for an afternoon's ride over his property. When he came back he had a son.

As he stood at my bedside, looking upon our son for the first time, I said, "Well, Senator Potter, what do you think of the junior senator?"

He kissed me, then the baby, before he answered.

"He has well-formed features—the Potter hairline and brow, but in other respects your facial structure, the set of the eyes, the wide mouth. What shall we name him? I don't believe we have discussed names."

"Discuss names? Why, I never thought of anything other than his own father's name. You wanted a son, didn't you, to carry on your name? Robert Potter, Junior, is his name, of course. The whole household has thought of nothing else. I don't like to call a child 'junior' though. We'll call him 'Bobby' while he's a youngster and 'Robert' when he's older—you've always been called 'Rob' so there won't be any confusion."

"Indeed there won't! He will not be named Robert! I forbid it! Do you understand? I forbid it!"

He turned away in sudden temper and walked to the fireplace. With his back to me, he stood there tapping his fingers irritably on the mantle.

I was startled and hurt. Then I became indignant and defensive for both myself and the child. Was he so touchy, I wondered, because in his first marriage there had been the afflicted child named Robert? After all, he had denied that child as his own. Then the boy had been taken from him by law and given another name. The mother was dead—the child, incurable and destined for a short life span—he had learned through letters from relatives and, in melancholy mood, confided in me. Now he was indulging in some dark mood of pride or shame that offended me deeply. It seemed dreadfully unfair of him to cloud this happy time with old ties and tragedies. I had given him a beautiful son to bear his name—another Robert Potter, perhaps to be a greater and more brilliant man than his father, to reflect his father's better self. Had he really wanted a son, after all? I asked myself. Was he carrying on some pretense with me, not so happy and devoted a husband as I had been thinking?

"If you're ashamed of your name," I said, "or ashamed for him to carry your full name, then I'm ashamed for us all!"

He didn't answer me, just tapped the mantle with his fingers faster and louder.

My anger rose in a sudden flash of response. "Well, do you want him to be named 'Potter', or will that offend you too? Is this some make-believe marriage? Am I some wilderness mistress, producing your bastard offspring?" I flung myself over on my face and began to weep wildly into the pillow.

He raced to my side. "Good God, Hatty! What's come over you? Just because I can't abide a namesake is no cause for you to have a tantrum. I shouldn't have spoken so sharply. I didn't realize your heart was so set on naming him for me."

He touched me on the shoulder. I moved away from his touch and answered through my weeping, "I thought you'd want it too."

"But I don't, you see." He became very gentle and persuasive and made quite a speech.

"I'm sorry, but it's something I can't change or explain. Stop weeping, Hatty. You've let yourself get upset beyond reason. And you've no cause to lash out at me on the point of marriage and make me out a villainous seducer. In the five years we've been together, have I ever withheld affection or respect, denied you support or protection, refused you the use of my name? Have you ever seen me look with anything but the greatest pride and fondness on little Lake? Have I ever presented you to friends or strangers as anything other than the cherished lady of this household? Have I not trusted you, confided in you, on all matters pertaining to my business enterprises here? And what was the first thing I told you when I came home? Weren't you listening? I told you to banish all worry about the legal aspects of our marriage. Didn't you understand that I purposely got the act passed to validate our union in the most permanent manner possible? Now, I'm going to read it to you, word for word, and you're going to listen."

He went to his desk, got out a pamphlet, and returned to my bedside. I knew he was waiting for me to stop crying. So, I stopped, and listened, but I did not turn my head toward him. He read this . . .

> *That whereas, any persons heretofore, previous to the passage of an act approved June the fifth, eighteen hundred and thirty-seven, had for the want of some person legally qualified to celebrate the rites of matrimony, resorted to the practice of marrying by bond; and others have been married by various officers of justice, not authorized to celebrate such marriages are declared legal and valid, to all intents and purposes; and the issue of such persons are hereby declared legitimate children, and capable of inheritance.*

When he had finished, he repeated the clause solemnly and slowly . . . " 'And the issue of such persons are hereby declared legitimate children, and capable of inheritance.' Do you understand now, fully and clearly?"

I indicated that I understood, but I did not turn over to face him. He reached over and gave me one of the fine silk handkerchiefs he always carried, and continued talking.

"And now what shall we name this exceedingly legitimate son of ours? Something literary? Historical? Biblical?"

I gave him no help.

"Matthew—Mark—Luke—John . . . All good names, sound well with Potter . . . Hatty! That's it! 'John' is the right name—'John D.' for your older brother John!"

I liked the idea. He knew I would. But I mumbled, "Maybe he doesn't like namesakes either."

"Don't be difficult, Hatty. You know he'll like it. The baby has a marked resemblance to you and should be named for one of the Moore family. You've told me what a tall, handsome fellow John is. He'll soon be here, settling near us. This should please him—and you. *John D. Potter.* You do like it, don't you? Tell me now. It isn't like you to pout."

I moved about and looked at the little one. He had slept peacefully through all the tumult. And gazing upon him, I lost all my resentment and disappointment. I thought of John and his loss of wife and child. The child Amy carried so happily might have been his son, and beyond a doubt *it* would have been named 'John David.' A nephew by that name would make up just a little—warm a spot in his heart. It would be something in memory of Amy, too—dear, lusty, lovely Amy.

I wiped my eyes and face with the silk handkerchief. I looked at Rob and smiled.

"Yes, Rob, I think 'John D. Potter' is a fine name. My brother will be pleased, very pleased—I'm sure of it."

Before John D. was a month old, Rob was called to Clarksville by his good friend Amos Morrill who sent word that the Traveling Board of Land Commissioners was examining the land certificates of Red River County and it would be well for Rob to be close by for any questioning that might come up. Neither of us felt any particular anxiety over the summons. Rob had asked Mr. Morrill to keep him informed on this matter so that he might clear title through patent as soon as possible.

It was an inconvenient time for him to be called away from Mulberry Shore, however. Spring planting was still to be done, and several of his best mares were due to foal. Abraham was too young for responsibility, and John hadn't arrived yet. We had received word from John that he was coming to the Point in company with a Mr. Rieves who was moving his family in; their plan was to charter a steamboat and come by way of Shreveport. This would be quite a venture since thus far no steamboat had come into Lake Ferry. The river would have to be right for such a trip—so planting might be well past by the time John arrived. Rob promised me that if his business took more than a week, he'd send someone from Clarksville. Perhaps Ames would come again, he said.

He explained to me that the main intent and purpose of the land board was interception of the big grafts carried out under fictitious names. Their work could not possibly affect his headright except to speed up the securing of patent by weeding out the frauds. Since he had, beyond all question, served the republic loyally in the independence struggle, he felt certain his rights would not be tampered with. But he was eager to know what frauds would be uncovered in Red River County. He suspected Old Rose of some monkey business, he said, in the settling of the Rose clan; some of them he feared, were already trespassing on the Potter headright.

He departed in high spirits. I knew his mind would be pleasantly occupied on the long ride with plans for his land, for his re-election, for his court cases with his partner Van Zandt. And I could imagine, too, that he would probably recite some speeches as he rode along, some in behalf of his own candidacy, some in behalf of his friend Burnet who was expected to run against Houston for the presidency. If Burnet could be elected, Rob knew some choice appointment awaited him—almost anything he might request. So, as he rode on to Clarksville, he probably mapped out the road to fame and glory that he expected soon to be traveling: Senator . . . Ambassador . . . President. Would I ever accompany him, I wondered, when he had attained these ambitions? Did I accompany him in his imagination? Or, was I always left behind at Mulberry Shore?

A few days after Rob left, the strangest man I ever saw came to my door. He was like something out of a legend. We stood staring at each other in mutual surprise. He towered above me. His big mouth so full of big protruding teeth reminded me of the wolf in the Red Ridinghood story, yet I was aware that the smile of it and the glow in the wide friendly eyes were no disguise. At his heel was a huge wolflike dog. Like his master, his expressions were friendly. Dusty and Domino were showing him proper respect, however, keeping their distance. Beyond the fence, I saw the tall mule he had ridden, and the two smaller white pack animals. His costume fascinated me: reptile boots, belt, vest, hat trim, and various ornaments. I had never before been aware of the fierce beauty of the little coral snake—had never seen it's hide stretched and finished so skillfully—would never have thought the copperhead's coloring could be such a glittery show—nor all the greens of nature so artfully displayed in a snake's protective camouflage.

His first words to me were: "In my mind, you were pine-tall, Brave Woman, and now my eyes behold you only flower-high."

"I am Mrs. Potter," I said, thinking this pronouncement might clear up his daftness.

"You are lake and forest woman . . . you are kishi-woman *sans peur!* Dee wah!"

"And who are you?"

"Tejas! Call me Friend, Brave Woman, and honor my life!"

"I have no reason to call you otherwise. But you do have a name, don't you?"

"My name is well matched with my face and my trade. I am the peddler Snake Seecher. My wares are from snakeskins. My trails are where I make them. Dee wah!"

"Welcome to Potter's Point, Mr. Seecher. Have you journeyed far?"

"From gulf waters to lake waters that I might stand here—before the bravest woman in the Republic of Texas!"

"Mr. Seecher, what improbable tales have you been hearing about me?"

"My heart sifts what my ears hear, and I know a kishi-woman has been in the forest. I know a kishi-woman dwells by the lake. Dee wah!"

I invited him in to show his wares and was surprised that he declined with many French and Spanish flourishes, and said he only wanted my permission to camp near the premises—that he had nothing to sell at my door. I offered him a cabin for which he thanked me in several languages before declining that also. His *amigos animales* who traveled with him would not understand, would be lonely he explained . . . and didn't I recognize in him a guardian in the camp of Caddi-Ayo, appointed to watch the bejeweled sky?

I almost answered him "Dee-wah!" and did reply from some urge to match his poesy of expression.

"I recognize in you one appointed by Caddi-Ayo to spread good will. And as long as you abide near us, we will feel bedecked with the jewels of your friendship."

My response awed him. He looked at me with a dazed sort of wonderment, bowed low, and turned away. Several times he looked back at me before he mounted his mule—and each time, he gave me a bow of reverence that had me feeling very self-conscious.

There was no doubt about the Indian strain in Mr. Seecher—but there were also inherited streaks of Spanish soldier and French trader banded into his personality as brightly as the stripes on the coral snake trim of his costume. How odd it was that a man of such chance mixture whose trade derived from serpents should be so harmonious in character—such a dweller with peace and beauty.

He camped at Mulberry Shore for several days. And it was while we were enjoying the pleasant diversion of his curious presence that Rob became embroiled in unexpected controversy at Clarksville.

In due course, I heard the story of what took place from Rob, from Charles, and from Mr. Morrill. Three men, each of different temperament, and I came to know them all so well, that I can recapture those scenes and stage them in my mind in full dimension and dialogue.

Rob rode directly to the house of his friend when he arrived at Clarksville and Amos met him at the gate. There was bad news written on his grave visage.

They shook hands and Rob demanded, "What's happened, Amos? Tell me at once."

"The board has rejected your certificate. They will not approve it for patent. They say that there is not sufficent evidence that you are the legal head of a family in this Republic—that evidence is entirely lacking that you were head of a family on March 2, 1836."

"Amos, are you sure?" Rob's lips drew tight and the blood left his face.

"I'm very sure. Come on in and we'll discuss the details. I had a talk with H. L. Williams, a member of the board."

Amos poured drinks and they sat before a small fire. Rob was slumped in dejection, shaking his head in disbelief, drinking, while Amos talked to him.

"Don't lose heart, Rob. We'll take it to the district court," Amos was saying. "The statute that created this traveling board provides that holders of rejected claims may bring suit in the district court and seek to recover their claims by presenting the same proof required before the county board. We'll claim that damage has been done you by this refusal and pray the court for clearance."

"My enemies have conspired against me," Rob groaned, "otherwise this indignity would not be heaped upon me. Certainly there can be no doubt of my service to the Republic, my loyalty through the dark days. I've given my time and energies to nothing but public service since my arrival at Nacogdoches in 1835. And now they try to make capital of my personal life, quibble over dates of family matters that would never be questioned except in malice. Who are they that desire to expose me to public scandal?" His hands twitched and his eyes flashed as temper began to feed energy back into his system.

"I don't know about your enemies at the capital, Rob. Every energetic legislator has some. Maybe some member of this board carries a grudge or a friend's grudge against you for something you've sponsored or opposed. And perhaps he examined your certificate with extra care in the hope of finding a flaw, however small, that would cause you public embarrassment, maybe put you out of the senatorial race."

"Yes, yes—it could be. There are some who rankle at my authority on the land laws and my probable chairmanship of the committee on public lands."

"Then there's your local opposition to consider—and I do know something about that. Your property location is choice and has aroused envy. There are those who would like to keep you out of the Congress, diminish your popularity."

"But no one has announced for my place."

"Plenty of time yet."

"Any rumors?"

"None yet. Your reputation is still too solid with the voters to invite a race. And your oratorical powers make you a formidable opponent. You have a neighbor, however, who has already made public declaration that he will support anyone who comes out against you."

"Which neighbor of mine?"

"A dangerous one—the Lion of the Lakes—Captain Rose himself."

"Now we are touching the core of this perfidy!"

"I'm convinced he was partially responsible for the board's decision against you. You know Old Rose. He doesn't whisper anything, slander or praise—he shouts. And he shouts quite openly that you're a single man and entitled only to a single man's bonus. He says that the lady residing at your estate is a Mrs. Page of Brazoria and not your wife. What do you say to that?"

"I give it the damned lie! That mangy old beast! I'll strangle him!"

"You'll have to keep calm, Rob, so we can think straight. You entered Texas, you say, in 1835?"

"July, 1835."

"Did you get the required certificate of character?"

"Indeed I did."

"How were you listed—your family status, I mean?"

"As a widower with family. Why question me on this? You know I don't like probing into my past."

"I'm assuming that you'll want me to help with your representation in court."

"Will you, Amos?"

"Of course. Am I the type of friend to go back to shore when the water gets deep?"

"Indeed not. Forgive me."

"When you got your bonus certificate in 1838, you represented that you were entitled to a family man's headright. Were you claiming your present wife, the former Mrs. Page, as a family?"

"Yes, but the oath I took referred only to time of arrival in the Republic, my service and my loyalty, as required by law, without reference to the who and where of my family."

"Did anyone on the board attempt to question you specifically—mention your North Carolina family?"

"Yes—but not for the records—prompted only by vulgar curiosity, hoping to prick my pride. I answered quite promptly that my North Carolina family consisted of two children 'by reputation.' " Rob gave bitter emphasis to the phrase "by reputation."

"What children had you then by the present Mrs. Potter?"

"Only my stepson, Joe. We had lost an infant son at birth."

"And now there's little Lake you've mentioned to me so fondly."

"Yes, and a son hardly two weeks old, born to us on February twenty-sixth."

"Congratulations! Now you have a better reason than ever to fight for your land and your reputation. What's his name?"

"John D. Potter."

"Having a son should put spine and spunk into you, Rob. Away with dismals! A toast is in order . . . Here's to the Senator from Red River and the Senator's son . . . Here's to success . . . the race to be run . . . the fight to be won!"

He and Rob settled down to planning the suit to be brought against the Republic. They must work fast. The spring session of court was near at hand. Rob forestalled Amos on further questioning about family data by admitting that circumstances had prevented proper documentation of his marriage to me. He explained that the union had been entered into in mutual good faith and proper intent which, he believed, was sufficient moral and legal commitment, although no entry had yet been made in public records. It had been his intention to do this following the recent enactment of a fitting statute on bond marriages. But now he believed that making such an entry would be too conspicuous, invite attention where it was least wanted. Didn't Amos agree with him? Amos did.

They further agreed that several attorneys of political importance should be brought in to sign the petition and present evidence and argument, attorneys with enough prestige and bearing to awe the judge and jury.

Rob said Isaac Van Zandt, his law partner, should be one. "Isaac has logic and delivery and his comments on my service in the Senate will command the best attention. And I will make so bold as to ask Thomas J. Rusk as well. I enrolled with the Independent Volunteers under his command during my early residence in Nacogdoches. He and J. Pinckney Henderson have recently gone into law partnership. Rusk and I have often been in opposing camps but there are reasons why at this time he's not likely to refuse me this favor. Yes. I shall get Rusk."

"It will cinch your case, Rob, if you can," Amos told him. "And may I suggest John B. Denton as a man of influence in your home district."

"You represent my home district in the best possible fashion, Amos."

"But I'm known more as your personal friend. Denton would be better along with Van Zandt and Rusk. I'll be on hand, of course."

Rob began to see in the suit a great publicity value for himself. "Amos, I'll turn this case to my own advantage yet. To win a decision from the Republic—that will enhance my legal reputation, further popularize me with the common people. It will be the first case of its kind! And to win it! Think what that will mean! I'll show those connivers!"

"Be careful of Rose, Rob," Amos warned. "You know his methods. He would like to excite you to violence and eliminate you in his own ruthless way. He's carrying his slander to ludicrous degrees, in the belief, I think, that you'll come running right into his gunfire. So I trust you to let humor dominate temper when I tell you this further thing: He says you comport yourself toward other women like a single man—that you have on occasion paid court to a woman of his family— his daughter, I presume."

Rob scowled, then laughed. "The women of his family are charming enough to incite the courting fever in the worthiest of men. Tell me, Amos, how is it that the most offensive ruffians can win for mates the most beguiling and fairest of women and beget offspring equally as lovely? I admit I've given his womenfolks the most courteous, and I must say, pleasurable attentions. The trouble with that scaly old billy goat is that he doesn't know the difference between courting and courtesy."

"Well, hereafter, you'd better make the difference very clear to any sires, sons, or suitors that happen to be around."

"Don't concern yourself on that score. If any Rose meets up with me, it will be on my own property or along my own path, and at his own risk!"

"Watch your every word and deed from now on, Rob. Hold your temper in check no matter what you hear that Rose has said or threatened. He's been so brazen as to say that since you are entitled to only a third of the land you claim, he intends to file on a part of it for a relative of his."

"I'll kill him if he does!"

"That's just the kind of thing you mustn't say outside this room."

"He should be entitled the 'Leech of the Lakes!' An aquatic worm! A bloodsucker!"

Amos waited patiently for him to subside.

"I know, Amos, I know. I can no longer afford the luxury of careless anger. I must learn composure in all the passions—and yet, man needs some stormy elements, don't you think, if he would play any role above the average?"

"Quite right, Rob. Fire is a good thing for warmth, but out of control it consumes and destroys."

"All right, Amos, I promise not to flame too high or spark too far. Now that we have our plans made, let's go see Doc and Isabella. To me there's nothing more cheering than their delightful company. I should not allow myself to be morose for a moment when I have such good friends as you and the Gordons behind me."

Dr. Gordon and his wife, Isabella, had entered into a friendship with Rob that meant much to him, and he was proud of the correspondence they carried on with him while he was in Austin. They were prominent citizens of Clarksville; Mrs. Gordon was wealthy in her own right, being formerly the widow of the Clark for whom the town was named. The political and literary discussions that took place at their fireside were always a feast in sociability for Rob, and their regard and approval were important to him as a lawyer and political figure. I had packed his finest attire for the trip, knowing he would be visiting with the Gordons. This included his fashionable blue "colonel" coat, a satin vest, silk scarf, and a fine high-crowned, fawn-colored beaver hat. So his grooming was as perfect as he could make it when he and Amos set out for the Gordons.

On the way there, he asked Amos about Charles Ames and learned that they were near his workshop.

"Take me by there, Amos. God knows when I'll get back to Mulberry Shore. I must see Ames and get him off posthaste to the management of my farm. Spring is such a demanding season."

"Do you think he'll leave his shop?"

"I'll persuade him."

So that was how Rob and Amos came to call on Charles. They found him at work with his chisel in the small one-room building he had rented for his woodshop. The room was fragrant with the odor of woods. Charles, in contrast to his callers, was dressed for comfort and work—sleeves of his cotton shirt rolled up, collar open, loose trousers, roomy moccasins. But this put no constraint upon them, Charles least of all. He greeted his friends warmly, removed tools and some shaped pieces of wood from a stool and a wooden crate that they might be seated.

"I guess you've heard of my fate at the hands of the traveling board," Rob mentioned at once, offering a cigar.

Charles declined the cigar and picked up his pipe. He answered Rob that this fact was public knowledge and regrettable. Then he brought coals to light their smokes.

"I suppose you're aware of the verbal dungcart Old Rose has been pulling around to make things more difficult for me." Rob continued.

"The captain is not secretive with his opinions," Charles replied. "And on matters concerning you his tongue has been extra loose and loud."

"I should cut it out of his head," Rob said, "but Amos here has turned me from violence temporarily." He was smiling that his friends might know he was speaking lightly.

He told Charles of the suit he planned against the Republic, and it was obvious that the taste of controversy was becoming sweeter with every word. Then he came to the purpose of his call.

"So, it will be weeks before I can return to Mulberry Shore. You know the needs there better than anyone else, Ames, and you have a knack for farm management. I appeal to you as a friend in need of a friend's assistance to go there at once and take over for me. I know you don't need such employment and that you're turning a talent to profit here—and I don't mean to take advantage of our friendship. But if my fields are properly planted and my good mares well tended through the spring foaling, there will be profit for us both. And your share should more than compensate for any losses here." He looked about the workshop in a way that implied Charles had little to lose and much to gain by granting his request.

Charles crossed and recrossed his legs, squinted, puffed on his pipe.

"Tell me, Charles, can you go at once—today?"

Charles looked at Rob, a long searching look, wondering if Rob might possibly suspect his true feelings and simply be using him to selfish advantage. But Rob's returning stare seemed to hold nothing but friendly eagerness waiting to flash into brilliant warmth if Charles accepted.

Charles looked around the room at the pleasant work he had

planned and hardly started. Despondency swept over him, and he felt overwhelmingly saddened. The future seemed a dark curtain that he dared not try to peep through. He rose to his feet, wandered about, pretended to be putting some tools in place, and, while he was facing away from Rob, he said softly, as though to himself, "I'll go."

Rob burst into happy thanks.

Charles turned to him and listened attentively to instructions on planting and care of livestock. At last, Rob spoke of me and the children.

"Tell *Mrs. Potter*," and he emphasized the title, making this his whole answer to whatever Charles might have heard about *Mrs. Page*, "that the legal matter isn't serious, but, that it will detain me indefinitely into the spring session of court. I don't want her worried. I trust you to protect her from the anxieties that any fuller knowledge might bring to her. Little Lake will welcome you and your forest tales. I'm jealous of the attentions I know she'll bestow on you."

Charles smiled gently, pleased that Lake had told her Daddy about the stories—had missed them perhaps—and for that little moment he and Rob were very close in their mutual affection for Lakeann.

"I've left my biggest and most pleasant news until last, Ames. I have a son—John David Potter, born on the twenty-sixth. You can understand that the desire of my heart is that my wife and children remain happy and unmolested. I can't tell you how it relieves me that you're going to them."

Charles spoke proper congratulations. There were admonitions and farewells, Rob concealing his eagerness to be off to the Gordons, Charles concealing the sad certainty that had engulfed him.

When the door of his shop was closed behind the two men, Charles moved about putting his tools away, piling unfinished pieces methodically, brushing up shavings, wishing he could will away the awful conviction that he was witnessing the beginning of a feud—the Rose-Potter feud—and that it would come to blood letting and death dealing in some ghastly finale. The two principals involved would not change in nature, in residence, or in purpose.

The first thing that Charles saw when he came into the big room at Mulberry Shore was the green reptile purse that Snake Seecher had presented to me in farewell. He walked to the table where I had left it and stood staring at it. I rushed over and placed it in his hands and began telling him all about my strange friend and his presents, which included a vest for Abraham and moccasins and belt for Joe.

When I paused, he said, "Dee-wah!"

"Charles! You know him!" I exclaimed.

It was the first time I had ever addressed him by his first name. It startled us both. I was embarrassed but he flashed such a happy smile in response that I could not say "Mr. Ames" again.

"Tell me all you know about this peddler," I demanded.

He admitted to having seen the purse before and told me of his traveling with Seecher and the conversation between them, or at least as much as he thought best to tell me just then.

"He heard from the Indians that you are without fear and that you can tame panthers—that's why he calls you kishi-woman—a very high form of praise. Seecher himself has made you a sort of high priestess in his cult of friendship. His Indian nature has idealized you into a forest and lake woman of goddess proportions—a type to worship."

"That's very strange!"

"Not so strange . . ." he said in a peculiar tone of voice, and then quickly inquired, "Did he tell you about rattlesnake steaks?"

"Oh, yes, how to prepare them for cooking and all that. I told him the Garden of Eden story had contaminated the snake in the eyes of most Christians. He asked me to repeat the story, and I did. He said to his ears it seemed that the apple was the contaminated food in that tale, and that if Eve had eaten the snake and left the apple alone, mankind might still be in the Garden. He cautioned me never to eat apples and snake steaks in combinations. It does sound evil, doesn't it?"

"Dee-wah!"

We both laughed.

"Certainly, his use of snakes either for skins or meat has left no evil mark on his nature that I could detect. Abundant friendliness is as much his trademark as the snakeskin. I confess to a feeling of affection for him and his beautiful friendly animals. He reminded me some of Prowling Bear—strolling about, looking at things so curiously. At other times he was not like an Indian at all. I saw him standing out on the bluff one day, and I thought of a lonely soldier on duty at a remote outpost of some ancient kingdom. My heart ached for him and I knew not why. I walked out and stood by him. We stood together silently for a while, looking out over the lake, and then he said to me, 'Ina, the Mother Earth understands all, Brave Woman. Behold her. Listen to her. Take counsel of her. She has wisdom for you. You are her favored child. She loves you.' And you know, Charles, the most wonderful feeling came over me. I felt myself a part of the earth under me, of the sky, of the water, of all things, and I was supremely happy in a holy sort of way."

This sharing of our feelings about Snake Seecher brought back an ease and comfort of friendship between us that we accepted as naturally as the happy tasks in which we became engaged. I was often with Charles or near him in the outdoors work. Delia and Hannah cared for house and children. I worked in the garden, tended the poultry, rode after the stock, milked the cows, watched Charles and Abraham at their field work, brought them buttermilk or berry juice to quench their thirst at midmorning and midafternoon, dug in the earth to see if the seeds were sprouting properly, and at noontime and evening asked Charles endless questions about plant and animal life in the forest which had been his home while I was still a city dweller.

At one day's end, after checking at the stables on the condition of a new colt, Charles and I walked together to the top of the steps leading down to the spring, moved by an unspoken agreement that the sunset was too glorious to turn our backs on. We stood watching the awesome display of colors deepening to crimson and purple, bringing to the lake reflections of incredible wonder. All the sounds that came to us were expressions of animal and human contentment. Joe was calling to Domino, then laughing in a joyous romp with the dog. Hannah's soothing voice was raised in some caution to Lakeann and was answered with a mischievous ripple of laughter. The chickens were flying to roost, cackling now and then gentle notes of false alarm.

I felt saturated with the beauty and peace of my surroundings, full of a gratitude that I must express. At that moment, Charles seemed to me the one most responsible for my contentment.

"Charles, you have been wondrously good to Rob and me—you are the dearest and closest friend we have. I must thank you for coming here to manage for us through these important weeks. I know you left off your own business to do this favor for us. I know too that you'll share with us in some of the profits, but kindness and goodness can't be paid for."

"The pleasure of serving dear friends," Charles answered solemnly, "is the most generous and lasting payment there is."

Silent moments passed while we continued to absorb the beauty around us. Charles had been standing with his hands in his pockets. He withdrew one hand and began an absent-minded display of restlessness with a stone he had removed from his pocket.

"What have you there, Charles?"

"Oh. Just a stone I picked up. See—it has the conformations of a perfect shell."

I moved closer to him to examine it. "Makes one think how old the world must be."

"And how little we know of life's processes. The earth beneath our feet is eloquent with meaning. If we completely understood everything that has happened to this stone—the life it was—the life it is—"

"It's painful, isn't it, Charles, not to know more about everything? Especially for a person like you with the truth mind and heart."

His hands were in restless movement with the stone again, and watching them, I spoke without thinking, "So much goodness in your hands, Charles,—as plain as the honesty in your eyes."

I looked up into his eyes and his gaze met mine directly. We stood locked in a mood of personal harmony that I had never experienced with another human being. It was an affinity that reached through and far beyond physical attraction.

Charles tried to speak but didn't. Finally, he turned aside, so that he was no longer facing me, stuffed his hands in his pockets, and said, wryly, "The first direct praise these unseemly big paws ever had. Thanks, kind lady."

"Charles, why haven't you married?" I asked. "Do you have some true love in your life, waiting for you somewhere?"

He didn't answer me at once. We were facing opposite directions— he toward the house now and I toward the lake.

When he spoke, I was surprised at his answer.

"Yes, I have a true love—as wonderful—as angelic a true love as a man ever had!"

It startled me too that he spoke so feelingly.

"You do?"

"Yes, indeed. Most angelic creatures, you know, have golden hair and blue eyes. But mine is not like that. She has black curls. Skin the color of beach-washed golden sand, eyes that sparkle like black stars, and the most adorable smile that ever graced feminine countenance."

Charles talking like this! Making love to me! Speaking in such an impassioned way that there could be no doubt of his meaning. Looking at me while he spoke: looking at my hair, my skin, my eyes, as he enumerated.

I was stunned. I wanted to cry out to him to unsay it—that it musn't be so. We were staring at each other in mutual distress. Close enough to touch, but not touching—unable to move—as though we had become statues with feeling in every cell but with all motion paralyzed.

It seemed an age before his words released us. There was a sound back of me. He was looking over my shoulder.

He said, in a husky voice, "And here comes that true love of mine right now."

I turned. There was Hannah and Lakeann. He had seen them all the time! Hannah put Lakeann down and she ran the last few steps to Charles. He swung the adorable little dark angel he had described onto his shoulder.

My feelings were in a tumult: anger, humiliation, and could it be—disappointment! Why had he tricked me so! It seemed a cruel prank. I had the impulse to run off from him—rush up the trail and make it evident that I was displeased with the joke, offended. But I thought better of it. I looked at him balancing Lakeann on his shoulder. She was clutching handfuls of his thick hair with great delight and she was amazingly strong. He seemed unaware of it. But on his face was an expression of pain—the stern set of controlled agony. Then, I understood. The little trick had started out as a gentle joke on himself. He hadn't intended to look at me as he spoke—doubtless he intended to mention Lakeann or thought I heard Hannah coming—and then the urge to let me know somehow, someway, had erased both humor and caution. Now he was sorry for what he had done—very sorry. I walked quietly by his side, hoping my presence communicated both my regard and my regret.

400

23.

Rob won his case against the Republic of Texas in the April session of the court. The petition to the court, carrying the imposing signatories of Rusk, Denton, and Van Zandt, specified no particular family. It stated simply that:

> *Your petitioner Robert Potter would respectfully show unto your Honor that he emigrated to the Republic previous to and resided in the same at the date of the Declaration of Independence, that he was at that time head of a family and entitled . . . to one league and labor of land . . . on the fourteenth day of March, 1838, he applied to the Board of Land Commissioners of Red River County and obtained a certificate for the same . . . that March 5, 1841, the Board of Commissioners appointed under an act to detect fraudulent land certificates refused to recommend for patent . . . whereby your petitioner is likely to be greatly damaged . . .*

The speeches of his attorneys citing his services to the Republic had the anticipated result on judge and jury, and reduced the district attorney's defense, so Rob told me, to almost inaudible routine. Judge Hansford presided, and in his decision announced that the jury had found Colonel Potter was entitled to the land originally applied for; therefore, the court decreed the recovery of this land and that patent be issued and that petitioner also recover from the Republic his cost in "this behalf expended."

With this victory, Rob's popularity and influence soared.

The "Lion of the Lakes" became ominously quiet.

Charles returned to Clarksville. My brother John arrived at Mulberry Shore. Fields and forest were in a riot of summer growth, and Rob was in a senatorial race that threatened to grow into a riot!

John B. Denton, who had represented him so ably in district court in the spring, became his opponent in the senatorial race a few months later.

The Lion roused from his den and roared again!

He roared approval and support of Mr. Denton.

He roared that the silk-skinned Potter was a notorious and infamous criminal.

Rob was the Peacock of the Pines, screaming, "Calumny! Murderer!" He branded Rose as a vicious killer, embellishing his crimes with spine-chilling details, and promised that he would personally see Rose prosecuted by the Republic of Texas if the law-abiding voters would return him to his place of authority in the Congress.

As the stories on each side magnified with circulation, Rob became genuinely worried. After all, the people would be voting on Denton, not on Rose, and though Denton was no match for Rob in oratory or personal magnetism, neither was he handicapped by the shadow of scandal that alternately dimmed and darkened around Rob.

Finally, resentment and desire for violent action built up in Rob so much that he went to Amos Morrill and told him that he was ready to silence Old Rose permanently.

"The only way to recover my self-respect and maintain respect in the public eye is to silence his lecherous tongue forcibly. He has besmirched me and mine until there are no words left for retaliation!"

Amos protested, "You'll ruin all chances of political ascendency. You'll disgrace your family and quite possibly lose your life."

"I'd rather lose my life than live it without public honor."

"Rob, you're allowing yourself to feel exactly as Rose wants you to feel—he's counting on some dramatic explosion of temper. I'll not allow you to feed such a dangerous mood, contaminating your true genius and promise of a great future. We'll think of something to counteract all this without violence of any kind—something good for your candidacy—something to squelch the gossip."

"Shall I ascend to heaven and come back with a halo?"

"Nothing that extreme. Have you had any social life at your home out on the point—any public gatherings?"

"Why, visitors come and go at all times, Amos. I maintain cabins for guests and feed them well. But if you refer to parlor socials—I've been on the road too much for that sort of thing."

"Don't you realize that people expect from a public figure some exhibition of family and home life and sociability? Have you ever made a public appearance with Mrs. Potter and the children?"

"Why, no. We can't leave at the same time. The distances are too forbidding—the development of our estate too demanding. There'll come a time, I suppose——"

"You've got to make a time—soon. Your public doesn't understand. It's almost as if you've kept Mrs. Potter in seclusion—that you hide or ignore your family. Please now—I'm speaking of appearances. I know your regard for your family. But do you realize that as close friends as we are, I have never met your wife, never seen your children."

"But that's your fault, Amos! You've been invited—once you were almost there——"

"Yes, but you never brought them to me. I'm just trying to point out to you——"

"I'm not equipped financially to entertain in the manner I consider appropriate. Now, if I had a town house here, and if——"

"Come down from your princely pinnacle, Rob. This doesn't have to be a court function! You don't have to give a formal dinner or fancy dress ball. Just give a barbecue! Have plenty to eat—invite everybody!"

Rob made one of his sudden transitions in mood. He slapped Amos on the back. He began to stride back and forth in a state of high excitement.

"Amos, you wizard! That's it—a barbecue; I've had my sights too high—you're right—putting off such an exhibition until I could sponsor the type of formal function I prefer. How foolish of me! I see it now—a politician's trick as old as time. Feed the people—feed them food, folk music, and humor. Show off family and possessions like exhibits at the county fair! How Hatty and my little Lake and John will shine! And Joe is a sweet appealing little fellow—and Hatty's brothers will be on hand! Why, we'll dry up the gossip and garner the votes all at one fell swoop! Amos—I'll tell you what—I'll even play the violin! And I'll scout the woods for some accompanying musicians. We'll have a frontier frolic! And I'll frolic right on ahead of Mr. Denton and back to Austin!"

Amos had turned the trick. Rob immediately set the date for the big barbecue at Mulberry Shore. In high spirits, he got off a long letter of instructions to me and sent it by special courier, sending at the same time a bolt of yellow silk from which I was to make dresses for myself and Lakeann. He requested that my brother John set off at once for Shreveport to purchase in barrel supply whiskey, white flour, sugar, molasses—and chewing tobacco, snuff, and cigars by the case—and a hundred pounds of coffee. Then he himself set off on a tour of invitation through his district.

Over two hundred men, women, and children attended the barbecue. This was enough to carry a detailed description into every home in the district. Every guest had a personal introduction to the family which Rob himself performed: "My lady, Mrs. Potter . . . my little lady, Lakeann . . . my boy, Joe . . . my son, John . . . my brother-in-law John David, and my brother-in-law Abraham."

Most came so great a distance that they spent the night. Women, girls, and babies were made comfortable on pallets indoors—men and boys bunked on blankets and buffalo robes in the yard for the few hours left in the short summer night after the frolicking was done.

Bear meat, venison, turkey, and great pots of squirrel stew made it unnecessary for Rob to offer more than one of his choice porkers and a single fatted calf on the political altar of barbecue. Molasses, sweet potato, and berry pies sweetened many an opinion. Tobacco by the plug and whiskey by the gourdful washed away many a suspicious thought. Fluffy white bread and buttered spice cake softened many a hard corn-pone heart. And an ornamental glass of snuff for each woman guest tenderized many a gossipy tongue.

Then the final touch of magic: music, with Rob the central figure —Byronic swirl of black hair, flashing eyes, bright blue coat and singing violin—and near him, by request, Lakeann and me, in our identical full-skirted silks, playing our parts quite naturally and merrily, giving the hero of the piece obvious devotion and adoration.

Need I record that he won the election?

When the Sixth Congress convened in early November, Rob had already been in Austin for several days working on matters related to presidential favor. Lamar's term as president would be expiring on December thirteenth and then Houston would be inaugurated— not Burnet as Rob had hoped. So Rob had to work fast in matters that involved action by the chief executive. It was well known that the cultivated Mr. Lamar often had a sympathetic ear for the courtly Mr. Potter's ideas. Rob once told me that Mr. Lamar had said not another member of his congress was so well read, could quote the classics with such wit and application as the Senator from Red River.

So it came about that when Lamar issued a presidential proclamation on November fifteenth offering a five hundred-dollar reward for the capture of Old Rose, Rob's energies in that direction were given full credit. The proclamation charged that Rose had assisted in the murder of the sheriff of Panola County in January and had murdered two citizens of that same county around September first. Old Rose's timing on these two killings in the fall had been in Rob's favor. Coming so near election time, votes were lost for Denton simply because of the Rose support, and Rob was given some high-burning fuel for his final campaign fire. And now, this posting of the "Lion of the Lakes" as a criminal wanted by the Republic so soon after the crimes was for Rob a campaign promise fulfilled in record time. Although Rob's action was judged to be as much personal vengeance as public service, there could be no denying Rose's guilt. He had been indicted for murder, but no officer of the region dared attempt his arrest. It was generally agreed that Old Rose would not submit peaceably to court trial for what he considered "lawful killings" of lawless persons. Whoever went after him would have to fight him. The reward, by making courage more profitable, was expected to bring lion hunters to the lakes from all over the district. Some would surely die, others be mangled, but in the end, the Old Lion would be caged or killed. . . . It didn't work out that way. The courage required to hunt Old Rose down was evidently a much more expensive kind. The proclamation was simply considered an open invitation to disaster. There were no acceptances.

I was greatly disturbed when I heard Rob's reaction to this. He was issuing verbal proclamations, right and left, that he himself would go after Rose when Congress adjourned. If he must do this, I thought, why couldn't he keep quiet about it? I felt that all these flourishing threats were simply putting Rose on guard and, since he lived so near us, exposing us all to his antagonism.

I suppose he thought his pronouncements might arouse someone to compete with him for the reward. What was the male population around the lakes waiting for, he wanted to know, in his letters to me and Dr. Pearce (one of his relatives in the area) and his Clarksville friends. Didn't the Red River citizens realize that Rose was setting up lynchers' rule over them just as the outlaw Moorman had done in Shelby County with his "Regulators?"

His questions were answered by continued inaction. They were waiting for Robert Potter to get home and do what they were afraid to attempt. Some were no doubt saying: This is Robert Potter's doing—let him take care of it. And I sensed the operation of an unwritten code: Since these two hated each other so much and had set this game going, let them play it out to the finish, and alone!

Rob made it quite clear that he would do just this. "I want Rose tried in court—forced to respect the laws and legal machinery of this country," he wrote. "If he resists arrest, then he should be killed—like any outlaw! If the duty finally falls to me to make this arrest, chastise this ruffian, I'll welcome the opportunity—and the five hundred dollars!"

From all accounts I have ever heard, the session of the Sixth Congress was a season of success and expanding influence for Rob. He held the important chairmanship of the Public Lands Committee. He pushed through a measure sponsored by his partner Van Zandt establishing Marshall University, a co-educational institution. He accepted with apparent good grace and compromise the installation of Sam Houston as president. He was even chairman of the committee to wait upon "His Excellency" during the inauguration exercises. It was Senator Potter who could be depended on to understand and direct the proper formalities of the ceremony. It was Senator Potter's committee who escorted the President and Vice-President to their places in accepted style and order.

There was another kind of popularity he achieved in Austin that was completely unknown to me at the time. Though he wrote me much of his legislative doings, he never spoke of his social life. Of course, I knew his manner of adorning any society in which he moved and would not have been surprised had someone told me that he was the central social attraction in Austin that winter, especially in the circle dominated by the Mayfield and Chalmers families. But I would have refused to believe any report on the web of personal intrigue that he was weaving around these two families—so deftly, so quickly, and so fatally. Outside the dangerous involvement with Rose, all I heard was good news—things that made me feel more proud and secure with him. He sent me a clipping from the *Weekly Texian* that published a description of him in its column of "Charcoal Sketches" on Senators in the issue of January 26. He explained that just the day before this was published he had received his patent on his land, duly signed by President Houston. January, 1842 . . . "This has been a month of achievement and recognition," he wrote. The sketch in the *Texian* was quite complimentary. It read:

> *Colonel Potter is well known in the usual acceptation of the word, and I believe but little understood in the true sense. That he has been organized with strong passions and propensities which have brought him into collision with the conventional rules of society, may be true.*
>
> *He is intellectual in a high degree, of great energy of character, of extensive reading and polished address and manners . . . a distinct enunciation and strong, clear and forcible reasoning, added to a happy tact at illustrating, by a good simile or story, creates a deep interest in the listener . . .*
>
> *He is sometimes too severe for the occasion, and satire and sarcasm seem rather too congenial to his temperament. Time is probably mellowing these shades of the picture. That he pursues a line of conduct in legislation marked out by settled and established principles, is clearly perceived; that some of which may be more theoretic than practical, may be true, but that they are ably sustained upon comprehensive views, is equally true. No one is more dignified and urbane in all that belongs to the duties of a senator.*

As January was his month of jubilation, February must have been his month of frustration. He began to realize that he must carry out the arrest of Rose himself. No one had even made an attempt to act on the Lamar proclamation. The Senator from Red River had made public commitments that he could not evade and hope to retain any of the authority he cherished so. He was not as confident about his ability to kill or capture the Lion as his peacock strutting and screaming had made out. If he had been, why would he have made out a deed to his property on February eighth and a will on February eleventh hardly two weeks after receiving his patent? At the same time, he began writing letters, cautiously recruiting assistance, assembling a company of men to go with him after Rose.

He was strangely preoccupied and quiet when he arrived home on March first. There were eight armed men with him, including Hezekiah. Nine more joined him at Mulberry Shore. He carried a copy of the presidential proclamation and a warrant for the arrest of Rose. He was not his lively dapper self and gave his family strained, indifferent greeting. I was much alarmed at the whole arrangement. I protested that he was too tired to undertake a mission so dangerous.

"Not so dangerous," he replied. "We'll take him by surprise. He thinks I'm still in Austin. And I happen to know that he's at home right now with none of his gang around him. We'll overpower him—take him without bloodshed."

"That's not likely, Rob. Rose considers the whole thing your doing —the proclamation your method of destroying him. He intends to kill you and you should know it! He knows—everyone knows!—that you've offered your services to plead the Republic's case against him if he's ever captured and brought to trial. You know he's like a mad dog with your tongue lashings already. He intends to shoot you on sight! Why don't you let some regular officer of the law take him in? If you aren't lucky enough to catch him unarmed, if you aren't alert enough to shoot first, he'll kill you! No matter how many men are with you, he'll kill you! I know he will!"

He turned his head away from me in stubborn silence.

"You'd better listen to me! At least, eat and rest a while before you go . . . you don't look well at all, Rob. Are you ill?"

"I'm not ill! I'll do as I see fit! Leave me alone!"

"You should not be so selfishly careless!" I countered, close to angry tears.

He left without further words between us. There had been no affection in greeting, no concern in farewell. I was depressed in the extreme—as though I were penned with stalking danger and there was no gate or stile in the fence.

It turned out that Old Rose was as surprised as Rob had anticipated. The story has been told and retold, printed and reprinted so many times through the years that it has become a legend of the lake country. What I record here for you is the way I think it happened though I didn't see it with my own eyes. I seemed to be gifted with perceptions that day that reached far beyond my physical eyes and ears. And when you know two people as well as I knew Rob and Hezekiah, much of this perception can be simple reasoning, and your interpretation of the things they tell you becomes the totaling of simple sums. I knew the Rose place and family too—not intimately, but the appearance and disposition of each was clear in my mind.

When Rob and his company of armed men approached the place, they didn't see Rose anywhere about. There was some land-clearing work going on—Negroes were piling brush and setting fire to it. The armed men began a systematic search of the place.

Now Old Rose was there. He knew what the men had come for and was completely unprepared for them. He had been supervising the work of the Negroes and was unarmed. He saw the riders before they had a view of him. He flung himself flat on the ground and told his Negroes to pile brush on him. This they did. He continued to issue whispered instructions from this brush pile. They were to go about their work at the same pace, pay no more attention to the spot where he lay than to the other piles. One was to stroll around in range of his voice. Keep the work going—set fire to some of the piles.

Rob sent several of the men to search the stables and lots. Preston Rose came out to talk to Rob. He was an honorable young man with his mother's disposition. He assured Rob that his father was not in the house, only his mother and his young bride. He hoped they wouldn't be molested or harmed. Rob told him there'd be no trouble of any kind unless his father resisted arrest.

"Why not tell us where he is and have the matter done?" Rob said.

But Preston stood with his back toward the brush pile and looked stubborn.

Rob told Hezekiah to search the house.

Mrs. Rose stood in the doorway viewing the whole procedure with fearless contempt. She was such a beautiful and such a godly woman that I always wondered how on earth she could bear to be wife to such a rough and riotous old man as Captain Rose. But, as it turned out, I was not to pass judgment on another woman's selection, considering the enormity of my own error.

Hezekiah didn't like the job assigned to him—didn't like it at all! He knew that if Rose were hiding in the house, his own chances of coming out alive were quite negligible. But he had obeyed Rob too long to defy him now, though he felt a surge of hot rebellion that his life was of so little consequence to his employer. It fed his anger against Rob for Mrs. Rose to be standing there defying him to enter with her frightened young daughter-in-law looking over her shoulder.

"Git outta my way!" he commanded them.

"Scum!" she said, looking him right in the eye.

He made a move to shove her before him.

"If you so much as touch me with a filthy finger, you'll answer to my husband!"

Rob was paying little attention to Hezekiah. He and several of his companions rode around the house and fired their guns, hoping to trick Rose out of hiding to defend his family.

Preston, feeling compelled to watch what was going on outside, called to his mother, "Let him search the house, Ma."

She stepped aside, and as she did so, Hezekiah seized upon a plan to protect himself in case Rose was in the house. It was plain that he was in the room alone with the two women.

He had his gun at readiness and he pointed it at Mrs. Rose.

"You git in front of me," he ordered her, "and you behind," he told Preston's wife. "If either one of you tries to mess me up, I'll hurt the other one, and bad. Now we look around."

He moved through the house, cautious at first, the two women kept close to him, then he became careless as he became convinced Rose wasn't there. Feeling mean and mad (and Hezekiah was not altogether mild or kind-natured), he looked around for some way to compensate for Mrs. Rose's scorn and Rob's indifference. He began to ransack the house, pulling off the bed covers and tearing down the curtains. On the dresser-top he spied a ladies' pin-on watch and noticed that Mrs. Rose was eying it with concern. It was something she treasured, was afraid he might take! That was just fine! He'd do just that. He enjoyed the sense of loss in her expression as he reached for it. He pitched it up playfully and then pocketed it.

"Small pay for a lota trouble," he said, and was puzzled that a woman could look so hurt over so small a thing. The score was even, he decided, and didn't feel as good about it as he thought he would.

He turned abruptly away from the women and left the house in a hurry. When he got on his horse, he said gruffly, "He's not there or I wouldn't be here."

The men gathered back around Rob to wait for his orders. He kept looking around the place trying to figure out where Rose might be.

His riding equipment and vehicles were all in the stalls. And Rob had had a report from one of the men with him only a few hours earlier that Rose was at home. He studied the landscape—felt very tired—the fatigue of long anxiety and continuous riding settling over him. Preston was talking to him, talking fast and hard. He hardly knew what Preston was saying.

Rob looked at the brush piles. The Negroes were acting mighty strange. Usually they stood still and stared at any unusual sight about the place. They kept moving about—watching the fires—acting as though nothing unusual were happening. Something wrong there. Preston's talking kept interfering with his thinking. One brush pile not lighted. Noisy old rooster circling around it. But just then a Negro squatted and sat the brush on fire. Something odd about that too. (If his mind had been clear and keen, his lawyer's concern with the significance of detail would have noticed that the pile was lighted on the wrong side, so that the wind blew the flame away instead of feeding it into the pile.) But the smoke itself completed the ruse. Rob's tired mind that might otherwise have hit upon the brush offering a place of concealment did not probe beyond the lighting of the pile, did not heed the rooster's chicken-language that said plainly there was something strange in that particular brush heap—his neck craning about, his feet raised so high and deliberate as he walked around the pile making curious little squawks. None of these plain signs reached Rob's weary brain. He began to listen more closely to Preston. He realized that the young man was desperately in earnest and was offering an easy solution. Let Preston bring his father in, as he was promising upon his honor, over and over, that he would do. The courtroom would make a better battleground. Preston even promised he'd warn Rob if his father got out of control and went on a rampage.

So Rob and his companions rode away, and the men dispersed as they went, until by the time they arrived back at Mulberry Shore, there was only Rob and Hezekiah.

I turn to other accounts for the facts of Old Rose's actions as soon as the riders were out of sight. First, he grabbed the old rooster that had so nearly betrayed his hiding place and wrung his neck. Then he put his Negroes on fast horses and sent them out as messengers with orders for certain men to join him at a place of rendezvous on Potter's Point. As for Preston and his promises, it took only a proper amount of parental tyranny to nullify such nonsense. Preston was sent out to spy on the retreating men and see if they took the branching trails to their own homes or rode on with Rob. Rose himself struck out for the residence of a "justice" who would do his bidding—aroused the sleepy magistrate from his bed to prepare a warrant of trespass to be executed by "taking the body," and then rounded up a constable to accompany his "posse." The Lion of the Lakes was fully aroused. The hunted was on the trail of the hunter.

When I heard Rob's account of his failure to find Rose, it was like an announcement of doom.

"Do you think he was there?" I asked.

"Not far away at least," he replied.

"You know how vengeful he is. He'll get his gang together and try to kill you. He won't wait. You should be prepared for an attack tonight."

"You're all keyed up, aren't you, Hatty?" His tone was derisive, "I thought you were the fearless pioneer woman. The wilderness must be getting on your nerves. I think you need a trip. Maybe you'd better return to the city. Live among civilized people again. Have friends instead of killers for neighbors. This isn't as romantic as you thought, is it?"

I studied him—really worried now. Nothing he had done or said this gloomy suspenseful day had seemed normal or right. I didn't resent his remarks, for I knew how tired he must be with the strain of long riding and imminent danger. But I was deeply disturbed over the immediate threat to his life and his indifference toward it. I felt that I must force him to take measures for protection against a raid that very night.

"You shouldn't have let those men disperse," I said. "They should have remained with you to meet the attack that's bound to come. Every man of you should have realized that Rose will make a fight of it now that you've challenged him. You're the first since Sheriff Campbell to try to hunt him down. It isn't too late to do something, Rob. Let Hezekiah and Abraham ride out for some of our nearest neighbors. At least six or eight of your friends could be here by midnight. Rose can't possibly get his gang together and get here before then. We're well supplied with weapons and ammunition. We can hold this place like a fort."

"Listen, Hatty." He spoke slowly in an effort to control his temper. "He couldn't possibly get his gang together for an attack any time tonight, even if he tried. And I've told you repeatedly what Preston said. He'll warn me, he promised, if his old man gets out of hand."

"He'll warn you! And where will his father be meanwhile? That means nothing—absolutely nothing!!"

"Preston is a good boy. He gave me his word on his honor as a gentleman!"

"Rob, don't prattle about words of honor and being gentlemen when Rose is on the prowl! It's positively childish!" I was having a hard time controlling my own temper. "Preston is a nice boy—we both know that. We both like him. But he's only eighteen. He'll be as helpless before his father's wrath as a newborn calf before a mad bull. He'll be lucky if the old man doesn't thrash him half to death for making such promises. Expect no warnings from Preston. He'll be right by his father's side, a gun in his hands."

"Get this through your head, Hatty. The subject of Rose is closed for tonight. I don't want to hear another word out of you. I want to be left alone—entirely alone—you understand. Let the baby sleep with Hannah. Be sure that Lakeann's asleep when you bring her in. I don't want any story-nonsense tonight. Bring me some brandy and go away. I want to be alone—alone! Do you hear me!"

I heard him well enough, and the temper warnings were all out. So I brought him the brandy and left the room. And I didn't come back until he was in bed and sound asleep.

I settled Lakeann comfortably in the middle of the big bed, not touching her father, then I lay down on the far edge, but not to sleep.

I lay there waiting . . . listening . . . waiting . . . hearing all the night sounds I knew so well: the crickets in raucous spring serenade—the dogs after coon or possum—the eerie call of an owl. I dozed once, then awoke with a start, thinking I had heard footsteps. And I must have, for at once the dogs set to barking as they always barked when strangers approached.

"Rob!" I reached over and touched him, then shook his shoulder. "Wake up, Rob! Someone is outside, sneaking around."

"How do you know?" he answered irritably, refusing to be separated from his slumber.

"The dogs . . . the dogs never make a noise like that unless strangers are around."

"The dogs be damned! Leave me alone! I'm tired enough to die!" His words trailed off as he sank again into deep slumber, muttering, "Go away, Hatty. Go away."

I lay in bed a while longer, interpreting every sound, and at last I was so certain of what the barking, growling dogs were telling me that I could bear the suspense no longer. I got up and dressed in the predawn darkness. No need to arouse Rob again until I knew what was in store for us.

I enumerated the firearms in the room with us: three pistols, the cannon, a double-barreled shotgun, and a blunderbuss—all loaded (I had checked that before I went to bed) and a good supply of ammunition near at hand. Refreshed by his sleep, Rob would be strong and alert for fighting if there was need of it, I thought. Just the two of us would be hard to take from this well-fortified room.

Everything became very quiet for a bit. The dogs subsided and I dared to hope that they might have been aroused by some prowler not connected with Old Rose. But I knew someone was outside there, waiting.

In small shedrooms on the back of the house were the sleeping quarters for Abraham, Hezekiah, and the Negro boy, George. These rooms were constructed on either side of a roofed runway leading up to the back door. If anyone were hiding about the place, it had to be at either end of the house or around the buildings beyond the runway. At the first peep of light, I felt I had to get the day started and dispel this feeling of being surrounded by evil and danger. I slipped out to George's room and awakened him earlier than usual and told him to go after the corn. If some stranger were waiting outside for breakfast or directions, George would discover him. I went back into the big room and waited. I heard George leave for the corncrib.

I waited longer than usual to hear the mill start grinding, but there was no sound of any kind to indicate what George was doing. The dark night began to turn into gray dawn.

I decided to awaken Abraham and have him check on George. I told him in a whisper that I had sent George out and he hadn't returned and I feared something was wrong. He said it was so inhumanly early that George had probably gone back to sleep out at the corncrib. I left him and went back to wait again. Then it occurred to me that he should not go out unarmed, but when I rushed out to tell him to take a gun, he was already gone. I regretted sending him and my anxiety mounted.

The morning light was still treacherous, and outlines of buildings and fences indistinct. I heard Hezekiah stirring. I waited for him. There was still nothing to be seen or heard from George and Abraham. When Hezekiah stepped out, on his way to feed the hogs, for that was his early morning chore, I stopped him.

"Wait, Hezekiah. There's something strange going on around here. Take a gun with you. George went for the corn quite a while ago and hasn't commenced to grind yet. I sent Abraham out after him and he hasn't come back. I want you to see what's happened. But be very careful. You'd better go armed."

He grunted, "All right," and shambled on out, ignoring my warning.

I was so provoked with him that I decided to investigate for myself, so I stepped out into the yard and started toward the kitchen, without a gun, doing what I had just warned Hezekiah not to do. I looked after Hezekiah—he was going over the stile—his dark hunched figure clearly outlined in the breaking light.

There was an explosion of sound almost in my ear. I saw Hezekiah go down. I whirled and ran back. Three men appeared, two from the kitchen and one from the corner of the house. They ran after me, snatched at me, had me in their grasp once, but I surprised them with my strength and twisted away from them. Several shots were fired before I was safely back in the house and had the door securely barred behind me.

Rob was awake and scrambling into his trousers. "What does this mean?"

"It means the house is surrounded," I said, "and we'll have to fight or die."

"Where are all the men?"

I was relieved to see that he was alert—ready for action.

"Killed, I suppose, I just saw Hezekiah shot." I shouldn't have said this. I have always regretted it. The statement shocked him, unnerved him, left him irresolute.

He moved around the room saying to himself more than to me, "I've got to get out of this house. It's not quite daylight. If I can slip by them, I can get away."

I ran to him pleading, "No! No, Rob! You must stay right here! We must fight! We can defend ourselves. I'll stand right by you as long as we both live!"

"Hatty, I'm going to get out of here. Don't try to stop me. And before I try it, I've got something to tell you."

"Rob, no!" I ran and got his gun—placed it in his hands. "We'll fight. You and I together. I can load as fast as you can."

He moved across the room toward the back door. He peered through a crack in the wall near the door.

"Too many, Hatty, too many. They're around in the back yard now concerned with those they've just slaughtered. I'll make a run for it—from the front. If I can reach the lake, I can get away. I can swim to safety. But there's something I must tell you first. Listen Hatty——"

"I'll not listen. You listen to me. We've got all these firearms—this cannon. They're all loaded. If you'll just kill Old Rose and Scott the trouble will be over, the others will go away. Most of those men out there are here because they're afraid of Rose—not because they want to see you killed. They won't fight without Rose. Just kill Rose, and it will all be over."

"Hatty, I'm leaving. Hush. But just in case—I feel that I should tell you——"

Lakeann had been whimpering, now she screamed out, "Papa! Papa! Don't go, Papa! Don' go 'way. No! No—oo—Pa—pa!"

"Oh, Rob, please Rob . . . Oh, for God's sake, you can't——"

He heeded neither my plea nor Lakeann's. He muttered, as he rushed to the front door, "They can't hurt you anyhow——" opened the door, and sprinted across the yard.

Six shots were fired at him and none took effect.

I rushed out into the yard after him. He stopped for an instant and looked back. The light was good now and he recognized Sandy Miller and Stephen Peters at the back yard fence.

He called out to me, "These are my friends."

"No! No, Rob! They're not your friends! Run, Rob—run for your life!"

417

Peters and Miller both fired at Rob as he jumped the rails, but neither hit him. I don't think they intended to. The rest of the group ran from concealment behind the house, and yelling like a bunch of wild Indians, they pursued Rob down the hill and along the beach under the cliff.

"Kill him—kill him—kill the damned rascal!" Someone was yelling above the rest.

But Rob raced on unhurt by the bullets sent after him. When he reached the beach, he doubled back toward the spring where the three big cypresses stood on the shore—here was sufficient depth at the lake edge for diving and swimming under water. He took time to prop his gun against one of the cypress trees, then dived in and on out of sight of his pursuers. Rob excelled in swimming under water. I now had high hopes for his escape—except for the gun. I was horrified that he had left his loaded gun so handy for some pursuer to pick up—wished now I had never placed it in his hands.

Scott, Rose's son-in-law, was closest to Rob and had just fired a harmless shot before Rob dived in. Now Scott wouldn't have to re-load. I started to run from the yard thinking I might divert him somehow. But Old Rose was right beside me. He had left all the running to the young and nimble. He leveled his gun on me and ordered me back into the house.

I didn't move. I was watching Scott. I saw him seize Rob's gun and hold it ready. When Rob's black head appeared out on the lake surface for an instant, he took careful aim and fired.

Rose hadn't intended for me to see anything. "Git back into the house, I say!"

"I won't move a step," I told him. "I'll watch every wicked thing that goes on here!"

He started dragging me toward the door.

Scott came back up the bank.

"What're you abusing Mrs. Potter for," he said to his father-in-law. "She hasn't harmed you any. Let's get outta here. We've done what we come for."

There was no way of knowing for sure if Scott's shot had taken effect. But Old Rose took it for granted that Rob was dead.

"Now what do you think of your pretty Bobby?" he jeered.

"I think he's a good swimmer and might have escaped from your clutches after all, and you don't like that, do you?"

"As a fighting man, he makes a good runner!"

I had backed into the doorway of the main room by this time. I stood by the table where the cannon was set up, loaded with buckshot. I yearned to set it off in the midst of these killers! I reached for the match that I had conveniently placed there, and it was gone. I felt a fury beyond all control.

"If only I had a match to touch off this cannon, I'd shoot your tongue down your throat!"

Rose said, "If you find old Hezekiah alive, tell 'im those buckshot in him are mine. I give 'em that dose of lead for man-handlin' my womenfolks." He turned to his son-in-law. "Scott, we outta do somethin' with this woman. She's a mean 'un, and she saw it all."

"Let her be, Pa. You couldn't git rid of her no way outside of killin' her outright. And I reckon she's too brave a woman to kill. Maybe she'll see it our way after a while. Maybe she'll come to think we've done her a favor by feedin' 'im to the alligators."

"The 'gators won't touch 'im. He's too pretty and too full of lily-liver," Rose said.

Scott got between his father-in-law and me—then, pushing and persuading, took Old Rose on around the house and out of my presence.

Some of the other men had released Abraham and George unharmed.

A grim quietness settled down.

The raiders didn't talk, even to each other. They didn't look in my direction or come close to the house as they left. They circled around to the front and on toward the woods where they had left their horses. I went to the front door and stood watching them go.

I knew them all—fixed each name in my mind. There were ten, counting Old Rose.

They felt my wrathful gaze on their backs, accusing them and condemning them—I'm sure of that. They were made self-conscious, awkward—especially Stephen Peters who stumbled and almost fell.

You should fall on your face and weep for shame, Stephen Peters, I was thinking. Colonel Potter was always kind to you, a good neighbor. You were in his debt for many favors.

It was a bitter thing to face the realization that these men were not a gang of outlaws. Except for the Rose family, Rob had considered them all his friends. Several of them he had helped to get settled on the point. He had loaned them money, sold them corn on credit, let them borrow his farm tools and field hands, secured the patents to their land without legal fee. But fear of Old Rose had been stronger than any sense of gratitude . . . Sandy Miller lagged behind, almost stopped, almost looked back, then disappeared with the rest.

And Preston was there too, with a gun, just as I had said he would be. . . . Kindnesses and promises nullified with gunfire.

Lakeann started whimpering again, pitiful little snuffles, coming out of the terrified silence she had gone into during the attack.

Hannah rushed in, John in her arms, saw that I was paying no attention to Lakeann, hardly hearing her.

"O Lawd Jesus, mah li'l lamb! Yo's safe, honey lamb, sweet baby, an' yo' Hannah's heah."

"Pa-pa. Pa-pa. I wan' my Pa-Pa, 'anna, I wan' my Papa."

"Sho' ya do. He be bak. He be bak." She lifted the sobbing child into her arms, and carrying both children took them out to the kitchen.

I went out the front door and back around the house, scanning the lake as I went.

George called to me, "Missus, ol' Hezzy alive."

I heard a deep groan from beyond the stile. I had thought surely Hezekiah was dead.

Delia and Tildy emerged from their cabin, big-eyed and kitten-quiet. Three field hands, sleeping in the lean-to, were too frightened to come out and were forgotten until later in the day.

Old Thomas Parsons, who was in charge of the hired help, and using the guest cabin, had watched part of the attack from his window, knowing nothing of what it implied.

I called to him to come help with Hezekiah. We got him to his bed, and I left Delia to dress his wounds, none of them very deep.

Hannah quieted the children, put George to work grinding the corn, and began to cook breakfast. The steel mill whirred and sang out on the morning air, its usual cheerful sound distorted by the double speed George put on—trying to grind away his fears—wondering—as we all were—with every whirr of the mill a rhythm to the thought: is he dead or alive? dead or alive? dead or alive?

I had already sent Abraham for the spyglass and set him to watching for any sign of Rob.

Joe had run down to the shore and was looking out over the water—but he couldn't see very far—he was crying too much.

After checking Hezekiah, I took over the glass from Abraham and sent him in to breakfast.

Hannah brought some coffee out to me and I sent her back with it. I couldn't eat or drink and look through the glasses at the same time. I couldn't have swallowed anyway.

There was no sight or sound anywhere on the surface of the lake to give us a clue to Rob's fate.

Finally, we took a canoe—Abraham, Mr. Parsons, and I—and began to search the lake over the distance Rob might have been able to swim. We searched the islands and the shore line. All day we searched, using the spyglass continually. All day . . . until our eyes ached with scanning the bright waters and our muscles were in spasms of pain from the continuous rowing. The Negro men would not go near the lake. Hezekiah from his bed ordered them out to the field— told them they'd better be found in the corn patch when the Colonel got in, but they paid him no mind. Hannah alone remained impassive, spent her time caring for the children, keeping them calm. Delia walked with Joe, endless miles up and down, up and down the shore along the point.

I did not give up the search or the hope that Rob was alive until darkness and storm clouds drove me from the lake. And as I gave a backward glance at that broad sheet of dark water, I wondered how I could ever have thought it beautiful. Now it was a horrible, greedy force, holding back some dreadful secret from me, refusing to give up even a lifeless body.

Storm clouds broke over Mulberry Shore that night. Thunder roared and crashed, shaking the buildings. Lightning flared continuously in great white sheets spreading an awesome illumination around. I sat up fully clothed the whole night long, as if keeping company with the dead.

At one time, I caught above the sounds of the storm a prolonged piercing cry that ran the scale of agony. I started to leave my chair and investigate, but Hannah, watching by the bedside where the children slept, stopped me.

"It jes' Delia, missus, wailin' fo' da daid. She da high-wailin' kin', ya know. Bes' letuh wail out. She too wil' ta look on when she let go."

The storm rose to a peak of fury and the noisy elements canceled out Delia's wailing and all other sound but its own. It seemed to me that the raging thunderstorm was some vaster expression of my tortured mind. When the rains were finally released, I could weep. I lay back in the chair and gave my body up to grief and a flow of scalding tears.

The storm lashing and churning the lake, as if in chastisement, delivered up Rob's body to the very spot where his tracks of the day before left the sand. I found him there in the earliest morning light when I had the men carry the cannon down to the lake for firing across the water. (This was supposed to attract a lifeless body to the surface—why, I do not know.)

I left no task to others that I could possibly do myself. I helped carry him up to the house where he was placed on the big bed in the main room. I examined the fatal gunshot wound in the back of his head. I removed his sodden clothes and found in his trousers pocket the big match I had needed to fire the cannon. I laid him out for burial in the clothes he liked best, using my scissors and needle with special care to make his well-fitted garments conform to the water-a-bused body.

Although the news of Rob's murder spread through the neighborhood at once as these things always do—and I learned later that there was no deadlier shot than Scott in the whole region and the whole gang could feel quite certain that Rob had been killed—there was no gathering of friends and neighbors, curious and concerned, at Mulberry Shore. All who might have come were either too fearful or too shamed. Rob's relative, Dr. Pearce, who had settled some twenty miles away, and Mr. Meredith who worked for Dr. Pearce, arrived not long after I had taken Rob's body from the lake and were the only outsiders present to assist me with the burial.

"Of the many he has befriended, only you two have dared to come and help me," I said to them. "They were all ready enough to accept his favors. But how do they repay him? Some by joining in the foul assault upon him—others by hiding out, too cowardly to offer a plank for his coffin or lift a spadeful of dirt for his grave. It gives me a holy chill to witness such betrayal! And it shall not go unavenged! I'll trick them—trap them—risk anything to bring the murdering crew before a bar of justice where I can tell the world every detail of the assassination! . . . You'll help me by telling all who inquire of you that I'm broken in spirit, helpless, fearful, and planning to leave the country. Tell them," I instructed Dr. Pearce, "that you advised me to take no action, to get out, leave it all behind me. I'm the only eyewitness to the murder outside the gang. They'll kill me if they suspect my intentions."

On a beautiful knoll in front of the house, where a clump of stately trees lifted lofty branches above the surrounding grove, we laid Rob in his grave. I recalled that he had said to me time and again, with strange insistence, "When I die, I would like to be buried on that spot of elevated beauty."

There was no one at his graveside to deliver a funeral biography and eulogy, to honor his love and talent for oratory with appropriate eloquence. But the tempest had already spoken over his body with a symbolic eloquence surpassing anything human tongue could utter. There were no singers with songs for the soul departed. But the tall trees standing round were a superior choir, more gifted in impartial song than any assembly of mortal voices could have been.

24.

The men who were now my enemies for what I had seen and might testify placed Mulberry Shore under a form of silent seige. They knew that if I intended to prefer charges against them I would go to Dangerfield, the nearest town where a magistrate resided. Dangerfield had been designated the county seat of Paschal County, a new county created for judicial purposes and including our property. It was fifty miles from Mulberry Shore and a raw settlement hardly two years old. The only road out led by Scott's farm. And the wilderness was so impassable, the road must be used. So, by day, they kept a sharp lookout on the road, and, by night, they posted sentinels around the house to watch and listen.

I had expected this dangerous attention. And I was fully aware of the night guard. Dusty and Domino told me plainly when the spies arrived and when they departed. I realized that I was marked for murder if anything they saw or heard indicated that I wanted to reach Dangerfield. I knew too that any night might bring an attempt on my life—that the temptation would be heavy on them to make certain of my everlasting silence. After all, Rob had influential friends at Clarksville and was a man of importance and popularity in the region. Once the evidence was before a court, there would be legal war, and quite probably some extra-legal skirmishes on the side, and either could end with bullet or noose for the killers.

My first step was to make secret preparations for defense in case an attack should come. Every evening, the household gathered together and the men were armed, even the Negro field hands. I had no claim on the loyalty of these hired slaves, and it was a calculated risk placing firearms at their disposal.

"I'm trusting you with these weapons," I told them, "expecting you to defend me, save my life if anyone tries to kill me. If trouble comes and you betray me or refuse to fight for me, I'll kill you before I die, have no doubt of it!"

They didn't doubt it. They knew I would. I was full of the determination for vengeance. Some kind of flaming force seemed to possess me. I had seen my husband murdered, with a deliberate aim at the head as in the slaughter of an animal. I had never before seen anyone killed in any manner or handled a dead body, much less a loved one with a bullet through the head. I was so full of a seething rage all the time that I would have killed any of them. But I would be over-

425

whelmed and have no chance to reach court. Instead I must play a role of meekness and fear.

I rearranged all the sleeping quarters about the place for greatest protection. Delia and Hannah and the four children slept in the attic. Mr. Parsons moved in with Hezekiah, and George had a pallet in their room. The field hands slept in Abraham's room with instructions to act under his directions during any emergency.

From all appearances, I settled down to stay at home, grieving and subdued. I was waiting for a time when the guards would tire of their vigilance and become vulnerable to deception. At night in the big lonely room I lay awake for long thoughtful hours, plotting, scheming how I might trick these men, slip past them, escape to Dangerfield. Each day I coached Abraham and Mr. Parsons on the conversation we would present some night for the benefit of our sneak audience. This dialogue was planned to quiet the fears of the killers, presenting me as a weak and weary woman, resigned and fearful and in failing health.

One evening before dark, we played the performance over so convincingly that I actually felt ill when it was done. After Mr. Parsons and Abraham were gone from the room, I fell into a deep despondency—felt sick of the whole sorry game—and actually wondered if I were strong enough to go through with it. The endless night stretched ahead. I always retired early so the watchers would not suspect that I was aware of them. Then I would lie awake the intervening four or five hours until the guard was gone. On this particular night I tried to cheer myself with the idea that someone might come to my aid. Someone might arrive at Mulberry Shore to share my burden, take me out under adequate protection. But, who? Certainly no one in the vicinity, for all who otherwise might have befriended me were either involved in the murder or were held back by fear of what would be done to them if they dared come to me. It would be weeks, even months, before Rob's personal and political friends in the far places would hear of his death. Then only rumors. I alone knew the full story. Who of them would set out on a long journey to find out how his widow fared, a woman most of them had never seen? The friends dearest to him were in Clarksville: Amos Morrill, the Gordons, Charles Ames. Morrill I had never met, and Dr. Gordon only once when he had joined Rob at Potter's Point for a trip to Shreveport. But there was Charles—blessed Charles. It was a comfort just to think about him. He had appeared twice before in my life at a dark-cloud time. Would some sweet chance bring him again to my side?

That night I dreamed of Charles. We were crossing a bridge together. There were swift gray clouds passing across the eastern sky from south to north. I said to Charles, "The clouds are lovely." And he replied, "They certainly are." That was all there was in the dream— our walking together and my feeling of relief from all anxiety, the clouds in motion and the single comment. I awoke with new hope and energy. During the early hours of the day, I worked in the garden. And it pleased me that there really were gray clouds scooting across the sky with breaks of blue and sunshine, and several times I said aloud, "The clouds are lovely," and almost expected Charles to answer me.

My escape from thoughts of murder and danger was only a brief release, however. I had a visitor all right. And he came that day. But not Charles Ames. "Grave" Bruton.

During his last stopover at Potter's Point, "Grave" and Rob had quarreled violently. Prior to the quarrel, Bruton had been around Mulberry Shore for several days, his presence endured because of Rob's policy of giving free lodging to boaters whose friendship and services were so essential to the prosperous development of the point. While Rob was busy at other things, Bruton had followed me around, just staring at me, and answering my sharp rebuffs with insolent grinning. Finally, he brought out from his ghoulish loot some Indian trinkets and offered them to me as "pretties." I refused them indignantly and felt that I had put up with quite enough. So I spoke to Rob about it and told him of Bruton's offensive manner toward me at other times. Rob was angered and drove Bruton away after there had been an exchange of threats. Rob called Bruton a filthy murderer and said he would expose him in the courts if he ever showed his face at Mulberry Shore again. That had put Bruton in surly retreat. When I asked Rob to explain this, he said he had recently been informed that Bruton had fled from murder charges in another part of the country.

Now murder and graves had a sharper meaning for me and the sight of Bruton had never been so hateful. And I knew he had come, knowing Rob was dead.

He arrived at noon mealtime and seated himself at our table in the kitchen house, without invitation and without removing his coonskin cap. His eyes smiled evilly while he told me that he was sorry to hear that Colonel Potter had drowned. The lake was treacherous as a woman, he said.

I got up from the table, saying only, "We need nothing from you, Grave Bruton."

Abraham and Mr. Parsons hardly knew what to do about Bruton. They didn't like him, but they knew nothing of his quarrel with Rob or his ugly attentions to me.

"Poor grieved woman," I heard him say as I was leaving. He had heaped his plate so high with food that it was spilling over the edges. "I guess I upset her, speakin' right out like that."

I turned to look at him, hunched down over the table as he began to eat. He had taken a knife from his belt, ignoring the cutlery I had by the plates, and with gluttonous dexterity seemed to throw the food directly from plate to stomach. It made me feel quite ill and I rushed away, hoping he wouldn't follow me.

I went on through the house to the front door and stood there looking out at Rob's grave. A raging anger began to build up within me, focusing on Grave Bruton. For two long weeks, I had held my emotions in check, remained painfully inactive, played the part of lassitude, endured the menace of the nights. Now here was another menace, another *murderer*. I ought to kill him!

Then I heard him enter the room behind me. I whirled about.

"Get out! Colonel Potter told you never to come here again."

"I don' pay much 'tention to dead men. But I got a wide eye for a real live woman!" He grinned broadly. "Now perk up, little lady. Don' be so huffy. Whut kin a dead man do fer ya? I gotcha a present, somethin' mighty fine." He reached into his pocket, brought out a necklace of polished pink shells and bright beads, held it out, moved toward me.

"Grave robber!"

"This ain't Indian junk—this is real jewelry. Look at it, woman, look at it." He dangled it before me, like bait.

I looked at it—with horror, for I recognized the beads—the blue ones I had given Tall Flower. She had strung them with pink shells and little Clear Water had worn them. Tall Flower had been very proud of this adornment for her daughter—had shown me the quality of the shells, every one hard and polished to a high luster. It was truly a beautiful string. Bruton had robbed the grave of Clear Water.

He thought my interest meant I liked the beads and wanted them. I backed away from him slowly and he followed me, unmindful of my motive and my fury.

"Let me put 'em round yer neck, purty woman." He held the rope of beads open with his two hands and advanced to put them over my head, for I was against the wall and could move no further away from him.

But he never touched me, and what happened to him was such a complete shock that he stood for a moment still holding the beads extended, just a shotgun's length from me, and there was a shotgun between us, held in my hands, with the end of the barrel against his belly. All the time I had been backing to a certain spot near the bed where I kept the gun propped in a crevice in the wall.

"Don't say another word to me, you river rat," I told him. "If you so much as grin, I'll kill you and I'll enjoy it. Put your hands up. Hold onto those beads. If you drop them, I'll pull the trigger."

I moved a step closer to him, letting the gun slide under my right arm some, my finger still on the trigger. I reached out with my left hand and jerked his pistol and knife from his belt and threw them on the bed—then I knocked his coonskin cap from his head.

"You'll show some respect for the living, and the dead, before I'm through with you!"

He was genuinely frightened of me—I could tell that. And he kept looking around, expecting someone to come in and put an end to my madness.

"Don't try to attract attention," I warned him. "They can't help you. I'm the boss here now. Colonel Potter probably wouldn't allow me to act this way. But he's dead, as you were just reminding me. Murdered! And so I'm running things. Now, turn around and go out the front door and down to your boat. I'm right behind you." I punched him with the gun barrel.

All the way to the shore, I lashed him with my anger and contempt. "Murderer! Think how it would feel to be shot." I gave him a hard jab with the gun. "Corpse thief! When you die, dogs should dig up your bones and gnaw them."

His arms became tired and he waved the beads around over his head in crazy fashion.

When he came to his boat, I saw four big Indian baskets there, filled with grave loot.

"Get in," I commanded him. "Move out into the lake until I tell you to stop. If you don't do exactly as I say, I'll shoot you. Try me, and see. I'd like to shoot you. You know that, don't you? Don't dare speak to me. Just nod."

He nodded.

"Put the beads in the basket there. Now, shove off."

He did as I told him, his arms stiff and awkward, fumbling in his terror.

When he reached deep water, I told him to stop.

"Now a ceremony of apology to the dead, Grave Bruton. First to little Clear Water. Pick up the beads. Break the string. You dropped some in the boat. Pick them up! . . . Now scatter some to the east (not too many) . . . and to the north (careful, not all at once) . . . some to the west for that's the way her soul traveled . . . and to the south. . . . Now the baskets: lower them one in each direction . . . Now bow in apology, toward the south, toward the House of Death— bow lower! . . . Look this way now—toward the grave of Colonel Robert Potter. Get down on your knees. Hurry up! Bow your head— in apology for insult—in respect to the dead—and don't raise it until I tell you or I'll shoot you through the head—just as Scott shot Colonel Potter. You and your cruel quip about his drowning in the lake! He was murdered! Do you understand? Nod your head, but don't dare raise it. Don't tempt me!"

He obeyed my every order, certain, I'm sure, that he had fallen into the hands of a maniac—and for a while there I felt like one.

Finally, I released him, "Get up and get out of my sight—and be as quick as you possibly can about it." He got into such a frenzy of effort trying to get the boat under way that he almost fell overboard.

When Bruton was gone from my sight, I collapsed on the sand and wept with an utter abandonment to weeping. I didn't wail like Delia, but I wished I could. I sobbed and moaned and clung to the earth for consolation. I wept for Tall Flower and Clear Water. For Prowling Bear and his primitive friendliness. For Ginny's grave on Galveston Island. For the infant grave on the hillside. And for the fresh grave in the tall grove—for all the beauty and love lost to brutality—the wild assault of violence upon goodness—the pitiful nakedness of ideals, dying, dying, leaving the mind as well as the heart bereft.

If my devoted friend, Snake Seecher, could have seen me there, he would have beheld instead of the bravest woman in the Republic the most desolate and defeated. I had met the day with hope of deliverance—and Bruton had come. Murder and graves . . . murder and graves . . . that was my life. *Death* of everything! I dug my fingers in the sand and gave up to another surge of physical grief-letting. Then something strange happened in my mind. The grief was closed out and I heard a voice in quiet commanding clearness, call "Hatty!"

My body became as still as my mind. I raised up to a sitting position and looked about me. No one was there. But there was a memory as clear as the voice. The memory was my mother saying, "You cry too easily, Hatty. Control your tears. Always use the good mind God has given you . . . I leave you in God's hands."

My grief of this day had reached back to the acute loss of that day when at ten years old my world seemed to end with my mother's death. And in that death scene was the strength of faith and goodness —sorrow softened with the hint of some vast truth and beauty, rising incomprehensible but oh, so reassuring from the life force—the part of it that doesn't die—that uses death as an entrance, not a departure.

I recalled the tranquil, completely fearless expression on my mother's face. And I recalled two other faces of goodness and strength that had meant comfort and deliverance to me: Mrs. Abit and Mr. Cloud. Mrs. Abit, who from her deathbed had sent Mr. Cloud to my rescue. Mr. Cloud quoting, " 'Whither shall I go from thy spirit? or whither shall I flee from thy presence? If I ascend up into heaven, thou art there: if I make my bed in hell, behold, thou art there.' "

I got to my feet, brushed off the sand, pushed my hair clean from my forehead, and walked down the shore to the spring. There I washed my face in the cool water and drank deeply. Then I went up to the house and told Mr. Parsons and Abraham that I had made plans to start to Dangerfield that very night after the spies were gone.

In the afternoon, we rehearsed what our conversation would be on this night of performance for "audience benefit." It would have to be convincing or we'd get no further than Scott's farm on the road out.

We made other preparations: packs of provisions were made up for living out-of-doors—Mexican blankets, buffalo robes, some extra clothing, food, coffee pot—all loaded on a mule. Three horses were made ready and a supply of shelled corn sacked and lashed to the back of each saddle. Weapons and ammunition were carefully checked—certain items of disguise decided upon.

The most painful part of my decision lay in the necessity of leaving the children behind. It would be folly to attempt taking the little ones on such a journey when they could be safe and comfortable at Mulberry Shore where Hannah and Delia had helped with their care since birth. Joe was twelve years old now, his riding and shooting up to adult standards. He didn't mind being left—felt he was being given manly responsibilities. But the babies . . . they might get sick . . . might fall or hurt themselves in some way . . . which reminded me that I must give Hannah some very specific instruction.

"Hannah, you must keep your mind on the children at all times," I told her. "When they both need attention, you will take care of Lakeann and Delia of John. And no soapmaking while I'm gone—remember that."

"Ah lubs ta mak soap!"

"I know you do. That's exactly why I'm saying don't do it until I get back. You always take half a day for it and you act as if nothing else is going on in the world but soapmaking."

"Ah make de puhtiest—de whites'—de bes'-smellin'——"

"I know very well how good it is, and I'm glad you can. But you wouldn't be noticing the babies—and boiling soap is dangerous with children around. Remember what I tell you now. I won't be gone long—four or five days. Perhaps a week—not long."

I left Joe with a man-sized lot of work to do. He was to pen the horses at night, feed and care for all the farm animals. George would help him, be his companion.

Hezekiah couldn't work yet but was well enough to supervise the field hands at the tasks I assigned to them.

Only Mr. Parsons and Abraham would accompany me—and only they knew that I was going to Dangerfield. The others thought I was going to visit Mrs. Swanson.

The Swansons lived across the lake and far back into the woods—an out-of-the-way place, off any public track.

That night when the dogs signaled curtain time, I began to play for my sinister unseen audience.

"I need a change," I whined to my brother and Mr. Parsons. "I've been thinking to pay Mrs. Swanson a visit. Maybe she'd help me forget my troubles. Do you think I could be spared around here for a while? Do you think I ought to try to make such a trip?"

"Nothing we can't take care of around here, Mrs. Potter," Mr. Parsons assured me. "I'm all in favor of it. You been stickin' too close—never givin' yourself any rest or pleasure."

"I think it's a fine idea, Hatty!" Abraham came in heartily. "Just what you need. You look a little peaked and run down. You don't have any life any more. It would do you good, sure enough!"

"I hate to leave the children behind."

"Leave all the old folks and kids behind—just enjoy yourself," Mr. Parsons insisted.

I sighed. "It's not an easy trip. I hardly feel up to it. The waters are too rough for a canoe—the way I feel, I couldn't stand it. But if you could borrow Mr. Rieve's skiff, Abraham, and take me across in it tomorrow——"

"I sure can, Hatty. Whatever you want."

We discussed the proposed visit at length. It was a balmy night and Mr. Parsons stood in the doorway, making sure he was heard, gazing at the stars, occasionally squirting tobacco juice toward a spot where he thought one of the eavesdroppers was crouched. I moved about the room at small tasks, pausing near Mr. Parsons or where Abraham sat in a rocker not far away to comment or ask for an opinion—what I would take—when they would send for me—what kind of gift would please Mrs. Swanson—how watchful they must be of Lakeann and John. Then I left the room, went to the kitchen for coffee, left the stage to the men for giving the final lines of misinformation.

"Don't you think your sister looks a little heavy, Abraham?"

"Heavy? Why no—I been thinking how bony she looks—no appetite a-tall—her eyes so hollow—her face all thinned out——"

"I mean heavy in a family way."

"Mr. Parsons! Surely you don't think Hatty's——"

"I shore do, son. I shorely do."

"Poor Hatty! What an awful thing!"

"I hear it's a lot harder for a woman in that condition if her man's passed on—liable to affect her mind, I've heard—sometimes she don't pull through."

"What can we do, Mr. Parsons?"

"Humor her in everything—try to keep her mind off her troubles. I guess that crew of murderers would be relieved to know about this——" Mr. Parsons got carried away with his part. "Nobody but a sick little woman bearin' a child to hold 'em to account for their crime . . . did you ever hear of a lower crime, Abraham? The killin' was bad enough —but shootin' him right before her eyes—leavin' his body in the lake to bloat and wash up at her feet with a bullet hole in the *back* of the head. I say damn 'em all to hell and then some! Damn 'em to the Comanche corner of it! Just plain hell is too good for 'em!" He jetted an amber stream that showered into his target bush and was certain of movement there. He turned back satisfied, toward Abraham who was frowning heavily at him, censoring his boldness in this unrehearsed bit of action.

The sentinels left their posts earlier than usual that night, and I dared to assume that my strategy was successful. So we moved on to the next step to find out for sure.

Mr. Parsons was jubilant as we made ready for our journey, packing the mule, saddling the horses, disguising ourselves and our mounts as best we could to look like a party of immigrants just coming into Texas.

"I wish I could a-been an actor," Mr. Parsons said wistfully as we went about our preparation. "I'd a made a good one. I hope Scott hisself was behind that bush. I hope I hit 'im right in the eyes!"

"I do too. But it's a wonder you didn't get shot. Don't brag about your acting until we're past the Scott house," I advised.

"The weather's in our favor," Abraham noted. "It's beginning to drizzle." My brother was obviously relieved at this advantage.

"You shore look funny in that big sunbonnet this time of day, Mrs. Potter."

Hats were our main items of disguise since we would be using big Mexican blankets for covering ourselves and our mounts. This was common enough traveling regalia and would be even more so on a rainy morning.

434

The bonnet I was wearing was Hannah's. Nobody had ever seen me in such a bonnet. I like air and sunshine on my head.

"You look ready to pick corn in that big straw, Mr. Parsons."

"You know what, Hatty, I believe this coonskin cap has fleas in it," Abraham complained. He had been assigned the headpiece left behind by Bruton.

"That oughta keep you hoppin', son," Mr. Parsons chuckled, as he helped me get seated comfortably on Sukey Blueskin and well wrapped in my Mexican blanket.

We rode out on the road only half an hour behind the guards, using this timing as a part of our disguise.

It was several hours before daylight. If no one was on the lookout at the Scott house, we could pass by without attracting notice. But watchful eyes accustomed to the semi-darkness would be able to see us pass, might be curious, might come out to question us.

We were not spared a final critical performance in our drama of strategy. There were lights at the Scott house—horses were tied at the front. Several men standing on the porch would be able to see us in outline, three riders and a pack mule.

"Keep the horses at a plodding pace," I told Abraham and Mr. Parsons. "We must not hurry past. And keep hunched down, like we're half-asleep."

We could see that the men were eating and drinking, taking refreshment after their night watch at Mulberry Shore. Their postures were lounging, relaxed. We could tell they had noticed us, were making some mention of us, but they didn't move from their places.

"They swallered our bait. They're feelin' better than they have in a long time," Mr. Parsons surmised, riding close by my side, breaking through the terrible suspense that gripped us.

"Thank God for the rain," I said, for now the mist had turned into a light but steady rain, so gentle and compassionate it seemed, a mantle of safety from curious eyes.

"Scott is probably saying, 'I hope them damn immigrants don't try to put up here.'" Mr. Parsons was feeling cheerful again.

"Can't we hurry now?" Abraham pleaded.

"Not yet."

Two miles beyond Scott's farm we could feel sure of our escape. The rain became a handicap now, making the trail hard to follow.

Now relief from strain, after a day and night of preparation and action, settled over us and we felt we must rest a while.

We decided to camp until daylight. We took the precaution of riding about half a mile down a deep gully. Here with some protection from the wall of the gulley, we made a fire for brewing coffee. As we sat and drank, we became cheered and warmed and the company of the fire was a pleasant thing. But soon we extinguished it as an extra precaution, leaving only the coals under the coffeepot. Wrapped in our buffalo robes, we were warm and dry. Those few hours of sleep before dawn were for me the most restful I had known since Rob came home to his grave.

The chief magistrate in Dangerfield was a disappointment to me. I had hoped to find a man of action and intelligence. He did not even know his full duty in a case such as I presented to him. His office was minor, his legal knowledge very sparse, he readily admitted. The newly created counties such as Paschal were functioning as judicial subdivisions with their authority not too clearly defined. But he acted as I requested him to and issued a warrant for the arrest of the men I named and prepared to send a constable to serve it. Then he became extremely cautious. I could tell that he was impressed by Rob's importance and the enormity of the crime. He was also impressed by the fact that Captain Rose was so much alive. He finally instructed the constable to bring in Scott and several of the others for questioning. This, I thought was a mistake, but he kept saying the matter required caution.

I remained in the dingy little office of the reluctant justice to hear the questioning. As it turned out, there wasn't any questioning. Scott just did the talking. He informed the magistrate that he had no right to issue such a warrant—that the men who went to the Potter residence on the morning of March second were a duly authorized posse with a trespass warrant issued by a justice of the peace and in the hands of a deputy constable. Potter had resisted arrest—had fired on the officer and fled.

"He did not fire on anyone, your honor!" I protested. "He was shot with his own loaded gun by this man!"

Scott ignored me, and so did the magistrate.

"This warrant you've issued is invalid," Scott was telling him, "coming as it does after the one we acted on that was issued in this same county, under your jurisdiction, by your associate justice. If you do not immediately release all of us, you'll be sued in the higher courts for false imprisonment, and I swear it!"

"No need to use threats, Mr. Scott. I didn't know you men was a legal posse. I wasn't told about the other warrant. You can go home."

"Is this a full release for all concerned?"

The magistrate assured Scott the case was closed.

I was stunned by this development. This was the first I knew that Rose had a warrant. It was hard to imagine how he had moved that fast. But it didn't alter the fact that Rob had been deliberately shot—that it had been a sneak raid with no pretense of trying to make an arrest.

I was trying to think this out when Scott addressed me. As on the day of the murder, he was not inclined to be abusive.

"You're a plucky little woman, still giving more attention to Potter than he ever deserved. But you go on home now—take care of yourself and your children, and you won't be troubled. Will you do that?"

"What else is there for me to do?" I countered bitterly.

He studied me for a moment longer with that special look a man reserves for a pregnant woman, and I realized that he was attributing my journey to Dangerfield to impulse rather than trickery. The fallacy that I was a weak woman in delicate condition still had some protective value.

I went on out to Abraham and Mr. Parsons who had stood nearby, waiting for me. As we walked back to our camp spot, I told them what had happened. We would remain in camp for a while, I decided, until Scott and his companions were out of Dangerfield and well on the way home.

And then what would we do? they wanted to know.

It was not easy to decide. Disappointment was too keen for clear thought. Maybe we'd go on to Clarksville—a long sixty-mile ride, but there I could talk to Charles and to Amos Morrill. I couldn't go back to Potter's Point with nothing accomplished—nothing at all!

A visitor came to the camp and made the decision for me—a young man who gave no name.

"I been carrying some mail, ma'am," he explained. "Just rode in from Boston yesterday. Judge Mills is holding court there. I'll bet he could help you out. You got a dirty run-around here, ma'am. But it's a long ride to Boston for a lady—some forty miles."

"I don't mind the distance. I'll ride anywhere for a chance to bring my husband's murderers to trial. But Boston's in Bowie County. Do you suppose Judge Mills would consider my case?"

"He's a district judge, ma'am, and got a lot more power than these ignorant backwoods county office-holders. Why don't you try it?"

"I will."

"I'd advise you to ride out of Dangerfield like you was going back to Potter's Point. About two miles out there's a lefthand trail—it's a cut-off back on the road to Boston."

He gave us full traveling instructions, wished us good luck, and galloped away.

Rob had been murdered on March 2, 1842, the sixth anniversary of his signing the Texas Declaration of Independence (What an irony that was!). It was on March twenty-fifth that I appeared before Judge John T. Mills and preferred charges against William P. Rose, Preston Rose, John W. Scott, Stephen Peters, Samuel Perkins, Sandy Miller, James Williams, William Smith, Isaac Jones, and Calvin Fuller for murder. By this action, I set in motion a string of events that kept me away from my home and children for six weeks and put me through tests of endurance beyond any yet experienced in my ordeal of living in the Republic of Texas.

I rode all night from Boston to Clarksville, a distance of forty miles, to carry Judge Mill's order of arrest to Sheriff Edward West of Red River County. I felt exultant satisfaction in the wording of the order for the capture of these men, *dead or alive, in or out of Texas*. I arrived in Clarksville just as the sun was rising and went directly to the Gordons. And for the first time since Rob's death, I knew the sanctuary of a safe and friendly house where my efforts were given immediate attention and support—where indignation and desire for justice matched my own. Dr. Gordon waited only for a hasty account of the murder and then took the warrant from me and delivered it to Sheriff West.

Amos Morrill and Charles came together to see me, and I repeated my story in more detail to them. Amos assured me of his legal counsel every step of the way, and Charles said simply that Amos and I were to command him in any way that he could be of service.

Within two hours, and while Amos and Charles were still with me, Dr. Gordon returned to say that the Sheriff with a posse of twenty men had already set out to capture the men charged and return with them to Clarksville.

To my great relief and surprise, the Sheriff was able to execute his order without bloodshed. Arriving in the lake region before daybreak, he surprised every man he sought, took each of them without resistance and brought his prisoners into Clarksville chained to their horses.

Mrs. Gordon and I watched from her doorway the procession of chained men being brought in.

"They don't look like bad men, do they?" I remarked. "It's hard not to feel pity for them, carrying all those chains."

"Pity, Mrs. Potter? I should think that sight would give you the greatest kind of pleasure."

"It is what I want, but I can't be as happy about it as I thought I could."

"Believe me, they won't show you any mercy, or give you any kind of pity. If they had believed for an instant that you could do this to them, you would be as dead right now as Colonel Potter. Don't get softhearted, Mrs. Potter. They'll give you a rough time before this is over. You can count on it. You won't be spared because you are a woman or a mother."

"But what can they do to me now?"

"You're a lawyer's widow. You should know. They can get bail—they can win a verdict——"

"Oh, but they can't—not when I saw with my own eyes——"

"Mrs. Potter, have you ever seen a murder trial?"

"Why, no."

"I have. It isn't resolved by what anyone has seen with his own eyes. Have you ever been involved in any kind of court case as a witness, or in any other way?"

"No, but——"

"You're a brave little woman. And you're going to have plenty of opportunity to call upon every bit of courage you have. Steel your heart and mind. Some bad things are ahead of you. I hope you win.

Robert Potter was my friend—the Doc's and mine. I hope you have
the tenacity to secure a full measure of vengeance for this atrocity
that extinguished the light of such a brilliant mind"—she turned her
face away from me for there were tears on her cheeks—"robbing
Texas of a future president who could have swayed the courts of
Europe in our favor."

There was no jail in Clarksville. So the prisoners were held in
chains. It was a week before the grand jury investigations were concluded and during that time I came face to face with the harsh
reality of Mrs. Gordon's prediction.

Rose and Scott had sent a runner ahead of them with instructions
to employ all lawyers so that I would be without an attorney. Amos
and a young attorney who worked with him refused to be hired. All
other available legal aid went to the men charged with the murder.
And to lessen the weight of my testimony before the grand jury, the
old slanders that had been used against Rob at election time were
revived. No matter how old they were, they were new as applied to
me, and the anguish of being publicly denounced as a paramour
swearing falsely to the status of wife was also new.

Amos counseled me to ignore the slander persecutions, engage in
no arguments, make no statements in defense of my reputation. He
explained that Rob had discussed our marriage with him and that he
was fully qualified to defend me in this matter, and that my case
would suffer no injury by these character defamations as long as the
court recognized me as Mrs. Potter—and he would see to it that this
was done! Since I was the only eyewitness and the one bringing the
charges, I must expect the opposition to be pitiless, he said, and the
efforts to discredit me unrelenting.

Since the chains holding the prisoners were not prison walls, their
statements were overheard and dispensed with more speed and cover-
age than any printed matter could have been, and were much more
abusive in the unprintable language used.

The Lion in chains had a more dreadful roar than even his roughest
companions had ever heard on the prowl, I'm sure. He could revile
and vilify with spine-tingling versatility and his insults were not wholly
limited to me.

"Dullards! Stoneheads with bug eyes and pig ears!" he stormed at the grand jury as they listened to my account of his abuse on the morning of the murder. "Fumbling fools callin' this woman 'Mrs. Potter.' That purty butcher never had but one lawful wife and he put her in her grave. All the rest were just willin' women. I'll prove it! You'll all look like a bunch of slobberin' idiots when I'm through with you and that evil-eyed little witch of a Page woman who'd take any man—"

"Sheriff, silence your prisoner," the foreman commanded.

The sheriff jerked out his knife, held the point of it under Rose's chin. "Use Mrs. Potter's name one more time—just one more time before this jury and I'll slit your big loose mouth from ear to ear!"

My endurance was rewarded when the grand jury on April sixth returned a true bill indicting seven of the ten men I had charged, who

> . . . not having the fear of God before their eyes, but being moved and seduced by the instigation of the Devil, on the second day of March in the year of our Lord one thousand eight hundred and forty-two, with force and arms at and in the County of Red River and Republic of Texas, feloniously, willfully, and maliciously and of their malice aforethought, in and upon one Robert Potter, in the peace of God and our said Republic, then and there Being did make an assault, and that said William P. Rose (and the others named) a certain Gun at the value of Twenty Dollars, then and there charged and loaded with Gun Powder and divers laden shot, which said Gun the said William P. Rose (and the other named) . . . did shoot and discharge . . . in and upon the back part of the head of him the said Robert Potter—one wound the depth of five inches and the Breadth of two inches, of which, said wound, the said Robert Potter then and there instantly died.

Charles, during this time, was held back from doing the things he wanted to do by restraints as binding as the chains that held the accused. Since he was the only unmarried man among my declared friends, Amos warned that he must be scrupulously careful that his services to me and comments on the case not attract attention. Otherwise he would only provide more fuel for the slander campaign, since Rose and other residents around Potter's Point knew of his employment at Mulberry Shore during Rob's absences. Since Charles was often with Amos, there were occasions now and then when the three of us could talk together, and Charles would lament his lack of legal wit and knowledge—that he was unable to assist Amos in court. There were five energetic attorneys for the defense, and only Jesse Benton, the district attorney, and Amos to do legal battle against them.

"And there'll be more before we're done," he declared.

"How long will this court fight last, Amos?" Charles inquired.

"That's like asking me to set the date of Judgment, Ames. It will last until five lawyers and any others they may enlist have exhausted all possible legal maneuvers for delays."

Charles did assist Amos by reporting every move that was being made outside the court, every threat or slander that was being passed out, and at night he kept Amos company, going over the papers in the case with him, and reading law books while Amos worked and planned.

Since Mr. Parsons and Abraham, as well as myself, were being held indefinitely for important testimony, I became much concerned about affairs at Mulberry Shore. Also we were in need of clothes and other supplies. Amos decided that it would be all right for Charles to make a trip for us if it could be done without public knowledge.

So Charles left one night for Mulberry Shore. He came by to see me before departure. I gave him letters for Joe and Hezekiah, lists and letter to be read to Hannah, and finally a more personal commission.

"Charles, will you hold John for a bit and tell him his Mama misses him very much? And will you tell Lakeann one of your lovely stories— and kiss her black curls for me?" Homesickness engulfed me and I could hardly hold back my tears. "Oh, Charles, this is the greatest pain of all—being separated from my little ones. You—you are the only person who can make them feel that I've not deserted them—impress them with my concern. Praise Joe for all he's doing in caring for the stock."

"I will, Harriet, I will! Trust me completely."

"And on your journey—if you should see any black haws in bloom— it's early, but you might see some——" I tried to smile, tried to tease a bit, "would you take a bouquet to your true love? You know how she likes white blossoms."

He tried to speak—just said "Harriet." He reached for my hands and held them tightly in his. "Harriet—I'll search every step of the way—for white blossoms—for my true love."

He left abruptly—his good-by phrase a mere whisper.

The legal delays Amos Morrill had anticipated ate up the whole month of April. First there were protests that the warrant had been issued in the wrong county. Then Rose and Scott through their attorneys prayed that the case be continued. They had been kept in such strict confinement since the charges, it was claimed, that they had been unable to make arrangements for defense witnesses. A long list of these witnesses was presented. On April fifteenth, the five attorneys for the defendants applied for bail. This was denied, and Judge Mills ordered the prisoners removed to the nearest jail, which was at Nacogdoches, two hundred miles to the south!

So the cavalcade of prisoners and guards, lawyers and clerks and witnesses, along with the curious and the concerned who could afford such a trip, set out on the long journey to Nacogdoches—the town where Robert Potter had first appeared in Texas, presented his character certificate, and offered himself for public office. The circle was closing, and I rode along the final segment with five men: my brother and Mr. Parsons, the district attorney, and Amos Morrill and his assistant.

Amos left Charles in charge of his office at Clarksville. It would not do at all for him to accompany us, Amos said. Also, it was arranged that Charles would make another trip to Mulberry Shore to keep in touch with my family and business. He had given me much relief with his report on the first trip. The children were all well—everything in good order. It was further arranged that we would send a messenger to Charles at Mulberry Shore about the middle of May, and there could be an exchange of reports if I were being detained beyond this time.

Now, Old Rose had no intention of taking up residence in the Nacogdoches jail, and the story of his intrigue along the road there later became a part of the legend.

One night during the journey, when the prisoners and their guard were being lodged in a wilderness home, Old Rose secured the friendly secret services of his host and was able to arrange for the delivery of a letter to Thomas J. Rusk. At that time, Mr. Rusk, former general and judge, was known throughout the Republic as an able attorney. Also, he was a native of Nacogdoches, and this would be an advantage.

That's how it happened that Mr. Rusk and his law partner, J. Pinckney Henderson, joined the Rose team of attorneys in Nacogdoches. And it turned out that they brought along copies of the fatal documents Rob had executed in Austin during February.

The attorneys began their defense of Rose with calculated delays.

Sheriff David Rusk of Nacogdoches refused to receive the prisoners on the plea that the jail was insecure. So Sheriff West had to leave his prisoners under guard and go to Shelbyville for instructions. District Judge William B. Ochiltree was holding court there.

The Judge was preoccupied with Regulator troubles, especially the feud-hanging of the McFadden brothers and was having to hold court with his pistols in easy reach. So he gave Sheriff West divided attention and a definite order: The Nacogdoches jail was all right and the prisoners were to be confined there.

The duel of delay between the sheriffs went on until Attorneys Rusk and Henderson had the stage set for release of the prisoners and could get Judge Ochiltree's full attention and presence.

In the meantime, I found my position in Nacogdoches a most painful one. In Clarksville, I had been surrounded by Rob's closest friends and admirers. Here I had only the men who accompanied me to offer encouragement and support. And even they began to act discouraged and strangely vague. I was under great strain every time I appeared in public. On every hand I met either open hostility or vulgar curiosity. I was repeatedly addressed as "Mrs. Page." I began to feel as if I were moving in a bad dream where no one recognized me, lost on a rough, forbidding road, encountering only cruel derisive faces that refused me directions of any kind. All the legal procedures seemed to be a web especially designed for my humiliation and confusion, torturing me with uncertain waiting until my longing to get back to my home and children was almost unbearable.

The sheriffs were still playing their game of the The-jail-is-strong-enough—It-is-not, when Judge Ochiltree got to town. At first, things looked better for me. The Judge was not too friendly to the Rusk and Henderson plea for a writ of habeas corpus on Rose. He had just been outmaneuvered by the Shelby County rascals who had managed to keep the grand jury from bringing in any bills on the slayings there. It was hard enough to get a murder indictment of any kind in this wilderness, he said, without one judge undoing what another had set in motion. But he listened carefully to their plea that Rose had cause—that Rob had threatened his life, had written letters engaging armed men to enlist against him—that Rose had acted in the company of a peace officer with a warrant. I don't know how they reasoned the judge around the fact that Rob was executing a presidential proclamation and carried a warrant for the arrest of Rose. Maybe Judge Ochiltree didn't like Lamar. Anyway, on May fourth, he granted the prisoners bail, setting Rose's bail at $25,000 and Scott's at $10,000. He made this concession principally, he announced, because of certain documents that had come to light, presenting some very surprising angles on the case not known in Clarksville. There were certain things that Judge Mills could not have understood without the evidence that Rusk and Henderson had presented.

After he had seen these documents, he refused to hear my testimony, and it fell to the lot of Amos Morrill to enlighten me as to the contents. He would not discuss it with me until we were alone in my drab little boarding house room.

"I have before me the most difficult task of my life," he said. "These papers are—a deed and a will—both executed in Austin only a few days after his patent was granted and less than a month before he was killed."

"Oh God help me, Amos. It's something disgraceful, isn't it?"

"Yes. Do you want to read it, or shall I read it to you?"

"I don't believe I could read just now, Amos. My head, my eyes, feel very queer indeed. I know it will pain you, but if you will——"

"It will pain me no more to read it than you to hear it—we'll share the agony."

He began reading in a legal monotone, not permitting himself a single inflection.

"The deed: Robert Potter to Mrs. Sophia A. Mayfield for a tract of land—dated the 8th of February, 1842—

Know all persons that I Robert Potter of the County of Paschal in consideration of my esteem for Mrs. Sophia Ann Mayfield and my desire to affix some lasting testimony of my respect and friendship and for the further consideration of one dollar to me in hand paid, the receipt whereof is hereby acknowledged, do give, grant, bargain and convey to the said Mrs. Sophia Ann Mayfield a part of my estate on Ferry Lake it being all that tract or parcel of land lying and situate on Ferry Lake in the County of Paschal and being Section Twelve as known and marked on the map of surveys made by the authority of the United States, in Range Seventeen (17) West, township Twenty (20) together with all that lot and parcel of land lying between the Western line of said section and the Lake aforesaid and also a part of the tract or parcel of land surveyed and located for me on said Ferry Lake as will be more fully shown by reference to the Patent issued to me for the same bearing the date January twenty-fifth, 1842, and recorded in the land office at Austin—To have and to hold the same to her, her heirs or assigns forever. In witness whereof I have hereto set my hand and seal this 8th day of February A.D. 1842.

Signed 'Rob Potter' and duly witnessed by C. Van Ness and J. S. Anderson."

"Who is Sophia Ann Mayfield, Amos?"

"The wife of Colonel James S. Mayfield who was a member of the Congress, in the House."

"What have you heard about her and Rob?"

"That they seemed much attached to each other—were seen frequently riding about Austin together during the last session."

"Does Mrs. Mayfield have children?"

"Five, I believe."

"Isn't it strange that Colonel Mayfield permitted the relationship?"

"It's all strange—incomprehensible."

"Now read the will, please, Amos."

"The will of Robert Potter—

In the name of God: Amen:—
I Robert Potter of the County of Paschal do make and ordain this my last will and testament—
1st I desire that my debts shall be paid by a sale of sufficient amount of my personal property.

446

2nd   As a testimony of my deep sense of the personal worth of Mrs. Sophia Ann Mayfield and my gratitude for her friendship and the happiness I have derived from her converse, I give and bequeath to her all that part of my estate on Ferry Lake known and described upon the map of the survey made by authority of the United States in Range Seventeen West, Township Twenty as Sections Twelve, Thirteen, and Twenty-Four, the latter being a fractional Section fronting on said Lake and being the place of my residence.

3rd   As a testimony of my deep sense of the personal worth of Mrs. Mary Chalmers, my gratitude for her friendship and the happiness I have derived from her converse, I give and bequeath to her all that part of my said Estate on Ferry Lake known and described on the map of aforesaid as Sections Seven, Eighteen, and Nineteen the latter being a fractional section, fronting on said Lake adjoining to and lying East of the Section on which is situated my residence.

4th   I give and bequeath to Mrs. Harriet A. Page all that part of my headright, being part of my Estate aforesaid lying North of Section Twelve before mentioned and West of Section six as mentioned, except one hundred acres to be set apart by Mrs. Page and reserved for her brother John D. Moore. I also give and bequeath to her two mares to be chosen by herself out of my stock, Forty hogs also to be chosen by herself, my stock of cattle and three Negroes to wit: George, Hannah and Matilda and also my household and kitchen furniture and farming utensils.

5th   As a testimony of my esteem for my long cherished and valued friend John W. Crunk I give and bequeath Negro girl Mary.

6th   As a testimony of my esteem for my friend Col. James S. Mayfield, I give and bequeath to him my favorite horse Shakespeare.

7th As a testimony of my esteem for my friend Dr. John G. Chalmers I give and bequeath to him all my estate real and personal that may remain after meeting and satisfying the several bequests and objects hereinbefore expressed.

8th I appoint my friend Col. Robert W. Smith my Executor. —In testimony of which I hereto subscribe my name and seal this the 11th day of February A.D., 1842.

Signed 'Rob Potter' and duly witnessed by M. C. Hamilton, F. Henderson, and N. B. Yancy."

"Amos, I don't believe Rob ever intended for me to find out about this will. He would have changed it if he hadn't been killed. I'm sure of it."

Amos looked at me with great astonishment. He had expected me to burst into sobs, I'm sure, and start berating Rob for this last and greatest of his deceits. Oh, I was bruised and shamed to the core of my spirit, but I kept thinking of Rob's several attempts to tell me something before making the run to the lake.

"Three times he tried to get me to listen to him——" I began explaining to Amos, "let him tell me something—before he made his attempt to escape. But I was so concerned with trying to persuade him to stay and fight that I refused to listen. He was probably going to warn me—tell me something that would explain these documents which must have been a camouflage for some political trade, a land transaction involving other property—you know, a deal of some kind legally concealed. It could even have been a gambling obligation— Rob did gamble sometimes—some impulsive commitment, perhaps. Oh, I know how charming he was to women, and there might have been some amorous diversion there—but if it were more than that, why did he leave Colonel Mayfield his favorite horse? Why did he mention Dr. Chalmers? There's a clue there somewhere, Amos, in his mentioning the men . . . He wrote me long affectionate letters every week, Amos. He was a devoted husband. He adored the children. The will itself is a deceit of some kind and not the greater deceit that it seems! I'm sure—oh, so sure, he wasn't tired of me, Amos. He loved me—he truly loved me!"

Amos did not agree or disagree with me in all my suppositions.

He let me complete the whole frantic circle of thought, trying to rescue some fragment of Rob's honor—some scrap of my pride from this abyss of shame.

"Of course, it could be as your silence seems to say it is: that he denied me as his wife, rejected his children, planned to be rid of us all for love of another. But what of his Sophia's husband and five children? How would they have been disposed of? It's all too ridiculous. I simply can't accept what he has declared there as the whole truth, even though I may have to accept the will. Is it final, do you think?"

"I know of nothing more final, more legally binding, than a man's last will and testament, especially one so perfectly in order as this one."

"Amos, I've had enough. Take me home to my children. I said *home*, Amos, and that's what I mean. I'm the one who stayed on that property and made a thriving farm of it—a beautiful home. Somehow, I'll keep it. But for now, just take me home."

"How about the case against Rose, Harriet? It's far from concluded. The men are under heavy bond. Though Ochiltree has allowed bail, it doesn't mean that he will look the other way on a matter of murder. I'm still with you if you want to continue to press charges. These documents do not alter what you saw."

"But they alter the status and identity of the person who saw it, as far as the courts are concerned. Judge Ochiltree has already refused my testimony as 'Mrs. Potter' . . . Well, I will not be sworn in as a paramour. I can spare my children and myself that recorded shame. Robert Potter has lost his own case. In such circumstances as these, I don't think he would expect Harriet Page to come to his defense, and Mrs. Potter cannot—so she's going home.

On the journey back to Potter's Point, I was escorted by the same five men who had left Clarksville with me. They made every possible arrangement for my comfort and convenience. Most of the time Amos rode by my side. I insisted on long steady rides and would agree to rest only at night time.

My long talks with Amos held some of my restlessness in check—I felt such a pressing anxiety to be home, experienced such regret that I had ever left my children to ride this long road of danger and defeat.

"I realize I must forever live with the certain knowledge of Rob's unfaithfulness," I said to Amos as we rode along. "As I look back on our six years together, I see a long trail of deceits, some dim, some very plain, and yet just as certainly I can say that he loved me deeply, that he was never unkind or overbearing beyond a few outbursts of temper. There was so much love between us, Amos. I cannot understand what was missing."

"Romantic love cannot stand alone, Harriet. Love to endure must have a character foundation, a spiritual significance. The same is true of abiding and fruitful friendship. I was close to Rob as a friend—no man has ever aroused me to expect more from him. I saw elements of greatness in him. I was highly stimulated and excited in his presence. So much talent, so much magnetism, made me feel that I was honored by the company of such a man—standing before genius. He betrayed that friendship as certainly as your love."

"None of us lacks faults, weaknesses, Amos. The seed of both good and evil surely resides in us all. People never do as much good as they want to, or as they intend to."

"It is my observation that every man is many men. In some men and women, the better self remains triumphant with only an occasional battle; in others, evil flourishes—while in most of us the war of the souls is forever raging. But in none have I ever seen the battle so awesomely balanced, both extremes so manifest, as in Robert Potter. My friend was a man of shining intelligence and cultural attainment. He comprehended the elements of hope and beauty in the arts, in religion, in philosophy—knew the warmth of kindness, recognized the responsibility of leadership. And yet, he acted as a criminal, a coward, a traitor, long practiced in evil deeds, as a primitive untouched by culture or compassion—depraved, mad."

"When my Negro woman Hannah can't figure out why something is so, she says, 'Hits de Lawd's business—de Lawd know why.'"

At sundown of the second day, we were twenty miles from Potter's Point and decided to stop at a neighbor's house for the night. Though the family here had not come to me at the time of Rob's death, they were especially kind to me on this occasion. But they made me quite uncomfortable by acting so sad and strained. Even though they knew of my plight and hardships, I would have welcomed more cheerful hospitality. I spoke of the beautiful Maytime scenery we had journeyed through that day and of my eagerness to see my children. The lack of response was embarrassing. Perhaps it was the scandal that made them so self-conscious, I thought, since their sympathy was so apparent.

I insisted on a very early departure the next morning and hurried the party along continuously. It seemed that they lagged and loitered, could not comprehend my happy urgency to have my children in my arms again. They were one and all in a dismal mood, and I tried my best to cheer them, planning the comfortable quarters and good food I would provide for them at Mulberry Shore to express my gratitude and erase their fatigue. Abraham and Amos looked positively ill and I began to wonder if we had taken some water or food that was contaminated. I could almost imagine I was feeling the same way when I looked at them, but as the trail became even more familiar with each landmark nearer and nearer my Lakeann and my John baby, I became more and more animated in spite of my weary male companions.

Near journey's end, we crossed a branch where the black hawthorne grew in abundance and the bushes were now showing the full beauty of their dainty white blossoms. I stopped my horse, gazed at the lovely bushes, food and drink to my soul.

"We'll stop just a moment here," I told them. "I must have some of these beautiful branches to take home."

No one moved to help me dismount (Gentlemen, you must be sick, all of you, I almost said, just in fun)—so I quickly swung from the saddle and began to break off some choice stems of flowers.

"Mr. Parsons, why don't you help me? You know how Lakeann loves these blossoms. You men! Doesn't this beautiful sight cheer you any? Hardly a smile from any of you for twenty miles. You've poked along all morning, and now when I stop for a few flowers, you all stare at me as if I'm delaying you."

Mr. Parsons got off, stiff and awkward, and came toward me. "Mrs. Potter, I wouldn't gather those flowers if I was you." His voice was unnatural and harsh. The other men began to dismount.

I took a good look at Mr. Parson's face and a great dread gripped my heart. "Mr. Parsons. Something has happened and you don't want to tell me."

"I don't want to, God knows. But I will. The others don't want to tell you either. I said to them, 'Well, I'm old and know all the hurts, and she's young and can bear 'em, so——' "

"Tell me."

"Little Lake is dead—dead and buried."

Mr. Parson's face twisted and he began to cry. "The folks told us last night."

Amos came to my side, tried to hold the flowers for me. I held on to them. I had to hold on to something. The whirling darkness— the pain—the awful devastating mother pain, pulling at all the inside of me, at the whole mind of me.

"Kill me, somebody. Let me die!"

I leaned against Sukey Blueskin, clutching the saddle, clutching the flowers.

"What happened?"

"She was scalded to death . . . Hannah had a pot of soap——"

"Oh God, I told Hannah . . . I told Hannah . . . I told Hannah . . ."

This was (and remains to this day!) the agony of my life.

I let the men help me into the saddle. I had no further word for them. No tears. I rode in a stony stupor the rest of the way.

When I rode up to the yard gate, Hannah came to meet me, carrying John, tears washing down her face.

I dismounted, handed Hannah the flowers, took John. He hugged and kissed me saying, over and over, "Mama! Mama! Mama home!"

I held him tightly and started walking slowly toward the grove— toward the graves. Hannah walked beside me.

"Missus, ah didn' bil' soap to pleasuh mahsef. Youse gone sa long— sa long, Missus—an' we needs soap. Ah hang da pot in da fiuhplaz, good an' tight. An' da chillums slep—Baby John middle da bed—Lake on da pallet befo' da fiuh, lak she allus do. She know 'bout fiuh, Missus—ya know dat—she da smaht 'un. Delia an' me, we's got washin' an' i'onin' in da shed. Delia fetchin' watuh when Lake scream. Delia gits dere fust—soap pouhed all ovuh . . . debbil-man done hit . . . debbil-man done hit as ah say . . . an' Delia say she saw he shadow!"

In my mind there was no place at all for thinking how it had happened—whether Lake herself had tried to stir it or whether this was the worst crime of all.

I just kept walking—slowly—the only function of mind to get my body to move on toward the grove.

I didn't say a word. Hannah kept on talking.

"Delia gone, Missus. Delia run cleuh away. She go plum' wailin' mad. Ah wants ta wail an' run mahself, Missus. Ah sholy do. But Baby John need me—Tildy need me—you need me maybe. Ah nevuh runs fum need, no mattuh whut."

We were close enough to the grove now to see the small fresh mound.

I stopped. "Take John, Hannah. Give me the flowers. Take the baby back to the house. Leave me alone. A baby should be happy, Hannah. Sing to him."

"O Lawd Jesus! She say sing to 'im."

I went on alone.

I sat by the grave so long without moving or making a sound that my friends feared for my reason. When they came to comfort me, they were driven away by the madness in my eyes. Actually, I never saw or heard them.

Then Charles Ames came.

He took me by the elbows and pulled me to my feet. When I stumbled, his arms enfolded me and recognition pierced the awful encasement of my shock.

"Charles," I whispered to him, "your true love is dead." Then I broke into wild sobbing.

He held me tightly until I had quieted enough to hear him. Then he said, "No, my dear. No, my darling. My true love is not dead. She is right here. Safe in my arms. And I shall never let her go."

Tricky shook her grandmother's shoulder and tried to wake her. Harriet was usually a peaceful sleeper. But on this night, she was moaning as though in a nightmare, and Tricky was finding it hard to arouse her. Her grandmother had seemed very bemused and sad the evening before, after staying in seclusion at her writing desk most of the day, and Tricky, disturbed by the mood, had asked to sleep with her.

If Gram could only hear! She hated to shake her so roughly. Gram was so small and fragile that she might come apart.

The moaning stopped and Tricky lay back in relief.

Then her grandmother started muttering. And Tricky raised up to listen. The words were distinct:

"White blossoms from the black hawthorne . . . white blossoms for a black-eyed angel."

It gave Tricky an eerie feeling. She herself was black-eyed and she loved white blossoms of all kinds. Her grandmother's voice had an unearthly quality. Tricky had never before heard anyone talking in sleep. She must get Gram awake. She gave her another little shake and spoke right in her ear, "Gram! Gram! Wake up! What's the matter, Gram?"

And her grandmother spoke again.

"Baby John slept in Hannah's lap . . . and she sang to him."

Tricky shook her again, harder this time. And her grandmother sat up.

There was no light in the room. Tricky thought she had finally aroused Gram. She leaned over close to her and said, "What were you dreaming, Gram?"

Then to her astonishment, her grandmother began to sing, softly and sweetly crooning in Negro dialect:

> Oh, ya libe a little
> An' den ya die,
> Dat's da Lawd's business,
> Da Lawd know why.
>> Bye, Baby, bye
>> Close yo' puhty eye,
>> Let da ole folks cry,
>> Bye, Baby, bye.

> Oh, da rivuh run wet
> An' da rivuh run dry,
> Dat's da Lawd's business,
> Da Lawd know why.
>> Bye, Baby, bye,
>> Close yo' puhty eye,
>> Let da ole folks cry,
>> Bye, Baby, bye.

454

Oh, some crittuhs crawl,
An' some crittuhs fly,
Dat's da Lawd's business,
Da Lawd know why.
    Bye, Baby, bye,
    Close yo' puhty eye,
    Let da ole folks cry.
    Bye, Baby, bye.

When she had finished, she lay back down, turned on her side, and her breath came quietly and evenly in her sleep.

Tricky lay back down too, awed and wide awake for a long time.

Tricky was busy making up the bed for her grandmother who sat nearby giving her careful instructions on how to punch and pat and mold the feather mattress. No servant ever made Harriet's bed. It was the one housekeeping ritual that she reserved for herself, for the feather mattress must always be handled just so and shaped just so for comfort and beauty. Occasionally she allowed Tricky to do it for her, giving as much attention to detail as an art teacher with a pupil at the easel.

"I like the feel of it, Gram. So soft . . . pushing the feathers around . . . shaping it up so pretty . . . and having it wait there for you to come and sink into the softness if you're tired, or sort of want to hide, or sort of gently think."

"Or quietly cry. You can hide a lot of pain in it, Tricky. It muffles and absorbs the sounds of grief."

"I suppose so."

"You'll find out, Tricky, that a bed is for sorrow as well as for joy. Such is the balance of life."

"Yes, Gram, I know about sorrow."

"You've only touched it, child. Only touched it. But remember what I say: it balances. Out of the great love of my life, I bore thirteen children in pain and gladness with that mattress under me. And nine of them, at different ages, one just your age, I watched through their last sleep there. And then your Grandfather Ames—he had his last earthy sleep there too."

"I never knew you had thirteen children, Gram. That's a dreadful many!"

"For some perhaps. Not for me. Actually, I had eighteen in all. Five before I married your grandfather."

"Gram! Eighteen!"

"I guess that does shock you, doesn't it child? Having grown up with no brothers and sisters and then only Cousin Claud in Uncle E.Y.'s home and only Cousin Frank here. I wish you might have had more children around you."

"Oh, I'm happy this way, Gram. I have you."

"I'm hardly a playmate."

"Well, the things I can't do with you, I can do with Tanya."

"You love Tanya very much, don't you?"

"I think I shall marry Gideon some day, Gram. Then I shall live at 'Gates Gardens' and have Tanya for a sister."

"Tricky!"

"Is it wrong to talk about marriage when you're only ten?"

"No, of course not. A little girl talks about marriage almost from the time she talks at all—to her doll—in her playhouse. My reproof is that your statement sounds greedy. You love 'Gates Gardens,' and indeed it is one of the most beautiful estates I know. You've heard Gideon's Grandmother Gates say as many times as I have, 'All this is for Gideon when he marries. And I shall die happy knowing that my son who has no need of it has given me a grandson worthy of such a legacy.' She's been saying that since he was two years old. I don't know how she can be so sure of his worthiness."

"Oh, Gram, everyone knows Gideon is wonderful!"

"Oh. So you wouldn't mind having to put up with him to get the Gardens and Tanya for a sister?"

"Gram, don't talk like that. You know I love Gideon as much as I love Tanya."

"You'll have to love him more and differently from that to make him a worthy wife and experience the true bliss of wedded life. Let me tell you something now—though you're only ten, you should know this—love is not a choice of surroundings or people you'd like to live with. Love is something deep and abiding between two people—them alone—something understood and cherished and trusted beyond all doubt—something——"

"Yes, Gram. What else?"

"I'm trying to explain too much too soon, dear."

"But, Gram, we have so little time."

She knows, Harriet thought. She knows without knowing she knows —without realizing.

"I'm not so sure about that. Something else I can't explain. But perhaps we have all the time there is."

"Because we're so much alike?"

"The links of love, I think, are eternal."

They were silent while Tricky spread and tucked the fresh sheets and then began to arrange the counterpane. Harriet knew there was a question poised in the air between them, but she gave Tricky no help in giving it word form.

"Gram—you said eighteen children—in all. What about the other five—before you married my grandfather? Do you want to tell me about it?"

Harriet was glad Tricky's back was turned. She almost laughed. Tricky's tone was offering the comfort of confidence, disguising, suppressing, the intensive curiosity that was always there concerning any matter of her grandmother's life.

And, after all, she is my comfort and my confidant, more than she realizes, Harriet thought.

She answered, "No. Not now."

"Did you have the magic mattress then?"

Harriet did laugh now, a laugh unusually clear and sweet for a woman her age.

"No, my dear. No mattress. Only hard reality. And as for the magic—there was some—but—it came to confusion."

"Will you tell me—sometime?"

"Sometime—yes—I promise. Now, go to the foot of the bed, the far corner, and pull the cover back from the mattress. Don't look so startled. You did it all right. I've just decided I should tell you now about the proper care of the mattress when it's yours. You see that finishing seam at the corner?"

"Yes, Gram."

"Inside that seam is a little pocket, and in the pocket are explicit instructions for washing the feathers, a job that you must do very carefully and all by yourself."

"Oh, I will, Gram, if you say so. It's an awfully big mattress though, and I'm not very big, you know, not as big as I want to be—not even as big as Tanya and she's only nine. Oh dear, Gram, I never heard of washing feathers . . . I don't know a bit of a thing about washing feathers . . . but I'll do it . . . I'll do it someway, Gram."

"Don't get so excited and burdened with the responsibility. With proper care, it doesn't have to be washed but a few times in a lifetime. And the explicit instructions are all there."

"Yes, Gram." Tricky's voice told Harriet that somehow this responsibility took the mattress into a realm of reality for Tricky that brought her face to face with the further reality that when she performed this task, her grandmother would not be there—she would be forever gone—dead and buried. With all of their frank discussions of death and heaven and the possession of the mattress, there had been a delightful veil of fantasy over the whole thing. Washing the feathers . . . the golden brocade covering ripped off and laid aside . . . no veil of fantasy here . . . no grandmother.

They looked at each other and faced the fact together.

"You'll not miss me much when I'm gone, Tricky. Your life will be full of other loves and big decisions. I will be nearer than you think, and you'll know that. And the things we've said and done will always be in your bright mind to take out and give deeper comprehension as time goes on. Now about this feather-washing. There's a bit of magic attached to that too." She saw the look of loss fade and the bright imagination reach out.

"On the first night of rest upon the fresh washed and sunned feathers, the one who lies there experiences a lightness and brightness not like any other night. You will seem to be without weight and floating on a feathery cloud. Your thoughts and dreams will have wondrous clarity. My mother spoke a little rhyme on the matter that went: *On the fresh first night, all dreams are bright, decisions right, and wishes might—come true!*"

Tricky repeated the rhyme after her grandmother.

"That's it. Now tuck the cover back carefully, and come here to me. I want to tell you something that won't be in writing. I want to exact a promise of you that will have no bearing on your life until you are grown—of marriageable age."

Tricky came and sat on a little stool, looking up at her grandmother.

"Before you answer any man 'yes' to a proposal of marriage, before you commit yourself to either formal or informal engagement— whether it be to Gideon whom you've known all your life or to some stranger whose presence puts a new rhythm in your heartbeat— sleep over your decision before you utter it—and make it a special sleep—a 'fresh first night' on the magic mattress with every feather washed and aired breathing brightness into you and over you. Do you want to promise me this?"

"Of course I do, Gram. It's a most beautiful promise—the most beautiful promise that ever was made. And I make it to you. I promise you, Gram. I shall wash the feathers, I shall sleep for a night on the magic mattress before I say, 'Yes, I will marry you' to any man. And, I seal it with a kiss."

Young lips touched old lips in all gentleness and love, promise and caress. And young cheek pressed against old cheek in a happy communion that death and time could not touch.

25.

Harriet Ann Purcelle, age eighteen and one day, sat at her grand-mother's writing desk. This room, since her grandmother's death, had become her study and her very private retreat. From a great array of birthday gifts, she had selected three to bring into the room with her, and these were before her now: one, an antique royal mantilla, short cape of velvet and lace, with a history of being worn by Marie Antoinette, was hung across the corner of the desk; another, a ring set with two rare and matching diamonds, sparkled from its velvet case open before her; and a third, a bouquet of eighteen sweetheart roses, short perfect buds, just now beginning to unfold, were arranged in a shallow ivory bowl so close that the fragrance seemed to go right to her heart with every breath and set her blood to tingling. Each of these gifts symbolized a road of life, a future, and she must make a choice, for she knew that she would take one of the three. The ring was Gideon's. He had presented it as an engagement ring to signify her formal acceptance of his formal proposal. He had been astonished and deeply injured when she had told him that she was not ready to become engaged—that she had more thinking to do before accepting his offer of marriage, or any other.

It had come as no shock to Gideon Gates that Tricky Purcelle had many offers of marriage to consider. But it did surprise him very much that she would seriously consider anyone but himself.

"What thinking could you possibly have to do that you haven't had time to do already through the years I've known you? Ever since I was fourteen, I've been telling you of my expectations. And you've never been coy with me. Your wholehearted affection I have always been as sure of as—as—well, as Tanya's or my parents' or my grand-mother's. We're family to each other, Tricky. How can it be any other way?"

"Perhaps it can't be any other way, Gideon dear. I'm not sure. I do love you. But is it marriage love?"

"Of course it's marriage love. I'm not repulsive to you, am I? In the countless times I've kissed you since the age of six, I've never had the feeling that I was."

"Of course you aren't."

"You wouldn't find being my wife an icy burden, would you? It was always you who grabbed me for a husband when you and Tanya played house and made me imaginary father to innumerable broods,

always outlandishly large . . . Trick, I simply don't understand . . .
I've always been so sure . . . Other girls have never appealed to
me——"

Tricky laughed and her eyes twinkled. "Never, never, Gideon?"

"Well, now, you didn't expect me to go around mooning like a
lost calf in public while you belled it with every eligible in New
Orleans? But you knew beyond any doubt, you'd be the one. You
must accept me, Tricky. I couldn't—I wouldn't know how to live in
this world without you."

"You'd always have the cotton exchange and the stock market,
dear, not to mention the horse races," she teased, for Gideon's reputation for financial wizardry and luck had given him such popularity
with the young and respect with the old that he had come into
spectacular prominence both in sporting circles and financial con-
claves. In all of New Orleans there seemed no young man so certainly
destined for wealth, and a happy combination of pleasure and authority.

There was another man besides Gideon himself who felt that Tricky
Purcelle must accept no other than the Gates scion for a husband;
her uncle, the eminent industrialist, E. Y. Ames.

He told his wife, "If I were God and fashioning the right husband
for Tricky, I'd make Gideon Gates just as He did."

"Don't be so sure God made him for Tricky. She'll decide that.
And don't be acting like God, dictating the match," his wife Grace
warned. "She's like her grandmother. Doesn't want anyone managing
her life. If some fly-by-night comes along and she gets the impulse
to wed him, she'll do it. Mark my word."

"Tricky has my mother's good sense, as well as her looks and
temperament."

"You must admit though, Edward, that your mother made some
big mistakes with men before she found your father."

"My God! Of course I admit it, Grace. I was a grown man when
that Supreme Court decision took her property and scandalized her
name. Charles and William and I all rallied round but without
Father's influence and judgment, we were helpless. That inability
to protect her when she needed it most has always been a thorn in my
flesh. That's why I've worked so close with Frank and Addie to keep
irresponsible charmers out of Tricky's life and Gideon so much in it.

462

She's the only girl in the whole family, and such a confounded duplication of Mother, I simply will not allow——"

"Don't let the thorn goad you into making unreasonable threats or promises."

"It takes a lot of self-control not to urge the marriage upon her. She's eighteen. What's Gideon waiting on? He doesn't have some other girl on the string at this late date, does he?"

"Not Gideon."

"What did he give her for her birthday? She didn't show me."

"And for good reason. A double-diamond ring, quite fabulously beautiful."

"An engagement ring, thank God!"

"Withhold your thanks a bit, my eager dear. She didn't put it on."

"Why? You mean it didn't fit?"

"My sweet ox! Would Gideon Gates buy a ring that didn't fit?"

"If she turned him down, I'll——"

"She didn't turn him down. She didn't accept him either. Addie says Tricky told her she wants to 'think it over.' Gideon insisted she keep the ring until her mind is made up one way or the other. She did."

"One way or the other? Who else in the name of heaven is she considering?"

"It might be that actor, Fame Kingston. He's certainly given her a lot of attention since they did that Shakespearean dialogue at the benefit. I think she overstepped there."

"What do you mean?"

"She was queen of the ball—that was enough—without becoming an actress, engaging in the sensation to attract the crowd."

"It was just for charity."

"Sure. Otherwise Fame Kingston wouldn't have lent his talents to baiting the money collection trap. But the press didn't praise Miss Harriet Ann Purcelle for her service to charity, they praised the quality of her performance opposite a great actor. And Fame Kingston didn't start courting her for charity either."

"Courting her? Nobody told me he was courting her! How could Frank and Addie allow it?"

"How could they help it? is a better question. You should know that Fame Kingston is no common actor. He's a great Shakespearean performer, and a mature man of cultured deportment. He must be at least thirty—there's something about an early marriage that ended in divorce. But no scandal pursues his private life and as a public figure he's a young maiden's dream-god, and, I understand, as inaccessible as one—until he did a benefit performance with Tricky Purcelle. You don't turn a man like that away from your door, you know."

"An actor! Divorced! Almost twice her age! I certainly would turn him away and with orders to stay away from my niece!"

"Oh, no, you wouldn't. He's a great man, I tell you. And he's not twice her age—only ten or twelve years older. Besides, he hasn't actually asked to pay court. He's simply called at the house a time or so—given them complimentary seats in the box for his performance— things like that. They had to ask him to dine, of course, as return courtesy. But, so far, he just visits with the family or strolls in the garden with Tricky in plain sight of Addie."

"Why hasn't anyone told me about this?"

"I didn't give it much thought until she didn't accept Gideon's ring—then I began to wonder."

"What advantage could such a person possibly have over Gideon Gates as a suitor?"

"Perhaps Tricky prefers a dark prince to a light one. And then there's theatrical glamor—and—a voice. Ah! That voice!"

"Glamor! That's not something for a girl to marry. And Tricky is not the type to be bedazzled. She sees right through false fronts— always has. As for voice—what's wrong with Gideon's?"

"Nothing, for ordinary speaking purposes. I don't know how he sounds making love, but I'm sure he's no Romeo or Lysander. If Fame Kingston sounds half as captivating wooing a woman as he does wooing an audience, I'm afraid——"

"No, Grace, no! A woman doesn't marry a voice."

"I'm not so sure. I guess I've never told you what your voice does to me—when you're making love——"

"Grace!"

"Just because you were a decorous old bachelor when I married you, don't keep acting like one. That beguiling voice runs in your family—your mother had it—you have it (that's why you're so irresistible in both bed and business—ah, you're blushing!)—Tricky has it (that's why the hulla-ba-loo over her Juliet, Hermia, and Miranda lines at the ball with Fame)—and our Claud has it (bless his captivating heart! What a time he'll give the ladies!).

"Grace! You've given me an idea. Claud. He and Tricky adore each other. She'll listen to him. He'll help me get Gideon's ring on her finger."

Grace laughed. "You blind eagle, you! Don't you know those two are first for each other, then for the rest of us. She's more likely to use Claud to soften us up if she turns Gideon down. By the way, does Gideon know, I wonder, about her 'manly accomplishments'?"

"I hope no one outside the family knows. I bought that tract of land adjoining the city park property for her and Claud to use just to keep the matter private and give Mother the country outings she craved. It's a good investment. I intended to hold it until the city needed it for park expansion. But I think I'll sell it right away. Now that Mother's no longer here to chaperone, it's hardly proper for them to be gadding out there with only the servants around."

"I agree with you. I don't like anything about it. Fishing! What a detestable pastime! All I ever get out of accompanying them out there is a lot of unsightly mosquito bites! I thought after Tricky's debut, her interests in such things would flag. But no! They've increased. I wonder what the elegant young gentlemen who clamor for her favor would think if they knew she could swim, fish, shoot, and ride with more skill and energy than most of them."

"Don't rub it in, Gracie. I had to humor Mother in that request."

"I wouldn't have minded the riding—ladylike riding. But a cross saddle rider I consider most unladylike—approaching vulgarity."

"Well, to tell you the truth, Gracie, so do I. But she wears ample skirts over her breeches and boots, just as the sidesaddle riders do."

"As far as we know she does."

"You think she might—uh—dispense with the skirt on occasion?"

"Ask Claud."

"Little good that would do. He's probably tied and gagged with promises. What makes you think she leaves off her skirt when they ride?"

"Just the expression on his face when I asked him about it."

"I'll put a stop to it."

"Too late now, Edward. That kind of nonsense should have been

465

stopped before it started. I don't think it's good for Claud either
to be so often in the company of a girl (even though she's his cousin)
who can so easily outdistance him in masculine pursuits. I've watched
them swimming. (She refuses to wear a skirt—only blouse and bloomers with the bloomers pushed up higher than any decent woman wears
them under her skirt). She always excels. And he readily admits she's
a better shot."

"Oh, well, he's younger. That's salve enough for his vanity."

"He doesn't really care—they have the greatest fun together—he
worships her. I shouldn't have to tell you that."

"It will be broken up soon. She'll forget all about these rough
exercises when she starts having babies."

"Get her married first, dear!"

E.Y. glared, then granted his wife a dismal smile. "I can't trust
myself to talk with her about it. I'll consult with Frank and Addie.
We'll plan something—plot something."

"I've never known you and Addie to plot anything that she didn't
unravel the whole thing before you got it done."

"Gracie, help me. Don't discourage me."

"I'm not trying to discourage you, dear. I'm trying to prepare you.
Tricky loves us all, but no single one of us, nor all of us put together,
will decide for her about marriage."

"If we can only get her promised to Gideon—she never breaks a
promise."

"That she doesn't. And I've never known anyone more cautious
about making one."

"It isn't just the Gates' wealth, Gracie, nor that Gideon's father
is my good friend and business associate. I wouldn't urge a marriage
without devotion and character involved. Why, Tricky and Gideon
have been devoted since childhood. The boy's level-headed and clean
and on his way to being a king of finance . . ."

"A golden-haired Apollo with a face that shatters a lady's composure
—and restless hands they yearn to hold——"

"Grace!"

"And no vice but lust for the races, and that but half a vice since
he usually wins. There we have Gideon Gates—the nephew God
made for us but only Tricky can give us!"

Tricky reached for the ring and put it on. It fit perfectly and its double radiance seemed to promise a double portion of happiness, seemed to grace her hand with all the elegance that would be hers on all sides as the wife of Gideon Gates.

She reached for paper and pen and set the ink out, then let her left hand lie conspicuous before her own gaze as she wrote out sample signatures with careful penmanship:

Mrs. Gideon Gates

A fine, important-looking signature, she thought.

Harriet Ann Gates

Harriet Purcelle Gates

Tricky Gates

Each variation, even the nickname, she decided, carried a certain distinction. She tried saying each one aloud—then the compound version: *Gideon and Harriet Gates*—and a tone of pleasant dignity seemed to ring through them all.

She thought of her last visit to "Gates Gardens" . . . the tour of the mansion, each room a repository of furnishing treasures . . . the stroll in the gardens, a kingdom of blossoming beauty, hedged with oleanders, perfumed with camellias and jasmine, roses and honeysuckle, magnolia and sweet olive, and drugging the sense of sight with exotic designs of flowering color, derived from a century of culture and continuous care. And by her side, Gideon's grandmother, speaking quite frankly of the marriage she wanted for her grandson.

"You'll soon be eighteen, Harriet Ann, and when Gideon proposes, don't keep him waiting. The boy needs a wife—you specifically. He's never desired any other, though he's been most shamelessly pursued. You've flitted about as a jeweled butterfly is entitled to do for a while, but I'm well acquainted with your virtures and good sense, and I've watched the steady gleam of affection always in your eyes for my Gideon. There are no barriers to this match, a rare good fortune that seldom comes to marriage. It will be approved, welcomed by both families. In proud tradition and sound wealth it offers the greatest possible happiness and security for you and all the sons and daughters that may bless your union. I promise you I shall not be in your way— shall give no orders outside my quiet and self-restricted domain in the east wing. You will be undisputed mistress of "Gates Gardens." I will enjoy my retirement. My advice will be given only when it's sought. I'll simply rest from responsibility and wait for my great-grandchildren as the culminating joy of my life."

Remembering this, Tricky sighed with the responsibility of so much happiness held in her hands to dispense to others. Did she need Gideon as much as he needed her? No one but herself to ask and answer this question. Must she feel bound to Gideon by the great-grandchildren a dear old dame already envisioned clustering about her? And Tanya . . . what of dear Tanya? Tricky smiled at the child-hood memories rushing in, sweet conspiracies and agreements: *Marry Gideon, Tricky. Promise. Then we'll be sisters.* It was hard to deny Tanya and she'd wanted to promise—but she hadn't, thanks to Gram who'd cautioned that she mustn't ever think of marrying Gideon just to get "Gates Gardens" as a home and Tanya as a sister. As a child, she'd thought Gram a bit unreasonable on this practical point. Now it was good not to be bound by any promise, even one given in childhood's fancy. Yet, she had to admit that the dreams of being mistress of "Gates Gardens" were not easily relegated to their proper place in seeking the true equation of her love for Gideon, and the temptation to place the weight of Tanya's eternal close friendship on the balance for decision was still present.

Why must she inflict this pain of indecision upon herself, especially when any other alternative would bring so much unhappiness to those she loved? Not a friend or relative, except Claud, who wouldn't be disappointed or deeply hurt if she refused Gideon's ring. Only Claud . . . Then why not forget the royal mantilla and the sweetheart roses —just pull a curtain across the window of thought—shut out the view on all that these gifts signified? Why not just rush to Gideon's arms, wearing the ring? . . . Rush to Dame Gates and Tanya for their happy embraces—let the flood of joy from her family and Gideon's sweep over her obliterating all exits from the life they desired for her— thrill to the social whirl of engagement and wedding parties—take the magic mattress to a place most appropriate for it—under the golden canopy of the great mahogany bed in the grand room where Dame Gates had so pointedly indicated she wanted her great-grandchildren to be born—sink into its feathery softness in the arms of—in the arms of——

The fragrance of the roses seemed suddenly to intensify.

"No, Peter, no!" she whispered, as though to a real presence, and pushed the ivory bowl back further on the desk. She gave the intrusion further denial by getting up from the desk and walking about the room, the ring still on her finger, stopping before the mirror, making the stones flash with special gestures, stopping beside the bed, punching and patting the well-shaped mound, moving to the window and back to the desk where she picked up the mantilla, placed it around her shoulders and went back for another view in the mirror. She was startled at her reflection—at the look of grandeur—at the dramatic intensity given her dark coloring framed in royal blue and the rich brown cream of the ancient heavy lace.

She began to speak with the sweet eloquence that had made a famous actor her suitor:

> "My good Lysander!
> I swear to thee, by Cupid's strongest bow,
> By his best arrow with the golden head,
> By the simplicity of Venus' doves,
> By that which knitteth souls and prospers loves,
> And by that fire which burn'd the Carthage queen,
> When the false Troyan under sail was seen,
> By all the vows that ever men have broke,
> In number more than ever women spoke,
> In that same place thou hast appointed me,
> Tomorrow truly will I meet with thee."

By her own provocation a spell was wrought and she was recapturing the excitement of her secret meeting with Fame Kingston . . . the day she had driven as usual to the conservatory in the family brougham for her music lesson, knowing very well her teacher would be absent that day . . . then Fame driving up at once as they had arranged, in a single-seat public hansom, side-curtained with driver in back. It had all been so deliciously conspiratorial. She had worn her big "motoring" veil enveloping sailor hat and face and tied in a big bow under the chin, thankful for so concealing a fashion.

She had felt no guilt—no fear of Fame. His intentions had been very clearly stated to her and would have been stated to her guardians had she permitted it. He wanted her to marry him *and* the theater— become his theatrical partner as well as his wife. He had even given her a theatrical name: "Annabel." *Fame and Annabel Kingston* was indeed a beautiful name combination.

This romantic conquest was unlike any other in her experience and gave her a sense of triumph that was blissful incense to her self-esteem. To have won a man of such maturity and accomplishment —won him so quickly and wholly from the very first meeting. He had been quite indignant when the arrangement committee for the performance at the ball had revealed the plan to have the queen of the ball presented in *Romeo and Juliet* dialogue with him. It was not his custom to engage in "cheap theatricals" he had said—there was no greater sacrilege to the Great Bard than to place his divine phrases at the mercy of some simpering schoolgirl elocutionist. He wasn't interested in her beauty—no matter how much she could *look* like Juliet, if she didn't *speak* like Juliet. The committee had suggested to Mr. Kingston that he hear her read, then consider. He had replied that he was quite willing to pass on her *inability*.

So Tricky had come to the audition, delighted with the challenge, fearing neither Fame Kingston nor William Shakespeare but with admiration for both and a studious knowledge of the art of each.

He had requested that she read with him first in the opening scene of Act III from *The Tempest* (Juliet must not be profaned by an amateur). She had felt the first tingle of triumph when his eyes had met hers with meaning beyond theatrical requirements as he read Ferdinand's declaration:

> ". . . Full many a lady
> I have eyed with best regard: and many a time
> The harmony of their tongues hath into bondage
> Brought my too diligent ear: for several virtues
> Have I liked several women; never any
> With so full soul, but some defect in her
> Did quarrel with the noblest grace she ow'd,
> And put it to the foil: but you, O you,
> So perfect and so peerless, are created
> Of every creature's best!"

And when she spoke the line: "Do you love me?", his answer was directed to her ear on a vibration of intimacy that caused her skin to prickle in response.

"O heaven, O earth bear witness to this sound,
And crown what I profess with kind event,
If I speak true! If hollowly, invert
What best is boded me to mischief! I,
Beyond all limit of what else i' th' world,
Do love, prize, honour you."

With her answering line, "I am a fool/To weep at what I'm glad of," the tears down her cheeks seemed no artifice at all. How easy it was to be awed by the true wonder of the theater in such an exchange of feeling with this dedicated performer! How difficult it was to determine the difference between good performance and valid self-feeling.

Still delaying her audition of Juliet, Fame had asked her to read Hermia to his Lysander in the sequence on love's tribulations from Act I, Scene 1, of *Midsummer Night's Dream*. Now, standing before her mirror, caped in his exquisite gift, releasing her imagination to full exposure of the Kingston charm, certain lines were like bright birds whirling in and out of her thoughts.

LYSANDER. Ay me! for aught that ever I could read,
      Could ever hear by tale or history,
      The course of true love never did run smooth:
      But, either it was different in blood,—
HERMIA.   O cross! too high to be enthralled to low!
LYSANDER. Or else misgraffed in respect of years,—
HERMIA.   O spite! too old to be engag'd to young!
LYSANDER. Or else it stood upon the choice of friends,—
HERMIA.   O hell! to choose love my another's eyes!

Finally, when he had allowed her to read Juliet to his Romeo in the famous second act delineation of "true love's passion," the communion he had established with the line "It is my soul that calls upon thy name," had reached her with a piercing sweetness that made the few remaining lines of the scene an ecstasy of lover's music and sadness completely outside her own identity.

When they were finished, Fame had remained silent for a long moment holding them together in the pitch of mood so perfectly achieved, until he was ready to return to himself. Then he had announced to her and the committee with abrupt decision that he would do all three selections for the performance. He had said good-by at once, with a manner of detached aloofness which Tricky considered a piece of acting far below Kingston standards, for, as his eyes flashed into hers just before his little polite bow of departure, she caught a flame flickering there that nullified any coolness of manner.

"It is my soul that calls upon thy name." Did his soul really call to hers with true love's deepest meaning and fullest passion, she wondered. Or, was he simply a master of emotion and sensation and she a subject of his art?

The ride to the park . . . the time alone in the arbor . . . that should have told her, but had it? She would search again, willfully retrace the experience through every sensation although some part of of herself seemed to forbid it, seemed to oppose such sensuous day-dreaming as a betrayal to—to——. She resisted the tug. After all, Fame too was waiting for the answer she had promised after her eighteenth birthday. She would not deny him any place in her thoughts until her mind was fully made up. If she said yes, there would be many elaborations upon the pleasures only intimated during that stolen hour. She was convinced that no man she had ever known, or could ever expect to know, would be capable of making such a lover's symphony of sensation, as Fame Kingston contrived, just within the limited privilege of holding hands.

Until that ride in the hansom, there had been only the touch of fingertips in greeting and parting. Strolls in the garden were always under the watchful eyes of Aunt Addie. She would have been in a frenzy could she have known that the sedate strolling and apparently casual conversation had been a fine bit of acting on both their parts, covering up the electric attraction that flashed between them and the impassioned descriptions Fame gave of what their life together could be like; traveling the world, playing the greatest theaters—*Fame and Annabel*. And family? In due time, of course—a theatrical family—establish a great family line of Shakespearean performers. Home: the theater. There would be money for tutors and nurses—mother-hood a minor role—reproduction was no talent, her voice was. All these things they had talked of in plain sight of Aunt Addie, without even a gesture of personal attachment. He had even confided that his brief early marriage had been to a young lady who thought she was marrying an architect and considered his theatrical interest and talent degrading. He had allowed her to get the divorce on the only cause legally acceptable: adultery. "My art was my mistress," he said.

"Perhaps your art is your true love, not your mistress," Tricky had replied, "and you should remain wedded to her alone."

"If I can ever have you one hour to myself, I will prove to you who is my true love and who should be my wife. Since you are so sure your guardians won't permit courtship, won't let me be alone with you, even though I state my intentions, can't you make some arrangement, permit me to declare my love in privacy? Permit me to touch you—to hold you—to caress you, all within the domain of your favor? You know that I wouldn't impose the gentlest touch upon you against your will, don't you?"

She had felt sure enough to make such an arrangement when her music teacher had canceled some lessons for a concert.

She was short-breathed with excitement as the driver quickly put his horse into a high trot to take them to the park in the shortest time possible, as directed. What would be Fame's first words, she wondered tremblingly—his first touch? He sat very, very still, letting the excitement build up between them.

Then he sighed, "Time is our enemy. Love's sweetness is not a nectar to be greedily and hastily downed." He began to remove his gloves, speaking as he did so.

"Every small fragrant honeyed drop should be savored by all the senses." His gloves were removed and placed aside.

She sat to his right. He reached for her gloved left hand, lifted it tenderly and brought it to rest in his left hand held palm upward in his lap to receive it.

"O your hand, dear love . . . the shape of it . . . the promise of it . . ."

She wanted to say, "And your voice, dear love . . . the promise of it . . . speak on."

He held her hand pressed between his two while her pulse raced faster than the hearty tempo of the horse's clop that carried them along so rapidly. She was glad to be so well veiled and even then looked aside through a blur of unreality at the objects in the street whirling past. She became aware, with a sense of shock, that Fame was removing her glove. She had the impulse to pull her hand away,

473

forbid him this intimacy. But, actually, what was so intimate about removing a glove? She had always removed her own gloves, that was all. You couldn't expect a man, granted permission to impress you with his courting, to hold a gloved hand. She should have removed them herself, as he had done, perhaps. But—this was—certainly was—more pleasant.

He made each touch on each finger while loosening the glove a separate, prolonged caress . . . and then paused an instant before pulling away the glove as though hesitant to reveal fully something so intimately lovely. And when he had made the final gesture of removal, supporting her arm at the wrist as he did so, her fingers began to tremble in a way she could not control.

"The desire of it!" he whispered, and guided her trembling naked fingers to repose in his palm again, pressing her hand again between his two, cherishing the testimony of the trembling fingers that had told him what she could not and would not have spoken.

No hand-holding with beaus, no arm stolen around the waist, no embrace of the dance transgressing propriety with stealthy stroke or pressure, no courting kiss permitted or snatched, from Gideon or any other, had been such an introduction to sexual appetite and sensation as Fame had given her in the simple act of removing her glove. And the lesson was hardly begun.

When her fingers had stilled under the pressure, he released them and began to stroke each one.

"Fingers of love . . . to play upon the glorious harp of a man's senses . . . each one like a note of purest passion . . . to be combined in a chord of such consummate harmony that a man would rather experience it and die than forfeit it and live!"

She had not spoken a word since being helped into the carriage and he reminded her.

"Have you no word for me, sweet love?"

She simply shook her head.

He began to stroke the back of her hand, and it was like a stroke that covered her whole body and gave her great unexpected sensual pleasure. She felt a need to deny it, but all she could do was move her hand in slight protest. The stroking stopped, and then she was sorry. She leaned back against the seat, closed her eyes, took a deep breath, and willed that her hand just lie still within his, not trembling, not protesting.

"Have I offended the hand of Annabel?"

She kept her eyes closed. She had granted this hour for his advantage and her enlightenment since she couldn't make up her mind about marrying him. Now, she must not retreat into some shell of girlish reticence. She was a woman grown, ready to make a choice of husband and mate.

She let her fingers close around his ever so lightly.

He immediately brought her hand to his lips, began kissing it with a language she had never known existed, and murmuring between each separate pressure.

"O the taste, the intoxication, that my lips find on your fair flesh . . . O the fragrance of it that I dare to breathe . . . O fingers that hold my heart's fate . . . O palm to dispense all the happiness I could bear and receive all that I could give . . ." Her fingers were bent back, his lips pressed to the center of her hand . . . and the final consuming gesture, the cuff of her shirt waist pushed back, "pulse of my life . . . pulse of fire" and his lips were a burning pressure against her throbbing pulse.

Then she had said, "No!" She had recovered her hand, and he had kept her glove. They were in the park. The hansom driver let them out near a latticed arbor, heavily draped with queen's crown and honeysuckle. He would signal them with his little bell at the appointed time.

She had sat down stiffly on a bench and Fame, laying gloves and hat aside, had seated himself beside her.

"My precious darling, I must fight your sensitivities as well as time's limitations, for the cruel minutes are beating me, lashing my heart and patience as they flash by. You trust me, I know. But you do not trust yourself. I cannot tell you the happiness I feel at what you reveal to me without saying a word—showing me that I can lead you into a whole glorious new realm of love's bounty. I want to make these moments so memorable that you cannot separate yourself from thoughts of me when I'm gone and cannot be content until we dwell together in the paradise we can only glimpse today from the pinnacle of our desire."

She had become quite calm and had smiled at him. She must

not turn away in bashful dismay. She must look this man steadfastly in the face—this man who might become her husband.

"You're hidden behind that veil. May I untie it for you?"

"Please."

So he had untied the big filmy bow with the same careful reverence he had removed the glove, putting so much of deferred caress into every gesture, that by the time he slowly raised the big veil up over her face to rest back of her pompadour on her abbreviated sailor, her cheeks were flushed and her lips tingling. He was going to kiss her, she knew, but not suddenly, not at once. In so brief a time she had already learned that it was his way to fast the impulse until hunger was at the proper peak for greatest pleasure. Was this the technique of true love? or, the technique of charting emotions through plot to climax? She couldn't tell—she only knew it was the most exciting arousal of the senses she had ever known.

He touched one of her cheeks, then the other with his fingertips.

"My own fair blush, by me aroused . . . treasure incomparable here in this bright color at my fingertips, treasure beyond gems or gold . . . treasure uncovered by sounds of love and thoughts of love—and touch of love." His fingertips slid from chin to hairline—then his palms came firmly against her hot cheeks, and he pulled her toward him slightly; his face came closer and closer to hers, his eyes so extra bright with a dazzling liquid glow that she closed her eyes against it and waited for the kiss.

(Reliving this experience, Tricky left the mirror to sit down again at the desk in her grandmother's chair. Her eyes were closed tight and her hands gripped the arms of the chair in trancelike captivity to the memory of Fame Kingston's kiss.)

When the kiss came, his lips did not greedily demand her response—rather, they explored, tempted, exposed her own appetite—a hunger she had not known was waiting there. Then when her lips, like her fingers, independently bore witness of the hunger aroused, his kiss covered and drew it out, compelling, absorbing it to nourish his own.

His hands left her cheeks, held her shoulders—then one strong arm reached around her shoulders, another around her waist, bringing her instantly and adroitly into position against him, firm and comfortable but tightly captive to his embrace where, with passionate phrases of love and deliberate delays of caress, he stored rapturous anticipation to painful capacity and then blissfully siphoned it off in a prolonged kiss.

When the driver's signal came, it was hard to admit the realization that it was important, must be obeyed. It had seemed like a travesty on life and love to break the embrace. Put on a veil that trembling hands (his as well as hers) could hardly tie, brush out wrinkles, try to look unruffled in apparel, casual in movement, when the body shrieked for release from all restraint, freedom to engage in this wild assault of the senses.

The ride back to the conservatory had not been a happy one. For Tricky the struggle between reason and desire was an experience as new as desire itself. She did not dare try to explain to Fame about Gideon and "Gates Gardens" nor about her childhood promise to Gram that she would wash the feathers and sleep on the magic mattress before saying "yes" to any man's proposal. And she certainly did not want to reject the life and love Fame was offering her.

So when they were back in the hansom, and her ungloved hand was locked in his—not passive as it had been on the journey out—and they were sitting in a closeness that would have caused Aunt Addie to swoon—he had said, "Now, will you marry me?" And his voice was very sure of her answer.

"I feel 'yes,' Fame. I want to say yes, but I mustn't. I'll be eighteen before your season's done here. I'll give you my answer then."

She had felt him stiffen—felt the vexation in his fingers—and he made no attempt to hide his chagrin.

"Do you even love me?"

Certainly you loved a man—if you found such uncontrollable pleasure in his arms—if you couldn't resist his kisses, yielded and responded at his bidding, lost to your own will. Surely that was marriage love—and yet—— So she said to him what she had later said to Gideon: "I love you. Oh, I know I know I love you, Fame, or else——" She didn't want to sound too childish and inexperienced. "I mean, I must think a little. Perhaps it isn't marriage love!"

"O God! You child, you!"

So she had made a childish answer, after all. And so Fame had a temper. Well, she had one too. She withdrew her hand—moved away from him.

"Perhaps so. That's a good reason for waiting until I'm eighteen."

477

"Then I do not intend to see you or touch you again until I have my answer."

Punishing her, was he? "I think that would be best," she answered crisply, pushing back the heavy thought of how long it would be before he kissed her again as he had today and what if she lost him altogether.

"I am no summertime dandy to be kept dangling. If you desire my presence at any time before the coy date you have set, send me a message—and no coquettish billet-doux—just a one-word message: Y*es*."

"You may expect no message from me until after my eighteenth birthday."

They stopped around the corner from the conservatory and he helped her alight.

She had expected a last-minute concession—a pressure of the hand, a quick tender kiss. But Fame's expression was dark—there was only the liquid glow in his eyes as they met hers, reminding her of the time of desire before the kiss when he had held her so close.

He said, "Good day, Miss Harriet," with a formal little bow, climbed in the hansom and signaled the driver without once looking back.

She wanted to call out after him, "Yes! Fame! Yes, yes!"

But there was pride, and the promise to Gram, and the necessity to probe her mind and heart for a better understanding of herself, and love, and desire, and marriage.

She had gone into such seclusion for a while that Aunt Addie had worried and tried to get Uncle Frank to prescribe a tonic. She did not go to parties nor visit at "Gates Gardens." She avoided Uncle E. Y. and Aunt Grace and cut out her usual trips with Claud to their private park. She lay on the feather mattress for hours, idly day-dreaming, feeding the desire to be in Fame's arms with imaginary courting scenes and possible marriage relations. She tried to do some honest thinking, but found it very difficult. Sometimes she felt compelled to send Fame the message he had demanded to bring him to her again. One time she got out her small scissors and started to rip out the mattress seam and consider the instructions for washing the feathers, then changed her mind. Fame was careful to keep her thoughts of him active. He sent no word, but every few days a gift came as poignant reminder of the sweet stolen hour: a pair of exquisite lace gloves in replacement of the one he had kept; a veil of sheerest silk, yards and yards of golden froth; a small water-color of their arbor of love, initialed as his own; and several volumes of love poems, with passages carefully marked for accenting her recall of all they had experienced together. Every gift was accompanied by the rarest and most exotic flower to be found in this city of flowers. She always took these things to Gram's room.

One day as she sat in the middle of the bed—a liberty Gram would not have allowed—but it was such a luxury spot—reading love poems aloud from Fame's latest markings, she became so overwrought with longing for him that she thought her heart would break. "Oh, Gram, what should I do?" she cried out, throwing the book aside and flinging herself into the softness of the mattress and into tears.

There was a knock on her door. She didn't move or answer.

Claud called out, "Tricky! Wake up, in there. Something important to tell you."

She quickly altered her appearance and let him in.

Claud was a tall sixteen. In features and temperament he and Tricky were much alike and were often taken for brother and sister.

"Are you all right?" he asked.

"Of course."

"What are you hiding from?"

"Hiding? I've simply been doing some reading and thinking."

"What have you been reading?"

"Love poems."

"That poison!"

"What's poison to sixteen may be ambrosia to eighteen."

"You're not eighteen."

"I won't feel any different a few weeks from now when I will be."

"Oh yes, you will. And I will too. Our good times together at the park will be over. Father intends to sell it as soon as you get married to Old Gideon. He says there are plenty of other places for me to exercise."

"He's pretty sure I'm going to marry Gideon just as soon as I'm eighteen, isn't he?"

"Isn't everybody?"

"Hasn't it ever occurred to you that I might not marry Gideon at all?"

"I don't know that it has. Why?"

"Well, I just might marry somebody else."

"Wouldn't blame you. Far as I'm concerned, you can give 'em all the gate and be an old maid. I didn't come here to talk about your beaus. I want to ask you, would you like to see an old Frontier Model Colt .45 with a barrel about as long as my arm and heavy as a shotgun?"

"I'll say I would, even discounting your exaggeration."

"Well, come along and leave your love poems behind. John Reagan is going to bring his cousin Peter Sky out to the park again today to use our pistol range. This Peter Sky is an older cousin of John's. He comes from Colorado. He's in the U.S. Division of Forestry. You know, business of forest reserves, national parks, and the like. I've been thinking I'd like that kind of work—John and I both."

"What treachery is this?" Tricky teased. "You and John are both solemnly betrothed to the banking business. If your fathers heard that statement, they would have companion strokes."

"Every man should be his own master."

"Easy spoken. Seldom done. How do we get out to the park unchaperoned so I can be out at the range to practice with you?"

"Mother is waiting downstairs to drive us out, but she isn't set on staying—just wants to give Leb and Lucy the same old orders about keeping us in line. She hates the mosquitoes and I've been telling her how bad they are lately. She won't hang around long. She doesn't know about John bringing Peter Sky out. I was afraid she might object. . . . Tricky, you should see that man shoot! He's also got a new Bisley Target Model—it's a lot like the Old Frontier—it's a .45 too, seven-and-a-half-inch barrel, and man, oh man, is it a target arm! It's equipped with adjustable sights, Tricky. I've never shot a gun like that before. I'll tell you it takes a strong wrist to hold those old guns steady!"

"Well, if you can handle it, so can I." Tricky's voice was both envious and eager.

"Of course you can! I didn't make a very good showing. I said to Peter, 'I have a girl cousin who could do better.' He thought I was joking. He said, 'Nobody's girl cousin could do as well as you did with a gun this size unless she's an Amazon!' "

"So that's what he said! We'll show him."

"I thought it would be fun. And something else, Tricky. This fellow is part Indian."

"Honest?"

"Honest. The real thing. His grandmother on his father's side is a Ute."

"Utes. Hmm. I don't know much about Utes. Gram always talked about Caddoes."

"He tells Indian stories that sound a lot like the ones Gram told—about people living underground in animal form before climbing up to the surface of the earth. Things like that. I wonder why it is that corn is always in these stories of creation. Caddoes say they brought it into the world with them. And Peter says the Ute story is that they climbed up a giant cornstalk to get here."

"Maybe Jack and the beanstalk was originally an Indian story."

"Could be. But don't just stand there, Tricky. Hurry and get ready. We must get to the park ahead of John and Peter so we can have Mother on her way."

"All right. Stop talking then."

They rushed off together . . . and the web of desire Fame Kingston had woven so tightly with his gifts and the denial of his company was broken.

26.

Tricky Purcelle, age eighteen and one day, knowing that she would marry one of three men: Gideon Gates, Fame Kingston, or Peter Sky—bringing each man before her in thought as she considered his birthday gift and his proposal of marriage—admitted Peter to the bar of decision last of all, and with some reluctance. It would be so much easier if she just refused to consider Peter—made her choice between Gideon and Fame. But having done with thinking of Fame —having closed the book of love poems, as it were—Peter came right in and quickly took over.

Peter was like that: quick! Quick of eye—so direct and probing. Quick of hand—so large and sure. Quick of mind—as though born with a legacy of natural wisdom.

Tricky pulled the bowl of sweetheart roses closer and took a long deep breath of their fragrance—then she removed one from the bouquet and began to toy with it: bringing it close to her lips and nostrils, holding it off with wistful gaze. Now the last of her symbols was brought close—the ring on her finger, the mantilla about her shoulders, the rose in her hand—two to put aside and one to keep—two for the past and one for the future.

"Peter Sky" sounded like a name for a whimsical character in a story for children, and "Mrs. Peter Sky" was for laughter—but sweet laughter. As for "Tricky Sky"—that was ridiculous—and the very thought caused Tricky to laugh out loud. But she choked on the laughter and almost sobbed at the expressions of shock and horror in the faces of her respective relatives, as she lined them up before her in imagination and introduced herself to each one: "I am Mrs. Tricky Sky." She let them all fall in a faint and be carried out of her mind for the moment—all but Claud—his face wore an expression of high delight.

Peter Sky . . . truly, it was a gladsome name, suggesting the strong and the free, entirely appropriate for a man whose eyes were the bluest blue of the spectrum and whose tread made of earth a ballroom floor with the stars as chandeliers. Yet Peter's feet undoubtedly could find toeholds along a mountain precipice with more ease and grace than he could guide a partner through a formal dance.

Her first meeting with Peter had been punctuated with one surprise after another. On the way out to their pistol range to meet John's part-Indian cousin from Colorado, Claud had briefed her on the guns she would be introduced to with little reference to their owner. She vaguely pictured him a wilderness man of weathered maturity . . . long hair . . . moccasins . . . two large guns conspicuously ready to draw . . . a big man, awed and inarticulate before her surprising display of marksmanship.

She was the awed one—from the moment of introduction. At the pistol range practicing with Claud when the two men rode up, she had pretended a modest indifference at their approach, not turning toward them until they were off their horses and Claud and John brought Peter to her side for presentation.

Her first awareness was that he was not awkward, or old, or big. He was just right. After that, the famous Purcelle poise for which she had been noted since early childhood deserted her, leaving her baffled and surprised as she reacted to his manners and appearance.

He startled her by taking her whole hand into his for a firm, friendly grip when she had extended it expecting only a fingertip acknowledgment. Then there was something shocking about his eyes shining so brightly blue from a face so richly tanned by heritage as well as sun . . . and in the unruly brown hair, lighter than his skin, with no fashionable middle part—trained for parting only with the wind—and streaks of sun bleach making small paths of light across his head.

His unfitted jacket was worn open and his shirt—merciful heavens!—had a soft turn-back collar and no tie!—the neck open—his throat exposed. This was such radical departure from the masculine must of chin-high stiff collar and tie among the style-conscious young men of her acquaintance that she found herself staring at his bare neck and greatly embarrassed for doing so. Why, this was more radical than her riding cross saddle without her skirt! At least her boldness was not exhibited in public, to strangers! Then smarting under her own prudery, she tried to meet his eyes with the gracious directness that was part of her charm, but when she encountered the expression of light mockery and pure comprehension in the look he gave back, she was undone, blushed, and looked away.

Immediately his sensitivity and kindness came to her rescue. He began to praise the park and its beautiful lagoon for boating and fishing, the cypresses with all their lacy drapes of gray moss and green fringe, the flowered bridle paths, the charm of oak and magnolia. His speech, neither ornate nor unpolished, was as direct as the gaze of his blue eyes. He spoke of the good construction of the pistol range and his pleasure in being a guest on their private grounds. In answer to their questions, he explained that after a few weeks visiting relatives in New Orleans, he would be returning to Colorado. He had just been to Washington making some first hand reports to the Division of Forestry on matters related to the extension of forest reserves and creation of national parks.

Soon, they were all at ease and engaged in a shooting exhibition with the small arms Claud had at hand. Tricky became annoyed that Peter dealt out praise and comment so impartially—no special tribute for a New Orleans belle who was also an expert marksman. Perhaps such an accomplishment was commonplace among frontier women, and she wasn't so unusual, after all. She was annoyed, too, that her aim was not as keen as usual, that her wrist had developed a muscular twitch and weakness most unnatural. Before this calm young man, she lost her self-confidence, became over-anxious to excel. When he went to his saddle for the revolvers Claud had described, she found herself shivering in nervous anticipation of handling the big guns. She knew that Claud was disappointed in her performance so far— it was not as great as his brags. She must—she would—get special attention when she got the Old Frontier Colt in her hands. . . . Frontier women! She'd show him! After all, wasn't she the granddaughter of a kishi-woman (that's what the Indians had called Gram), and hadn't her mother and father been born in the Texas wilderness? She'd show this forest fellow a few things! She'd show him!

Since Peter had already explained the guns to Claud and John, and they had fired them, he brought them now to her. They were buckled around his waist. He had removed his jacket and rolled up his sleeves exposing sinewy arms as deeply brown as his face, and she found herself staring at him more than at the gun he held out to her. The weight was so surprising that she almost dropped it. He was telling her that the gun in her hand had belonged to his father and had been one of the first double-action revolvers produced back in 1877. She was thinking how cumbersomely large the stock was in her small hand and how awfully far away the trigger seemed. Could she possibly hold steady such a weight, balance, aim, and fire? She held it out tentatively and felt the uncertainty in her wrist. She handed it back and asked that the men shoot first that she might study their form. She must decide

whether to risk a very poor shot or refuse to handle the gun at all.
Regardless of her skill or strength (both of which seemed at low
ebb), her hand was simply too small for so large and heavy a gun.
But Claud was depending on her. She looked at him and saw the
disappointment plain in his face. She must not let him down. She
massaged her wrist and carefully watched her three companions make
their shots. Peter's form was smooth and accurate but he did not preen.
John was evidently having wrist trouble too!—the gun obviously
trembled in his hand and his aim was far off. Claud was not so bad,
and she had a feeling he made no special effort in order that her
try might look better. Finally, the gun was in her hands again. Peter,
standing on her right, was concerned for her, she knew; their eyes
had met briefly and there was no challenge in his. His kindness
irritated her and gave impetus to her will. She gripped the gun
firmly, raised it, compelled her wrist to steady, quickly took aim,
stretched her finger to proper position and pulled the trigger. The
result was highly satisfactory, a close partner to Peter's bull's-eyes,
but before the gasps of admiration were out, there was an awful aftermath. Her wrist in a spasm of weakness caused her finger to touch
the trigger a second time as she lowered the gun in an awkward arc.
There was the unexpected shot, a spurt of dust, and she looked down
in dazed bewilderment at Peter's foot. Dust covered his boot and
her heart stopped in anguish with what she had done. They were
all staring in a stillness as acute as if she had shot them all dead.
Peter moved his foot a little as if testing, and she saw a small brown
root that had been severed just at the toe-tip of his boot. The relief
of knowing the bullet had not pierced his foot was so acute that she
became quite dizzy.

Peter spoke, and she looked into the blue glow of his eyes now
bright with wry humor. "A number of people have threatened to
shoot my feet off at various times, but this is the closest anyone ever
came to it!"

Tricky could not laugh and found it hard not to cry. "Oh Peter!"
she said (when she should have said "Mr. Sky") "Oh, Peter."

The gun still hung in her hand. He reached over and took it from
her and holstered it.

He chuckled and gave her the praise she had craved. "A fair shot,
fair lady. First you match me, then you chastise me for doubting

your prowess. I am"—he bowed with teasing humility—"your humble servant."

She couldn't rise to his humor—was too honest to take refuge in it. The good shot had been an accident, the poor one a near tragedy. That this nimble-footed young man of forest trails and mountain paths had narrowly missed being made a cripple because of stubborn vanity——

The tears did come—she couldn't hold them back. So she did what she had never done before in the presence of a young man: She whispered, "I'm so sorry," and fled.

She whirled around and disappeared in the shrubbery just back of the clearing where they stood. She made her way, stumbling and crying, snagging her skirts on the undergrowth, thinking she must circle around someway and get to Leb and Lucy and their little caretaker's house. They would take her home—get her away from here and she'd never have to face Peter Sky again!

She heard Peter call out, "Miss Harriet, wait! Please!"

Oh, surely he wouldn't come after her! He mustn't! She couldn't talk to him ever again. She'd hide, she'd hide forever!

But Peter was coming after her. She heard him! She gave up the idea of getting to the house and concentrated only on hiding from Peter. Though she knew the park, all its paths and secret clearings, there were acres of thick undergrowth and entanglements she must avoid. But tearful as she was, desperate as she was to elude Peter, she became confused and found herself in a pathless area thick with vines and rank growth. She tried to push her way through, became trapped when her skirts caught in some reeds, and fell. Peter, more agile than she in such surroundings, was right on her heels. He crashed to his knees beside her.

"Miss Harriet! Miss Harriet! You mustn't feel this way. I'm all right—perfectly all right. I'm quite uninjured. It was all my fault. I knew your hand was too small for the gun. I should never have placed it in your hand. I was tempted to see what you would do. It was all my fault! Are you hurt?"

He reached over and grasped her shoulders and she must sit up and face him. So she did. "It wasn't your fault. I knew quite well I couldn't handle the gun as it should be handled. But I must try!

487

I must be a show off! And—and you might have lost your foot to my vanity!"

"If I had, it would have served me right." He pulled out his handkerchief and gave it to her. "Please stop crying. Your tears wound me far more than your bullets."

So she wiped her face with his handkerchief, and he smiled at her. What a wonderful smile he had! She smiled back. They sat there among the reeds, just looking at each other, and she was quieted. Somehow they came to understand each other without questions and answers, and without self-consciousness at being so newly met and so alone together. Finally Peter spoke as if summing up after analysis.

"You don't belong in this corseted, landscaped society."

"Where do I belong, Peter?"

"In the high country, by some mountain lake, I think."

"Why do you say that?"

"It's just a feeling I have."

"I have a feeling that you don't like cities at all."

"You're right."

"Your spirit can't breathe in a city."

"Yours hardly can."

"Oh, yes, it can, Peter. I love New Orleans. I truly do . . . the gardens—the romance—the shops—the theaters—it's—well, it's home."

"That's because you haven't known the mountains. Your eyes are for distant views from mountain peaks—your feet should dance on forest floors—your spirit should flow like a tumbling stream between the trembling aspens——"

"What is an aspen?"

"A lovely proud little tree—little beside its timber-sized companions—that is always and continuously vibrant. And when it's nipped by frost, it stands in a shimmering gold of glory among the changeless green of the pines."

"What makes it tremble all the time?"

"Well, there's a Ute legend about the aspen: why its leaves quiver so—even when there seems to be no breeze. They say that the Great Spirit once planned a special visit down to earth during the full of the moon. It was a great occasion for all living things and their anticipation was so great that they were set a-trembling at this sacred honor. But the proud aspen stood quite still unawed by the event. The Great Spirit was angered that this tree alone paid him no homage. So he willed that forever after, the leaves of the aspen would tremble before any eye that gazed upon it."

"Do you believe that?"

"Do I believe it?" He was amused. "It's a legend. Legends sometimes have significance and hidden meaning. Sometimes like a poem the meaning is beauty. Let's just say, I like them."

"I thought perhaps——"

"Being part Ute I might accept the legends literally?"

Tricky was confused that she had brought this personal matter into the discussion, and he sensed her confusion.

"I am not ashamed of my Indian blood. Does it offend you—make me less worthy in your sight?"

"Oh no . . . no, no." She spoke too hastily. She was trying to reassure herself. For, though the fact was not exactly offensive, it was disturbing.

He arose and held out his hands to help her to her feet.

"We must go back to the others. Your cousin will be concerned about you."

Tricky did not admit to herself until several days after the accident at the park that she wanted very much to see Peter Sky again and that she was disappointed that he had made no effort to see her. Yet, she knew very well why he had not made any such effort and why he never would. He would not step over into her world without specific invitation. And how could she issue him any sort of invitation? She could not be coquettish with such a man, and to seek his serious attentions was against all her better judgment and training. Yet she kept hoping——

It was Claud who resolved matters—or made them more complicated—depending on your viewpoint. He had told her on their next outing at the park that he planned to have John and Peter out for fishing, and Lucy and Leb would make a big fish fry for them, and she could come too if she liked.

"If you like Peter so much, why don't you ask him to dinner at your house—John would like that. You haven't had John over since Peter came, have you?"

Claud looked embarrassed, and Tricky was quick to accuse him.

"Why not? Are you afraid he might not wear a tie? Or, that Uncle Edward might find out he's part Ute and scold you? Don't you think he's smart as we are—good as we are? Do all your friends have to be banker's sons? Are you just a high-collared snob?"

Her tirade took Claud by surprise and hurt him too. "You know that isn't so. You know I think Peter's great and would like to have a job like his—like to be the kind of fellow he is. And I want him to meet Dad and talk about forestry—but, honest, Tricky, if he should come to dinner without a tie, Mother would be stiff and horrible, and Dad would be polite enough, might even be interested in him, but would consider him a rude non-comformist. I can just hear him saying afterwards, "That's all right for the wilderness or the plow—but in cultivated society—in the presence of ladies—and so on and so on."

"Peter is kind, considerate of others. He wouldn't embarrass you or me for his own comfort. He just isn't a slave to fashion. Ask him. I dare you. Ask me, too. I don't want to miss anything."

And so the invitation had been issued . . . and accepted. And Claud and Tricky had been so nervous over their project, once it was launched, that they found the waiting through several days—then through the hours of *the* day—almost unbearable. Tricky couldn't remember what she wore or what Aunt Grace served at that particular family dinner. But it was easy to recall the cold sweat of anxiety during the last few moments of waiting for Peter, almost hoping he wouldn't come, and the great surge of relief when she was able to spot a tie about his neck as she peeped through a window at his approach. True, he was no fashion plate, and there was a Western casualness in his attire. His collar was not high and stiff, but a soft turndown. His shirt, however, was white, and his tie black, and his hair slightly subdued. So she wouldn't have to despise herself and Uncle E.Y. and Aunt Grace for what might have happened if Claud's fears of a no-tie dinner guest had come to pass.

But she and Claud were only half-done with anxiety after discovery of the tie. Uncle E.Y. was a fluent conversationalist and adept at drawing out a guest. He would ask many questions before the meal was done, encourage all manner of discussion about Colorado and forestry—and Indians perhaps. Would he learn that Peter had a Ute grandmother? And how would he and Aunt Grace act after that? Courteous, of course. But Peter was astute and sensitive to bigotry. She could not bear it if his pride must be injured, his station demeaned in any way by withdrawal or insinuation. Oh, why, why on earth had she brought this painful meeting to pass? Claud would never have invited Peter but for her. Why must she champion Peter? Nothing unpleasant or difficult could have happened if she had just been content to forget Peter Sky and gone back to reading love poems or retreated to "Gates Gardens" for a tranquil weekend with Tanya and Gideon.

But there was no retreating now. And finally the question she and Claud both were dreading, came, and she had difficulty swallowing the food in her mouth when Uncle E.Y. uttered it.

"Having any more trouble with the bloody Utes out there?"

Why, oh why, did Peter look at her before he answered? She did not avoid his look nor try to hide the pain in her own.

He answered very quietly, his voice tiptoeing among sleeping giants.

"They have given no trouble for over twenty years—not since I was a child."

"How many of them left?"

"A thousand or so, counting children."

"Got them settled on a reservation, I suppose."

"Unless something is discovered on their territory that the white man wants."

"What do you mean by that?"

"The Colorado mountains were the Ute homeland. The white man violated agreement after agreement, pushed him back and back from one reservation to another just as soon as his pastures became desirable or minerals were discovered in his canyons."

"A savage warrior deserves no better. The Utes were notoriously a warrior tribe" Uncle E.Y. was proud of his knowledge of history. "I think our government has shown remarkable forbearance with the Redman on all frontiers."

"The Utes fought Indian intruders from their mountain passes just as they fought the white man, trying to hold their beloved high lands for themselves—as all men of all ages have fought for the land they occupy and love," Peter answered firmly.

Tricky tried to think of some way of stopping the conversation. She looked at Claud and John. They were as dumb as she. Aunt Grace was listening carefully, and frowning.

"The bounty of God's creation should not be left to the dominion of the savage."

Tricky saw Peter's expression darken, his lips tighten. After a bit, he answered softly. "Is savagery as much a characteristic of race as it is a quality of mankind? Is it not a matter of circumstance and environment where and how it becomes manifest either in a man or a race? If exhibitions of savagery can be considered valid reason for extinction of a race, then what races would be exempt? You're English, are you not, sir? 'Ames' is an English name, I believe."

"Why, yes, yes." Uncle E.Y. sensed that he was being trapped. "English and some other bloodlines, I'm sure. I'm no bigot about race. My niece here——"

Tricky jumped. Oh Lord, now she was into it.

"She has French blood—'Purcelle' is French, you know. My sister, Adeline, married to Dr. Marreo, has given me a nephew who is half-Spanish. In my business as a financier, I have many Jewish associates. I respect them. We dine together—on occasion we meet socially."

Oh, stop it, Uncle E.Y., Tricky pleaded in her mind. You're only making it worse.

"But you consider the tomahawk and the scalping knife, Indian atrocities and massacres, no matter what the provocation, as placing the Indian beyond the pale of humanity?"

"Exactly."

"I have some English blood, too, sir."

Oh no! Peter, no! Don't go on. Stop. Please, stop. Don't tell him you're part Indian. I can't bear it!

"And I must consider among my ancestors the savagery that caused a king to behead one wife after another to feed his lust and fancy."

Tricky dared not look at the shock she knew was on Aunt Grace's face.

Peter was not finished. "Is the knife that strips the scalp any more savage than the blade that severs the whole head?"

Uncle E.Y. for once had no answer. Peter expected none and hardly paused in his argument.

"The French too were happy with the guillotine. They even delighted in watching the heavy blade fall upon the fair white neck of a lovely queen. Skull-splitting and head-severing have often been the accepted mode of punishment and warfare among the so-called civilized tribes. The Indian used his tomahawk to the same purposes, true. But does it matter, sir, whether the blade cuts vertical or horizontal when evaluating the degree of savagery?"

What ghastly talk for dinner table! Tricky dared not look at Aunt Grace. But, after all, Uncle E.Y. had started it with his reference in the bloody Utes. When, oh when, would Peter stop? He wasn't done.

"As for the Spanish. How much of fair young flesh and bone, good mind and courageous thought became fodder for the fanaticism of the Inquisition, glutting the torture chambers with terror and mutilations? Would you say that the race and the church under which this refinement of depravity flourished should have been exterminated, or at least confined to a barren reservation in retaliatory torture? Did the American Indian ever devise torture more hideous than the Iron Maiden of Nuremberg? Or slay babes of the enemy any more callously than Herod slew the firstborn of his own race?"

Uncle E.Y. decided that the time had indeed arrived to close the topic.

"Young man, you missed your calling. You should have been a lawyer. Grace, forgive me for launching such a topic into the dinner conversation."

"And forgive me, sir, for pursuing it. I got carried away. You see, sir, I have had occasion to encounter both wisdom and virtue among the Utes. Mrs. Ames, forgive me . . . Miss Harriet, my apologies."

Tricky had never known such relief. Her eyes met Peter's again in thankful understanding. He had not been carried away. He had purposely given them all much-needed instruction.

The dinner proceeded smoothly after that, but Aunt Grace did not fully recover. She eyed the young guest of her son with uneasiness and alarm the rest of the evening in spite of his efforts to please with discussions of Colorado wild flowers and trout fishing.

Tricky had no private word with Peter on the occasion of the dinner at Uncle E.Y.'s—nor at their next two more pleasant meetings at the park where she was riding and boating companion to the three young men and eager audience with Claud and John to Peter's tales of mountain and forest land, of mighty rivers, fantastic canyons, grand mesas, worlds above the world, and deserted cliff dwellings of ancient Indian settlements.

It was she who suggested to Claud quite humbly—"That fish-fry you planned, Claud. Could we have it out here before Peter leaves? We haven't done any fishing in a long time."

So the date was set. They would meet at the park in the early afternoon—fish, and then Lucy would cook the catch. Tricky awoke early and it seemed forever until afternoon. On her bedside table was a white orchid that Fame had sent by messenger the night before. Attached to the orchid was a poem—written by Fame himself—and the last two lines were: "Remembered kiss—love-pulse of life, O taste of bliss that may be wife." She remembered the kiss, as he intended, but the demand was not the same. Instead, she had a wanton thought: What would it be like to kiss Peter? Would it be more exciting, more promising than Fame's kiss? Should she try to find out? She didn't dare dwell on such a plot. She got up and went to breakfast without appetite and miserably restless; then decided that just to be in the park would be soothing. She'd go on out and fish alone before the others arrived and assure a good supply of fish for the fry. She'd have Uncle Frank take her by on the way to the office. The family had been inclined to humor her recent fancy for frequent outings and she knew why: they were relieved at Uncle E.Y.'s plans to sell the park, breaking her off from these excursions altogether, getting her safely settled into marriage. Well, she would humor them too by pretending no awareness, making no objections.

After Uncle Frank let her out, she took a long swim while Lucy sat on the bank and scolded at her diving and underwater antics and made Leb stand close by ready for a rescue if anything went wrong. Then she went for a ride, cross saddle and unskirted, with Leb trailing in customary attendance. And the anticipation of loss rode close beside her—loss of the sweet freedom she had known in this dear spot—freedom from corsets and conformities—freedom to act and think within the true orbit of herself. And what about the further growth of this self? Where would she find greatest fulfillment of all the stirrings within—something beyond superficial happiness—some challenge beyond the immediate? Was the wing-spread of her best and most expansive self too wide for "Gates Gardens"? Was it wide enough for the demands of a dedicated theatrical career? And what of Peter's analysis that she belonged in high country—that her spirit was for mountain lakes and tumbling streams, snow-born and spring-fed. When desire was quiet and motherhood accomplished, what inner demands for self-growth would a woman face?

Still in riding breeches and shirt, but leaving her boots on shore, she got into the boat barefoot and rowed out to her favorite spot in a deep and shady area of the lagoon. Lucy would call her to lunch, and then she'd dress before the men arrived.

She hooked four large black bass and decided this was enough. She put the tackle aside, lay down on her back in the bottom of the boat, and mused on the designs of leaves and branches above her. She thought of Gram and her love of leaf patterns. It was a sad thing to give up places you loved as well as people you loved. She had let Gram go . . . and now she must let this place go . . . it would be taken from her beyond recall as Gram had been . . .

"Miss Harriet . . . "

Why, that sounded like Peter.

Then again, alarmed, "Miss Harriet!"

She raised up in the boat and there he was, standing on the shore, alone! Could she be dreaming? But no . . .

"I've been fishing," she said lamely.

He laughed. "Fishing for dreams."

"No. Really fishing." She pulled the string line up to the top of the water exhibiting the four large bass.

"The evidence! Cleopatra of the mystic lagoon. Am I challenged to an angling contest?"

The classic reference irritated her.

"Sorry I have no perfumed sails, Mr. Sky, or other exotic tricks to help the illusion along."

"I thought your family might have some good reason for calling you Tricky."

She couldn't respond to the teasing. He wasn't being his natural self. He was covering up his feelings. She felt uneasy, sad, and at the same time impatient and reckless.

"Why are you here so early? Where's John?"

"I'm here to tell you good-by. I've been called back to Washington for a few weeks and must leave this afternoon. John has gone after Claud."

"How did you know I'd be here?" Good-by!

"I only hoped."

"Oh, Peter!" She stood up in the boat.

"What is it? Careful there, Miss Harriet—you might——"

She did. The boat swayed and she toppled into the water.

Peter threw off his jacket, jerked off his boots, jumped in and swam toward her.

Tricky swam under water a short distance, realized she shouldn't try to swim across the lagoon in such heavy clothes and turned back to a shallower spot near the bank where the boat floated. She let down in water just below her shoulders. Peter swam to her side, then touched bottom near her, facing her. Faces gleaming, hair dripping, they looked at each other.

"Why did you do it—Tricky?"

"To show you I could swim, I guess."

"Not quite."

"To startle you—into something. To ease something in myself— a ghastly impulse, that's all!"

"I think I understand."

"If you do, why don't you"—she had the impulse to say—"kiss me, Peter," and then—oh, how could she possibly have done it—realized she had said exactly that. And now that she had, surely he would, oh surely. She would die—would drown herself right on the spot if he didn't!

"No, Tricky, no. I won't kiss you under any such compulsion. But I'll tell you what I will do. I'll marry you. What do you think of that?"

"Oh no, Peter, no!"

"Then why the kissing urge—just playing?"

"No, Peter, no!"

"Investigating?"

She couldn't answer.

"No need for that, Tricky. If we must endure parting, then let's don't add to the pain of it with greater knowledge of loss."

There was no reality about this standing here face to face in the water talking about marriage.

"If I could go with you, where would our home be, Peter?"

"We'd homestead at the very rim of the sky."

"Peter, I'm an orphan. I have nothing but a beautiful feather mattress that belonged to my grandmother."

"With my own hands I'll make you a beautiful bed of Basthina for your feather mattress."

"What is Basthina?"

"The sacred red cedar."

"I would love such a bed, Peter. But could I ever rest upon it, if my being there was a great unhappiness, almost a disloyalty, to others?"

"Your guardians?"

"They have given me everything. I have given them nothing."

"And now they would give you a husband?"

"Yes."

"Are you promised to him?"

"No. But it is taken for granted—with both families. And we have—all my life—been like one family."

"You care for him—this family's choice? Does he personally have a claim on your affections?"

"He is dear to me as a part of many things that are dear to me."

"Would he build for you a very special bed for your feather mattress?"

She smiled at the idea of Gideon building a bed. "No. There's one waiting, generations old, canopied with traditions as elaborate as the mahogany and satin tester itself."

"Have you never considered marrying any other?"

She could not—would not—tell him about Fame. But she found it impossible to be evasive with Peter.

"Yes."

"And what kind of bed did he offer for the girl with the feather mattress?"

Why, she hadn't thought until this moment, what would become of the feather mattress if she married Fame? He read her startled expression.

"Perhaps no bed at all except the bed of desire?"

Her face flushed scarlet.

"Now I know."

She did not ask him what he knew.

"And he no doubt keeps me company outside the family circle.

But the spot where I stand is much further from circle center than he is, for the blood of the Ute elongates the radius of my position. Will you marry me, Tricky?"

"No, Peter. No!"

"Have you ever said 'No' so quickly, so frantically to any other suitor, I wonder?"

She didn't answer.

"Are you afraid to think 'Yes'?"

"My grandmother taught me not to fear."

"Then unbar the door of your heart and let me stand on the threshold for a while."

Leb and Lucy appeared on the bank, became frantic with concern at what had happened. Tricky called back that she had fallen in and Mr. Sky had come to her rescue.

"I do not consider the rescue yet complete," Peter said as they pushed the boat before them making their way side by side across the lagoon.

He hasn't made love to me at all, Tricky was thinking. He's just asked me to marry him. I feel cheated. Why doesn't he say he loves me? Why?

"When will you be back, Peter?"

"In about three weeks."

"Will I see you again?"

"Will you?"

She hesitated.

He repeated harshly, "Will you?"

"Yes . . . I'll be eighteen then."

"Is that fatal?"

"I'm expected to—I'm going to decide—about marriage."

"Would it be easier for you if I just go now—and don't stand on the threshold, after all?"

"No, Peter. No."

"I like that negative better than the last two."

They were close to the bank now—close to Leb and Lucy. There would be no more privacy. This was the parting moment.

"Peter, I haven't really said 'No' to you until I've said 'Yes' to someone else. And the door of my heart is open."

498

Peter's reply was given with his eyes. And in the blue radiance of them and in the wonder of his smile, she knew his love and felt his kiss.

Tricky kissed the rose in her hand, carefully placed it back in the ivory bowl with the others. She removed the ring from her finger, held its multi-colored brilliance before her for a moment, then returned it to the case. She stood up to look at herself in the mirror again before removing the mantilla from her shoulders and hanging it back on the corner of Gram's desk.

She sighed deeply with the burden of decision that now seemed heavier than ever. If only Gram were still with her . . . she could tell Gram everything. Gram must have known a lot about man and woman love. She needed Gram's wisdom and experience at a time like this. Or her mother. She felt excessively lonely for her mother, a feeling most rare, for Alsheena Purcelle was more a dream mother, known best through Gram's loving references to her. There were times, however, when the dim sweet vision of early childhood seemed to clarify and stand quite near, loving and protecting her. If her mother were alive, what would she tell her daughter now about love and choice of mate? Was the brief idyll of love her parents knew, and of which she was born, the true, the perfect love? She didn't know enough about it to make comparisons. "Alsheena was as fair of soul as she was fair of face," Gram always said, "and the love she and your father knew was, I suppose too sweet for mortal abode. So they were transported." Gram was idealizing, of course, but how wonderful, how enlightening it would have been to have been close to such a love all her life.

She sighed again. Gram and her fair daughter Alsheena were simply dreams of the past. Nothing left between her and them except a promise to Gram—sweet, foolish little promise about washing feathers. Keeping it was the last small thing she could do for Gram. She opened an upper drawer in the desk and took out a pair of delicate, sharp pointed scissors.

She went to the foot of the bed, pulled the covers back and began a slow and careful ripping of the seam Gram had shown her long ago. Excitement stirred. She began to feel that Gram was very close,

watching her in pleased anticipation. The mood so often existing between them—delightful sharing of thought, enchanted vistas of imagination—slipped over her. No telling what she'd find in the magic
mattress. It wouldn't be like Gram just to leave plain instructions—
there'd be something special to share between them—something saved
until now. She could actually hear Gram's voice reciting the little
rhyme:

> On the fresh first night,
> All dreams are bright,
> Decisions right,
> And wishes *might* come true.

Finally, it was in her hands—the slip of instructions—just a single
page of simple directions for washing the feathers—and then—at the
end—just as she had expected:
"Secrets between us are not done and I am still near you. There's
a long pocket on the far side between brocade and ticking. Investigate. Be careful not to snag the brocade."
She hastily stripped the covers from the bed, exposing the golden
brocade of the mattress in a lustrous beauty that seemed accented
for this occasion. She ripped out the long seam with extreme care,
amazed at the skill with which her grandmother had fashioned the
pocket so that no hint of bulk or rustle of paper could give clue to
what was hidden there. Her hands shook as she took out the packets
and stacked the manuscript in proper order. She stacked it on the
bed, then seated herself on the soft throne of down and began reading

A LETTER TO MY GRANDCHILD, HARRIET ANN PURCELLE

New Orleans
April 15, 1890
Dear Tricky,
*You have just left my room, an eight-year-old child, but this
letter is for you to read as a grown young lady. Since it is the
privilege of old age to see visions, I am now addressing Harriet
Ann, a renowned New Orleans Beauty (it will not be your
Uncle Edward's way to let you go unnoticed). Suitors are the
biggest concern of your life at this time. You would like to*

ask me many questions about men and their ways. It is my intention that in my experiences and opinions recorded here you will find some of the answers . . .

Tricky read on through the rest of the day and most of the night: Read of Solomon Page, and Robert Potter, and Charles Ames . . . read of Harriet, the Brave . . . read of beauty and brutality . . . of love and loss . . . of love and betrayal . . . of love triumphant.

And after the reading, she felt proud and strong . . . ready for the exacting task of washing the feathers until each one bloomed into new downy lightness . . . and when this was done, ready for the "fresh first night" of magic repose.

Was it enchanted sleep or beautiful awakeness or some new strata of dreaming that enfolded her that night? Whatever the spell, at dawn there was happy decision and as many lovely wishes as a woman's heart could hold for an offering to the future.

And when she arose from the mattress, she went to Gram's desk where the bowl of sweetheart roses were in full bloom, and a ray of sun through the shutters enriched the royal blue of a Marie Antoinette mantilla and ignited the double diamonds of the ring into a sparkling fantasy of iridescence.

She opened the stationery drawer and took out three envelopes and three sheets of paper. She addressed each envelope carefully— then very slowly and thoughtfully wrote three notes, checking again each address as she placed the matching note within.

Two gifts were rejected, one accepted. Two hearts would be saddened, one made glad. The one made glad would soon be at her door.

> *Her dreams were bright,*
> *Decisions right,*
> *And wishes might come true.*

She sat very quiet, hands folded, dreaming of the love that would come to claim her. She felt the nearness of two approving presences, one just over her left shoulder, one over her right.

There was no question about their identity:

Alsheena, the Fair. And Harriet, the Brave.

And there was communication between them, reaching through her into the now.

"*She understands, Alsheena, my daughter. She understands about love.*"

"*She only touches understanding, Brave Mother. No one ever understands all about love.*"